THE TRUST

To Anne Marie —

Thank you so much!

A NOVEL BY SEAN KEEFER

2012

AN OLD LINE PUBLISHING BOOK

Printed in the United States of America

ISBN-13: 978-1-937004-17-0
ISBN-10: 1-937004-17-1

This book is a work of fiction. Any references to real people, events, establishments, organizations, or locales are intended solely to provide a sense of authenticity and are used fictitiously. All other characters, incidents, and dialogue are drawn from the author's imagination and are not to be construed as real.

Old Line Publishing
P.O. Box 624
Hampstead, MD 21074
Toll-Free Phone: 1-877-866-8820
Toll-Free Fax: 1-877-778-3756
Email: oldlinepublishing@comcast.net
Website: www.oldlinepublishingllc.com

PROLOGUE

I opened my eyes to silence.

Generally I expect some sound when I first open my eyes in the morning. Especially on those mornings when I am at my home. Perhaps the chirping of a bird, a distant horn, a dog barking... maybe even the sound of someone sleeping on the other side of the bed. Any of these things would have been expected, even appreciated, but today there was nothing save the silence. While I was puzzled at the lack of sound, I was not so cavalier as to think the silence meant it was a calm or peaceful morning. In fact, I was keenly aware that such a thought would be wrong. Completely wrong.

It was a fall morning, and though the coast of South Carolina is better known for the persistently humid summers that last long past the traditional notions of the season, this particular morning was cool, crisp even – a rarity for this time of year. The tropics had hinted at unrest and continued their threat of a hurricane, but so far with the weather, all had been calm. Under normal circumstances, on this alone, I might have been tempted to call it a perfect day. Football weather some would call it. In fact, as I was clearing my head to the morning, I was confident that legions from across the state would be flocking to Columbia for a day of South Carolina football, which was a ritual for the Gamecock faithful around the state. But the past week had insured that this day, and many to follow, would be far from normal for me.

I'd slept with most of the windows in the house open and could smell the salt air as I walked past the large table in the dining room toward the back door. That was one of the things I loved about living near the ocean – the wonderful array of scents and aromas nature offered. The salty smell of the marsh and ocean, the sweet lingering smell of the jasmine and magnolia, the freshly cut grass, the electric scent that precedes a summer rainstorm -- the list goes on. It's easy to find yourself lost in all that makes the coast such a wonderful place to live, but to say I had been slightly distracted as of late was somewhat of an understatement.

The work from the night before, and countless nights before that, was where I had left it on the dining room table. All things considered, I don't know that I would have been too terribly disappointed had someone made their way into the house through one of the open windows during the night and helped themselves to everything that I had left on it from the evening before. I found myself standing in the doorway staring at the loosely organized chaos before me, a slight breeze rustling a few of the papers. I'm not really sure how long I'd been standing there when I was pulled back to reality by the gentle yet persistent nudging of Austin, my Australian Shepard, who was patiently waiting to begin our morning ritual.

"Come on, boy," I said, and we walked toward the back door.

THE TRUST

Most every day started the same for Austin and me. Austin has to go outside and perform a spot check of the backyard that makes up his domain before anything else can occur. Once he makes sure all is well with his world then he can turn his attention to more important endeavors, like eating and napping.

After he got my attention, Austin led/herded me through the house, pausing every few feet to glance over his shoulder and make sure I was in tow. He pranced ever so slightly at the back door in anticipation of going out. I opened the door, and in a flurry of paws and fur he launched himself onto the deck and down into his backyard. I followed, watching him from the deck as he ran his inspection of the yard, sniffing, searching and the like.

The breeze was more pronounced outside, carrying its wonderfully intoxicating scent as it rustled through the palmettos and swayed the Spanish moss that hung from the large oaks in my yard. Austin busied himself with the scent of a squirrel that had vanished up one of the trees.

I went back inside and put some food out for Austin, completing the rest of the ritual. I sometimes wondered if he believed that while he was out roaming about that his food magically materialized in his bowl, as if delivered by house elves. Hearing his knocking on the back door I let him in, and with another flurry of paws and fur he rushed to his food.

This left me to the work in the dining room. It wasn't going to go away, nor was it going to get done on its own. Nor was the body count going to go down.

I guess the best way to explain the mess that had invaded my dining room and let you know all that it entails is to tell you a bit about myself, and how I came to find myself in my particular situation.

I am a lawyer.

THE TRUST

In the grand scheme of things there's not really anything special about being a lawyer. Sure, you have to go to school a bit longer than most, but at the end of the day it's a job, not unlike any other. From time to time people need lawyers, not unlike they need a mechanic for their car. Most times, people feel about the same going to see a mechanic as they do an attorney. Sometimes people find they need some degree of specialized assistance only a specific lawyer can provide and, on that day, that lawyer will become a much-needed commodity. Me, I've never really been a commodity.

As to my particular practice, I don't specialize. I don't work for a huge firm with posh offices, and I don't turn the television on at night hoping to see my latest commercial. I just practice law, trying to help out the people that find their way to my office.

Most people seem to think lawyers are rolling in cash, but I will quickly assure you that I am a testament to the invalidity of that statement. What most people don't realize is that while a number of attorneys do generally reap the rewards -- sometimes vast rewards -- of a successful practice, there are some, like me, who are quite content in not having their very existence being defined by their work and are willing to sacrifice a few dollars and a lot of headaches to achieve that. I like being a lawyer, but I also like being me and being able to enjoy spending a bit of what I do earn on things that I like, dare I say, love.

In all honesty I'm probably not the first person people would think of when the "I need a lawyer" thought enters their head. Truth be told, I have a pretty general and relaxed practice - some divorces, real estate closings, minor criminal cases and, what caused the situation with which I was presently confronted, a little probate work.

Probate Court is where you go when you have to deal with cleaning up the aftermath of a person's life after they die. If you're lucky, when a person dies they leave a will that will hopefully provide some guidance with what should be done with their stuff.

A little earlier I explained that mine is not the name that comes to mind when someone decides they need a lawyer. Old clients refer new cases to me, or my criminal clients, at least those that I helped avoid jail, generally call me for their subsequent go-rounds with the system. Nothing like good repeat customers. And, on seemingly rare occasions, I get a call that results in a new client. However, it wasn't quite a year ago that I had a new client come in to see me whose path to my office could not have been more puzzling.

He had a will.

And that is how everything began.

CHAPTER 1

"It's a simple question, Mr. Parks. How did your name come to be in this will?" he said.

"I'll say it one more time - I have no idea, Mr. Thomason. And I think it's time you leave my office," I said.

That's how my relationship with Steven Thomason started.

Steven Thomason walked into my office for the first time on a day when my secretary had decided her day would be better spent elsewhere. In fact, in retrospect, I'm quite sure it was a day that I felt could have been better spent elsewhere. The beach, a bar, anywhere other than my office. It was this day Steven Thomason chose to walk into my office. Without an appointment, I should add.

My general rule is that I don't meet with unscheduled, unannounced people who just stop by. My thought is that if something is important enough to go see an attorney, then it is important enough to pick up the phone and make an appointment.

However, this concept, simple as I thought it was, apparently eluded Thomason.

Given that I was alone in my office on the day he decided to insert himself into my life, dressed for the gym and facing a desk already full of plenty of other things I could be doing, I really had no desire to deal with a walk-in. After all, I didn't run a beauty salon.

So when I heard the office door open I cursed under my breath and rolled my eyes before I walked out into the lobby to see what surprise awaited me.

There I found that a man who looked to be about sixty had made himself at home in my lobby. He was dressed casually in a personally tailored way - pressed khakis, a pale blue oxford button down and lace up, toe-capped shoes. He had an aura of confidence and sophistication about him that was accentuated by his full head of gray hair and rugged complexion. He sat with his legs crossed. I looked at him a moment and realized that, while the chair he was in was a garden variety waiting room chair, the manner in which he was sitting in it made it look as if it had been custom built for him. He was reading a newspaper, a steaming cup of coffee to his side, briefcase at his feet. I was momentarily taken aback by his appearance as most people who simply arrived at my office didn't look quite so refined.

I glanced down at my tee shirt and shorts and put on a smile. "Hello. May I help you?"

He raised his eyes from his paper and looked over the reading glasses perched on the end of his nose. He studied me from head to toe then back again before locking on my stare. I guess my wardrobe justified the added scrutiny.

"Noah Parks?" he said.

I glanced over my shoulder, my eyes falling on a sign to the side of the receptionist's window that read "Noah R. Parks, Attorney at Law." I turned my gaze back to him.

"Yes. And you would be?" I said.

Ignoring my question, he put down the paper. "Attorney Noah Parks? From Myrtle Beach?"

Now this was interesting. It was not often that I found myself both perturbed and curious. This was certainly an exception to this rule as both of these sensations were growing by the moment. "Yes, and generally, yes."

He contemplated me for a moment more, allowing the silence to linger just long enough to make me notice, folded his newspaper, then stood. He brushed his pants and spoke again.

"Is there somewhere we could sit and speak? There is a matter at hand with which I require your assistance."

Brash. I forgot to mention brash, another characteristic my guest exuded.

I was still perturbed, but the curiousness I was feeling had started to change to intrigue. This encounter was shaping up to be at least potentially a bit out of the ordinary. I had found that sometimes out of the ordinary, in addition to occasionally being interesting, could also be profitable. I wasn't expecting anything earth shattering, but I decided to go with it and see what this man had to say.

"Certainly, but I didn't catch the answer to my question."

He paused in silence for another long moment.

"Steven Thomason. And if you don't mind," he said as he looked back toward my conference room. "We have a lot to cover."

I waited another moment to see if he would finally offer his hand, but as the moment stretched thin, I stepped to the side around him and walked toward my conference room, still without a handshake from my guest.

He stooped to retrieve his briefcase and followed.

~~~~~~~~~~~~~~~~~~~~~~~~~

I always liked having my first meeting with potential clients, (even if they were unannounced intruders), in my office conference room. Something about the formal mahogany table and the rows of books made me feel more lawyerly. Especially when I was wearing gym clothes. The funny thing about all the books was that in the decade plus I had owned them, I wasn't sure if I had opened any of them. Computer research has generally made the stereotypical law books obsolete and little more than the bane of first year law students, but every attorney I knew had a similar room with row after row of books. Those attorneys basically used them the same way I did -- image. It's all about image. That and I had paid a fortune for the table, so books aside, I always jumped at the chance to use the conference room.

Thomason walked around the table and took a seat before I had a chance to offer. He also refused my offer of a drink. I sat, pulled a yellow legal pad from a drawer, removed my Mont Blanc from the pocket of my shorts (which probably looked a bit odd), and sat back. The yellow legal pad, along with my Mont Blanc, are two other little image touches I like to think complete the lawyerly picture. As Thomason arranged several folders on the table that he had taken from his briefcase, I put on my interview face and began.

"So, Mr. Thomason, what brings you to my office?"

"Mr. Parks, I have a probate matter with which I need your assistance. It seems…"

I was suddenly feeling let down. I'd been hoping for something a little more interesting. Probate work? On the interesting and exciting scale, probate work generally hovered somewhere a bit higher than watching paint dry, but only slightly below waiting for water to boil. Hearing that he'd come into my office for this purpose I launched into my canned overview of the probate process, not paying attention to the fact that I'd cut him off. I also completely ignored the fact that after he put down his pen, he rolled his eyes and started staring around the room. With a deep breath, I began explaining how one began the probate process, where it would lead, and generally what to expect as an estate was first opened and ultimately ran its course.

Overall, the probate process was not terribly complicated, and I generally had the opinion that a monkey could do the work. It was loads of paperwork and lots of waiting for not a lot to happen. After all, the main focus of the probate process is the administration of the estates of the recently deceased. Given all of this, I at least had to make the process sound a bit complicated to justify a decent fee. I'd given this speech countless times, and was about to switch gears and begin the delicate work of explaining my fee when I sensed that the good Mr. Thomason wasn't hearing a word I was saying, and hadn't for some time.

"Any questions so far?"

He took his glasses off and rubbed his eyes. "Mr. Parks..." he started.

"Please, call me Noah."

He looked at me a long moment before he started again. "Mr. Parks, thank you for that rather abbreviated overview. However, I am actually quite familiar with the probate process, having practiced in the field for a number of years." He paused and stared for a moment. "Yes, I'm an attorney. However, the process you have so aptly summarized for me is not the reason that I am here. I am sure that you were soon to tell me that overall the task, while not always demanding or terribly complicated, is however quite

16

detail-intensive and will require a significant deal of attention to ensure that all of these details are adequately addressed and that your surely modest fee will amply ensure that the estate receives all due considerations and attention." He looked at me with a gaze just this side of glaring, laying a nice slice of deafening silence on the table for me.

I looked back and contemplated him for a moment. I always hate it when I find that I don't have control of a meeting, especially when it's my meeting. I guessed he knew that, or at least suspected it. I also hate it when I'm manipulated by someone I don't even know. I was quite sure that he knew this. I was determined not to break the silence, but after the impression I'd made thus far I was sure there would be no retainer coming from this case anytime soon. I decided to attempt the salvage of a modicum of pride.

"Well then, that being said, tell me how exactly I can assist you, Mr. Thomason." I set my pen down on the legal pad and crossed my arms.

"Mr. Parks, allow me to explain."

"Absolutely," I said. "But humor me on one point if you will. This practice of law tends to generally be quite formal, often painstakingly so. I try to dial back the formality whenever I have the chance or when I'm some place, say in my office, where I feel formality actually adds tension. Feel free to call me Noah. Please, I insist."

As if I had not even spoken, he continued.

"Mr. Parks, for you to understand the purpose of my visit, you need some background." He took a deep breath and continued. "A number of years ago, I first met a gentleman who became one of my most loyal clients. He also became a dear friend. My work for him covered an array of issues, not the least of which involved the drafting of a comprehensive Last Will and Testament.

"Now, some years ago I left the full time practice of law, but maintained my friendship with this gentleman and continued to provide him legal counsel. During this time, I refined his will a number of times. Actually, he and I simplified it as he consolidated and minimized his affairs for when he left us. Unfortunately, that time arrived a little more than a week ago."

I shifted in my seat and gave him a look encouraging him to continue.

He stared back for a moment and resumed. "I was contacted by his family, few that there are, to finalize his affairs. I returned to South Carolina and, after attending his memorial service, met with his two children.

"They presented me with his will that they had collected from his home here and asked me to coordinate the management of his estate. This did not surprise me as I knew that I had been named as the Personal Representative of the estate. I explained to them the process as you did to me a few minutes ago and then the next day sat out to begin my work. I visited the Probate Court here in Charleston, and after opening the estate returned to my hotel. It was then that it occurred to me that I was perhaps taking something for granted.

"I realized that I had not reviewed the will that I had just filed. I cursed at myself for making such a foolish mistake. While I was confident about the will, having not reviewed the actual document that I had just filed was concerning to me. I took a copy out of my briefcase and skimmed through the first few pages. Thankfully, all seemed to be in order."

I was getting annoyed sitting in silence. "So it was the will you'd done for your friend?"

"Well, as I finished the document I looked at the final page, the signature page. On the final page where years before I had signed as a witness, where my signature should have been, there was another. Then I noticed the date of the signatures. The date was five years later than it should have been."

I took a deep breath and said, taking advantage of the pause in the story, "I do apologize, but while I do find it fascinating, I don't see where you are going with this or how I can be of any help."

"Bear with me if you will."

He shifted slightly in his seat and continued.

"Realizing that the will I was examining was not the one I had watched my client execute, I sat down to scrutinize it. It was not until this reading that I found the sole difference between what I had done and the document that I held in my hand.

"The main substance of the will had not been altered. In fact, there was only one difference. And that addition, Mr. Parks, is where you come in."

Having said that, he reached inside his blazer and removed an envelope and slid it across the table to me. I looked at it without moving.

"Go on."

I considered it for a moment, then took it. It was a garden-variety envelope, unsealed. I looked at him and he gestured toward it with his eyes. I reached for it and removed a document from inside. It read "Last Will and Testament of Leonardo Xavier Cross" across the top. There was a sticky tab several pages in that I turned to, hoping to save time. I saw that several lines of the text were highlighted in yellow. The passage that was highlighted was substantially all of a section that was headed "Legal Representation."

I began to read.

"I direct that my Personal Representative herein named

19

engage the professional services of Noah R. Parks, Esquire, of Charleston, South Carolina, as legal counsel for my estate. As compensation for his services, in addition to his normal hourly rate, Mr. Parks shall take charge of the entirety of the contents of the safe deposit box held in my name at the Bank of Charleston's Broad Street branch. Said contents, for purposes of my estate, are to be valued at $1.00.

I further direct that the then manager of this branch, upon presentation by Mr. Parks of the closing documents relevant to my estate, provide to him access to such safe deposit box held in my name. In the event that any person other than Mr. Parks, even with purported authority from Mr. Parks, attempt to obtain the contents of this safe box, even under Court Order, such contents shall, under the terms and provisions of this will, become the property of the Bank of Charleston and the Bank of Charleston is instructed to destroy the contents of this safe deposit box without review of the same."

I'd never heard of this man sitting in my office. I flipped back to the first page of the will. I'd never heard of the dead man whose will I was holding.

"So, Mr. Parks, would you be so kind as to explain that to me?"

"I can't."

"It's a simple question, Mr. Parks. How did your name come to be in this will?"

"I'll say it one more time -- I have no idea, Mr. Thomason. And I think it's time you leave my office," I said.

He didn't move.

"Mr. Parks. It's time to explain this to me."

I threw the will on the table in front of him. "Me, explain it to you? Somehow, I think I should be asking that same question of you. No, wait. Actually, I can explain it to you. Quite quickly. I don't have any idea what you're getting at with this," I said as I pointed to the will. "So why don't you tell me what this is about." After a short pause, I added, "I think we might be finished here."

I waited for him to say something. He leaned forward across the table and stared at me with a piercing gaze that drew me in and did little to make me feel like I was running this meeting. In a patterned, staccato tone, he spoke as he stared.

"You're telling me you don't know anything about this?" he said as he rose slightly in his chair, giving me the feeling he may actually come across the table at me.

"Not a thing," I said as I leaned in toward him, not wanting to show that he was making me feel nervous or apprehensive.

"Mr. Parks, I find that rather hard to believe. So, you'll pardon me if I do not accept a simple, 'I don't know.'"

"Prepare for a bit of disappointment, because even if I wanted to tell you something else, I couldn't without it being a lie. And some of us in this world still have a modicum of manners left, and for me to lie to you would just be rude. However, it isn't the least bit rude of me to think you need to leave."

I'd had quite enough of this little display, and I rose completely out of my seat to address him.

"Not without some answers."

"Sir, again, as I just said, I have no idea about any of this. The little I do know, you just told me. But you have a tone that I don't particularly like. So, as interesting as this all seems, I trust you'll understand that I don't care to have strangers who refuse to use my first name come to my office unannounced to ambush me with accusations of unethical and inappropriate behavior. Now, if you will excuse me, Mr. Thomason, I feel certain you can find your way out."

I moved toward the door, leaving the will on the table in front of him.

He stared at me for a moment as that all too familiar silence crept back in. Then a smile crossed his face. This was certainly not the response that I expected.

"Noah, I never said you were anything less than ethical or had done anything inappropriate. Please sit."

I looked at him a moment. He smiled. Now that was something I hadn't seen from him yet. Not knowing exactly what else to do or say, all I could get out was an "Okay." I sat.

"Prior to coming today, I did some looking around - a lot of looking around - and could find no connections between you and my friend. If I had I wouldn't be here, mind you. While I learned a bit about you, I didn't find anything at all connecting the two of you. I realized that my only option as to finding out why your name appears in that," he pointed to the will on the table, "was to follow the instructions you just read. After seeing your reaction, that is exactly what we shall do. After all, the decision has already been made for you to represent the estate."

I looked at the will again. I scratched my head a moment and looked back at him.

"So, Noah, do you have any questions of me?"

"I must admit I'm a bit confused here. A man I have never met comes into my office and shows me the will of a man I've never heard of. He thinks he drafted the will. Then he tells me he actually didn't draft the will, but interestingly enough, this mystery will directs that I be the legal counsel for this man's estate – the man I have never heard of. Oh yes, I almost forgot, for my services I receive the contents of a safe deposit box. A safe box that I gather you not only didn't know about, but have no idea as to what's inside. That about it?"

"Precisely. So why don't we get started. The sooner we get through, the sooner we can open that safe deposit box and see what this is all about."

So that is how I first met Steven Thomason, and how this all got started.

CHAPTER 2

I actually told a bit of a lie when I said I'd never opened any of the books in my library. There's one that I open quite frequently, actually on many occasions. My copy of Black's Legal Dictionary. It didn't occupy a place of prominence on the shelves of my library and there was nothing unique about it. Upon first glance, were you to even notice it, nothing about it would really even catch your eye. In all respects, judging by its cover, it was really nothing more than a well-used dictionary. While I hadn't used it to look up any words or phrases lately, through my law school daze the dictionary had never been far from my side.

The study of law is as much about learning another language as anything else, and Black's, as it is called, is the cornerstone of this language. In law school I had taken to highlighting each word or term I looked up in Black's. In the three years I was in school, I'm pretty sure that more of the entries had been underlined than had not.

THE TRUST

On the day I graduated from law school, after the ceremonies and fanfare had ended, I was standing alone in the quad. A rather large oak leaf floated down and landed at my feet. For some reason I picked it up and put it in the pages of my Black's, where it has remained since. In the years that have passed I've placed other items in the pages of the Black's from time to time - a letter, a note, a ticket stub, a passage from a book or magazine, perhaps a photograph. Looking through the pages of the Black's always gave me a perspective on the practice of law.

On the day I met Steven Thomason, I felt the need to look at the Black's. I took it from the shelf and flipped through the pages, reading the occasional letter or article, my eyes falling from time to time on a highlighted term that took me back to my days in law school. I even passed over and brushed the oak leaf. After staring at the dictionary for some time, I made a copy of the will. Returning to the library, I separated the pages of the will, randomly inserting them into the pages of the dictionary. When I was done, I placed the book back on the shelf after collecting all of the papers that Thomason had left. I turned off the light in the conference room and went back to my office.

~~~~~~~~~~~~~~~~~~~~~~~~~~~~~~

After Thomason had laid out the reasons he was in my office and before he left, he and I discussed the specifics of the estate. He'd already made all of the filings that were required by the Probate Court – much to my relief, as the paperwork to open an estate was my biggest dislike of the whole probate process. It was a mundane, paperwork intensive process that was dictated by bureaucrats. However, in the days following, while he was still in town, Thomason and I met on several occasions and I quickly began to learn more about the estate and the man behind it. However, Thomason hadn't been quick to volunteer anything about Cross, ultimately leaving me to ask him about the man.

"Very well, let me tell you about my friend," he said.

And so it was that I began to learn about Leonardo Xavier Cross. Leonardo, Leo, as Thomason referred to him, had lived the last years of his life in Charleston, South Carolina, after having been raised in the mid-west and having worked for many years in Chicago. He hadn't achieved any great fame or notoriety and, in fact, had been a virtual recluse in his final years. But the more I learned about him the more interesting I found him, primarily because the more I learned about him the more questions I had.

Charleston is a moderate sized southern city with a population in the area of a hundred thousand. So while I didn't know everyone, generally I knew of or had heard of those of prominence or means. However, this was not the case with Mr. Cross. He'd made his money in publishing. I learned that Cross had owned a Chicago publishing house that published technical manuals for use in the manufacturing of electronics. In the 1950's and 1960's, if it was electronic, Cross had likely published the instruction manual for it. He'd sold the publishing house and made a fortune.

He had remained in Chicago with his family until his wife died. Then he moved to Charleston, purchased a home in the downtown area and largely kept to himself for the remainder of his life. From what I could tell, sometime after he sold the business he became good friends with Thomason and the whole will process started.

From what I was learning, Cross did little outside of day-to-day business in Charleston. He had done his local banking at the Bank of South Carolina – Broad Street branch, of course – where he apparently, at some point in his life, also rented a safe deposit box. However, the bulk of his banking, investing, and other affairs remained in Chicago area banks or institutions, though administered through national brokerage houses that had offices in Charleston. This struck me as rather odd as it seemed that Cross would have wanted to keep things local, but seemed to be of little concern to Thomason.

Cross' wife had died in an automobile accident, so his only heirs were his three children. Much of the work on the will was a product of Cross' concern that his children would squander his estate. As I learned more of his children, I started to think that the children may pose a problem with the probate of the will by contesting it or challenging it. Thomason didn't share my concern; in fact, he was almost dismissive of it.

"No, it's not that I expect any problems from them. But the goal of the will was to balance what the children received, leaving them each a modest sum but allowing the rest of the estate to be put to positive ends," Thomason said.

"So the children are okay with the will?" I asked one day soon after we had begun work on the estate.

"I really have no idea."

"How's that?" I said.

"You have to understand the relationship Cross had with the children. They were not overly excited when Cross sold his publishing business. They were even less excited when he moved to Charleston. When they were growing up they had everything handed to them. Cross spoiled them, so I can understand their disagreement with the move. See, they fancied themselves as pedigreed members of the Chicago socialite scene. In truth they were little more than delinquents who had never worked and accomplished little other than spending their father's money."

"That must have made things interesting when it came time to move south from Chicago."

"In a word, they said 'no' to the move. When the children refused to accompany him to Charleston, Cross gave them an advance on his estate and then cut off their funds, effectively canceling their membership in their social circles. He was terribly upset over their refusal to move with him, but he went on with his life and let the children do the same with theirs."

"Interesting. So tell me about the children?" I said.

Thomason put down his pen and looked over at me. "Why are you interested?"

"Oh, just basic curiosity. Humor me."

"Noah, you entertain me. They are spoiled children, nothing more, but if you must. There are, or should I say were, three: Chase, Anna Beth and Daniel."

"Were three?"

"Oh, now you're impatient. Do you want to hear about them or not?"

"I do, go on."

"Thank you. Chase was just greedy. Chase took advantage, or rather attempted to take advantage, of his ties to the Chicago social scene and opened an upscale nightclub. He soon realized his membership in the social circles meant little. He had upscale customers, but they didn't want to pay." Thomason took a drink of his coffee and continued. "His so called friends, despite being very wealthy, expected Chase to give them his hospitality. The general public decided if the rich people were coming it had to cost a fortune so, in the end, the people who came didn't spend any money and the ones who would have spent their money stayed away. He lost all of his money and is now one of many managers at the Chicago Hard Rock Café. Of course he blamed his father for everything."

"So he's broke and you don't think he'll be a problem with the will?" I said.

"He won't. Neither will Cross' other son."

"Why's that?

"He's dead. Daniel was his name. He had contact with his father from time to time, but it was never friendly. He would show up unannounced in Charleston to confront Cross about what a terrible father he had been. I heard he had planned on going to law school, but he was killed in a mugging in Chicago several years back. Cross didn't take it well at all. I think he felt that Daniel, as his youngest child, may have ultimately reconciled with him, but it was not to be."

"So a pissed off son and a dead son. What did Chase think about his brother's death?

"I have no idea. His father didn't say."

"So you don't know the children?" I said.

"No, I know them, just not personally. I've never had a reason to spend any time with them."

"I see. So, things as interesting with the daughter?"

"You could say that."

"Meaning?" I said.

"She married not long after Cross moved. I hear she was quite happy until it was discovered that her husband was, in addition to being a pedophile, quite insane. She filed for divorce and in exchange for keeping the lurid details of the scandal out of the tabloids, she received an attractive settlement. She is quite comfortable in Chicago. She distanced herself from her father and, as I understand it, wants no part of the estate."

"Poor guy. Three greedy kids, lots of money, and he dies alone."

"I would hardly say he was a 'poor guy.' He was always quite happy and content."

"That would be quite a feat given the story you've just told. And you're sure that neither the son nor the daughter will be coming after the estate?"

"Positive? No. But even after he gave them the money years ago, he's allowing them each another one million dollars in his will."

"That should ease the pain of his passing a bit I would imagine."

"That was our goal. That and to get them to ignore the trust he created," he said.

"Trust? Dare I ask?"

"You're the attorney for the estate, of course you ask. In fact, I would expect you to."

Thomason was quite literal, and my sense of humor was lost on him.

"The remainder of his estate is in a private trust. Last I reviewed the financial statements, it was valued at about eighty-five million."

"I'm sorry? Did you say eighty-five million?"

"Yes, more or less, depending on the markets," he said.

"And you don't think that will change the children's feelings about the estate?"

"I would imagine not. They simply don't want to be involved."

"I do hope you're right, but it seems to me that the trust gives us about eighty-five million reasons why they would want to get involved," I paused. "So, trust. Eighty-five million?"

"Yes," he said.

"Like you said, I'm the attorney for the estate. Tell me about it."

"There's not much else to tell. It's headquartered in Ohio in a little town called Oxford where Cross attended college. It engages in general philanthropy, made reports to Cross during his lifetime – now the reports will be made to the board of directors." He leaned toward me. "And if you're wondering, yes, I'm on the board."

"Actually, I had just assumed you were. So, some money for the children, the trust. What else is there?"

"Not much. His house. The safe deposit box. That's about it."

"All right, another question."

"You seem to have a few today. Go ahead."

"You knew Cross for what, like twenty years or so?" I said.

"Twenty-four, to be exact."

"What's in the safe deposit box?"

"I have thought long and hard about that," he said.

"Me too, though perhaps not as long. And it is frustrating me like you wouldn't believe. I've even found myself hoping that Cross is the long lost uncle we all dream about."

"Amusing, but no. Remember, I checked you out quite thoroughly. Nothing at all in your past, or your family's past, connects you to Cross. You come from southern Americana, Cross from a more refined upbringing."

"More refined upbringing?"

"Yes, more refined."

It was lost on him that he might have offended me. Lost, or he didn't care.

"You really have no idea about the safe deposit box?" I said.

"No."

"Anything missing from his personal possessions? I mean, anything glaring that you've seen from going through the inventories?"

"Nothing glaring, but I'm certainly not an authority on his possessions, which I should remind you need to be finalized."

"Yes, I've been taking care of that," I said.

~~~~~~~~~~~~~~~~~~~~~~~~~~~~~~~~~

Since the time of Cross' death I had visited his house several times, both with and without Thomason. Every time I was there it was under the watchful eye of Martha Burkes. Ms. Martha, as she liked to be called, had been employed by Cross for almost as long as he had lived in Charleston, and one didn't dare call her the maid. She liked to be referred to as the house manager. She'd worked at the house literally from the moment he moved to Charleston. After having spent some time with her, I got the feeling she believed she really owned the place. He hadn't left her anything in the will, but Thomason and I learned she had been paid handsomely during the years of her employment and had been left quite well off. There had even been discussion that she would buy the house when it went on the market.

I always enjoyed a trip over to Cross' house. The first time I'd been there was one random day around lunchtime. Ms. Martha had a nice spread waiting for me. Seems it was something she always did, and she wasn't going to let a little death get in the way of tradition. So I enjoyed a nice lunch, and after that I tried to plan my trips around lunchtime. Ms. Martha caught on pretty quick, but I think she enjoyed the company, and I realized just as fast that she knew the house as well as anyone.

One day I was finishing up a lunch of pork chops with cornbread and macaroni and cheese.

"Ms. Martha?"

"Yes, Mr. Noah?"

"Question for you. Mr. Cross ever mention a safe deposit box?"

She turned from the stove and rested a hand on her hip as she contemplated my question. "Safe deposit box? No. He liked to talk a good bit, not always to me, mostly at me, but never mentioned any safe deposit box."

"Hum. Let me ask you this, you ever notice anything significant around here go missing?"

"The only thing to ever go missing around here that I noticed was all that food I'd have to buy. That man could eat, let me tell you. But no, nothing special comes to mind. In fact, not that I been snooping or nothing, but most everything here been here and stayed since I got here. Why you ask?"

"Oh, you know, I just have to account for everything for the Court and I figured you'd know if anyone would."

"You're right about that. If anyone would know I would, but I figure that you got some reason other than just paperwork there, Mr. Noah."

"Now, Ms. Martha, you know I'd never try to put anything over on you."

She smiled as she turned back to the stove.

I left Cross' house pleasantly full and headed back to the office to gave Thomason a call.

"We need to decide what to do with all of the stuff in the house," I said

"I agree with you. I plan on coming into town next week, so we can discuss it then if your schedule will allow it," he said.

"Certainly, plenty of availability," I said as my paralegal, Heather, walked into my office with an envelope that she placed on my desk. Though I was on the phone with Thomason, she spoke to me.

"Might want to take a look at this," she said.

Heather was a part-time law student at the Charleston School of Law, and while quite bright, often seemed to forget the meaning of support staff. Not that it was a big problem, but it wasn't unusual for me to get the occasional instruction or direction from her. Actually more often than occasionally. Sometimes this annoyed me; however, this time she seemed to be correct in her advice.

"Hold on a second," I said into the phone as I looked at the envelope. It was a legal size manila envelope with a return address from the Charleston County Probate Court. On the envelope was a reference to the Cross estate.

I could tell Thomason was not accustomed to being cut off mid-thought. "What is it?" he said.

"Something from the Court."

I detected an air of impatience in his voice. "Noah, tell me you haven't missed something."

Thomason had a talent for being able to push the envelope on annoying me with the slightest degree of effort, but this time I was more curious as to what was in the envelope.

The probate process is one of strict procedure. It was Thomason's opinion that Cross' estate would run its course and there would be no claims made against the estate - by the children or anyone else. So far, this opinion had proven correct. Little did I know that this was about to change.

"Hang on a second, I'm going to put you on speaker."

I hung up the receiver after turning on the speaker. "Most times when I get a notice from the Court at this point in the game, it means a claim has been filed," I said.

"This isn't most times, Noah. There are no claims to be made."

Inside the envelope there was a letter that I took out and scanned.

"Want me to read it to you?" I said into the phone.

I was rewarded for my question as Thomason's voice poured out of the speaker. "I would be quite satisfied if you would just let me know what we have to do as a result of whatever this may be."

THE TRUST

"It seems that a Mr. Chase Cross of Chicago, Illinois has formally contested the validity of Cross' will."

CHAPTER 3

As my words hung in the air, Heather took a seat in my office. I couldn't tell if it was to provide moral support or to watch the fireworks that no doubt were soon to launch from the speaker.

I waited for Thomason to say something. Anything. Anticipating the coming storm, I was met with silence. Happened a lot with him, the silence.

"It appears that I shall have to travel to your fair city sooner than I anticipated," he said. "I shall plan on meeting you tomorrow, your office, say 9:00 a.m. If you would be kind enough to contact my hotel and let them know that I shall arrive in the next few hours. Also, I trust if it was not included, you will obtain a copy of the formal pleadings filed with the Court."

Noah Parks, Attorney at Law and Personal Concierge, I thought to myself.

"Have them right here. I'll call the hotel and let them know you'll be here later tonight," I said.

"Very good then. I shall see you in the morning."

The phone's speaker emitted a staccato tone indicating that the line had gone dead. I was a bit surprised at our conversation, or should I say lack thereof. I had anticipated the fireworks.

I contemplated Thomason for a moment. I realized that while I had been acquainted with him for many months, I actually knew very little about him. He always looked like he had just visited Brooks Brothers. I knew he had been Cross' attorney. That was about the extent of it. It seemed that the only personal thing I really knew about Thomason was that he'd only stay at the Planter's Inn when he traveled to Charleston. We'd never met outside of my office, never discussed anything but this case – I didn't even know where he lived, though I suspected Chicago. I only had a cell number and a post office box address for him.

I must have been lost in thought, or at least looked like I was, because Heather cleared her throat. I looked to her.

"He certainly took that better than I expected," Heather said.

"I know, surprising actually. I just knew he was going to blow."

"You want me to call Planter's and let them know that he'll be arriving tonight?"

"Do you mind? I'm going to read over the pleadings Chase filed and get things organized for the morning so I can at least try to get a good night's sleep."

"Plans for tonight?" she said.

I had shifted - almost - my attention to the pleadings, but as soon as she said this I raised my eyes toward her and paused. This was becoming a frequent question for her.

I often wondered what she would have said or done if I had said, "No." But for any number of reasons, even though I was single and found her attractive, I resisted. Though I will admit it was with a degree of reluctance, more so recently.

"The usual, exercise, deal with the dog, off to bed, you know. An exciting evening of who knows what." I braced myself for her stock answer.

"Sounds fun." She caught and held my gaze for a moment, just enough to make me feel like I was an eight year old with his hand in the cookie jar. She wandered out of my office, glancing back at me and flipping her hair gingerly over her shoulder as she did so. She left me with a smile.

Heather was attractive in a librarian sort of way, a really unique kind of librarian sort of way - a really unique attractive librarian. She was smart, and a good paralegal that appeared to know how to have fun. She was easy to talk to and even easier to look at. Sometimes I got the feeling when I walked in and surprised her or caught her on a personal phone call that maybe there was something more to her below the surface that I was missing. Something maybe I should explore. But I never could quite put my finger on it and never took that next step. Whenever I did stop and wonder, I realized that while I spent as much if not more time with her than I did with anyone else, I really didn't know her – not even how old she was. She was generally reserved and kept personal details to herself. Like I said, she was attractive, and even the way she dressed hinted at something more. I was pretty sure she flirted with me from time to time, but that could have been me subconsciously fishing.

From what I had been able to piece together, I was pretty sure that she had another job a couple of nights a week and I think she was from Georgia, but I wasn't really sure about that. Suddenly, I realized that the two people that I had been spending most of my time with were people I really didn't know.

After Heather left my office I looked at the letter from the Court. In sum total it was only the letter from the Court and the pleading that had been filed several days earlier. There was a hearing set for the end of next week.

I flipped through to the end of the document and read the name of the attorney who had filed it. I expected an attorney from Chicago, or at least the name of an attorney at one of the big local firms who would have been associated by a Chicago firm, but it was a local attorney with a solo practice, hardly the type a big city firm would associate and hardly someone that Chase Cross would randomly select. I knew him from cases we'd had together through the years. Robert Seabrook was his name. I tried to call him, but he was out of the office. I left a message and asked him to call me in the morning. Before nine.

I turned back to the first page of the Demand for Hearing he had filed for Chase Cross. I read through it. It presented a claim of duress and undue influence - against Thomason of all people. Essentially the claim was that Cross had been taken advantage of by Thomason who made him sign the will unfairly depriving Chase of his rightful inheritance. The theory was that Thomason had befriended Cross and, through the years, in a carefully planned and orchestrated fashion, slowly exercised his influence over Cross to induce him to ignore his children and leave his entire estate, through a sham trust, to Thomason. I followed the theory to a point; however, the theory fell apart as there was a weak link at best between Thomason and the trust. Sure Thomason was on the board of directors, but he was only one of the directors, and not even the chairman. But as I thought about it, it made sense. Other than what Thomason had told me, I hadn't been able to ascertain anything about the trust. Up until this point I hadn't needed to know anything more. Now, from reading the allegations contained in the challenge

Seabrook had filed, he knew even less than I did about the trust. He was banking on the court being shocked and offended with his story about how a conniving Yankee had induced a resident of our fair city to divert millions to a nebulous trust in another state that happened to be well above the Mason-Dixon Line.

It was thin, but I also knew that Seabrook didn't care. It was his style to stir things up, push the envelope to the ethical limit, then get the other side to pay his client enough to make the "situation" go away. This would make Chase Cross happy because he'd have fresh dollars to spend and could leave the world of Hard Rock management. This result would definitely make Seabrook happy as he would've earned at least a third of what Chase received. This could potentially devastate the trust, but Seabrook didn't care. Once he had the dollars in his sights he wouldn't let go, no matter who suffered.

I had to admit that the whole estate was rather odd, but Seabrook's theory fit together quite well in the grand scheme of things, if you overlooked the fact that he had no facts to support his position. Since the estate was generally unique, to have heightened scrutiny or attention focused on it was to potentially place the entirety of the estate at risk. It could be made to face the reality of tremendous taxes, diminished value and excess attention that could potentially cost the trust millions. Seabrook's theory was geared toward this and structured in a fashion that would have the estate pay Chase to go away before allowing the trust to fail or be exhausted.

I felt confident that ultimately Seabrook's efforts would fail. I suspected that Seabrook had been given marching orders from Chase to shake some money loose from the estate. I smiled as I realized that Chase had bypassed the Chicago legal machine and headed south, which meant one less attorney to pay, thus giving him more money at the end of the day. I'd already made up my mind that I would advise Thomason to fight this; however, I expected that he'd tell me just the same when we met tomorrow. Thomason would take it personally, being accused of this by Chase and Seabrook. From what I could see, Cross felt abandoned by his family but still had a sense of obligation to them, even if this trust was to receive the bulk of the estate. But apparently this was not enough to keep Chase from digging a little deeper.

I reviewed my notes for my meeting with Thomason the following morning, then I decided to head home. When I looked at the clock, I was a bit surprised to see that I had been working for more than five straight hours. I had a vague recollection of Heather leaving, but I couldn't remember exactly when. I rose from my desk, turned off the lights and headed out. I found one very aggravated canine awaiting me upon my return home.

~~~~~~~~~~~~~~~~~~~~

I awoke at first light and felt like I had closed my eyes only moments before. I got up and went through the morning ritual with Austin then left for work, arriving at the office just after 7:00 am. Heather hadn't beaten me to the office, but a message from Robert Seabrook had.

I picked up the phone and called him back. I wasn't at all surprised when he picked up the phone on the second ring.

"Robert Seabrook."

"Robert, Noah Parks here. You're in the office early."

"Well, there's work to be done, you know."

Dead air. I spoke again.

"I got your demand yesterday and wanted to give you a call."

"Noah, how are you doing? You already got it? I just drafted a letter for you to send it over, but I guess the Court does a bang up job of getting things out." He laughed to himself, apparently amused. "Sorry I didn't let you know sooner that I was on the case. I thought I had at least another day. Unfortunately, I won't have the element of surprise."

He sounded almost disappointed.

"Now Robert, why would you want to surprise me? I'd gather your case is strong enough to not need a surprise."

"Of course it is, but I always love surprises. So, I take it you've looked things over and are calling me to settle," he said. As preposterous as this was, I knew he believed it as he was saying it.

The thing about Seabrook was he liked to be as big a pain in the ass as possible. It was his entire approach to make the other side look at the ultimate settlement of a case as a sort of salvation in that it was a mechanism to rid themselves of him and his nearly daily diatribes. An escape hatch, a way out. I knew of more than a few attorneys who had done just that to salvage what little existed of their sanity after he had run his course. However, even knowing this, I didn't let it bother me. I took the approach that if you pressed back with Seabrook he'd finally cave because he really hated to actually do any work. He could give with the best of them, but never wanted to be faced with taking any of his own medicine. So I planned to be as big a pain in the ass to him as possible in hopes that he would tire of the work and set his sights elsewhere.

"Actually, I just wanted to talk with you generally and see if we could clear anything up prior to court so I didn't have to spend too much time down there with this before trial."

"Of course. If you would like to talk about how much we will need for settlement, I'd be glad to take your offer to my client. In fact, last time I met with my client I told him what a pleasure it was to work with you. It was funny, may have been the humidity, but I got the idea that he thought we might be a bit too friendly. Anyway, I convinced him he was in capable hands with me and that with you on the other side, we certainly should be able to quickly work this out without any problems."

"I hate to disappoint you, but I don't think we can work it out. My client's way past adamant about not paying anything on this. He's taking it personally, you having accused him of all those things. The unethical allegations especially. You have to meet this guy to understand how that gets to him. Point is, he won't authorize me to settle – won't even entertain it. He wants trial dates and wants to sit second chair."

I knew this would send Seabrook into orbit. He hated going to trial – it took away from time he could spend harassing other lawyers. That and he wasn't really that good in court, so the thought of two attorneys on the other side of a case, one being retired with nothing but time and a cause, made it worse. I also knew I was inviting him to tell me about how strong his case was, which generally meant the opposite.

And he did just that.

He did, however, stop just short of threatening to go after me personally, but he was kind enough to warn me that he really didn't want to see me get "roughed up" in court.

"So, I take it that you won't go ahead and drop this?" I said.

"That's not the issue. If your client's going to be so stubborn then it'll cost him big." He sounded like he was spitting into the phone. "Not only will the estate have to pay, I may have to go after him personally. Noah, I'm surprised that you would involve yourself with such."

"No problem, then. I can get ready for trial."

"Wait, wait. Why would you want to do that?" he said. "What good would a pretrial or depositions do when we haven't even discussed settlement?" Seabrook also didn't like it when anyone filed anything with the Court or did anything that could possibly point out the weaknesses in his case. "Tell you what, let me talk to my client. We can talk again and see what we can work out?"

"We have your hearing next week, so I'll look to hear from you and we can go from there. I'll get a letter out to you," I said. He was starting to say something as I hung up.

With Seabrook, it was important to leave the ball in his court.

~~~~~~~~~~~~~~~~~~~~~~

I reviewed my notes again from the prior evening in preparation for Thomason. Heather arrived and gave me her normal cheerful, "Good morning, Noah." I was just finishing getting everything together when I heard Thomason come in.

"Good morning, Ms. Davis. Would you let Mr. Parks know I'm here? I'll be in the conference room."

"Of course, Mr. Thomason. How was your trip?" I didn't hear a response, but couldn't tell if he was being aloof or perhaps simply hadn't heard her.

I went to the conference room. Thomason was waiting for me.

"Good morning, Noah. So what do we have?" He was all business. No, "How have you been," or "Things going well?" Right to the point. I felt like I was back in law school about to get grilled by a professor.

"Would you like to hear about the allegations or the attorney that made them?"

"Based on that question, start with the attorney."

"Robert Seabrook," I said. "Been practicing for a good while. He's certainly competent, but also knows where the line between ethical and unethical behavior is as he spends most of his time toeing it. Let me see, he hates court and his MO is to be as big a pain in the ass as possible so we'll throw some money at him to make him go away. Crappy way to practice, but he's made a career of it."

"Interesting. I would have guessed that Chase Cross would have retained a Chicago firm that would have associated local counsel of a substantially different vein. His financial straits must be more dire than I expected. Very interesting. So, the allegations?"

"I'd expected Chase to do the same thing, as in hiring a Chicago firm, given the amount of money we're talking about. However, I'm starting to suspect Chase has no idea how much money his father actually had. I think that Chase's choice of lawyers is either random or calculated to Seabrook's style. Chase wants cash and Seabrook's style is to get as much as he can as quick as he can."

"Surprisingly, I don't disagree with that analysis," he said.

"At first blush, your relationship with Cross could easily provide the basis for some degree of undue influence. Older man, few friends, abandoned by his children, befriended by an attorney who retires but continues to do work for him on his will. A will that creates a mysterious trust. I gather you assisted in the creation of this trust, and being on the board of directors only adds to the conspiracy." Thomason nodded as I continued. "However, as you know, if Cross wants his estate to go to a trust, he gets to do that. And while we haven't discussed it yet, I am quite confident that the entire development of this will is very well documented, by you and Cross."

"You are correct as to that, but go on."

I was on a roll, and for what I think was the first time since I had been working with Thomason, he appeared to actually be listening.

"I have a few thoughts. First, like I said, I don't think Seabrook or Chase has a true picture or even a thought as to the actual size of the estate. Basically, from what I see he's doing what he does best: allege something, then start shaking the tree until the dollars start to fall. If Chase had any idea at all about the number of dollars we are talking about, we'd be dealing with someone else."

"Noah, I am impressed. I must admit, I did briefly consider such a possibility as you just outlined, but I also considered a number of other scenarios more possible. Most of which centered around a local attorney who was being directed by a higher authority located somewhat further north. Go on."

"When I called Seabrook he did nothing but convince me that what I just laid out is exactly what's going on. I told him you were taking it personally and that settlement was not something you'd consider. He also said something I found interesting. He said that he had a conversation with Chase and told him that I'd be a good attorney to work things out. That tells me two things. First the obvious, Chase has met with him, probably here, and that Seabrook is pulling from his regular play book."

"Very good, Noah. If Seabrook had been retained by a Chicago firm, Chase wouldn't have had that conversation with him, much less have met with him at this point. Let me ask you this, the pleadings, did Seabrook draft them?"

"Ninety-five percent certain he did."

"Even better yet. If your Seabrook drafted the pleadings, then he is calling the shots and there is no Chicago firm. So what do you suggest we do from this point?"

I was almost speechless at the question. I was used to him telling me what we were going to do. Not that he had ever been offensive about it, but he always was rather matter of fact.

"We have our hearing next week. At this point, with Seabrook and the Court, we do nothing. I'll file a general denial of the allegations and ask the Court for a hearing on the merits. The Court will schedule it rather soon, I should hope. That'll drive him nuts and likely push him to the point of offering to settle. If he does that, we'll cross that bridge when we come to it."

"I agree. I will be in town for another day. I have another matter that I have to attend to, and then I will plan on returning for the hearing. Why don't we take some time now and review the closing documents for the estate so we can get them filed as soon as the claim period runs."

I was surprised this had gone so easy. I was also surprised that he had let me take the lead without any discussion or question.

We spent the rest of the morning and part of the afternoon looking over the closing documents for the estate, making sure everything was in order for filing when the time came. When we finished and he left, Heather wasted no time in coming in to find out what had happened. I think she was a little let down that things had gone so smoothly. She was even more surprised when she learned that he had basically deferred to me on the strategy for handling everything for the hearing.

I started out on a draft of the denial of the allegations so Heather could send it out by courier. As usual at the end of the day Heather was leaving before me, and I have to admit that I was a little bit disappointed that she didn't ask me if I had plans. For some reason, this was the one day where I may have actually varied a bit from our normal script and actually accepted or at least offered to do something. I guess it was a lesson in opportunities and how you have to be careful with them.

I didn't have any idea then about how true and important that concept was soon to be for me.

~~~~~~~~~~~~~~~~~~~~~~~~~~~~~~

On the day of the hearing I was in the office early. Thomason met me and we left for the hearing. We arrived fifteen minutes early. I always do that as I find fifteen minutes just enough time to allow me to relax and get focused. It was also the perfect amount of time to keep clients from trying to engage me in small talk.

Our hearing was at 11:00 a.m. and the Charleston County Probate Judge, Judge Lawrence Oscarson, never started, or ended, late. At 10:55, the bailiff came out and told us we could come into the Courtroom to set up. I was surprised Seabrook and his client weren't there. At 11:02, the Judge came to the bench.

"All rise," the bailiff said.

"Be seated. Okay, appears we have a hearing demanded by an heir today. It also appears that we have an attorney for the estate – Good morning, Mr. Parks – and I gather we have a Personal Representative, Sir," he said, nodding his head in greeting to Thomason. "Gentlemen, thank you for coming. However, it seems we are missing at least one disgruntled heir and his attorney – Let me see, Robert Seabrook. Not like him to be late. Bailiff, any idea where Mr. Seabrook and his client might be?" Oscarson said.

"No sir. I just called the case in the hall and no Mr. Seabrook," the bailiff said.

"Mr. Parks," the Judge said.

"Well, your Honor, I've not spoken to Mr. Seabrook today, but it's not like him at all to be late. Traffic perhaps?"

"Perhaps, but the fact remains he's not here. We'll take a short recess, say ten minutes. Please feel free to wait in the Courtroom, then we will resume."

We waited exactly ten minutes.

"All rise," said the Bailiff.

We stood and watched Oscarson walk to and adjust himself on the bench.

"Sit, sit. Most interesting. I called his office and got a machine, then called his home and got a busy signal. Tried several times in fact. Dug up his cell, but got voice mail. I guess I should have tried the golf course or marina."

There was silence in the Courtroom as he shuffled the file about. He continued.

"I'm at a bit of a loss, but I'm also feeling a little bit ignored. So, let's go on the record," he said as his court reporter sprang to life. "We're here for a hearing in the matter of the Estate of Leonardo X. Cross. Present today is the Personal Representative of the estate and his attorney, Noah Parks. Not present and quite unaccounted for is the party contesting the validity of the will in this matter, a Mr. Chase Cross, decedent's son, and his attorney, Robert Seabrook. As the Court has received no request for continuance in this matter, no information as to the whereabouts of Mr. Seabrook or his client, and generally no information as to why Mr. Seabrook is not here, I'm going to dismiss this matter without prejudice. I'll prepare an administrative order and forward it on to you, Mr. Parks."

I looked at Thomason and then to the Judge.

"Certainly your Honor. Thank you," I said as we rose to leave. "Bailiff, who's next?"

CHAPTER 4

"That was interesting," I said, as we exited the courtroom.

"I certainly don't know your Judge, but yes, that was actually quite amusing. Seems like no matter where you go, judges never do like being ignored. However, once Seabrook and his client surface, I would wager a new hearing will be demanded, likely before the Judge files the order."

I looked at my watch and was about to suggest that we go have some lunch.

"Seems we have some time, Noah. Unless you have something pressing, shall we go have a bite to eat? It will give us a bit of time away from the matter at hand."

I smiled and thought to myself that it seemed impossible to surprise this man.

"Something amusing?"

"No, not at all. I was actually just thinking the same thing. Any preference?"

"There is a wonderful place in the hotel."

Why didn't that surprise me? Thomason liked the restaurant at the Planter's Inn as well.

"One of my favorites," I said.

After a short walk through the lovely Charleston humidity, I was looking forward to lunch. Mainly to be inside, but also in anticipation of learning a bit more about him. Then my attention was drawn to the sound of the television over the bar.

"And now more breaking news from downtown where an accident has closed the Ravenel Bridge," the news anchor said. "We go to Morgan York downtown. Morgan?"

The news anchor's face was replaced with that of a lively blonde near the edge of the harbor. In the background I could see the bridge spanning the harbor between Charleston and Mount Pleasant. Traffic on the bridge had stopped, and from the abundance of multi-color flashing lights scattered about the scene, there were obviously a number of emergency vehicles there. Two helicopters moved in and out at the top of the frame.

"Thank you, Rebecca. As News 2 has reported, a little more than an hour ago there was a multi-vehicle accident on the Arthur Ravenel, Jr. Bridge. At this time authorities don't know the cause of the crash, but News 2 has confirmed there are at least five disabled vehicles on the bridge that have been involved in the accident. This has caused both lanes of bridge traffic to be closed, leaving several hundred cars stranded on the bridge. In addition to these five vehicles on the bridge involved in the wreck, it appears at least two vehicles have gone over the bridge into the Cooper River near Town Creek. From my location, just over my shoulder, you can see that a section of the bridge has been damaged at the point where we believe the vehicles went off the bridge. More rescue personnel are traveling to the scene, but the traffic on the bridge is making this extremely difficult. We have also been told the Sheriff's Department has an underwater search and rescue team en route to our location. We don't have any word on fatalities, however, as I said, two cars have gone over the side of the bridge. Traffic is backed up on the entire bridge as no cars can get around the wreckage. Authorities have closed the bridge and are diverting all approaching vehicles. We'll keep you updated as we learn more. Morgan York reporting live for News 2 from the Cooper River."

"Steven, I found Chase and Seabrook."

"I'm sorry." He turned from the maitre de's stand and walked into the bar. "What was that?"

"Seabrook's office is across the bridge in Mount Pleasant. Looks like traffic is backed up on the bridge from a pretty bad accident with no sign of getting anywhere anytime soon. Guarantee they're in that." I pointed to the screen.

"We can count on him re-filing this afternoon."

"Mr. Thomason, your table is ready," the maitre de said.

We walked away from the news anchor as she promised to keep us informed as further updates became available. I was glad my office was downtown and that I didn't have to face bridge traffic every day, especially today.

Thomason and I walked into the mostly empty dining room and were seated at a table in the rear of the room. A busboy appeared and poured us each water. I studied the menu.

"Let's assume that the notice will be re-filed by the end of the day. Can you get a copy today?"

As always, right to business, I thought.

"Sure, I'll call my office and have Heather take care of it. Will you be staying overnight? If you are, I can drop a copy off here for you at the desk."

"I will be staying at least one more night and would appreciate it if you would get a copy to me today. Do you think I did anything improper with the will?" he said.

Direct as ever.

"Not that it matters, but no. Given the bizarre nature of this entire thing, I don't think that you did anything other than spend a lot of time helping a friend. But tell me this, did his children ever try to work their way back into his good graces?"

"Why do you ask?"

"I'm curious if perhaps Chase tried to reconcile with his father. If he did and it went poorly, it may have a bit to do with why he's appearing now. I mean, didn't you meet with him and Anna Beth after Cross died?"

"I did. But there was no mention of concerns with the will or any reconciliation for that matter," he said.

"I see. How'd you get the will?"

"They gave it to me, the children. They contacted me when Cross died and gave it to me after the memorial service. From there you know the rest of the story. Why?"

"That's how I thought it went. No problems with them? I mean, any sign of things to come?"

"Actually, no. It isn't that I expected problems, but let's say I was anticipating them and was prepared for contingencies. You're thinking something," he said.

"I am. I've been kicking it around for a while now, but it all started with a question. Why do you suppose that Chase waited six months before he did anything? He's been estranged from Cross for years – what, almost twenty?"

"Almost."

"My thought is that if he was going to do anything, he'd have long ago decided to jump as soon as he got the chance. So why wait like he did?"

"I hadn't thought about that, actually."

"We can ask him that when we take his deposition. But, one other thing I've been wondering about – where is Anna Beth in all of this?"

Thomason kept going as our food arrived.

"Anna Beth is a horse of a different color. Not to compare her to a horse - she is truly a lovely woman - but after her father cut off the children's funds, she was the only one of the three that realized that if she was going to make it, it would be her that made it happen. No one else. She was young, only seventeen when her father moved, and I was very surprised that she didn't move with him. She had been the closest of the three children, but nevertheless stayed behind in Chicago."

"Do we hear from her next?" I said as Thomason stopped to butter a roll.

"No, I would think not. As I've said before, she has her own life now with her own money. Her road is her own, and while she will likely take the proverbial money and run, I doubt she will push for anything more."

"Well for now we have Chase to deal with. And we'll probably be back in court within the week. I wouldn't plan on Oscarson forgetting about the events of the day, though. How's lunch?"

"Quite good."

The rest of the lunch was generally silence punctuated with his thoughts on the weather, the city or Chicago's transit authority. However, nothing specific about him, Cross or the children, despite some subtle prodding from me.

~~~~~~~~~~~~~~~~~~~~~~~~~

I arrived at my office to find Heather with the television on, talking on her cell with two lines on the office phone on hold. She smiled as I walked in.

"Gotta go," she said into her cell. "So how did it go?"

"Seabrook was MIA. I think he's stuck in that mess on the bridge."

"Mess is right. Like two hundred cars have been stranded on the bridge for three hours, and it looks like they'll be there awhile. Traffic's screwed up all over town."

"Just another reason why we work downtown. Hey, could you call the courier service and have them go by the Court this afternoon? Have them get a copy of the re-filed notice that Seabrook'll be filing?"

"I'll do it right now."

Around 5:00 o'clock I heard Heather shuffling around outside my office. She appeared in my doorway.

"I'm heading out. I am hooking up with some friends to watch the sun go down on the bridges with all the cars still up there."

"Seriously?"

"Yea. It sucks for them, but how often do you get to see something like this? Wanna come?"

"One day. One day I'll take you up on your offer."

"One day, huh?"

I wrapped up several things I was working on and headed home. It hadn't been that hectic of a day, but I was exhausted. I should have played with Austin, but after a quick bite, I was out for the evening.

I rolled out of bed a little later than usual the next morning, though it was still dark outside. I grabbed a robe and walked to the end of the drive to get the paper. Austin was waiting downstairs at the door for me when I returned and we began our morning ritual, though we had to run through it a bit faster than normal. I decided to skip my morning run to get to the office early. I showered, got dressed and decided to eat breakfast at the office. As I was walking out the door, I turned around and grabbed the paper.

I arrived at the office a little after 7:30, well ahead of Heather. However, the after-hours drop box was empty. I was a little surprised that the courier had not delivered the notice, but the bridge had been closed for almost eight hours and that may have had something to do with it. I gathered Seabrook hadn't had a chance to file anything, but he wouldn't let the morning get by without doing it.

I always liked the office best first thing in the morning when there was no one there and the phones weren't ringing. Thinking about this and expecting silence, I opened the door to the sound of a ringing phone. I normally don't like to answer, but I made an exception given the hour.

"Noah Parks."

"Noah." It was Thomason's voice on the other end of the line.

"Steven. Good morning. How can I help you?"

"Was that him?"

"Steven, um, I'm sorry, it's early yet and I'm not following you. Pretend for a moment I don't know what you're talking about?"

"Seabrook, was it him?"

"Steven, again, I have no idea what the hell you're getting at."

"Have you been watching the news? Is our Seabrook the Seabrook they are talking about?"

"Seabrook? What? Who are you talking about?"

"Noah, whatever have you been doing since you got up?"

"Steven, not to be rude, but just tell me what you are talking about."

"Sit if you will and I shall spoon feed you." He paused while I situated myself at my desk. "Are we ready? Very well. It seems a local attorney named Seabrook was in one of the cars that went off of the bridge yesterday in that accident we saw at lunch. Is there another attorney named Seabrook in town?"

"Yes, Robert's cousin," I said as I glanced about my office for my newspaper. I spied it on the chair by my door. "Hang on, let me grab my paper."

"Go."

I spread out the paper on my desk and read the headline on the front page.

"LOCAL ATTORNEY DIES IN BRIDGE CRASH."

I started to read through the article but didn't have to get too far until I had the answer to Thomason's question.

> *"A local attorney, Robert Seabrook, died when his car plunged into the Cooper River after going off the side of the Arthur Ravenel, Jr. Bridge in a seven car accident..."*

"To answer your question, yes, that was him," I said. "Hang on a moment."

I read on.

> *"Authorities have released little information or other details about the wreck. However, witnesses have indicated that one of the vehicles involved in the multi-car accident appeared to have lost control and caused a chain reaction. Seabrook's car, along with one other, appear to have been thrown from the bridge as a result of the accident. After leaving the bridge, the vehicles fell more than two hundred feet into the Charleston harbor below. While reports are unconfirmed, Seabrook is believed to have had a passenger*

in his car at the time of the accident..."

"Steven, I'd gather you would've suspected this, but looks like Chase may have been in the car with him."

"You are right, I had suspected as much. I guess we will have to wait for confirmation, but that may very well be the end of the problem with the Court."

"True," I said, thinking it a bit odd that this was his first thought following the confirmation of their deaths.

"I have some calls to make, but keep me posted if you hear anything else," he said.

"I will. Anything else I can do?" I said as I was trying to read more of the article.

"No. I will give you a call later today, just find out what you can."

I hung up the phone and finished the article. As was generally the case, there was a long story but not a lot of details. Lots of witnesses had been interviewed, but everyone reported basically the same thing – things were fine, then all of the sudden there was chaos and cars were, as the paper quoted one witness as saying, 'flying everywhere.'

The rest of the day was a bit of a blur, and I got little done. Most of my time was spent talking to other attorneys about the wreck or Seabrook. It seemed tragedies such as this served to feed everyone's morbid curiosity

~~~~~~~~~~~~~~~~~~~~~~

The next day Seabrook's car was pulled from the harbor. All of the local stations provided live coverage of the car being raised on television. I watched along with Heather. The car was pulled slowly from the water and raised to a barge with a screen to shield the curious onlookers. Divers attached cables to the car and a crane on a separate barge slowly pulled it from the water. It was guided toward the waiting barge by ropes that disappeared behind the screen. As the car, a silver Mercedes, dangled at the end of the crane's cable, it rotated toward the camera despite the ropes attempting to hold it steady, and for a brief moment you could see the outlines of the car's two occupants. The ringing of the phone startled me. I heard Heather answer it. A voice came across my speaker.

"Mr. Thomason is on the line for you."

"Hello."

"You watching this?"

"I am. Chase, is that him?"

"Yes, it is. I have several matters to attend to which will keep me occupied until after lunch. I know that the closing documents for the estate are not due for about a week, but I would like to go ahead and get everything signed so they can be submitted. I will not be able to meet with you the day they are due, so I would like to get them signed in advance. Shall we say three today at your office?"

"That will be fine," I said.

Three o'clock came fast. I joined Thomason in my conference room just after he arrived, having previously arranged our work on the room's table.

"Should we do anything, contact anyone?"

"I called Anna Beth and informed her last night, at least of the likelihood. I called her again this morning and confirmed it," he said.

"Will she be coming into town?" I said.

"Anna Beth will coordinate things, and while it is unfortunate, this rather clears the air as to our finishing with the estate, would you not agree?"

"Looking at it like that, yes, I would tend to agree," I said as I gathered the necessary documents for him to sign. From his demeanor, I could tell the conversation concerning Anna Beth was over.

After Thomason signed the papers and departed without further comment, I made them ready for filing with the Court the following week.

~~~~~~~~~~~~~~~~~~~~~~~~~~~~

Following Seabrook's death, I found myself paying more attention to the news than I usually did for the next few days. Something drew me to the story. As was generally the case in town when a big local story came along, it was treated much like a dead horse. First there were the stories about the crash, then the stories about the raising of the cars from the harbor. Of course that gave way to a sidebar on the technology of underwater salvage and a flood of stories on bridge safety. Then came the coverage of the funeral. It was a local attorney who had died, and in the few days since his death he had gone from being just another name in the yellow pages to an esteemed member of the bar. It was also discovered, (though I already knew), that it had been a client who had died in the crash with him, and that this client was the son of a local resident who had recently died.

There was an investigation as to the integrity of the bridge that raised a few questions, but ultimately showed nothing. The police did an investigation as well, but at the end of the day the accepted conclusion was that one of the cars veered out of its lane, clipped a car in another lane and started a chain reaction that led to two cars being thrown from the bridge.

Perhaps the most disturbing thing out of this for me was a picture that ran in the local paper. One of the photographers caught Seabrook's car as it was being moved from the barge in the harbor to a pier and waiting wrecker. While it was swinging in the wind. There was nothing graphic or inherently morbid about it, but you couldn't see either of the occupants clearly. Seabrook's hand was visible, caught on the Mercedes' steering wheel, which gave the photo an eerie feel. You could tell that both of the men were still in their seatbelts, but, in either the plunge to the bottom of the harbor or the trip up from the bottom, anything in the car not fastened down had come to rest in a chaotic fashion intermingled with random marine life. It even looked as if one of the papers that had been in the car had attached to Seabrook like a bib. This photo bothered me even after the story of the accident and their death faded from the headlines. However, the day I delivered the closing documents to the Probate Court, even the thought of a morbid photo couldn't keep the smile from my face. We only had to wait for the arrival of the official discharge papers from the Court and I could visit the Bank of South Carolina.

CHAPTER 5

The days following the filing of the last documents required to close the estate seemed to have gained more hours, growing longer, crawling by. It was always the same with the Court. They got to things in their own sweet time on a schedule that few, even those involved in its inner workings, could discern or even pretend to understand. So while I waited I tried to find things to do to keep me occupied instead of dealing with the increasingly frustrating anticipation of being able to open the safe deposit box. Through the months leading up to this, during all of the time I was working on the estate, I had wondered in passing about the safe deposit box. Now, with nothing to do but wait, I found myself often daydreaming about what was waiting in the bank's vault downtown.

In times like these I found it interesting how the human mind worked, mine in particular. For months my work on the estate had been sporadic, a little here, a little there. The work had always been there, and whatever was in the safe deposit box was there waiting like a carrot at the end of a rope. I do have to admit that from time to time I wondered about the contents of the safe deposit box, but those thoughts always faded to more concrete and immediate ones, usually related to a phone call from Thomason or Heather asking me out again.

Then there was Thomason. Sometimes he could be a bit much to deal with. When he called he really expected that my entire office come to a halt for him. He expected things to be done then and not a moment later. In fact, if things were done immediately that could potentially be a little slow for him. Fortunately he didn't have any unrealistic expectations, nor did he ask or expect me to perform miracles on every occasion we spoke.

One part of the estate process that I always found fascinating was inventorying personal property in the estate. It gives you a chance to learn about someone you'd never met. A person's property says a lot about them.

I have handled estates where I had to go through box after box. Some estates seemed to have nothing, but it seemed that in almost every estate there was something that helped to paint a picture of the deceased.

From all I had learned about Cross - the problems with his children, his isolation, living in near total exile for the later years of his life - I was expecting to find he had lived a life of regret. But I was surprised. I learned a few things about him, but mostly, all I found were questions. And more questions. In life, Cross had been a very private person. Now, in death, the same was proving to be true.

One thing I did find was that Cross had a lot of possessions. Rare books, artwork, furnishings, rugs, collectibles and many other physical possessions. However, I didn't find anything truly personal. His house, thanks in part to Ms. Martha, was immaculate, but quite impersonal, telling nothing about the man. It was almost like being in a personal museum. I was able to admire everything, but I couldn't connect with the person behind the property.

There were a lot of odd things about Cross' possessions as well. The truly odd part of it all was that I have never been around someone's home so devoid of personal photographs. There wasn't a single photograph of Cross, his family, or anyone for that matter. The only photographs were fine art photographs of buildings or landscapes. It was as if he didn't want to be reminded of his children or life before he came to Charleston.

There were plans for an auction in the coming months, after Anna Beth Cross was given the opportunity to look through a list and obtain any of the property she wanted. Then the house was to be sold.

So after everything was filed and the waiting set in, I occupied myself with other work in the office. Even still, I found myself continually asking Heather if she had checked the mail. That is, until I started to notice her eyes rolling. After that I just checked for myself.

One day, several weeks into my wait, I was contemplating calling the Court when I heard footsteps approaching my office. I looked up to see Heather leaning against the outside of the doorframe, only her head and hand visible from where I sat.

"Noah?"

"Yes?"

"Everything all right?" she said.

As she said this her hair fell from her shoulder, outlining her face. I was surprised to feel my heart speeding up.

"Yes. Why do you ask?" I said.

"Well, you've been wound up like a, what is it you say? A

cheap watch?"

As her words hung in the air she walked into my office and sat across from my desk. She crossed her legs and leaned slightly toward me, her hands on her lap.

"Ever since you closed the Cross estate you've seemed a little bit obsessed about it. So, basically, what's going on?"

"Funny you should say that." I looked away from her toward the chaos of papers on my desk. "I was just getting ready to call the Court and check on things, unless you've checked the mail for me."

"Oh, now don't do that. You know how that always makes it harder for me to get anything out of them when we really need it."

There was silence for a long moment, then she spoke again.

"I do have a question."

"And that would be?" I said.

"What's the hurry? It'll be back soon enough."

I contemplated her for a second. I hadn't told her about the safe deposit box before. It wasn't that I had avoided it, I simply hadn't. "Well, I'm mentioned in the will."

"I know."

I must have looked surprised because she sat up in her chair as soon as she spoke.

"I'm sorry," I said. "How's that?"

"Mr. Thomason told me. One day a few months back he said you get something in a safe deposit box downtown."

"Really, now?" I shifted in my seat and put down the papers I had been holding. My heart rate was increasing again, but for different reasons. Why would Thomason tell her this and not mention it to me? I could tell she knew she had wandered into a delicate area.

"Yes. Um, I'm sorry. Should I have kept my mouth shut?"

"No, no, not at all. I just didn't know Thomason had told you.

Not that it matters. I guess I'm the one who should be apologizing."

"So you aren't mad at me?" she said as she peered through a lock of hair that had fallen to her face. She brushed it aside.

"Good heavens no. Not a bit. I mean, I'm curious why Thomason didn't tell me, but I'm not concerned about you knowing at all. I mean, after all, you know more about what goes on around here than I do most of the time."

"Just as long as you aren't mad," she said, showing a slight smile.

"And sorry if I have seemed distracted. I guess I hadn't been thinking about it all that much until recently when I started to realize the estate would be closed soon."

"So?"

"Remember how Thomason first came in? And how I told you Cross' will basically said I was the attorney for the estate?"

"Yes."

"The will says I'm to be the attorney for the estate and I told you that, but that's not all. You see, after the estate is closed, there's a safe deposit box downtown. I get what is inside. Whatever's in it."

"Seriously? That's actually quite cool, sorta like a movie."

"I can't say I've thought about it like that, but I'll admit it's certainly something that doesn't happen every day."

She shifted in her seat and crossed her legs. She put her hands together and raised them to her lips.

"So? What do you think it is?"

"I haven't the slightest idea. Could be anything."

She lowered her head to look at me. "If you get rich, do I get a cut?"

"Maybe," I said, trying to be cool and flirtatious at the same time. The silence that followed made me wonder if I had just fallen flat on my face.

"Well, so what are you going to do?"

"I think I'll just take a deep breath and be patient."

"Patience doesn't always pay off, you know?"

"I know, but this time, I think I'll just wait," I said.

"What's the fun in that? Why don't you just go for it?" she hesitated and stared at me. I held her gaze for a moment, then she looked away. "Why don't I just call one of my friends down there and see if I can't speed things up?"

"No, it's been a couple of weeks. It'll be closing soon. I'll just try to stop obsessing. But let me ask you this."

"What's that?" she asked as she stood, smoothing the front of her skirt before she looked toward me.

"Could you go check the mail?"

~~~~~~~~~~~~~~~~~~~~~~

I waited as the days crawled by. I realized it had been a while since Thomason had called which was quite odd, particularly given that things were so close to being finished. I figured that he'd be obsessing even more than I, so I reached for the phone and dialed his number. He answered on the second ring.

"Noah?" If it had not been for the omnipresence of caller ID, I would have thought this evidence that he was psychic.

"Yes, Steven, how are you doing?"

"Good, thank you, and how are things in your fair city?"

"Very good actually. I wanted to call and give you an update."

"Very good. Do we have good news?"

"Well, if you consider no news good, then yes, but in all actuality, there's nothing to report. I just wanted to call and let you know that I was still waiting to hear."

"Then thank you for keeping me updated even if there is nothing to report."

"How did things go with Chase and things related to that?"

A silent pause on the line.

"I really have no idea. I didn't hear anything to the contrary, so I expect they went as well as could be expected." I waited to see if he would volunteer anything else, but he didn't.

"I'll keep you posted and call you the minute anything comes in."

"Very good then, I hope to hear from you soon."

I was staring at the receiver in its cradle when Heather's voice came through the intercom on the phone.

"Noah."

I was momentarily startled, but answered. "Yes."

"There's a call for you on line one."

"Could you take a message?" I didn't want to speak to anyone at the moment as I was reflecting on my conversation with Thomason.

"I think you want to take this one. It's Mr. Cross' daughter."

I took a drink of water and picked up the phone.

"This is Noah Parks."

"Hello Mr. Parks. My name is Anna Beth Cross, and I understand that you have been handling the estate of my father, Leonardo."

She sounded nothing like what I had imagined, but then again, I really don't know what I had imagined, if anything at all. I have always found that most people believe they can imagine how a person will sound prior to meeting them and hearing their voice. However, when people finally meet, most realize that the person's voice actually sounds nothing at all like what they had imagined. This thought morphed to one of me wondering what it must be like to have lost two brothers and a father in such a short time. Apparently I got lost in this thought a bit longer than I realized.

"Mr. Parks?"

It was like being called on in class after you had been daydreaming. I snapped back to reality.

"Yes, I'm sorry, yes, you were saying that I represent your father's estate, that's correct. How can I help you?"

"I'll get right to the point. I'd like to arrange a meeting with you so we can discuss some matters related to my father. I am sure you're aware that my brother recently died?"

"Um, yes, I am." I left it at that. It wasn't my place to go further on that subject.

"Mr. Parks, do you keep your own calendar, or should I speak to your assistant to arrange an appointment? That is, if you will see me?"

"Of course I'll see you. Let me look at my calendar. When will be good for you?"

"I am in town now and have no commitments, so whenever is good for you."

"Why don't we say tomorrow morning, at 10:00?" I said.

"That will be fine. I shall see you then."

"Good then…" I was saying as she interrupted me.

"Mr. Parks, I look forward to meeting you tomorrow. And Mr. Parks?"

"Yes?"

"When you speak to Steven, please give him my best," she said. The line went dead.

Once again, in a span of less than ten minutes, I found myself holding a dead receiver. No sense in disappointing her, I thought. I clicked over to another line and dialed Thomason. I got him on the first try.

"Steven?"

"Yes, Noah, did you forget something?"

"No…" I started, only to find myself cut off again.

"So have you heard from the Court?"

"No, something else has come up, so to speak."

"And that would be?"

"I received an interesting call as we were saying goodbye. Anna Beth Cross just called and asked to see me. About what, I have no idea. I mean, she told me it was related to her father, but that was it. No idea what she wants to speak to me about."

"Really now? That is interesting."

"Yes, I wish that I had more, but I don't. Except for one thing."

"What was that?"

"She said to say 'Hello' to you."

"It doesn't surprise me that she called, but I do admit that I am curious as to her agenda and motive. However, I am confident she is aware of your puzzling involvement in her father's estate. It also doesn't surprise me that she suspected you would report immediately to me and, by the way, thank you for doing so. I am sure that she believes you to be little more than my agent in this affair."

"I certainly picked that up from her tone."

"Take no offense, Noah. Forces were at work long before you became a factor in this matter. Well, when do you meet with her?"

"None taken, and ten tomorrow morning."

"I trust you will give me a full report. A word of caution, though. She is smart, street savvy, deceptive, quite capable of taking care of herself and especially beautiful."

"Not worried about me, are you?"

"Actually," he said, then paused. "Yes."

"Don't be. I think I'm quite capable of looking after myself,

Steven. She's just a daughter and sister who's lost a father and both of her brothers."

"True, but trust me, there is much more to Ms. Anna Beth Cross. Just watch your step."

"I'll be sure to give you a call as soon as I wrap up with her."

I looked up at the clock as I placed the receiver back in its cradle. It was time to go home.

~~~~~~~~~~~~~~~~~~~~~

I was in my office early the next morning, wondering how my meeting with Anna Beth would go. I was particularly intrigued by Thomason's description of her, especially the beautiful part – frequently the description of beautiful varied from one person to the next. So I found myself in my office busying myself but really doing nothing in anticipation of her arrival. The sound of the intercom on the phone broke my feigned concentration. Heather's voice sprang forth from the receiver.

"Noah, she's here."

"Tell her I'll be right there."

I started to pick up her father's file, but I decided against it. I straightened my tie and headed toward the lobby.

She sat in the furthest chair from the door. Sandals, a white tee shirt showing a bit of her firm stomach, and a pair of tight low rise khaki pants. Her long brown hair was pulled back in a ponytail. She sat upright with her legs crossed, staring at the floor.

No briefcase or files. Good, I thought.

As I walked toward her, she raised her eyes to meet mine. She looked as if she could have been right at home on the cover of any fashion magazine. The funny thing was, despite her beauty, she looked very approachable and not the least bit aloof. Then I saw her eyes. I felt a surprisingly enjoyable feeling in my chest that lingered before it faded. Her eyes matched the color of her hair, and from the first time I saw them I knew they could be dangerous. Thomason certainly got the beautiful part right. Of course, that meant it was quite likely that not only was the rest of what Thomason said true, but it was even more likely that he had neglected to tell me a few things about the lovely Anna Beth Cross.

"Good morning Ms. Cross. I'm Noah Parks." I held out my hand to her. "Pleasure to meet you."

"Hello Mr. Parks," she said as she stood to shake my hand.

She was quite tall, almost as tall as me. She also appeared to be quite athletic, but not in a masculine way. Immediately I noticed that she exuded poise and grace. Even a blind man would have picked up on this as it was so obvious, but there was something else there that I couldn't quite get a handle on. Something inviting, but at the same time something that made me hesitate. I realized that I'd never been told how old she was, and even as I looked at her only a few feet away I couldn't really be sure of her age. She could have been as young as twenty-five, or easily older. It was clear that she took care of herself, and while she didn't look to obsess over her appearance, it was easy to see she was quite conscious of how she presented herself and that she was quite confident with herself.

"Please, call me Noah. Let's go back to my conference room where we can talk."

I led her through my office, opened the door to the conference room, turned on the lights and motioned for her to sit.

"Please accept my condolences for your brother's death."

"Thank you," she said as she sat comfortably in a chair across the table from me. I took out a legal pad and my Mont Blanc.

"Well, Ms. Cross, I'll be candid with you and please don't read into this that it is any sort of inconvenience to meet with me. It is just that normally when people see me I have at least a general understanding as to what they wish to discuss. While I can hazard a guess here, I really have no idea how I can be of assistance to you. So, to avoid wasting your time, I guess the question we need to start with is, what can I do for you?"

"Thank you for your candor, Mr., I mean Noah." I thought I saw a hint of a smile. "I have a few questions about my father, some about my brother and, I guess, a few other things generally related to their deaths that I want to talk about. But mainly, I need to talk to someone about all of this, and you seem the best choice."

I guess my silence or expression told her more than I realized.

"Noah, rest assured, I'm not crazy. I'm sure that Steven told you a bit about our family, and you probably know my father and I had little in the way of a relationship. It was much the same with my brothers after my divorce. So, this leaves me with two options as to people that are even mildly acquainted with the affairs of my family now – Steven, and you. I'm sure he let you know that while we are quite civil toward one another, we don't get along too well. So, that leaves you. I have some things I'm trying to work out, and I'd like to talk to you about them. And don't worry, I have a therapist in Chicago."

She smiled as she mentioned the therapist.

I took a deep breath and put my pen down. "I don't know what good I can be, but I can certainly try. Tell me what's on your mind."

I certainly didn't think such a simple question could end up being so complicated.

"I believe my father and brothers were murdered."

CHAPTER 6

There comes a time when it's best to take a step back and spend a moment in contemplation of the path that has led you to your present situation. In these times, I find a moment of reflection gives me a degree of perspective. It also gives me a pretty accurate glimpse of where I might be going.

From time to time I take such a pause and, more often than not, I'm able to realize when things are about to become complex. Whenever this happens I generally have a feeling deep in my gut, not unlike the feeling I was currently experiencing looking at Anna Beth Cross. As it had before, this feeling was telling me to turn and run. And, as was also becoming habit with this case, I found myself completely ignoring the feeling.

A few weeks ago I'd been enjoying an uncomplicated life. The most unusual thing I had to deal with was the estate of a person whom I'd never heard of. That and an overactive canine, neither of which were beyond my ability to handle. I'll give you that my being mentioned in Leonard Cross' will made for a situation with a bit of texture, but overall I was up to the task.

So, until recently this was the extent of my life's complications, and with that I was just fine. In fact, for most people the perplexing situation that Cross' will offered would have been about enough intrigue for one sitting. Actually, thinking about it, I was one of those people.

Even with the Cross' will, I was happy with my life. I imagine most people would have been, given the low stress level that came with it. If my practice and Austin weren't enough, for added enjoyment (and maybe a bit of complication) I did have my on-again-off-again crush on my paralegal. Generally, I was satisfied with my life to the point that if I had been able to put it up for auction on eBay I imagine that the bidding would have been quite competitive.

But then, just like on a favorite shirt or coat, a small thread appears in the fabric that you pull at just a bit, and then things start to unravel. It's something that you hardly notice in the beginning because it's so innocuous. Even as you continue to pull and pick, you really don't notice what you're doing, but the next thing you know your shirt only has one sleeve. And tell me this – how many people do you know that parade around in shirts with only one sleeve not looking a bit foolish?

I think the metaphorical thread first appeared when Thomason walked into my life. I was afraid to speculate on exactly when I first started to pull at it, but as I sat here with Anna Beth Cross, I expected to look down and see that my shirt was minus a sleeve.

As I look back, my life had been the epitome of enviable. Then, in a flash I'm in the middle of wrapping up an estate that has more questions, unexplained events, bizarre overtones, and now this mysterious woman. Now, granted the reason she was mysterious was that I'd only just met her and knew little about her, she was, nevertheless, perhaps the most mysterious woman I'd encountered as of late. Of course, the fact that within ten minutes of meeting her she tells me that she believes her father and brother had been murdered only helped to raise her mystery rating.

Overall, not only was this a lot for me to process, but it was also a most interesting way to begin a day.

As I thought all of this, I realized I was staring at her. Not to be outdone, she was staring back with the most interesting of looks on her face. As I stared I found that my head cleared, and I was focused only on her face.

The look on her face told me I'd been staring at her just a bit too long for her liking. The silence that had been blanketing the moment grew thick and obvious, then cleared as she spoke.

"Is there a problem, Mr. Cross?"

I broke my stare as the last of the wandering thoughts left my mind.

"No, not at all. May I call you Anna Beth?"

"Certainly."

"So, Anna Beth. I think the important thing here is perspective. That and complete candor. I apologize for my little lapse there. I want to hear exactly why you think your father and brother were murdered, but first I want to explain my position, or at least my thoughts on all of this."

"That's fair enough, I guess," she said.

"Good. The first thing to understand is that I'm a pretty basic person. I like things simple. I love what I do, but like to enjoy lots of other things too. To cut right through things, I have a pretty predictable life. Then one day I find myself in this very room with a generally pleasant but rather overbearing gentleman..."

"Steven can be that way," she said. I paused. She looked almost as if she wished she hadn't spoken.

"So one day I find myself in this very room with Steven Thomason, and I can safely say that my life's otherwise pretty okay. There's this will. I'm in it. I can handle that, but it starts to get odd when no one is able to tell me just why I'm mentioned in it. I don't suppose you know why I'm in your father's will do you?"

"Actually, I was going to ask you that," she said.

"I didn't think you would, but I had to ask. Anyway, things just keep stacking up, body count included. You appear and tell me that in addition to everything else, we now have two or more murders on our hands." I took a deep breath and put my hands on the table. "So, I guess you could say I'm feeling just a bit overwhelmed and maybe a bit confused about all of this."

She smiled at me.

"Good," she said. "If you felt any other way, I'd be concerned."

I found myself wondering why every time I met someone new related to this bloody estate it was as if I had to take and pass a test. I locked eyes with her, shifted my lips from side to side and tapped a finger on my conference table.

"Anna Beth, let me just say one thing because you look like you're about to become rather serious."

"Please."

"It's important for you to know that I'd never heard of your father, Thomason, or anyone else associated with this whole thing before I found myself right in the middle of it all."

"I realize that. In fact, I…"

"Let me guess, you checked up on me?"

"Yes," she said. Her look that told me she was surprised I'd have any questions about something so obvious.

"That certainly doesn't surprise me, actually seems par for the course," I said as I leaned back in my chair. "Go ahead, please."

Apparently she took no notice of the smirk on my face.

She continued. "Okay then, I guess the first thing would be for me to know exactly what you know."

"By that I guess you mean about you and your family."

"Yes," she said.

"I know your father moved here some years back after your mother died, but you and your brothers stayed behind in Chicago. He cut off your funds and you and your brothers had little contact with him through the years. Let's see, your youngest brother died a few years back and your other brother died only recently. Failed businesses, divorces, bitter feelings, the like. Oh yes, and I'm also coming to realize that your father was a very private man. So that, in a nutshell, is it."

"Given that you probably learned that from Steven, that's a good summary. For now. But, I am certain that Steven wasn't quite so general, or kind, with his details. "

"How's that?"

"Mother did die. There's no conspiracy that she was murdered. It was a car accident with a drunk driver. Yes, Father moved, we stayed. Chase longed for a carefree lifestyle and Father would have probably given it to him if he'd shown just a little appreciation. I was young and even when Father left - I thought it was how it was supposed to be. Daniel, for reasons I never really understood, blamed Father for Mother's death."

I had more than a few questions but I kept quiet, not wanting her to stop. She took a breath and continued.

"When Father announced we were moving to Charleston, Chase refused to go. After Father told us, he just walked out. Chase had less and less contact with Father after that. What started out as his chance to prove himself turned out to be Chase learning that all along he'd really been living off Father."

"He didn't like what he saw, I take?"

"No, not at all. Funny thing is, Father tried to give Chase help through the years, but Chase seemed to always refuse. Then Father stopped offering and Chase started demanding. They rarely spoke after that. They were both just so stubborn."

She paused a moment.

"Daniel was quite the opposite. He was so angry. He thought Father was giving up on us and didn't think we could live in Chicago without Mother. To Daniel, leaving Chicago was the same as leaving the memory of our Mother. But for Father, he couldn't be in Chicago without every sight and sound haunting him. He needed to leave to escape her ghost. I'd just assumed that we all were going to move, then Father asked me to stay with Daniel in Chicago. I did."

"Was it difficult? Being separated from your father?"

"I didn't really notice. I'd already been living in my own apartment, so even though Father was hundreds of miles away it was really no different than it had been with him just across town. With the trips to Charleston, it sometimes seemed like I saw him more," she said, her voice trailing off.

"You mean you saw your father after he moved? In Charleston?"

"Of course! See, Steven really isn't the authority on all things Cross. But that doesn't really surprise me. Sometimes Father painted a less than complete picture. He could be selective with his facts from time to time. Anyway, it took several years for Daniel to come around with Father, but he did. After he started classes at Miami, his relationship with Father was great."

"I sense a 'but' coming."

"Well, not really a 'but.' Actually, though, one of the questions I'm trying to figure out. Daniel was doing wonderful at Miami. I'd finished my first year of law school, but decided to get married. My quitting school and getting married wasn't exactly a high point in our relationship. Father was thrilled when I decided to go to law school, but he had quite the opposite opinion on my decision to get married. As I'm sure you're aware, my marriage wasn't what one would call a success. I'm sure anything Steven told you about that is entirely accurate."

I nodded, not sure what to say. She paused again before continuing.

"But back to Daniel. He was doing quite well in school. Announced his plans for law school, was getting along great with Father, and then out of the blue he decides to take a year off from school. I just knew that Father was going to be livid. But the bizarre thing about it was Father completely supported him. In fact, they traveled together a good bit – all over. I don't think Steven even knows about this. Then…"

"He was killed."

"Yes. Murdered. To say Father took it poorly is an understatement."

"How's that?" I was quite fascinated by all of this. I found it intriguing that I was so curious about this dead man that I had never met. For months I'd been yearning for more information where there was none. Then in walks his daughter. The nothingness starts to fade. There were still questions, but questions about a situation I was starting to understand.

"He just shut down. I was still getting over my marriage, so I probably wasn't the most helpful of people with Father, but after Daniel died Father withdrew completely. I think after Daniel's death Steven was probably one of only a very few people that had any contact with Father."

"One problem. I'm still not sure how I fit into this," I said.

Without acknowledging what I'd said, she continued. "I know much of what I've told you is different from what you've already heard. I know that you'll tell Steven what I've said. He'll tell you to be cautious because I have some other motive, and I do, but not what he thinks. All I want is to find out what happened to my brothers and my Father. That's it, that's why I'm here."

We sat in silence for a few moments. I waited to see if she was done. When she didn't speak, I began.

"I'm flattered you'd tell me that. But I want to say this; even if all of that is true, I am still not sure about your father and brothers being murdered. I guess I should say your father and Chase because I think everyone agrees that Daniel was murdered. Did they ever charge anyone in connection with his death?"

"No. And please understand that I realize you probably don't believe me. But Father was quite careful in what he told people. What Steven and I have told you is likely quite different. What I'm trying to say is that Steven has told you what Father told him. Maybe Father's given me a different version of reality, but what I've told you is what I know. All that aside, I'd like your help, even if you do end up reporting it all to Steven."

Strange as all of this was, I could almost understand how she would come to me. I could even see how her story could be true, or at least how she could believe it. Of course, I could also see how her story could be a complete lie to work her way into the mix of things. Stranger things had happened when fewer dollars were involved. The mastery of her tale was that there was no quick way to verify it, but there was also no quick way to verify what I already knew. However, her timing was her biggest ally. If she had wanted to throw a wrench into things, the way to do it was through the Court as Chase had. Now there was really nothing she could do to disrupt the process with the Court.

81

Apart from that, the whole thing was so intriguing to me that I really wanted to get to the bottom of it. I decided that if I was careful, little harm could come from helping her. After all, the things she was asking me to help with could only help me understand the big picture.

"You think about things a lot, don't you, Mr. Parks?" she said, stating it more so than offering it as a question.

"Funny thing is I really don't, but lately things have gotten so strange I really can't help myself. So, I'll tell you what. This whole thing's been confusing from the start, but I'm intrigued. I don't know how much I can help you, but as long as it doesn't pose a conflict with the estate, I'll do all I can. How's that sound?"

"Given the circumstances, Noah, I think that's more than fair."

I liked the way it sounded when she said my name.

"Good. Here is the way I see things. There's only one or two ways I can help. After the estate's closed, there's a chance there may be some information in the safe deposit box that may hopefully answer some of your questions. But, the best bet is probably to have you help finish going through your father's house. I think that's the most likely place we might find something. How's that sound? I mean, provided you can be around Steven and he doesn't mind."

"Noah, I assure you that I can be around Steven without any problems. We haven't always gotten along, but we certainly don't dislike each other. And yes, that approach sounds perfect. I take it you'll be calling him in the next little bit, so please tell him I said hello and that I look forward to seeing him. If not, you and I can decide on another approach."

While I felt that I should have been surprised at her last comment, I really wasn't. I actually thought it sounded quite logical.

"That sounds fair enough. So, how long you think you'll be staying?"

She stretched in her chair as she spoke. "I was thinking of staying for a few weeks. I'll probably rent a beach house on Sullivan's Island. I like the Planter's Inn, but the beach would be a bit more private and relaxing. I'll leave my number with your assistant when I have it and you can keep me posted."

"Actually sounds quite nice. I think Thomason was planning to come down fairly soon so we could finish everything all at once, but I'm not sure when that will be."

"I'll plan on staying a few weeks, and if there's nothing by then we can go from there," she said as she rose from her seat. She walked around the table and offered me her hand. "Thank you, Noah, for taking time to see me and for agreeing to help me."

I moved toward the door, opened it and walked her to the front door. "Well, hopefully I can be of some help."

"I hope so too. I'll look forward to hearing from you." She paused a moment as if she was going to say something else, but only smiled then walked out. She didn't look back as she walked to her car.

I closed the door and walked back in the office where I was greeted by Heather, who wasted no time in offering commentary.

"Wow, she's beautiful. And you walked her out to her car. Who said chivalry's dead," Heather said.

"She is quite attractive. And rather interesting."

"So, what were ya'll talking about back there for so long?"

"She thinks her father and brother were murdered. She tells a different story than Thomason and wants me to help her find out what happened between her father and her youngest brother and see if her father and Chase were murdered. She even went to law school for a year."

I took a deep breath and explained to Heather all she had told me.

"Noah, this just gets better and better."

"I'll give you that."

"You believe her?" she said.

"I don't know, but I also don't know that it matters. Regardless of what I believe, she should be able to see her father's stuff, and if her answers are anywhere, they'll be there. But for now, I guess I better go call Thomason. Mail here yet?"

"Funny. You know I'll let you know as soon as the stuff comes."

~~~~~~~~~~~~~~~~~~~~~~

I walked around my desk and picked up the phone, dialing Thomason from memory. As usual, I got him on the first ring.

"Well, Noah, it's almost one o'clock. If you met her at ten, you and Anna Beth must have had quite a conversation."

"Yes, Steven, we did. And how are you today?"

"Most anxious to hear what the fair Ms. Cross had to say. Please, Noah, don't keep me in suspense any longer."

His tone was sharper than normal, and his lack of the usual pleasantries was a departure for him. I started to point it out, but thought better of it and decided to give him a summary.

"She wants to know what happened to Daniel. She seems to believe that he and Cross had some reconciliation a few years before his death and wants to know about that. She tells a somewhat different version of events than you. She doesn't appear to want anything that can't be had by a look through Cross' personal effects. And she also told me to give you her best when we spoke."

For some reason, I decided to leave out the part about her believing that Cross and Chase had been murdered.

"Ever the clever girl. I told you to be careful with her. Were you?"

"Well, yes. Without feeling like I have to defend myself, I've thought through what she's asking and I see no harm in it. I mean at this point, since the time to contest the estate has passed, she can't hold things up, and I don't see what harm can come from her learning about her brother's death."

"On the surface, I agree. But let's not forget, there are many millions of dollars in question here. Anna Beth may have a comfortable life at the moment, but I dare say that she would not pass up the chance to make it even better. I had not expected her to become involved, but it appears I misjudged her motive. Now that she has appeared, I'm not sure what she has in mind."

"I don't disagree with you, but at this point, I say why not let her find out what happened to her family. I mean, look at it from my perspective. I have two different people telling me two different stories. Regardless of the truth, it doesn't seem to cause a problem, what she is asking." I realized I had risen from my chair and was pacing.

"My, my, seems the lovely Ms. Cross made quite an impression on you. I've never heard you speak like that."

"I have to admit, I want to get some of these questions answered."

"I take it that you are asking for permission to have Anna Beth help finish with Cross' possessions?" he said.

"I told her I'd run it by you and you certainly had the final say, but again, I don't see the harm."

"Noah, I think the lovely Ms. Cross has an ulterior motive, but I also agree that there is little she can do to hold up the closing of the estate. So give Anna Beth my best and tell her I would be happy to have her aide us. After all, Cross accumulated much in the way of possessions and another set of hands couldn't hurt."

"So let me ask you this, do you have any desire to get together, the three of us, to meet for any reason?" I said. I had expected this to be a bit more challenging.

"Why?"

"No reason in particular, just thought it might be helpful."

"Excuse me, Noah." I hadn't noticed Heather standing in front of my desk.

"Steven, pardon me a moment."

"I'm sorry to interrupt you, but I just got back from dropping some papers off at the court. I ran into one of my clerk friends, and they told me everything would be signed off today. It's done," Heather said.

"Steven, Heather told me she just got the heads up that the judge had just signed off on everything. It'll be sent out tomorrow. We're done. When can you get down here?"

"Tonight, I'll leave tonight. Call the hotel and let them know I will be arriving?"

"Certainly."

"And Noah, why don't you see if Ms. Cross can join us for lunch tomorrow. Noon at the hotel. Then," he paused. "You and I can visit the bank."

"I'll call and let her know."

"Do that," he said. "I'll plan on meeting you there."

CHAPTER 7

Given the way the day had progressed, I really didn't find it the least bit unusual that I'd receive word that the estate was being closed on the same day I met Anna Beth Cross. Actually, it seemed par for the course, even though I really didn't even like golf. So, I picked up the phone, called the Planter's Inn and asked for Anna Beth's room. She hadn't yet returned. I left my office and cell numbers and a message that we were to have lunch with Thomason the next day at noon. I also let them know that Thomason was going to be visiting them yet again and needed his room. Apparently his visits weren't that unpleasant for the staff of the Planter's Inn as they seemed quite pleased to hear he was to be in town once again. I told Heather we needed to have the courier service pick up the documents from the Probate Court as soon as they were ready.

"Is Mr. Thomason coming?"

"He is."

"Do you need me to call his hotel?"

"Nope, already took care of it," I said.

"What does he do every time he's here? He lives in Chicago, but he comes down here all the time. I mean, you have clients that live just across town that we don't see that much."

"You don't miss much, do you? Same thing crossed my mind more than once. I know he does something down here, but I haven't been able to figure it out. Who knows though, he doesn't strike me as the kind of guy that goes shopping or hangs out with the tourists. Who knows, maybe he has a woman down here, or maybe a guy he sees."

"He's gay? Did he come on to you?" she said.

"No, no, nothing like that. I mean, he may be. I don't know though, he just seems he's got stuff he's doing when he comes down. Other than this stuff," I said as I motioned to the estate file on my desk. Heather nodded in agreement.

"And you know what, every time he tells us he's coming he has us call the hotel, but he never has us get a car," she said.

I leaned back in my chair. "I think this whole thing has me suspicious. The will, Thomason, now Anna Beth? But I know what you mean about him. Has he said anything to you?"

"No. I mean, he has chatted with me a little, but mostly just being polite I think. This may just be me, but I think he may have actually been checking to see how much you've told me about things."

"Really? Like what?"

"Oh, like little things. If you had me helping with this or that, or he would call and ask me something saying he didn't want to bother you," she said.

"That doesn't surprise me, but at least this thing is almost done. Just make sure to call the courier and have them deliver the stuff from the Probate Court A.S.A.P."

I wanted to call the Bank of South Carolina's manager and let him know I'd be there before noon tomorrow to collect the contents of the safe deposit box. Heather looked like she had something she wanted to say, but I cut her off.

"Give me a minute, I need to make a quick call."

"Um, okay. I'll go call the courier."

"Thanks."

I had checked a few weeks after I started on the estate and learned that the manager of the Bank of South Carolina was named Anderson King. I had a private investigator check up on him to see if there was any connection to Cross. We came up empty. As we worked through the estate, we learned that the safe deposit box was the only connection between Cross and the bank. In fact, King had only been at the bank several months. We also learned that there had been four managers since the time Cross had signed his will, and checking on them turned up nothing either.

"Good morning, Bank of South Carolina," a cheery voice said. I loved that there were still banks you could call and actually get a real person on the phone.

"Good morning, my name's Noah Parks. I'm an attorney here in town, actually just down the street. I need to speak to Anderson King, please."

"One moment," the voice said.

After a moment, another voice came on the line. "Hello, Anderson King here."

"Yes, Mr. King, Noah Parks here. Do you have a moment?"

"Certainly, Mr. Parks. And please, call me Anderson."

I explained why I was calling, then he asked to put me on hold.

"Sorry for the wait, Noah. Now, this is a somewhat unique, but not impossible situation. Unfortunately, I can't even let you know if there is a safe deposit box in that name here. However, I think we can quickly get past that issue. Our policy here is that with a letter of authorization from the Personal Representative, a Certificate of Appointment and an original copy of the death certificate, we can address any issue that need be discussed."

"I certainly understand," I said, having run into this before. "I gathered that would be the case. Tell you what, if the personal representative is present in person with the necessary documentation, will that be acceptable?"

"Of course."

"Then in that case, will you be in your office tomorrow? Say after lunch – around 2:00? If possible, I would like to arrange to meet you then."

"Certainly, and I shall look forward to it," he said.

I hung up the phone and swung around in my chair. Heather was in the doorway, against the door-frame in what was becoming one of her signature poses – shoulder against the frame, arms crossed, weight on one foot, the other crossed, toes resting lightly on the floor.

"I called the courier. He should be here around ten tomorrow." She walked into my office and sat across from me.

"So, you're done?" she said. "Done with the estate, that is."

"It would appear so." When she had been in my office a few minutes before, her hair had been pulled back in a ponytail as she usually wore it, but now it was down, falling to her shoulders. I'd seen it this way a few times, usually when she was leaving for the day, but never during the middle of the day. I actually preferred her hair down, but kept that opinion to myself.

I wondered if she was trying to compete with Anna Beth. Both of these women were attractive, in different ways. I'd be hard pressed to pick one over the other. In a way, I felt a bit embarrassed for that run of thoughts, but at the same time I could feel my crush on Heather flaring up. She reclined in the chair. I shuffled some papers, trying to busy myself so I wouldn't stare.

"Let your hair down, I see," I said, immediately wishing I could pull back the words back.

"Like it?"

"I'm sorry, how's that?"

"My hair, do you like it down?" she said.

I was still shuffling my papers. As many times as I thought she'd been flirting with me in the past, even I, who wouldn't see the snake until I was about to step on it, was pretty sure this time.

I raised my eyes to meet her. "Yes. To what do I owe the honor?"

Silence. Sometimes I really liked it. Other times, like now, it was deafening and seemed to go on forever.

"So, I'll be bold. Let's close early and go have that drink we keep talking about?" she said.

"Sure," I heard myself saying. She looked as surprised as I felt. "Tell you what, why don't you lock up. I'll call the service and let them know we're gone."

"Already did it," she said.

"Confident, aren't you?"

"No, but I was prepared to use force to get you out of here."

"So, where to?" she said.

"You tell me, anywhere you like."

I'd let this opportunity pass me by many times before, and I guess I should have felt lucky to keep getting second chances. A moment later, I found myself in my car with her. Funny thing was, I was wondering what Anna Beth Cross was doing.

I backed out of my parking spot and turned onto Broad Street.

"You're being quiet, Noah. Everything alright?"

"Actually, yes, everything is fine. It's nice to be able to leave a bit early and take the day off. Though as many times as I turned you down, I'm surprised you offered again."

"Call me persistent," she said, with a smile.

"Well, the name suits you. So what? How about lunch?"

"Sounds perfect."

"Well, then let's park and walk," I said. She started grinning.

"What's so funny?" I said.

"You. You realize we just drove around the block just to park again?"

She faced me in her seat, her hair falling down, framing her face. I found myself thinking how amazing she looked. It was hard to believe that this was the same Heather that was telling me how beautiful Anna Beth Cross was only an hour ago. Anna Beth? Hadn't I just been thinking about her? I headed back to my office.

She was still giggling when we arrived back where we'd started – my parking spot. She brushed her hair from her face and shifted slightly in her seat. Our stares locked, and we sat in silence looking at each other until she spoke.

"I just realized I've never been in your car. Almost a year and I've never been in your car. Why do you suppose that is?"

"I'm not really sure. But you never asked," I said.

She seemed restless as she shifted again. Her hand lightly brushed my arm as she reached over, turned off the engine and removed the keys from the ignition.

"No, I never asked," she said as she dropped the keys in my hand. "Is that what I have to do if I want something?"

I decided that there probably wasn't a good way to answer that question.

"You never know."

"Noah, are you sure everything's all right?"

I thought about her question for a moment and was about to answer when she spoke again.

"How about you not answer that right now."

"Deal. Let's go grab a bite to eat," I said.

We got out of the car and walking from my parking spot, headed down State Street, turning onto Unity Alley toward East Bay.

There were a couple of neat restaurants where I knew we could sit and have some privacy. We chatted while we walked, mostly people watching, talking about the tourists that were wandering the streets. On almost every corner we would see a small group of them, huddled together, squinting at a map that one of them was turning round and round in a feeble attempt to orientate it to their position. Then, like clockwork, one or two of the group would raise their head and point off in the distance, then return their attention to the map. In the past I had always considered it part of my civic duty to help out the lost and wayward tourists I encountered. However, in recent years, the attitude of the visitors to the city had changed to the point that when you tried to help them they looked at you as if you were held with the same regard as a telemarketer. We chuckled, then she surprised me when she wrapped her arm around mine. We walked past a group in heated debate over a map that appeared to be not of Charleston but of our sister city to the south, Savannah. We turned off of East Bay and walked down a side street.

"Here we are."

"Jimmy Dengate's?"

"Absolutely, nothing but the best."

Jimmy Dengate's, or Dengate's as it's known about town, is a Charleston institution of sorts. While the location and owners had changed through the years, it remains a constant in the city. During the day until early afternoon it was home of the Blue Plate special –

a meat and three vegetables with Charleston table wine, commonly known as sweet iced tea. But Dengate's did sweet tea right.

Sweet tea is an art form. You get too far north, or even too far west, it is commonly, albeit incorrectly, presumed that sweet tea can be sweetened at any point in the process and survive as authentic. This is just wrong. Sweet tea has to be sweetened with pure cane sugar when it is still hot from being brewed. Any other way and it is ruined, little else than brown water.

At Dengate's after lunch, people come for more than just sweet tea. The landscape at Dengate's changes. During the night hours, it's the cornerstone of Charleston nightlife. However, during those transitional hours after lunch until the nighttime crowds arrive, Dengate's is one of my favorite places. Overlooked by the tourist and generally only frequented by regulars, it's little more than a dark bar where one can get away for a bit, relax and generally be left alone. It seemed like a good place for Heather and me to go.

"Noah, this is perfect. You come here much?"

"Enough to know Paul will probably be waiting for us."

I opened the door for her. It was as I had expected, virtually empty. We got a booth on the side and were soon greeted by Paul, the seemingly ever present bartender.

"Hey, Noah! Oh, hey Heather! What's up guys?" he said.

Heather and I looked at each other and we both laughed. "What did I say?" Paul asked.

"Nothing," I held back a laugh and looked at Heather. "Sorry, Paul."

"So what can I get you guys?" he said

"Miller Lite," Heather said.

"Two," I said.

"Back in a flash."

"So, come here often?" I said as I watched Paul walk across the floor. I turned back to Heather, who was leaning on the table toward me.

"Enough to know Paul would be waiting on us."

"Well, I'm surprised we never ran into each other," I said.

"I like it here, especially at this time of day. You can come in and pretty much be left alone if you like. I like Paul, too. Quick with a joke and a light of your smoke."

"A Billy Joel fan. I'm impressed. So what else have you been hiding?"

"Maybe, you never know…" She was about to say something, but trailed off. I looked as Paul arrived with our drinks. He offered menus. We declined and he returned to the bar.

"So, I have a question."

"Yes," I said.

"Why did you say yes?" She wasn't looking at me while she spoke, her attention was focused on the Miller Lite bottle in her hand as she started to peel off the label.

"I'm not sure. Should I have said no?"

"No, you made the right choice. Actually, you should've said yes sooner."

"Why's that?"

"Now you don't really want me to tell you that, do you?"

I paused and looked at her. As attractive as she was, something about the way the conversation was going was even more enticing than her looks. I smiled. She smiled back.

Sure, she worked for me, but it wasn't like I had a huge office staff to get jealous and cause problems if we were involved. Involved? Now where did that come from? But, what if we did get involved? If things didn't work out, all I'd have to do is to get another secretary. And she was in law school, which meant I was going to have to get a new secretary in time anyway. I could… The sound of her voice broke my train of thought.

"Noah?"

"Sorry. I sorta zoned out for a moment."

"Yes, you did, a long moment. I'm not boring you, am I?" she said.

"Far from it, far from it."

Paul was back with two more beers for us. We started talking, and I did what I did best - I listened.

As she peeled the label off of her second bottle of beer, she told me about growing up in Savannah and spending weekends on Tybee Island. She told me about going to college at a little school there called Armstrong State. She told me how she left after she graduated and traveled Europe before she headed to California, and about hitchhiking up the Pacific Coast Highway until she ran out of steam and the wanderlust faded. She came home to Savannah only to find that it wasn't the Savannah she'd left. Friends had moved, married, disappeared, and mostly just grown up. The places were all the same, but the faces were all different. She didn't feel at home in a place that was so familiar but so alien at the same time.

One day she decided she was done with it. She walked out of the bar where she'd been working, right in the middle of happy hour, packed her car and drove to Charleston. She stopped at the first bar she came to, drank till dawn, and rented an apartment the next day. She signed up at a temp agency that landed her at my office less than twenty-four hours after she had hit town. Since then, she had taken the LSAT and started law school. She'd been busy.

"You're easy to talk to," she said as she took a drink of her beer.

"All I'm doing is listening. Mind if I keep doing it for a while?"

"And why would I mind? Excuse me a minute."

I watched her walk toward the bathroom. I counted the empty beer bottles on the table, half of them with no label. No wonder I was smiling. A check of my watch told me we'd been there for more than five hours. I'd been enjoying myself, not wanting it to end. I thought of all the times I'd imagined being with her. Maybe it was the alcohol, but I found myself wanting it even more. Funny how that worked. She slid back into her seat and smiled at me. I'd finished my beer while she was gone. She emptied her beer, putting the bottle, minus the label, back on the table.

"So, want another?" she said.

"Depends. You hungry?"

"Maybe. What would you like?"

I thought of a dozen good comebacks to the question, but heard myself saying, "What do you feel like?"

"I don't really know. How about we get out of here and see what looks good. After all, this is Charleston. I think we can find something to eat if we can fight off the tourists," she said with a smile.

"Cool. I'll go pay Paul."

"Did you just say 'Cool?' Can't say that I've ever heard you say that. Kinda cute." She reached out and touched my hand. I felt a tingle as she ran her finger down the back of my hand. "And don't worry, I already paid him. I don't want you to think I'm out for your money," she said as she pulled her hand back.

She slid out of the booth, stepped around to my side and offered me her hand. I looked at her for a moment, then took it. We headed up East Bay and took a left into the heart of the tourist district. This time of day the Market was almost tolerable. Most of the visitors were either out to eat or back in their hotel rooms wondering how they could quickly cure a case of sunburn. The few that were left had likely either just arrived in the city or had had a bit too much fun the night before and were only just rising for the adventure of a new day.

The Market in Charleston is an interesting place. It spanned about three blocks in the middle of the city. Basically it was several open air buildings that had been around for centuries. It was no secret that Charleston, a few hundred years back, had been one of the main stops on the slave trading routes. At some point in the years since slavery went the way of the carrier pigeon, it had become an accepted, yet absolutely false point, that the Market had been where the slaves were auctioned off. I can't say that there were never slaves sold in the Market, but in reality the present day Market had been the more traditional open air market - fruits, vegetables and the like. If you wanted slaves, you had to travel up the street, off the major thoroughfare, around the corner and to a cobblestone street and a small nondescript building that still said "Old Slave Market."

These days the Market retained some of its past flare. You could find cigars, trinkets, tee shirts, sweet grass baskets, hot sauces, and just about any other tourist memorabilia you wanted. About the only thing you had a hard time finding in the Market was a native Charlestonian.

I was still holding her hand as we walked past a small group of people near the heart of the Market. As we walked, she pulled me closer. We crossed Meeting Street and headed toward King Street, the heart of the business district. We were generally wandering about as I was deciding on a place to suggest for us to eat when she stopped. She removed her hand from mine and turned to face me. We were standing on King Street between a closed boutique and a coffee shop. I looked over her shoulder and saw that there was an unmarked door behind her. She was only inches away from me, her head tilted up to mine. She crossed her arms.

"Still hungry?" she said.

I glanced up and down the street and then over her shoulder to look at the door.

"Sure."

"So, want to come up for a minute?"

"Where are we?" I asked as a crowd of people, likely from Ohio, walked by.

"My place."

"Oh, looks nice," I managed to say.

She turned and opened the door to reveal a set of stairs leading up from the street into the darkness of the building. She looked like she was going to say something, but just smiled as she disappeared up the stairs, leaving me alone on the street. I heard the words "I think so" drift back down toward me.

I waited for a moment and looked up the dark stairs. No sign of Heather. A landing was illuminated by a light from an open door. Opportunity appeared to be knocking, or at least it seemed to have left a door open for me.

The sound of Miles Davis rolled down the stairs.

I stepped off the street, walked up the stairs and stopped outside of the open door. An apartment. It was a small place, decorated in an appealing yet sparse fashion, making it look rather roomy. Modern furnishings and interesting art gave it a very comfortable look, where subdued colors made for pleasant yet subtle accents. Several canvases of contemporary artwork and a lot of photography that I assumed came from the cameras in the corner of the room balanced the decor. I could see a half bath to the side of the kitchen, and I guessed the closed door was the bedroom.

What I didn't see was my host.

"Hey, make sure the door to the street is closed and come on in," her voice said from somewhere in the apartment.

I peered out to make sure I had actually shut the door. I turned back to the apartment and walked to the kitchen, not entirely sure what I was doing. Two beers and a bottle of wine awaited me.

"I didn't want to be presumptuous, but care for a drink?" I heard from behind me.

I turned. She'd changed and was wearing a long loose shirt and I think a pair of shorts. She had her hair pulled back up again in a ponytail. I guess the surprise showed on my face.

"What?" she said.

"That was quick," I said, motioning toward her outfit.

"I wanted to get comfortable. Don't mind, do you?"

"No, not at all," I said, looking back to the beverages on the counter.

"So..."

"Have a preference?" I said.

"Actually, yes."

She walked to me, stopping just short of touching me. In fact, I was curious how she was able to get as close as she was without actually making contact. I turned to reach toward the bottle of wine. She ran a finger down my arm and the back of my hand as she had done at the bar.

"Still hungry?" she said.

"Maybe." I turned to face her and ran the back of my hand along the contour of her face, stopped at her chin, then reached behind her neck and pulled her hair out of the ponytail. It fell to her shoulders.

"I still like it like this," I said.

"I was hoping you'd do that. But you should have done it sooner. Months ago."

"Really? Why didn't you say something?"

"Noah, really now. I think I said a lot. A whole lot."

I still had my hand behind her neck, under her hair, and was unconsciously rubbing her neck.

"Ummm. Feels good," she said.

She rubbed her hand on my chest, reached behind her head and pulled my hand to her lips and kissed it. She turned, not letting go of my hand, and led me out of the kitchen.

"Let me show you around." She turned toward the bedroom, letting my hand fall from hers. She disappeared into the room.

I stopped at the door. She was standing beside her bed near one of the windows that overlooked King Street. She turned back to me. I wasn't sure, but I think a few of the buttons on her shirt had found their way undone.

"Hi," I said as I waited by the door.

"Hi to you too. You can come in if you want. I promise to play nice."

I walked into the bedroom to the opposite side of the room, where I put the wine and glasses on her dresser. "Nice room."

She turned around and walked to the end of the bed, then leaned against one of the bed posts.

"All right, I'll go out on a limb here."

"Okay, go ahead." I leaned back against her dresser.

She took a deep breath. "So will you think I'm being too cheesy if I say I've wanted this and thought about it a time or two?"

"No, of course not. Why would I think that?"

"You didn't seem to be taking any of my hints, so, I figured I better take advantage while I had your attention. It was either that or walk into your office naked, and I just couldn't see myself doing that."

"I admit that would've been interesting."

"So, you okay with this?"

"Very okay. Very okay," I said.

"Well, come here."

I walked to her as she stepped forward, meeting me halfway. I felt a stirring and my heart started to beat a little faster. I reached down and took her hand, running the other gently down her other arm. All of the buttons on her shirt were unbuttoned. No bra. In the fading light of the day, I could just make out the outline of her breast. I slid my hand inside her shirt over an amazingly firm stomach and around to the small of her back. No shorts, either. She took a deep breath and pulled me closer, this time touching me. I could smell the intoxicating scent of her hair and feel her breath on my face.

My heart started beating faster and I felt a stirring. From the way she pulled me to her, I was sure she felt it too. She ran her hands across my shoulders, down my back and pulled at my shirt.

I pulled her closer to me. She looked up at me. I was just about to kiss her as my cell phone rang, vibrating in my front pocket that was pressed against her.

"You have to be fucking kidding me," we said in unison.

I looked at her and she rolled her eyes. "Go ahead and answer it. Just my luck," she said.

I looked at her and she made an expression that confirmed that I should take the call. I pulled my cell phone out of my pocket and answered.

"Noah Parks."

I hadn't recognized the number.

"Noah, its Anna Beth Cross. Have you got a moment?"

I looked at Heather. She was buttoning her shirt, and I noticed she was bending over to pick up a pair of khaki shorts from the floor.

"Um, yes." I watched Heather walk into the bathroom.

"If you're busy, I can call you tomorrow."

"No, not at all, please," I said.

I truly had no idea what to say. To say I was uncomfortable would be an understatement. Heather walked out of the bathroom with another shirt on. And the khakis. She walked over to me and motioned for me to cover the mouthpiece on the phone. I did after telling Anna Beth to hold on a moment.

"Take it, it's okay."

She walked out of the bedroom. I couldn't tell if she was upset, but I was sure my evening with Heather was likely over.

"Sorry," I said into the phone as Heather walked away.

"Noah, are you sure I didn't call at a bad time?"

"No."

"I'm sorry, I didn't know who to call."

"No, no," I said. "What's wrong?"

"I, I'm not really sure. Please don't think I'm crazy, but I think someone's been following me."

"What?" I said.

Silence.

"I'm sorry, I shouldn't have called."

"No, Anna Beth. Wait. Are you okay? Where are you? "

"Just outside my hotel."

"Listen, there's a coffeehouse just a few doors down from your hotel. Go there now and wait for me inside. I'll be there in ten minutes, okay?"

"Thank you, Noah."

The line went dead.

I hung up and walked into the kitchen where Heather was busying herself.

"Shitty timing, I know."

"I sorta expected something to happen." She had opened the wine and poured a glass. "Seems every time I go out on a limb like that something like this happens. And I'm kinda embarrassed."

"No, don't be. It was Anna Beth, and something odd is going on. She thinks she's being followed."

"Followed? By who?" she asked.

"She didn't say. Don't think she knows, and I'm starting to wonder if she might not be a little crazy and…"

"And," she reached up and touched my lips. "As much as I don't want you to leave, you should go help her, see what is wrong with her. There will be a next time for us. We were moving sorta fast."

"Promise?" I said.

"As long as you promise not to wait for another six months, I think we can pick up where we left off."

We walked to the door, and she kissed me on the cheek after I said goodnight. I turned on the landing as she shut the door.

I should have kissed her.

CHAPTER 8

I know a song - goes like this –

'Radio still plays, forever on my mind. I think about the loves I've lost and the ones I've yet to find....'

I've always wondered about that song, what the words really meant. And as I walked away from Heather's toward Anna Beth, I began to get an idea of what the songwriter may have been saying. Earlier today I was wound up about the whole thing with the Cross estate, not knowing what to think of it. Anna Beth Cross walks into my life. Then Heather decides to, well, do whatever it was that she'd just done. Then Anna Beth calls, and I'm not sure what's going on with any of it. But, here I've found myself, in between these two women, not knowing if either was interested, not knowing what either wanted, riding the tide of fate with them. At least that was how I saw it.

But…

As I walked down King Street toward Anna Beth's hotel, I couldn't get my mind off of Heather. Talk about sneaking up on me, I'd be lying to say I hadn't spent more than a few evenings wishing for, or at least thinking about, what just happened. Sometimes thinking of more. Tomorrow would be interesting at the office, hopefully not too awkward. Might have to close early and go out for a drink again.

But…

I remembered where I was going and who I was about to see - Anna Beth Cross. Thoughts of Heather faded, replaced by those of Anna Beth. Was someone really following her? And what would Thomason have to say about seeing Anna Beth away from the office? I'm sure he'd consider this proof positive of Anna Beth's ulterior motive.

It was an unseasonably cool fall evening. Most people, tourists anyway, would have said it was hot and stifling, but we were in Charleston, and humid evenings where the mercury rested above one hundred degrees were not uncommon. But tonight there was a pleasant breeze, and the temperature couldn't have been more than seventy-five degrees. While there had been few people out downtown when Heather and I had been strolling about, now the streets had come to life. People shuffled about, eating, drinking, generally having fun, taking it all in, paying attention to nothing and no one, especially not a local attorney wandering the street with a smile on his face.

I crossed over Meeting Street and headed toward the coffee house where I was to meet Anna Beth. I stopped outside and looked in through the window. There were a few people inside, and a guitar player in the corner. No sign of Anna Beth. I reached for the door.

"Noah," a voice whispered.

I turned and saw Anna Beth standing in the shadows of an alcove just down from the coffee house. She looked a bit on edge, a bit anxious.

"Are you okay? What's wrong?" I said.

"Something happened."

"What?"

"It's probably nothing, but I wanted to talk to someone and, well..."

"I know. I'm the only person you can talk to."

"I'm sorry," she said as she stepped in the direction of her hotel. "I shouldn't have called."

I grabbed her hand as she went by, and with a slight pull stopped her.

"No, no, wait. That came out wrong. Let's go inside, sit – talk for a bit," I said.

"Okay, I'm just upset. I apologize," she said without looking back at me.

This was an entirely different woman than I had met this morning. Maybe there were a few issues that needed to be worked out for Ms. Anna Beth Cross. She'd told me she wasn't crazy, but I was starting to worry about denial.

"Come on," I said.

We went inside and I walked her to a table. I headed to the counter for coffee. After the afternoon at Dengate's, as I smelled the aroma of fresh ground coffee brewing just behind the counter, a cup of coffee sounded really good. I looked at her and held up two fingers. She nodded. I picked up some sugar and cream and walked back to the table with our drinks. Anna Beth smiled as I sat down. She hadn't changed clothes since I had seen her this morning, but her demeanor certainly had.

"I called your office earlier in the day, but they told me you had left. Not meaning to pry, but did it have to do with Father's will?"

"No," I said.

There was a moment of silence.

"I want to tell you something, but I'm afraid you may think I really am a mental case."

"No, not at all," I lied. "Go ahead, tell me what's going on."

The guitar player in the corner had started in on an instrumental medley of Clapton songs.

"Someone was in my hotel room when I was at your office," she said. "Housekeeping had already made up the room before I went to see you. When I got back it was like I had left it, almost, but something was off. Some things had been moved. Things in the bathroom, my luggage had been unpacked and packed again, and my clothes had been moved in the closet."

"You sure?"

"Yes. Positive."

"Did you call the police?"

"No, the last thing I want is to have them think there's a crazy woman at the Planter's Inn. And what could they do?"

"Anything taken?" I said.

"No, nothing. But I know someone was there."

I explained that I'd heard of hotel maids coming back and polishing up, but I don't think she bought it. She believed someone had been in her room. We finished the coffee and, not wanting more, got up to leave. The guitarist was into an Allman Brothers medley as we left. I told her I'd walk her back to the hotel. She didn't object.

We walked past the concierge, and he smiled as we went by. I found myself scrutinizing him, as if I thought he may have had something to do with what Anna Beth had just told me. I caught myself mid-thought not wanting to fall prey to an over active imagination, which after an afternoon of Miller Lites was a distinct possibility.

We walked up to the elevator and I stopped just short of the door. Anna Beth reached out and pushed the up button.

"You going to be okay?" I said.

She looked at the floor then looked up toward me. "Will you walk me up to my room?"

Twice in one night? I was on a roll. I dismissed that thought.

"Sure," I said, hoping my expression hadn't given away my thought. I waited for her to say it wasn't necessary, but the words never came. We rode up in silence, neither of us looking at the other.

The elevator stopped on the third floor, the doors opened, and she headed down the hall toward her room. I followed, stopping behind her as she paused outside of what I gathered was her door. I just knew Thomason was going to stick his head out of a door down the hall, infuriated.

"I know this seems silly and I hope it isn't out of line, but I'd feel better if you'd come in and take a look around. Make sure I'm not losing what little sanity I have left," she said, then flashed a nervous smile.

"I'd be happy to." Maybe I *was* on a roll.

She pulled out her key, a real key on a big heavy key ring, not a plastic key card like you get at most hotels. She put it in the lock, turned it, then paused. She looked at me over her shoulder. I motioned to her to go in.

I followed her inside and looked around. I realized that I'd apparently not been staying in the right places when I traveled. To call her hotel room a room was like calling a yacht a canoe. There was a sitting area larger than the apartment I'd just left. A separate den with a fireplace, a large kitchen, what looked like two bedrooms, and a huge balcony overlooking the Market spread out before me.

"Up to your room, huh?"

"What?"

"Little cramped here, don't you think?"

"Not really, no," she said.

"Right, yes," I said. "But a really nice place."

"That's what I really like about it. It doesn't really seem like a hotel room."

"I was just thinking that," I said. "I'll look around and get out of your hair. Anywhere I shouldn't go?"

"If you could just check around. I know there's nothing here, but it'll make me feel better. And no."

I looked at her a moment as she was putting her keys and purse on a table by the couch. I walked past her into the expanse of the room. I looked in all of the rooms and closets, out on the balcony. I even looked in the shower, the huge shower. The room was large enough that even looking around quickly took me almost ten minutes. She followed me as I moved from room to room, often peering over my shoulder. I finished, finding nothing.

"Well, I'm done and ready to give my report."

"Noah, I'm serious. Someone was in here."

"I'm sorry. That's just my sense of humor. I'm quite certain there's no one here other than us."

"I know, I know, and now I'm completely embarrassed."

I sat down in a chair across from her.

"Don't worry. Now that we know there's nothing here you'll be fine. After I leave, lock the door and pull the safety lock. If there's any problem, call the police, then call me. How's that?"

She sat down across from me. She began arranging the

magazines on the coffee table that separated us. We sat for a few minutes in silence.

"Shit."

"What?" I said.

"I'm not crazy. Someone was in here. I don't know why I had to have you come up here, but thank you for doing it."

She looked up at me. Here I was, alone with a beautiful woman for the second time in one night. She had started to cry. She wiped her eyes, sat up straight and took a deep breath.

I looked about, spotted some tissue, reached for the box and offered it to her. She shook me off, wiping her eyes with the back of her hand. She offered a nervous laugh.

"I do apologize. Any chance we can pretend like none of this happened?"

"Probably not, but think what a great story it'll make in a few years."

"I can hear it now. Okay, let me make it up to you. Can I offer you a drink?"

"Will you hold it against me if I say no thanks? I have an early day tomorrow. And so do you, sort of."

"I do?" she said.

"You do. After you left today I got word that the estate closed. We're going down to find out what's in that safe deposit box. And Thomason asked if you wanted to join us for lunch beforehand." I looked around for her phone. I spotted it in the corner, the message light flashing. I pointed to it. "See?"

"Really?" she said.

"Yep, really. That's if you care to join us?"

"Well, if you are going to shoot me down on my drink offer, I guess you can redeem yourself a little bit by asking me to lunch. Even if it is with Steven."

"How about tomorrow, here in the hotel? Noonish?"

She nodded in agreement. "Sounds great."

I stood and walked to the door. "We could have a secret knock if you want, for the next time I come back, so you will know it's me." I paused, waiting for the laughter. Silence. Faint smile. "That was a joke, by the way."

"I know, and a bad one. That's why I'm smiling. I'll look forward to seeing you tomorrow. And Noah…"

"Yes."

"Thank you again. You made me feel a lot better."

I smiled as she said that.

I walked out of the hotel and back to my office. The tourists were still out roaming about the streets as I walked behind my office to my car.

My trip home was, thankfully, much less eventful than my day had been.

I could tell Austin had been waiting a while to see me based on how high he was jumping at the door begging to go outside.

"Sorry dude," I said as I watched him race into the night.

~~~~~~~~~~~~~~~~~~~~~~~~

I awoke the next morning to the sensation of a paw being gingerly applied to my face. As I opened my eyes I saw that the paw was attached, as I expected, to Austin. Apparently I'd slept a little too late for him. I climbed out of bed, took care of him, and after grabbing a quick bite to eat headed off to the office. I'd slept a dreamless sleep, which was surprising given the events of the previous day. I was a little interested to see how Heather would act and even more interested in seeing Anna Beth at lunch. I had no designs on wooing two different women, but it had been a goodly time since I had to worry about even one woman. But that is a different story for a different day.

I arrived at the office just after eight, stopping to get the mail on the way in. I sorted it and then checked my email. One would think that the Cross estate was my only case, but unfortunately, that wasn't the case. I should have come in even earlier and tried to catch up. Fortunately there were no major issues to deal with. I typed a few letters - yes, I still did most of that myself. I also answered a few emails. I thought about calling Thomason but decided he probably could use the sleep after his dash into town the night before. Around 8:45, Heather showed up.

"Morning," I said.

"Hi," she said through a tight grin. "Got a minute?"

"I do."

"I want to talk about last night."

"Okay."

"Here goes – I had a lot of fun yesterday..."

"So did I, and..."

"Don't interrupt," she said as she shifted slightly in her seat. "I had a lot of fun, but I hope that I didn't embarrass myself. I mean, I literally threw myself at you."

"Well, I certainly didn't try to stop you."

"No, you didn't," she said.

"Can I ask you something?" I said.

"Of course."

"What's on your mind?"

She smiled. "If you really want to know, a lot actually. Some of it I'm still sorting out."

"Good stuff I hope?" I said.

"Yes, really good stuff."

"So what then?"

"You tell me."

"No pressure, huh? Well, I thought about it a lot this morning. I smiled a lot, too. How's this – why don't we go out to dinner? I have a place in mind, and we can go from there? Maybe tomorrow night?"

"Really?" she said.

"Really. I'd like it a lot."

"Good, so would I, but only if you promise to turn off your cell phone after dinner," she said as she rose.

"Good then. Now back to work," I said with a grin. The day was looking up already.

I told Heather to run down the pleadings from the Court, which she quickly did. I also had her hold my calls so I could accomplish something through the morning. Before I knew it, it was almost noon. I headed to the door and told Heather that I'd be gone for a few hours to meet Thomason for lunch and then to go to the bank. I grabbed the pleadings and asked Heather if he'd called once I realized I'd not heard from him all morning. That was odd for him. I thought of giving him a call, but since I was due to meet him in a few minutes I decided to just head over to the hotel. Heather smiled at me as I left.

As I walked down the street, I noticed that the cool breeze from the night before was still there. Fall was on the way, and I was feeling great.

I arrived at the Planter's Inn after the short walk and headed back to the dining room. I spied Anna Beth being seated across the room just as she caught my eye. It suddenly hit me that the last time I had been in here was the day her brother died. I told the maitre de, who was not near as friendly as before, that I was with Anna Beth. He directed me toward her table. She smiled as I approached.

"Good morning, Noah."

"And a good morning to you as well."

"Perfect timing, too."

"Wasn't it? Have you seen Thomason?" I said.

"No, I assumed he was with you."

"Actually, I haven't spoken to him since yesterday afternoon. I expected to hear from him this morning, but nothing. I'm sure he'll be here soon."

"That's not really like him."

The waiter approached and explained the daily specials as a busboy filled our glasses with water. We began to look over the menu and made small talk while we waited for Thomason, but there was no sign of him. After fifteen minutes I found myself looking over my shoulder every few moments for a sign of him.

"Are you okay?" Anna Beth said after a few minutes.

"Well, yes, but this is puzzling."

"What is?"

"You've known him longer than me, but he's never been late for anything."

"No, you're right. Are you sure he knew to meet us here?"

"Oh yes, this is the only place I've ever known him to go, or at least the only place he ever mentions to me. But I guess he could be somewhere else."

"No, not likely. He's a creature of habit if there ever was one. Perhaps something came up," she said.

"But what? I'd like to think he'd have called. Hang on a second."

I pulled out my cell phone and called the office. Heather answered and I asked her if she had heard from Thomason. She hadn't. I checked my watch - it was almost 12:30.

"Be right back." I got up and headed for the front desk.

I leaned on the counter of the front desk as I waited for the attendant to finish his phone conversation. He looked at me as if to say one moment, then finished his call.

"Tell me how I can help you, sir."

"I was to meet a gentleman, one of your guests, for lunch today, but he hasn't arrived. I was wondering if you could call his room and direct the call to your house phone."

"Certainly sir, what's the guest's name?" the attendant said as he began pecking away at his computer keyboard.

"Steven Thomason."

He stopped typing and looked up at me. "Mr. Thomason is not a guest with us at the moment."

"Are you sure? I called yesterday and let you know he would be arriving last night."

"And you are?"

"Noah Parks?"

"Oh, Mr. Parks, yes, pleasure to meet you. You frequently call for Mr. Thomason. In fact, we've spoken before. But I see here that his room was canceled yesterday evening."

"Really, um, can I ask by whom?"

The attendant looked puzzled. I couldn't figure out what was causing his concern.

"Apparently you, Mr. Parks."

I tried to put on my poker face and thanked him for his assistance. I headed back to the dining room and Anna Beth.

"Where did you go?"

"Front desk."

"You look confused."

"Then the look fits. I just learned the most perplexing thing. Apparently I called yesterday and canceled Thomason's reservation. But for those of you keeping score, that would be the same reservation I'd just made yesterday."

"Why did you cancel his reservation?"

"That's just it, I didn't cancel it. Hang on."I reached in my pocket, pulled out my cell and dialed Thomason's number. For the first time ever, I heard his voice mail.

"This is Steven Thomason and I can't get to the phone. Please leave me a very brief message and I will return your call as soon as I am able."

I did just that.

"Now that is strange. I've never gotten his voice mail before."

"So what do we do?" she said.

"Good question." I looked at my watch and saw it was quarter to one. We, or I, in any event, had to be at the bank in just over an hour. "Well, I have to go to the bank, but we might as well have lunch since we're here. If you want?"

"Sure."

The waiter appeared and we ordered. The food soon came out and we ate. We talked about Thomason and what we each knew of him. We laughed a bit as well. As odd as it seemed, we both had a very similar picture of the man. We both also agreed that he played a substantial role in Anna Beth's father's later years. At least she seemed to agree with me, but Thomason's warning kept coming back to me. I decided that I needed to be a bit guarded as to what I told her or what I let her see. However, I also decided that it would be a good idea to have her come to the bank with me to witness what happened there as I tried to talk myself into the safe deposit box without a personal representative. The check came after we finished and she grabbed it before I could reach it.

As she was paying it, I asked, "Want to go with me to the bank to see about getting into the safe deposit box?"

"You don't mind?"

"No, but you'll be helping as much as watching," I said. "I was supposed to get an authorization from Thomason, but didn't bother since he was supposed to be here. Since he's not, I'd still like to go over there, but I'm going to try to sell you as the next best thing being the daughter of the deceased." I grinned as I finished.

"You mean my father?"

"Yes."

"Not to seem trivial or dramatic, but I would prefer it if you wouldn't refer to him like that," she said in a very cutting tone that was quite different than what I had come to expect from our conversation that day.

"Um, I'm very sorry and please forgive me. That was completely inappropriate."

"I understand that you deal with this quite often, but please remember that I don't," she said.

We rose from the table and headed to the door. We walked in an uncomfortable silence toward the bank. It was only a few blocks away, but it seemed like miles when we finally got there. I held the door for her as she walked in.

The downtown branch of the Bank of South Carolina was an impressive building that had tones of both Classical and Greek Revival styles. The building was nearly two centuries old, and had been the site of a carriage maker, a bottling plant, and even a shoe manufacturer through the last century. At one point it had even been the home of a tire company that had destroyed the beauty of the building's façade. However, when the bank took over it was restored, and was now a testament to Charleston's famous preservation drive that sustained the historic personality of the city.

I told the receptionist who I was and that I was there for a meeting with Anderson King. She picked up a phone on her desk.

"He will be right with you, Mr. Parks."

I looked over to Anna Beth who sat, actually more so perched, on the edge of a couch in the lobby. I walked to her.

"I'm sorry for that at the hotel," I said as I stood before her, my hands in my pockets, head hung down toward her.

"I know you didn't mean anything by it, but I'm still getting used to the fact that he's dead. I didn't mean to snap at you, but it would mean a lot if you didn't say that again."

I found myself reaching out to place a hand on her shoulder. "I won't do it again," I said.

"Mr. Parks?" I heard a voice said.

I turned to see a gentleman I presumed to be Anderson King walking toward me, adjusting his paisley bow tie that matched the braces that framed his shoulders. He looked at me over rimless round glasses that worked with his slightly receding hairline to give him an air of sophistication. The manner in which he carried himself made his generally stuffy standard pin stripe suit pants and crisply pressed white Oxford shirt seem almost casual. I was still worried that I would have a problem without Thomason, but I held a glimmer of optimism after having seen him. He approached me with a smile and an outstretched hand.

"Yes, Mr. King?"

"Pleasure to meet you. Why don't we step into my office."

"Certainly." I turned to Anna Beth, told her I would be right back, and then followed Anderson King across the lobby to his office. I explained the dilemma to King in a brief, concise manner, and he listened with what seemed a sympathetic ear. As I was telling him of Thomason's most unusual absence, from his mannerisms and understanding looks I thought I was making some progress. I finished by offering up Anna Beth as Cross' only surviving child. He looked over his desk at me and spoke.

119

"Mr. Parks, I appreciate your situation completely. However, as an attorney, surely you understand that I can only assist you given the proper authorization. However, I can also assure you that once you do that, we can quickly move toward conclusion."

I smiled as he spoke. All progress gone. I'd forgotten I was dealing with a man who routinely sat across a desk from people and, with a smile on his face and in a genuine tone of sincerity, told people that while he understood their plight, he was unable to loan them any money. It had probably been recreational for him to tell me, an attorney, that he couldn't help me.

"I suspected as much Mr. King, but I only realized this a very short time ago and wanted to at least come by and meet you."

"It has been my pleasure, and I'll await word from you when I can be of assistance in the future." He was walking to his office door as he said this. He didn't stop there, but walked me over to the couch where Anna Beth was sitting. He introduced himself to her and walked us to the door of the bank.

"No luck, I take?"

"No, I have to find Thomason. I'll walk you back to your hotel then go see if I can't run him down."

"Noah, how long has it been since you spoke to Steven?" she asked.

"Yesterday morning."

"You've called all of his numbers?"

"Yes, why?"

"I may be being paranoid, but I know finding out what was in the safe deposit box was important to him. He wouldn't have missed this. I also know that he would not have missed an opportunity to tell me how Father had missed me in his final years. I want to call the police."

"The police? Isn't that a little bit sudden?"

"I'd feel better if there was a report."

I thought about it for a moment.

"Let me make a call. Hang on."

We stopped in the lobby and I pulled out my cell phone. I called a friend who happened to be a local detective. He told me he'd send over two uniformed officers to take a report. I thanked him and told him Anna Beth's room number.

"I have a friend, a local police officer. He's going to have a couple of officers come by and take a report," I said.

"Thank you. It might be premature, but Steven is never late for anything. Ever," she said.

We passed the front desk attendant and concierge as we headed to the elevator. I wondered as we went by what they would say when two police officers arrived.

We got off the elevator and walked to Anna Beth's room. She went into the bedroom and I onto the balcony. I was impressed as I looked down. It had been less than five minutes since I had spoken to my friend and already two uniformed officers were getting out of their car and walking into the hotel. I called to Anna Beth and told her the officers were on their way up. A few minutes later there was a knock at the door.

I answered it and two officers identified themselves. I invited them in and went over a summary of what had happened concerning Thomason. They took notes, nodded a lot, and said they would file a report. They also said they would talk to the front desk attendant. Mostly they told us not to worry, that it wasn't unusual for things to come up and people to get side tracked. They took our names and numbers.

"Shouldn't you check the airlines and see if he made his plane?" Anna Beth said as they were about to leave.

"That's something we will certainly look into, Miss," the first officer said. I always found it interesting how most cops could answer a question without saying a thing.

"If he doesn't show up by this time tomorrow, give us a call back," the other officer said as he handed Anna Beth a card with his number on it. "That's my cell number. You can call later and see if we have found anything."

Great, I thought. First I put my foot in my mouth at lunch, and now a cop I got was hitting on her. She's going to just love me. The first officer turned as I was thinking this.

"Say, one thing though, you said you did try to call, right? Try him again. Never can tell, you might get lucky and get him this time."

He stared at me for a moment as I realized that he was asking me to go ahead and call Thomason as we were standing there. I knew he was hoping that I'd get him on the phone so he could not only give me an 'I told you so,' but also pick up some attorney joke fodder.

Anna Beth was speaking to the first officer as the second walked around the room tapping his finger on the back of his iPad, mostly staring at Anna Beth. As I reached for my phone, I thought back to when cops used note pads and didn't make their flirting so obvious. I dialed Thomason's number.

It was a strange sensation when his phone started to ring, almost stereo, a bit of a delay with a touch of echo. No answer. The phone kept ringing. I glanced over at Anna Beth, who had a curious look on her face and a cell phone in her hand. The two officers were looking not at me, but to the large dining table across the room. I followed their gaze.

There was a cell phone in the center of the table.

It was ringing.

CHAPTER 9

It's a funny thing how realization happens to a person. First you have confusion. Then, slowly, confusion fades to partial clarity. Then the fade reverses itself, clouding things again. Then, sudden enlightenment.

In my case, the confusion was the strange ring and echo quality to Thomason's phone. Ringing first quietly in one ear then louder in the other. Somewhere between the juxtaposed ringing the fade started, and I looked at Anna Beth. I expected her to be looking at either the officer or me, but she was staring over my shoulder. I looked to the officer she had been talking to. He was looking in the same direction. I turned to the other officer, same thing. I was the only person in the room not staring at the table. The ringing and echo continued as I followed the path of their collective stares and saw that they converged on the dining room table and the cell phone that rested there. That was when the sudden fade focused. The stereo effect stopped at the same time the ringing did. It was replaced by Thomason's voice in my ear. The enlightenment hit. I started to speak.

The officer nearest the table spoke first. "Is this your cell phone, Ms. Cross?"

"No, mine's here." Anna Beth was holding up a cell phone.

"Any idea who owns this one?"

"No," she said.

"Sir?" the officer said as he looked toward me.

"I don't have any idea," I lied, having a pretty good idea who it belonged to but figuring it best to keep my mouth shut.

"Did you just call Steven Thomason's cell phone?" the first officer said.

"I did."

"Would you please call it again?"

"Really?"

With a stern look, the officer said, "Yes, really."

I hit the send button to call the number again. The ring and echo started again, but this time without all the confusion. I held the phone out for the officer to see.

The first officer spoke into his radio. I couldn't hear what he was saying. The second officer walked back toward us. "Folks, I'm going to have to ask you to come with me back to the lobby."

"Why?" Anna Beth said. "This is my room."

"This way." He was holding the door, offering no explanation.

I motioned to her as I walked toward the door and put my cell phone in my pocket. The officer escorted us into the hall outside of the room.

"Wait here and, sir, could I please have your cell phone? And the lady's, too?" Anna Beth gave me a look of protest, but I reached out, took her phone, and passed it along with mine to the officer. He turned and walked away, stopping just a few feet away to speak into his radio again. His partner came over and escorted us toward the elevator and the lobby, where he had us sit in a small room. At least it was comfortable, containing several nice couches. He remained outside. We waited several minutes and watched more officers come into the building. We waited.

I broke the silence. "That was Thomason's cell phone in your room."

"Yes, I realize that. How did it get there?"

"I haven't the slightest idea, but I am confident we'll both get a chance to answer that question in a few minutes."

"Who's going to be asking?"

"A detective most likely. The phone, did you notice it there before, on the table?"

"No. But I didn't look, either."

~~~~~~~~~~~~~~~~~~~~~~~

I knew we'd be questioned. However, I was a little surprised that they let us remain together. I took advantage of the time and told Anna Beth to be careful of the questioning, but generally not to worry.

We'd been there for about forty-five minutes, alone in our little room (but under the watchful eye of a uniformed officer), when a familiar face appeared in the lobby among what was becoming a sea of uniforms.

A tall African-American man was scanning the lobby. Given that he was at least six inches taller than almost everyone else he was rather easy to spot, but Emmett Gabriel was rarely picked out as a cop, much less a detective. He looked more like a basketball player. He was well over six feet tall, close to seven, all lean muscle. Today, as most, he was dressed in his standard uniform -

khaki pants and a short sleeve knit shirt. Unlike most Charleston plain-clothes police officers he didn't wear a clip-on badge, and when he carried a weapon, he carried it in an ankle holster. He smiled all the time, even when he was arresting someone. But as tall and striking as he was he always seemed to blend into a crowd, even though he towered above everyone else.

He spotted and greeted me with his eyes. He briefly spoke to another officer, then walked over to us. He contemplated each of us for a moment. I glanced at Anna Beth and could tell he was making her nervous. He stopped in the door to the small room where we had been waiting.

"Damn, see, this is how come I never go out down here. All the chairs they lay out are made for you short folks." I found most people expected a booming baritone from him, but he was very soft spoken. He smiled at me, then turned his attention to Anna Beth.

"Ms. Cross, Emmett Gabriel, pleasure to meet you." He smiled as he spoke.

"Charming as ever, Gabriel."

"Noah, I've always said you're a piece of work." He reached out to shake my hand.

"You two know each other?" Anna Beth said.

"Certainly do. We were roommates back in college, before Noah got sidetracked with law school." He looked back at me. "I always told him I expected him to go south on me and end up having me chase his butt down, but damn if I ever figured he'd be the one calling me to turn himself in."

"What do you mean?" Anna Beth said.

"Emmett's the friend I called who sent over the officers."

"Oh."

"Gabriel, what the hell's going on?" I said.

"Tell you what I got so far. It seems we got this call asking for a couple of officers to come over and take a report on some guy that didn't show up for an appointment or two. Officers show up, figured the guy missed a flight or something and pretty much decide there's nothing to it. They're getting some information when one of the people calls the missing guy on his cell. Now, here's where it gets funny." He takes a couple of steps toward me and puts his hands in his pockets. "The missing guy's cell phone starts to ring right across the room from where the guy's making the call."

"Strange, huh?" I said.

"You think? I've got to ask something. Can you give me chapter and verse on where you were since you talked to this guy yesterday?"

"Sure. I was with either Anna Beth or my paralegal all day till I went home."

"Ma'am?"

"Where was I?" Anna Beth said.

"Yes."

"Well, I was with Noah yesterday morning. Then I was house hunting or shopping. I had dinner at the hotel – alone. Came back to the room and saw Noah again for a short time, and after that I went to bed."

"Anything unusual happen yesterday?" Gabriel said.

I wasn't sure if he was talking to me or Anna Beth. If he was talking to me, I was sure that he didn't need to hear about my evening.

I decided to answer. "When I saw Anna Beth last night, she felt like someone had been in her room. I came up, looked around, didn't see anything that made me worry."

"Did you see the phone on the table?"

"No, but I wasn't looking for it, and I don't think I'd have said anything if I had seen it."

"Ma'am, why'd you think someone had been in your room?"

Anna Beth explained to Gabriel as she had to me. Now with the phone turning up in there, she was absolutely convinced someone had been in her room. I had to admit that the timing was interesting, but I was also thinking about Thomason's warning to me about Anna Beth.

"Some officers and crime scene techs are looking around up there just to be on the safe side. Noah, I'll shoot straight with you. This is downright odd, but it doesn't really mean anything except you don't know where this guy is and you can't call him because we have his cell."

"So, what are you going to do?" I said.

"Give us about half an hour and you can have your room back. I'll call if I need anything or find anything. In the meantime, let me know if this guy shows up."

"Sure thing."

Gabriel stood to go. "It was a pleasure meeting you Ms. Cross. Noah, hang on a moment. Excuse us if you would, ma'am."

I followed him into the lobby.

"This is a strange one. That guy got on the plane from Chicago and rented a car here last night – don't know where it is, but we're looking. He didn't check in, but seems his cell did. Apparently he stays here enough that everyone knows when he's here. Watch yourself here, something's not right. Your solid on where you were last night?"

"Completely."

I knew Gabriel well enough to understand that warning had several layers to it.

"You go ahead and get back to that lady in there. Tell her what you think she needs to hear. She doesn't need any more bad news coming from strangers."

"Great, and what am I?"

"Don't know, but better you telling her than me," he said as he walked off toward the lobby.

I went back to Anna Beth and told her a toned down version of what Gabriel had just told me about Thomason's flight, the rental car and the hotel.

"Noah, what's going on?"

"I wish I knew, but Gabriel's going to be checking up on us, where we were last night. Good thing you're staying in town a while."

We waited for another half hour until the first officer we had spoken to told us they were through in Anna Beth's room and that we could go back upstairs.

I walked with her back to the room. We looked around inside and, contrary to what you usually hear about police, there was no sign that they had been in the room. Except Thomason's cell phone was gone. Apparently they were a bit neater when they visited the Planter's Inn.

Anna Beth and I talked for a few minutes about what had happened. She called the leasing agent she had met with the day before and told her she wanted to move into a house at the beach the next day. I offered to help her, but she politely refused. I told her I'd call her to check later and said goodbye.

I got back to the office just after five. Heather was on the way out the door as I was coming in.

"Don't suppose Thomason called, did he?"

"No, you okay? You look exhausted. Where have you been?" She set her purse down on a table in the reception area. I sat in one of the chairs. She sat across from me.

"Thomason's missing."

"What?"

"He was supposed to meet Anna Beth and me for lunch and didn't show. He didn't show at the bank, either. So now, I'm done with the estate, but can't get in that accursed safe deposit box."

"I'm sure he'll turn up," she said.

"I hope so, but it's weird." I stopped myself and decided not to tell her about the cell phone. I didn't feel like going through the whole afternoon again.

"What's weird?"

"Oh, just him, of all people, skipping out on two appointments. It's not like him."

"It doesn't seem like something he'd do. Listen, want to go out and do something?" she said.

I looked at her - her hair was down and she was leaning forward, arms resting on her knees, staring. I thought back to the night before. A long lock of her hair fell into her face and she blew it out of the way. We both laughed.

"God, I really want to, but I'm exhausted and don't think I'd be much fun. I promise we will go out soon."

"Hey, I had to try. After all, things are looking up a bit." She stood up and stepped toward me. She reached down and picked up my hand and looked at it for a moment. "Nice hands." She walked out the door, stopping to look back toward me, holding my gaze for a long moment.

She was an interesting girl and certainly had my attention. I fought back the urge to reconsider her offer, but I needed to go home and get some sleep.

I sat for another ten minutes, then walked out to my car and headed home to Austin and bed.

~~~~~~~~~~~~~~~~~~~~

I talked to Gabriel a number of times as the days passed. I attempted to avoid thinking about the worst, but it was tough. Two weeks passed after Thomason stood up Anna Beth and me, with no word from him. The Charleston police called the Chicago police and had them go to Thomason's home, but there was nothing out of the ordinary. Of course, there was no Thomason, either. They knew he had arrived in Charleston and rented a car. No one could find the car. Gabriel kept me posted, but he was only able to tell me that there was nothing new – not because he couldn't tell me, but because he didn't have anything to tell me.

Anna Beth got settled into her rental house on Sullivan's Island. I stopped by one day after work following a meeting I'd had nearby. The place was beautiful. It was on a huge ocean front lot. One of the really old homes on a long slender lot. The house stood three stories high, and since Sullivan's Island was so narrow, from the deck on the roof it was no problem to see the Atlantic Ocean on one side and the waterway on the other.

We'd talked about what to do if Thomason didn't show up. Basically, we decided that since all of the matters regarding the estate were finalized except the contents of the safe deposit box, we'd go ahead and make sure all of the assets were distributed and not worry about the safe deposit box for the moment. We could always petition the Court to have Anna Beth named personal representative and get into the box later.

Things had stalled with Heather. The odds of fate, as the song went. A family member had gotten sick and she had gone to visit her parents just after Thomason ditched Anna Beth and me. She had called several times, but there had been no discussions of "us."

Without really having to work on the estate, I'd been able to make a lot of headway toward getting caught up on my other cases. The weather was becoming cooler as September got underway. I was in my office on a Wednesday morning when the phone rang.

I answered it. "Noah Parks."

"Noah." I recognized Gabriel's voice.

"Hey! So what's up?"

"I think I got something on that guy that's been missing."

"Interesting way to start a conversation. You do know I've never heard those words from a cop and had things end up good. Tell me this time's different."

"Can't do that, my friend. Meet me at the station. We'll take a ride."

I hung up the phone, hit a new line and started to call Anna Beth. I had dialed the first five digits, paused, then hung up. I decided it would be better to know the answers to a few of the questions she'd ask before I tried to answer them. I didn't want to lie to her.

I called the answering service and told them I'd be out the rest of the day. I drove down Broad Street toward the Ashley River, past the old homes on the Charleston harbor. In the last several years the property values had done everything but rise. There were a lot of homes for sale in downtown Charleston, but many of the homes, including those not for sale, were vacant. It had become common for out of town buyers from the North, or even Europe, to come to town and buy a southern mansion. Trouble was most of these people didn't call Charleston home. On a typical night you could drive through the old neighborhoods that had once been filled with families and have it seem like a ghost town, dark and empty.

I followed Broad Street around by the river until it turned into Lockwood Drive, then drove up to the police station beside the local minor league baseball park named after our mayor who had been in office for as long as anyone could remember. The new police station and municipal court had just recently opened, replacing the station that had been around since the 1940's. I parked in a visitor's spot and had the desk sergeant call up and let Gabriel know I was there. He was down a few minutes later. He had to tilt his head a bit as he walked out into the lobby.

"Sorry to up and ruin your day," he said as he put on his sunglasses and walked out the door. We headed off to his car, an unmarked Crown Victoria.

"Not going to open the door for me?"

"Get in if you're coming."

We drove off toward West Ashley, past the neighborhood where I lived, past the city limits. Gabriel was quiet as we drove.

"Little past your jurisdiction aren't we?"

"Well, if it hadn't been for that damn cell phone business that you got me in, I'd be home in the garden."

Gabriel spent all his spare time in a small Zen garden out back of his house. He was obsessed with the Japanese bonsai trees. I guess it had something to do with how big he was that made him so interested in the tiny trees. When he wasn't out fighting crime and corruption or dispensing law and order, you could bet he was in his backyard garden studying and caring for his tiny trees.

He turned down the volume on his police radio. "The car your friend was driving, we found it. At least county thinks they might have it off Boat Landing Road. They're going to pull it up any time now."

"Any idea where Thomason is?"

"It doesn't appear he's in the car. At least, the diver didn't see him."

We drove on in silence past the marshes and over the creeks. We turned off of Highway 17 and headed inland. The two lanes of asphalt continued winding through the marshes interspersed with pockets of live oaks, pines and sweet gums. The occasional house broke the pattern. Several miles after the turn-off, Gabriel veered off the main road to the right. The entryway to the boat landing was hardly more than an open spot in the trees. The pavement stopped as we headed down a single lane dirt road. I looked up out of the window. The live oak canopy covered the road and, even though it was the middle of the day, filtered out enough light to make it appear as if it was twilight. We continued down the road for about a mile until it opened up to reveal a clearing of at least three acres.

It was all coquina, a tabby like gravel substance made from partially fossilized sea shells that was mined in South Carolina. Boat landings like this were scattered throughout Charleston to give recreational boaters who could afford a boat but not the exorbitant dock fees a place to put their boat in the water. On most weekends through the summer the three acres of coquina would be packed. The boaters would back the trailers with their boats into the water, pilot their boat off the trailer and have a friend park the vehicle and trailer in the lot, where it would wait for the boaters until after they had had ample time to travel the waterways drinking themselves into a stupor. I'd been here a few times riding with police friends while on their patrol. When the boaters put their boats in the water, it mostly went quite well. When they pulled them out, or tried to at any rate, that was usually when the problems started. More than one drunken boater had backed their truck and trailer too far into the water and watched it slip below the surface. But today, while there were no trailers awaiting the return of their boats, the clearing was far from empty.

At least a dozen marked and unmarked police cars, a Sheriff's Department search and rescue van, several news trucks, an ambulance and a fire truck were scattered about the landing.

We pulled up to the police line where police tape kept the media and several onlookers back. A uniformed officer, recognizing Gabriel, lifted the police tape so he could drive through. We stopped beside a line of police cars.

"Watch yourself. May want to stay back a bit."

"All right," I said. He walked toward a group of uniformed officers.

A huge tow truck was backed up to the waterline. A cable led from the rear of the truck and danced to a point some forty feet from the water's edge, where it disappeared below the surface. Beyond where it went into the water, a steady rise of bubbles broke the surface. The bubbles soon gave way to the masked head of a scuba diver, who flashed a thumbs up sign and began to swim to the landing. He came out of the water and, after removing his mask and fins, walked to the group of men where Gabriel was standing and spoke to them. Heads nodded. One of the officers walked over to the tow truck operator, who then nodded and engaged a lever on the truck's side control panel. The cable began to crawl from the water.

I got out of the car but stood back from the others, watching as a car slowly appeared from below the surface. Chrysler 300M. Nice car. As it came into view, water began to run from the bottom of the doors and out of an opened window. I was becoming entirely too familiar with how cars were raised from the water.

When the car was largely clear from the water, the winch was turned off and the driver drove the truck forward to completely pull the car from the water. I studied the car. From where I was standing, it didn't appear that anyone was in the car. The diver walked over to the car door and opened it. Water poured out, but it was otherwise empty. Several crime scene technicians walked to it.

I watched.

After a short time, one of the crime scene techs came over and spoke to the officers with Gabriel. He turned and walked toward me.

"Guess you can see, he's not in the car."

I looked past him at the technicians taking pictures of the car's interior. They'd been working on it for about ten minutes. "Keys in the ignition?"

"What? Keys? Don't know. Hang on." He turned toward the group of men he had just left. "Hey Dave, keys in the car?"

One of the deputies, presumably Dave, shouted something toward the car. One of the technicians lowered his camera and peered inside the vehicle, then nodded to Dave.

"So, you want to take it for a spin?" Gabriel said.

"At the risk of having you raise your eyebrows, what about the trunk?"

He looked at me through slightly squinted eyes, rubbed the bridge of his nose with his index and middle finger of his right hand and slightly shook his head from side to side. He turned and walked back to the other officers and said something to them. The one that had answered when Gabriel had called to "Dave" walked to a crime scene technician who was holding the keys. He walked to the back of the car and opened the trunk. Dave and the technician looked inside for a moment. As Dave motioned for the other officers to come over to the car, the technician stepped back and raised his camera. It flashed. The other officers and Gabriel walked to the car, stared, spoke and stared some more. Several of them glanced in my direction.

The sound of Gabriel's voice carried toward me. "Noah, come over here!"

I looked around, hoping some other Noah would part from the crowd, but no one appeared. Gabriel met me as I walked up to the car.

"We may have found him. You ok taking a look, let us know if it's him?"

Although I'd lived behind a funeral home while growing up, I was never really a fan of corpses.

"I can if you need me to."

"It would help," he said.

We walked to the back of the car and the other officers stepped aside. I looked in the trunk and saw Thomason looking as if he'd been discarded like yesterday's news.

"That's him."

Often you hear people speak of how peaceful or content a person looks in death. I have never, nor will I ever, understand this. Nothing about death is peaceful. Eternal, everlasting, forever, sure, but not peaceful. And there was certainly nothing peaceful looking about Thomason as he lay there. Chrysler may market large trunks, but with a full grown man inside, roomy isn't a word that comes to mind.

His body was wedged toward the rear of the trunk, his features distorted and barely recognizable. An hour in the water can make you look like a prune, two weeks and you get an entirely different phenomenon of which there are no redeeming attributes. Thomason had been the epitome of composure and poise in life. In death, it was quite the opposite. I turned and walked back to Gabriel's car.

CHAPTER 10

Half an hour later, Gabriel headed back toward the car. Thomason's body had been removed and placed in an ambulance that departed for the coroner's office. In the fading light of the day I could see the crime techs still at work processing the car. My gaze shifted to the door as Gabriel opened it and sat down behind the wheel.

He put the car in gear, turned it around and drove off in silence.

"That was a bad one," he said as we turned back onto the main road.

I didn't say anything.

"Were you close to him?"

"No, actually not at all. He was the personal representative for an estate I've been handling."

"Had you known him long?"

"Around a year."

"Tell me why you wanted to look in the trunk?"

"No one else had."

He glanced at me. "You're not mixed up in this are you, Noah?"

"Actually, yes, I'm pretty sure I'm right in the middle of the whole thing. Only trouble is everyone else keeps turning up dead. But as far as the body count, I'm pretty sure that I'm okay on that."

"Body count?"

"You remember a while back, that accident on the bridge? Couple of cars went over the side?"

"Yeah, my day off. I was in the garden."

"Well, how much do you know about it?"

"A little bit. An attorney, Robert Seabrook, wasn't it? He died in one of the cars."

"Right. You know who was in the car with Seabrook?"

"Who?"

"The estate I was working, the one Thomason was involved with, was for a guy named Leo Cross. Ever heard of him?"

"Can't say I have. Wait, Cross. That was the name of the guy that died with Seabrook."

"Yep, Chase Cross, Leo Cross's son. Thomason and I were actually waiting for them at court when they died."

Gabriel had that "so what" look on his face that cops tended to get when someone was rattling off a theory to them.

"Here is what I am getting at," I said. "Seabrook and Chase Cross die. Now Thomason is dead. I know that Cross's death was supposedly an accident, but I'm pretty sure the verdict on Thomason will be different."

"Okay, I'll give you that. It has a funny look to it."

"Funny? You're kidding, right? It's bizarre, too coincidental. Until now I believed that Seabrook's accident was really an accident."

"Noah, you know how us police don't like the whole conspiracy theory thing."

"I know, I know, I don't either, but when you add in someone claiming to be me calling and canceling Thomason's reservation the night he disappeared..."

"So I guess you want me to do something for you?" he said.

"I don't know. I just feel like something's been overlooked."

"Dammit, Parks, you can be a pain in the ass. Tell you what, I'll go back over the Seabrook thing and see if I can come up with anything. Thomason's will be county's, but since you got me involved, I'll be in the loop."

"I'd appreciate that," I said.

"But word to the wise, that lady friend of yours is going to have a few more questions to answer now that we have a body. I mean, I think her alibi is solid, but count on them wanting to see her again."

"Have them call me and I'll have her where they need her."

We arrived at the police department. He stopped by my car.

"I'll give you a call if I hear anything. And Noah?"

"Yea?"

"Remember, you're the one that gets them out of jail. I'm the one with the badge."

"Thanks, mom."

He waved to me as he pulled around the station to the secure lot, leaving me standing in a near empty lot by my Jeep.

~~~~~~~~~~~~~~~~~~~~~~

I got in my car and headed toward home. Austin was his usual happy-to-see-me self as I took him into the back yard for some well deserved play. As I was throwing the tennis ball for him, a thought came to me. I stayed outside with him for a bit, then we went

inside. I fed him, then headed out to my car. Drivin
neighborhood and heading north on Highway 17, I
through Mount Pleasant, past the historic old village an
the beaches, passing over the old swing bridge towar
With less than a half a mile to go before the beach, I p
that read "Sullivan's Island City Limit."

Sullivan's Island is a small spit of an island no m
miles long and at most a half a mile wide. It had a hi:
before the Revolutionary War, but for many years wa
than a deserted island, cut off from the main land an
Charleston. Sullivan's housed Fort Moultrie that, alo
Sumter in the Charleston harbor, guarded the city in tir
Moultrie's main claim to fame came from the Revolt
There was an abundance of Palmetto trees on the is
soldiers used to construct the walls of the fort. Unknov
the time, the trees were quite fibrous. This made for ;
outcome when the fort was hit with cannon balls fire
on the harbor - they just bounced off. The fort's sec
fame was that it was one of Edgar Allen Poe's duty :
he was in the army. He penned "Gold Bug" while he
there. In the years since, Sullivan's Island had gone fr
island with a primitive fort, to a sleepy beachfront c
an escape for the wealthy who had the capital to affor
finest beach homes on the east coast. The place had
way. No wonder Anna Beth Cross had rented a house

I hadn't been to the house in more than a week, a
had only stayed briefly, not even going inside.

Tonight, the lights were on as I pulled up to the dr
The house, built over an open garage, rose three
balconies on each of the floors. The front was almost
and overlooked the ocean. I climbed the stairs to the

ork of art carved out of some tropical hardwood. I reached for the
ll and then changed my mind. I knocked instead.

Nothing.

I knocked again.

I saw a shape inside through the opaque glass on the side of the
or. The light came on beside the door as it opened and the shape
vealed itself. Anna Beth.

"Noah, what are you doing out here?"

"Can I come in?" I said.

"Certainly, please." She stepped out of the way and I walked
side, stopping just inside the doorway.

She walked past me. I followed her into the kitchen.

"I was just opening a bottle of wine. Care for a glass?"

"I'd love one."

She stood on the tips of her toes as she opened the cabinet and
ached for two glasses. She was barefoot, wearing a pair of jersey
awstring shorts and a tee shirt. Her long brown hair cascaded
wn her back. As she turned with the glasses, she caught me
aring.

"Shouldn't stare," she said, smiling as she walked to a bottle of
ne on the counter. "I apologize for being so casual, but I wasn't
pecting company. Forgive me?"

I walked over and picked up the bottle of wine. Manzantas
eek Sauvignon Blanc. "Nice."

"Could you open that? Top drawer, just to your left."

I retrieved an opener as she walked out of the room. I heard the
und of a computer shutting down in the next room. She walked
ck in just as I finished with the cork and was pouring the wine.

"So to what do I owe the honor?" she said as she reached for a
ss of the wine.

"Nice house."

"Thanks, but I'm guessing you didn't come by for a tour. Or did you?"

I took a drink of my wine. "Thomason's dead."

She walked across the kitchen, pulled out a chair and sat at the breakfast table overlooking the ocean. I waited for her to speak, but she sat in silence. I sipped my wine and watched her as she stared out the window onto the moonlit ocean.

"How?" she said.

I walked over and sat down across from her. "Well, I don't know."

"Meaning?"

"I got a call from Gabriel this afternoon. Sheriff's department found his car in the water off of a boat landing just out of town." I didn't tell her that I had been there when they pulled him up.

"So he drowned?"

"I'm guessing the answer to that will be no."

"You hesitated."

I looked at my wine glass and stared out toward the ocean, hoping to find an answer there. It didn't work. "Guess you won't let me get away with keeping quiet on this?"

"Just tell me." Her tone told me that my trying to lighten the situation wasn't quite what I should be doing.

"He may have drowned, but they found him in the trunk of the car, so I'm guessing the coroner will call it a homicide."

I expected questions, tears, some emotion, but I got more silence. Silence and her staring at the ocean.

She took a drink of her wine. "Thank you for coming."

"I couldn't just call and give you news like that. And I needed to talk to you."

"Needed to talk to me? About?" She raised her eyes to look at me, and I got the feeling that I may have just sent the wrong signal.

"No, nothing like that…"

"Like what?" She shifted her chair to face me. "Noah, what's the matter?"

I lied. "I wanted to talk to you about what's going to happen over the next few days."

"Okay, but let me ask you this. Does your friend have any ideas about what happened?"

"No, but he won't be investigating it, either. The sheriff will. And with the phone from your room, they'll be starting with you."

"You're serious?"

"Very. And they'll be focusing on your alibi."

"Alibi? You mean I'm a suspect in Steven's death?" she stood up as she spoke.

"I'd say no, but the cell phone is a logical starting place for them. I'm going to talk to Gabriel again about the rental car. I also told him to have the sheriff call me when they wanted to talk to you."

As if she hadn't heard the last part, she asked, "What about the rental car?"

"Well, it was rented after he flew into town. Question is, when was he killed? For the most part, I'm your alibi. You called me around 9:30 and we were together until almost midnight."

"Oh."

"Listen, I'll talk to the police about this. What I'd like to do is head them off so they don't even talk to you."

She picked up her wine, drained the glass and looked at me. "More?"

I looked at my empty glass. "Sure."

She walked to the counter, picked up the bottle and walked back to the table.

"Thank you for coming. You didn't have to, but it was very

thoughtful. I've had a lot of bad news lately, and you're the first person that had the decency to tell me in person. I was making something to eat. Join me?"

I liked the sound of that and found myself saying, "Yes."

As she cooked, we talked. We talked about Thomason some more. She was rightfully worried about the police questioning her, so I minimized the process. This calmed her down some. We also talked about her. I'd thought I had a picture of her, but as is usually the case, there was much more beneath the surface.

She had lived alone for most of the last decade after her divorce, and she'd remained quite private over the years. Initially I'd thought it a bit odd that she was going to stay in Charleston in an opened ended fashion, but it turns out that being alone was pretty much the status quo for her, so living alone in a large beach house wasn't that different from her Chicago apartment view, I imagined. She was still alone. The scenery was all that had changed. I found myself watching as she moved around the kitchen, cooking, talking, and occasionally smiling. I really enjoyed the smiling. Dinner was simple, but wonderful. We enjoyed it at the table overlooking the ocean.

"It's getting late," I said as I finished the last of my wine. "Let me help you clean up."

"No, I'm just going to leave it 'til the morning."

I looked at my watch and stood. "Thanks for dinner."

"Thank you for coming, and thanks for the company. I like the privacy, but it's nice to have someone to talk to."

"The pleasure was mine. Anytime, call me."

I walked to the door and she followed. "Are you okay to drive?"

I looked at her for a moment and had a fleeting thought that she may be about to ask me to stay. Then I decided it was just the wine.

I decided she was just looking out for me, being nice. I assured her that I was. She asked that I call her when I made it home.

I looked at my watch as I pulled from her drive and saw that I had been there for almost six hours.

The island gave way to the streets of Mount Pleasant, the Cooper then Ashley rivers, then the neighborhoods of West Ashley. I made it home without incident and called Anna Beth. To my surprise, I got her machine. I left a message thanking her for the evening.

~~~~~~~~~~~~~~~~~~~~~~

The next morning I headed into the office after a run and had a message from Gabriel. I called him back first thing.

"You called?"

"Morning to you too. Came by your house last night, but guess you were out."

"I was. Did I miss anything?"

"I talked to the guys over at the sheriff's office and they want to talk to your girl. I gave them a run down on what I had from the day you called me. I don't get the feeling that she has anything to do with this, but I have to let the sheriff make up his own mind."

"You check that phone for prints?"

"Now, Noah, really man, give me a bit of credit."

"So, question for you? Get any prints?" I said.

"Yeah, Thomason's and one of the officers from the scene. Stupid rookie touched it before the techs got there."

"Probably the one hitting on Anna Beth."

"Say what?"

"Never mind. So no one else's?"

"No, why do you ask?"

"Was it wiped?"

"Didn't appear to be. Why you so curious?"

"Here's what I am thinking. Anna Beth was with me from about 9:30 until probably past midnight. I'm guessing that the desk clerk could put her in the hotel the rest of the night."

"You representing her?"

"No, not yet, but I'm getting the feeling that she isn't involved in Thomason's death."

"Well, I think the same, but the sheriff's got things now."

"You talk to the detective?"

"I did and didn't accomplish a thing. Henderson's on the case."

"Great. You do know how to make a day."

Bruce Henderson. Pretty much a black mark on the Sheriff's Department. I'd had several cases where he'd been the lead detective, and they were memorable to say the least. He was sloppy, jumped to conclusions and made a lot of arrests. His theory was to arrest them all and let the Solicitor's Office sort out who they were going to prosecute. All he cared about was clearing cases. If he was wrong, and he usually was, when the case bounced back it usually went to another detective. He kept his arrest numbers up and that kept him his job.

"You did tell him to call me if he wanted to talk to her, right?"

"I did, but you know how much good that'll do."

"I do. I'm going to give him a call. Thanks, and let me know if you hear anything."

"Will do. And Noah, watch that girl."

I hung up the phone without saying anything else. Gabriel worried too much. I'd known him a long time, and while he was a great friend, he could be over protective. Sometimes a bit too much. I dialed the sheriff's office, was transferred to investigations and was told that Henderson was unavailable. I left a message, knowing that he wouldn't return the call. For some reason it was nearly impossible to get a cop to call you back. Well, most of them, except Gabriel. However, Henderson wasn't one of these and, unfortunately (or maybe fortunately) he didn't return many calls. It was his little power trip over attorneys.

Next I called Anna Beth and told her what I'd learned from Gabriel. As I expected she wasn't at all happy with the news, especially the part about me not being able to get in touch with Henderson. I told her I'd come over to her house later, but that if for some reason he showed up before I had talked to him she was not to say a word. I could tell she was nervous. I told her that it would be okay, and after a few minutes I got the feeling that she was starting to believe me. The trouble was, I wasn't doing a very good job convincing myself.

I walked out of my office and looked to see if Heather was there. No sign of her. I tried her cell and got her voicemail. I was starting to get a little concerned with not being able to get in touch with her. She'd been with me for awhile, and it wasn't like her at all to just disappear, but then again I had never almost hooked up with her before. I needed to look into it, but I decided Anna Beth got priority today.

I went back into my office to do some work, but found concentration beyond my grasp. Looking at documents, reading letters, sorting through phone messages from my answering service, my mind wandered to Anna Beth. I decided that it would be best to check in on her. I called the service and locked up.

~~~~~~~~~~~~~~~~~~~~~~~

Charleston to Mount Pleasant is just across the bridge and, as long as there aren't wrecks on the bridge, the trip's a quick one.

And Mount Pleasant isn't that far from Sullivan's Island. Actually, except for the Intracoastal Waterway separating them, they're adjoining towns. Problem is, though, Mount Pleasant's population has exploded, and it seems like everyone that has moved there has three cars and they're all on the road at the same time. What should have taken thirty minutes took almost an hour. I was glad I lived in Charleston and could fight the Mount Pleasant traffic at the times that I chose to do so.

I arrived on Sullivan's Island and drove up to Anna Beth's. I was surprised and more than a little perturbed to see an unmarked police car and a patrol cruiser parked in the yard. There was also a deputy on the front porch of the house. As I parked, another deputy arrived. I knew Henderson was in there with Anna Beth, and I was pissed he hadn't called me. However, I was more surprised there wasn't a Sullivan's Island police officer there as Henderson was in their jurisdiction. Officers from competing departments never liked it when outsiders, especially from other agencies, dug around on their turf. It had a way of creating problems between departments (which meant that it rarely ever happened), but Henderson didn't care about professional courtesy. He was showing his colors early on this one.

I stood outside of my car for a moment to see what the deputy would do. He stared at me through mirrored glasses, his face showing no expression. I walked up the steps. The deputy greeted me, if you could call it that.

"Can I help you?" he said.

"No thank you, deputy. I'm here to see Ms. Cross."

"Not today, you're not."

I stood for a moment. I knew that Henderson had told him in no uncertain terms that no one was to get through the door. In all likelihood, Henderson's instruction had included specific instructions that 'no one' particularly meant me.

"Get Henderson, tell him that Ms. Cross' attorney is here."

"I don't think you heard me Sir, I…"

I put up my hand.

"Get. Henderson. Now."

The deputy stood for a moment - he appeared to be balancing his next course of action. I could almost hear both of his gears turning ever so slowly in his head. Stand between an attorney and his client and risk getting a case thrown out, or go tell Henderson that his party was over. It seemed like an easy choice, but the deputy was struggling.

"Now," I said.

The deputy took off his sunglasses and walked inside. He tried to shut the door, but I caught it and followed him inside.

I saw that I'd made a mistake not having Anna Beth elsewhere for the afternoon. As I walked in behind the deputy, I heard Henderson's elevated voice from the living room. I walked past the deputy into the room and saw that Henderson had Anna Beth seated in the living room. She was on the couch with her head in her hands, Henderson standing over her. He was holding his sunglasses in one hand, jabbing a finger at Anna Beth with the other. His thinning hair was combed straight back, gelled stiff to his head. His collar was at least half an inch too small, and it looked as if it was squeezing out the fat on his neck. I had a lovely profile view of him which, given his stomach bulge, was less than flattering. Generally it took a good bit of work to make an expensive suit look like crap, but Henderson pulled off the feat with little effort. A deputy stood in the corner of the room looking like he'd rather be anywhere else other than there.

"Sir, there…" my deputy began.

"Henderson, what the hell is going on here?" I said.

Henderson turned to face me. "Noah Parks. And what are you doing here?"

"I'll be asking the questions, deputy. And by the way, you're done here. Anna Beth, go wait for me in the kitchen."

Henderson turned back to her. "You stay your ass right there."

"You arresting her?" I said as I stepped between them.

"Can't answer that."

"Then Anna Beth, go to the kitchen and don't say a word to anyone."

She rose and walked out of the room without looking at him. He glared at her, then back to me. She disappeared into the kitchen.

"Let me guess, you just forgot to call me?" I said.

"Must have slipped my mind."

"I'm sure it did. So, arrest her or leave," I said.

"Parks, I…"

"It's not a hard choice. And she's invoking her right to counsel, so no more questioning her without me. If I decide to let you," I added as I took a seat on the living room couch.

Henderson didn't move.

"Can I help you with anything else, deputy?"

"Parks, you're being a real pain in the ass, you know. I'm just getting started with her, so let's go sit down and talk. I'll let you watch."

"Sorry Henderson, we're done here. Let me walk you out. Or, actually, you're a detective, you can probably find your own way out." I stood and walked to the living room door.

Henderson looked at me, spoke to the deputy in the corner, then turned to the door.

"Parks, you just made the list." He walked by me, headed out the door and down the steps, collecting the deputy waiting outside. I watched them get in their cars and leave. I locked the door and headed to the kitchen.

She was standing at the island in the middle of the room.

"You okay?" I said.

"He just showed up and came inside. He said he had some background questions about Steven. I believed him."

"First rule with Henderson, never trust him. What did you say to him?"

"Nothing, just like you said. He came in and started asking me about why I was down here and where I was the night Steven came to town. When I wouldn't answer his questions, he started accusing me of killing him."

"Gabriel called him and I left a message. He obviously ignored us both. That won't happen again."

"What did he want?"

"He wants to make an arrest. The sheriff's department doesn't do a very good job solving murders, so if he can clear one up, then kudos for him."

"That doesn't seem like any way to be a policeman."

"It's not, but you have to know him. He is not a very good detective, but he makes a lot of arrests. That and his uncle was a state senator, which is how he got his job."

"He can't think I had anything to do with Steven getting killed, can he?"

"Unfortunately, yes. He seems to have you in his sights. You're not going to talk to the police anymore. He'll try to get to you again, but we won't let him. Course, all of this is assuming you want me to represent you."

"Of course I do, but should I be worried?"

I walked to the other side of the island and leaned over toward her. "I won't lie. If he came out here, his whole goal was to try to trick you into saying something that would give him an excuse to arrest you. If you'd given him anything, you'd probably be on the way to the jail. Like I said, he's lazy. Once he realizes that I'm not going to let him talk to you, he will most likely piece together anything he has and arrest you."

"You're being serious?"

"Unfortunately yes. So let me tell you what to expect and what we'll do. I'll contact Henderson's captain and let him know that if you are to be arrested, you'll surrender in person."

"I really can't believe this. How did it all happen?"

"I can't answer that question, but here's what we are going to do. I'm going to have one of my PI's talk to the staff at the hotel. You're alibi'll be solid."

"Noah, thank you so much." She reached across the island and touched my hand.

"Don't thank me yet, we still have a ways to go. I also think we should rethink our approach to your father's will."

"How so?" she said.

"We need to get the safe deposit box open and see what's in it."

"I take it you have a plan?"

"As a matter of fact, I do. First thing, we keep Henderson away from you. Next, I get you appointed as the PR of your father's estate and you give the permission to open the safe deposit box."

"You can do that?"

"The PR part is simple. It'll take a week or so, but that I can get done. Henderson will be a pain in the ass no matter what."

"Then, let's get going. What can I do?"

I explained the papers I would get together and what they would do. We also talked about the possibility of her getting arrested. I told her if she was arrested then she would need to have access to a large amount of money, maybe as much as half a million dollars for bail. This shocked her, but I explained that because she lived in Chicago and had access to lots of money she could be considered a flight risk. Since the estate was otherwise discharged, the two million from her father's estate was available to her. It was being held in an investment account on which she had already been named. We decided that I would be added to the account in order to access funds in the event she was arrested. That way we could make sure she would be able to get out of jail.

We talked through the evening, though without wine this time. This time it was all business. I ran out of steam on things after several hours and rose to leave. She walked me to the door and thanked me. She stood beside me at the door as I turned to go.

"Noah?"

I turned to face her and started to speak. She put her finger to my lips, stopping me from speaking. She put a hand on either of my shoulders and raised herself onto the tips of her toes and looked me in the eye.

"Thank you again," she whispered in my ear. Then she kissed my cheek.

CHAPTER 11

It didn't take long to complete Anna Beth's application to have her appointed as her father's PR. Fortunately, the coroner signed off on a death certificate for Thomason, and with that it was only a procedural hurdle with the Probate Court. In Cross' will he hadn't named an alternate PR, so Anna Beth, according to South Carolina law, was the next in line for the job. I'd spoken to Anna Beth several times since the run-in with Henderson and she was holding up pretty well – much to my surprise. Even more to my surprise, I hadn't heard anything from Henderson, but I didn't really call that good news. I'd spoken to Gabriel about Henderson and the stunt he pulled at Anna Beth's house. Apparently, Henderson, knowing Gabriel and I were friends, had called Gabriel's captain and complained that Gabriel was feeding me information. Since the captain liked Henderson only slightly less than I did, this didn't accomplish anything but get word to me that Henderson was on the warpath. That, and the captain told Gabriel to keep on top of the investigation, which meant that I still had a conduit for information.

To no one's surprise, the coroner ruled Thomason's death a homicide. He'd been dead when the car hit the water. The coroner determined a severe blow to the back of the head killed him. His stay in the river only served to destroy whatever other evidence was in the car. They were running a toxicology screen on Thomason, but no one thought that would show anything.

I'd been keeping my fingers crossed about Anna Beth and the murder investigation while I was waiting for her appointment as personal representative of her father's estate to come back from the Court. We would have another problem if she was arrested for his murder. However, I was really beginning to worry about Heather. She'd been gone two weeks with no word. That was unusual for her. I called her, but there was no answer at her apartment or on her cell. I decided to drop by her apartment and see if she was home.

I left my office early that day. Seemed I'd been doing that a lot lately. After driving downtown, I parked behind a friend's restaurant and walked over to Heather's place. The door to the stairs off King Street was unlocked. I looked up and down the street, almost feeling a little guilty for snooping around. It also looked a lot different during the day when I wasn't being invited up by an attractive woman after having been out drinking with her for hours. I opened the door and went upstairs. There was a note on the door from someone dated four days earlier.

"Call me. Jen."

I knocked. No answer. I tried again. I turned to the door across the landing from Heather's and knocked on it. No answer there, either. I decided I could check with the property manager and see if he knew anything, but there didn't seem to be anything here that helped me with where she was.

I decided to call a friend at the law school and see if she had been making her classes. I pulled out my cell and tracked him down at home and got him just before he started dinner.

"Hello?" a familiar voice said.

"Tony. Noah Parks here." It was always a pleasure to talk to Tony. He'd been a Family Court Judge when I first started practicing, but he left the bench to take a job at the law school when it first opened several years back. For reasons none of those who knew him understood, he took a job teaching property and seemed to love it. He had a reputation as a difficult but fair instructor.

"Noah. How are you doing my friend?"

"Well. And yourself?"

"Quite good actually. So, to what do I owe the honor?"

"Actually I have a question about one of your students – Heather Davis?"

"Yes, yes, I have her in a property planning class."

"Thought you might. She's my paralegal," I said.

"Hum, may I ask you a question, Noah?"

"Certainly."

"Ms. Davis is a very bright student, but I haven't seen her for maybe two weeks. Is she okay?"

"Your question answers mine. I haven't seen her in about two weeks myself. Her mother became ill several weeks ago and she went to visit her. She called several times, but nothing for two weeks. It's almost like she dropped off the face of the earth."

"That's about how long she has been out of class. Is there anything wrong?"

"I wouldn't worry about anything. Heather has a flair for drama, and it wouldn't be the first time she has just picked up and left," I said.

"I'm not sure if I've helped too much, but I want you to know if I can do anything, please let me know."

"Thanks Tony. Best to Rachel."

Now I was starting to worry, despite my lie to Tony.

~~~~~~~~~~~~~~~~~~~~~~~~~

The next morning I walked into my office and went straight to Heather's desk and began looking for anything that would offer any information about where she could be. I called the temp agency, but the person I needed to speak with wasn't there. I left my number. There was a surprisingly small amount of personal information at her desk. I contemplated looking on her computer, but something about that didn't seem right.

I picked up the phone and called Gabriel. He answered on the first ring.

"Noah, how you doing today?"

"Pretty okay. Yourself?" I said.

"Heading to the garden as we speak."

"You up for a little company? I need to run something by you."

"You know I'm always up for a little company. Come on by."

"See you in a few."

I left the office without calling the answering service. Gabriel lived just out of downtown in an old home that had been in his family for more than a hundred years. He'd worked on it practically all of his life to make it the beautiful place it is today. The original structure had been little more than a three room building, but over the years it had been expanded to more than four thousand square feet. In a neighborhood of small middle class homes, it was a mansion. His father had been a longshoreman and Gabriel his only son. His father had done quite well in all his years. Gabriel inherited all of it and owned the house free and clear. That allowed him the opportunity to improve and add to his home as he had, but he hadn't stopped with that. In his spare time he was on a community board working to rejuvenate the rest of his neighborhood. His work on the police force and a lot of volunteer time had cleaned the neighborhood of drugs and gangs, and he had been able to help take a neighborhood that was on the brink of despair and help make it a great place where people wanted to settle down.

I parked in the drive behind his unmarked police cruiser then walked up the few steps to his porch. I banged on the door and looked through the windows. No sign of him. I heard a dog bark around back of the house. I went down the steps and followed a path around the house to a gate in the fence to the back yard. As I swung it open, I was greeted by Rudy, the beagle, who was one of Austin's buddies.

I bent down and scratched his head while he licked my face to say hello. "Hey Rudy, where's your dad?"

"That you?"

I saw Gabriel walking toward me from across the yard with a pair of small clippers.

"Rudy, you're a mess. Leave Noah alone and go play with your ball."

At the mention of the word 'ball' Rudy dashed across the yard to the back porch, where he raced up the stairs and pushed the door open. I heard him rummaging around looking for his ball.

"Come on over while I trim a bit."

I followed him across the yard.

One of the things that made Gabriel's yard so neat was that it was so big. When his great-great something grandfather had first built on the lot he had ended up with about three acres of land, something that is unheard of in or around downtown Charleston these days. Through the years, through some selling, trading and basic generosity, Gabriel was down to just over an acre, but that was still estate size by local standards. His house sat on the very front of the lot, a privacy fence enclosing the backyard. Most of it was basic landscaping, some natural, some Gabriel inspired – buffering, plush grass, sego palms and oaks. However, in the far corner there were a number of Japanese fire maples whose leaves turned a brilliant red in the fall, even in South Carolina. They were flanked by bamboo that Gabriel kept trimmed and manicured to form a natural barrier. The maples formed sort of the gateway to a formal Japanese garden just beyond. There was more manicured bamboo, sand, gravel paths, a fountain with a stream and carefully sculpted mounds of earth on which were planted about a dozen bonsai trees of varying sizes. Several large stones surrounded the center and doubled as benches. On the far side of the garden a traditional Japanese structure housed all of Gabriel's garden equipment.

We walked through the maples into the garden. The only sound was that of the running water from the fountain.

"I can't believe how far you've come with this place." I could remember when his bonsai obsession had started many years ago. In fact, he had taken me with him when he bought his first tree, and for years afterwards pretended he was Mr. Miagai as he sat on his back porch trimming the little trees.

"Thanks. You know how much time I put in it. I think I'd have gone bananas if I hadn't had this. Most of the guys at the station think I'm going soft on them when they see it, but screw 'em. If you want a beer, I just put a fridge in over there." He pointed at the building to the side of the garden.

I heard a 'woof' from behind us and turned to see Rudy sitting between the maples with his paw on a tennis ball, tail wagging.

Gabriel looked at me, "He won't come in here." Then to Rudy,

"Hang on a sec, boy." Rudy immediately lay down with his chin beside the ball.

"So, wha'cha got?" he said.

"I need your advice on something."

"And that would be?" He was leaning over the sloping mound, studying a small bonsai about halfway up the rock.

"You remember my paralegal, Heather?"

"Cute brunette?"

"That would be her."

"Then, yes, I do." He looked as if he was contemplating some trimming, but wasn't actually doing anything other than staring. I had discovered that the trimming of the little trees often involved more thought than actual cutting.

"Well, she seems to have disappeared."

Gabriel looked up at me. "You've got to be kidding. You lost another one?"

"Here's what happened."

I proceeded to tell him about the night Heather and I almost hooked up that ended up being the night Thomason was killed. I told him that she hadn't been to work for about a week after that, but that Thomason's disappearance had distracted me so I hadn't been able to really talk to her. I told him about her mother getting sick and Heather leaving. I also told him about not getting an answer on her cell or home phone and also not getting any call backs. Finally, I told him about her not going to class for the last two weeks.

"Hum, you do realize the girl's probably just embarrassed or maybe even just pissed at you."

"I know, that thought's crossed my mind, but her missing school isn't like her."

"I'll give you that." He had risen from studying the bonsai and was sitting on one of the rocks across from me.

"So, should I do anything?" I said.

"You got a number for her mother?"

"No, actually I don't. I figured I'd look up the number in Savannah and maybe call the temp service that I got her from and check contact numbers. Got any other ideas?"

"Why don't you do that, and if she doesn't show up in a couple of days let me know and I'll nose around a bit."

We sat in silence for several minutes while Gabriel looked at the little trees. He sat down on a rock several feet away from me.

"So, can I ask you a question?" he said.

"About?"

"About this woman."

"Which one?" I said.

"Which one do you think?" he said.

"Anna Beth, I take. What about her?"

"Parks my friend, I know you too well."

He never called me Parks unless he had something serious on his mind.

"What are you getting at?"

"You remember what happened last time?"

"I do. You know I do."

"I just don't want to see you go through anything like that again. I thought you were never going to bounce back. I guess she just brings back some memories for me, stuff I hadn't thought about in a while," he said.

I looked at him as he sat there looking at me. He was a good friend, and I knew that he was right.

"Noah, damn it, you're not going to even try to tell me you haven't thought about this," he said.

"And if I have?"

"I'm your friend and I worry about you. I don't want to see you have to go through that again."

"I know. I hear what you're saying."

Rudy had started whining. I rose and walked to him. He pushed the tennis ball toward me with his nose and backed up a few feet, his body shaking in anticipation as I threw the ball. He tore off after it.

Gabriel appeared from the garden with two beers. Rudy came back with the ball and dropped it at our feet. Gabriel handed me the beers and heaved the ball across the yard for Rudy. I opened the beers and handed one to Gabriel.

We watched Rudy chase across the yard in silence from the gate of the bonsai garden.

~~~~~~~~~~~~~~~~~~~~~~

I left Gabriel's shortly after that and headed home. There were no messages on the machine, but Austin was happy to see me. He studied me carefully, smelling Rudy on me as if he wanted to be upset at me, but he couldn't be upset finding a familiar scent.

I went to bed, exhausted. What seemed less than five minutes later, the phone rang. It was so early that Austin didn't even stir on the bed as I reached for the phone.

"Noah Parks," I managed to get out in a gruff voice.

"Parks, good morning."

I let the voice echo in my head, but it didn't register at all. I guess the gap in the conversation clued whomever it was that I didn't know their identity.

"Parks, I've decided that I don't need to talk to Ms. Cross again. I'm arresting her. But since you made such a big deal about it, my captain said I have to call you and give you a chance to surrender her."

Henderson. I looked at the bedside clock - not yet 5:00 am.

"When do you want her to surrender?"

"Well, if she's not there by, say 6:00, I'm coming to get her."

"Henderson, don't be an ass."

"Parks, Captain said all I had to do was call and give you an opportunity to get her in. Better hurry. And on a personal note, I told you not to screw with me." He chuckled as he spoke. "Got anything you want to say, got you on speaker phone so everyone can hear you."

"Yes, as a matter of fact, I do. See you at Bond Court at 9:30." I could hear Henderson yelling 'God dammit' as I hung up the phone. I'd have bet that my name followed the 'God dammit.'

I jumped out of bed, let Austin out and raced through the shower. I was out of the house fifteen minutes after Henderson called. I dialed Anna Beth as I drove. Her machine picked up. I hung up the phone and called her cell. Voice mail. Henderson was probably already on his way to her house. If I didn't make it there before he did then he'd arrest her and she'd spend a day or two in the jail before I was able to get her out. I dialed her home phone again. Busy signal. As I was pressing the "End" button on my cell, a call came in. Anna Beth. I answered.

"Noah?"

"Yes, sorry to wake you. Listen, get dressed. Fast. I'm on my way over."

"Noah, it's barely 5:00 in the morning. Can't this wait?"

"No. Henderson called and he wants you to surrender today. He's going to arrest you."

"Oh, Jesus."

"Listen, get dressed – comfortably, just in case. Call me when you're ready. I want you to meet me somewhere."

"But, Noah…"

"No buts, get going."

Fortunately there wasn't a lot of traffic as I headed toward Anna Beth's, but even with no traffic it was a thirty minute drive. I was hoping that with a little luck I could get her out of there just before Henderson graced us with his presence.

The phone rang in seven minutes.

"I'm ready and in the car."

"No police?"

"No, will there be?" she said.

I lied. "No."

"Ok, where am I going?"

I gave her directions to a friend's house in Mount Pleasant as I changed direction to meet her there. It was off the main highway and also had a huge garage where we could park our cars away from prying eyes. I called him but he wasn't home, which wasn't a surprise as he traveled a good bit. Fortunately, I had a key to the house. I arrived a few minutes later and opened one of the doors to the four bay garage. I stood in the drive and saw Anna Beth come around the corner. I motioned for her to pull inside. She did and I shut the door. She jumped out of her car.

"Noah, what are we doing here? If I'm wanted isn't this like hiding?"

"Come with me, we're not hiding. We have to consult – legal term."

The house was on Shem Creek, a large tidal creek that cut through part of Mount Pleasant from the Charleston Harbor. The home was four stories high with more glass than brick. It commanded a beautiful view of the creek, the Charleston Harbor and the ocean beyond. Under normal circumstances the view alone would have been enough to captivate the senses, but today the view was the last thing on either of our minds.

"Do you want anything?" I said.

"No, I'm too nervous. Why did you call me so early?"

"Henderson called me at home and gave me till 6:00 to get you to the jail. I told him we would be there at 9:30. I needed to get to you before he did. He may come looking for you, but he won't find us here, and as long as we are there by 9:00 he'll get pissed at me but can't do anything to you since that's before bond hearings start."

"You seem to keep appearing just in time lately."

We stared at each other for a very long moment. Neither of us moved. I finally broke her stare and spoke.

"You need to call and get bail money arranged. If Henderson charges you with murder bail will be high, and I want you to have enough to cover it."

I expected her to question me or perhaps protest, but she pulled out her cell and dialed. She already had the routing numbers to my escrow account and moved the entire two million there. I tried the office on the slim chance Heather was there. No luck. I spied a laptop on the coffee table, and I noticed it had a wireless internet connection. I logged onto the county's web page and checked the judge at the bond hearing. Judge Robert Carver. Seemed my luck was turning around. I'd known him as long as I had been practicing. Not that my knowing him would give me any advantage when it came to his setting Anna Beth's bail, but he didn't like Henderson either and that couldn't hurt.

I looked to see that Anna Beth was off the phone and was staring out one of the windows overlooking Shem Creek. She was crying. I walked over to her and put my hand on her shoulder.

"Hey, hey, it's going to be all right."

She turned to look at me, stepped to me and laid her head on my chest.

"You can take care of this?'

"I have a few things that I think will get it squared away. I can't make it all go away today, but I think we can get to the bottom of it pretty quick." Another lie. "You shouldn't have to be at the jail more than a few hours."

"I'll be there that long?" she said, obviously not looking forward to the prospect of a day in jail.

"It'll take a little while to get you processed, but I'll get the bail posted and get you out."

I explained how the process would work. She was nervous and scared, and I couldn't say that that was the wrong way to feel. I did the best I could to calm her down, and after about an hour of talking (and even a little laughing), she looked at her watch and said it was time to go. I couldn't tell if she was feeling better or was just a good enough actor to convince me she was okay.

We walked out of the house, got in my car and headed across town to the county jail. We rode in silence and arrived about twenty minutes later. We parked and I looked toward her. She flashed a smile and said, "Let's go."

~~~~~~~~~~~~~~~~~~~~~~

The sign on the door read "Central Bond Court." We went inside. I looked around and saw a deputy that I knew. I didn't see Henderson.

I looked at Anna Beth. "Stand here and don't talk to anyone."

"Omar," I said as I walked toward the deputy.

"Noah, what you got today?" he said.

"Here to turn in a client. Can you square me away? Supposed to meet Henderson." There was no love lost between most of the other deputies and Henderson.

"Love to. That her?" he said as he nodded toward Anna Beth.

"Yeah, name's Cross. Anna Beth Cross."

"Hang on a sec. If the warrant's in the system, I'll start her processing." He disappeared.

I walked back over to Anna Beth. "This might go a little bit smoother than I thought. Henderson's probably out at your place or at my office looking for you. Omar can get you processed and in the courtroom. You'll be handcuffed, but Henderson won't be able to slow things down."

Omar returned from the administrative office holding a warrant. "Second degree murder. Henderson's rolled this one up. I'll get her started then call him and tell him you're here. You know Carver's on the bench?"

"That I do."

"Hold on for a few, I'll get her right out," he said.

"Thanks, Omar, I owe you."

He turned to Anna Beth. "Ms. Cross, if you would come with me. And I apologize, but I have to put these handcuffs on you. We'll put them up front."

Anna Beth looked at me and I nodded to her. She disappeared with Omar after he loosely locked the cuffs on her wrists in front of her as opposed to behind her. She winced as they clicked shut. She didn't look back as he led her to the processing area.

I walked through the metal detector and back to the courtroom. Judge Carver was already on the bench doing hearings. Whenever a person is arrested they have the right to a bond hearing. At this hearing, a judge learns what crime the accused has allegedly committed. Ultimately the judge makes a decision on an amount of bail that will motivate the accused to stay in the jurisdiction until the charges they may be facing have been resolved. The theory behind this process is that if the accused has money on the line, they'll stay around. If you disappeared, you lost your bail.

Henderson would oppose bail. He always did. Everyone he'd ever arrested was the worst flight risk he'd ever seen. I was also pretty sure that the judge would set a substantial bail, but bail nevertheless. Judge Carver acknowledged me when I walked in the courtroom with a nod of his head.

I'd been sitting about fifteen minutes when Omar led Anna Beth in. I was glad I'd run into him. If Henderson had processed Anna Beth, to get back at me, he'd have planted her in an interview room and left her there all day until the Judge left the bench. Then he would've held Anna Beth overnight until the next morning, or maybe even the next afternoon. Since she was already processed in, photographed and fingerprinted, she could be heard as soon as Henderson arrived and could be out in a couple of hours.

Omar sat Anna Beth in the front row, right in front of me. Omar motioned for me to come out of the courtroom. I told Anna Beth that I would be right back and followed him out.

"I called Henderson and told him that she was here and to meet me in the courtroom. Be ready to go."

"Thanks, Omar."

"No, he'll be pissed. Thank you." He smiled.

I went back into the courtroom. As I sat down behind Anna Beth, Judge Carver finished up a case and turned in my direction.

"Counselor," he said in greeting. I nodded my head. "You have a case today?"

"I do, I'm just waiting on Deputy Henderson."

"As soon as he gets here we can go."

Turns out Henderson had been at Anna Beth's place on Sullivan's Island and was taking his time getting to the Court.

After about thirty minutes Judge Carver looked over my

direction, and then to a security deputy. "Henderson not here yet? He know we're waiting on him? Go find him. I'd like to clear things by noon."

A smile crossed my face. Carver was already upset at Henderson and he wasn't even here yet. About ten minutes later, after Carver had been alternating glances toward the door of the courtroom and the clock on the rear wall, Henderson walked in.

Carver was in the middle of a bail hearing, but stopped as soon as he saw Henderson.

"Deputy, how nice of you to join us. Normally I'd make you wait, but as Mr. Parks and his client have been here for almost an hour, we'll take the case next."

"I'm sorry, your honor, but I was delayed. If I could ask the Court for some time to get everything together, I think I can be ready after lunch," Henderson said.

"After lunch?" the Judge said.

"Yes, sir. If not then, shortly there about."

Classic Henderson. He took more than an hour to get to the Court, kept the judge waiting, and was now trying to delay Anna Beth through the day.

"Deputy, let me finish this hearing and we can address that. If that's okay with you?"

"Okay, Judge." Henderson said, not working at all to hide his anger.

Judge Carver returned his attention to the hearing he'd been conducting when Henderson walked in. He finished about ten minutes later.

"Okay, let me see here. Mr. Parks, what case is this?"

Henderson had been standing against the wall of the courtroom talking to another deputy, but jumped forward when he heard my name. "Judge, we're going to push this off 'til later today, I believe."

"Whatever gave you that idea?"

"But, she's not even processed in yet..." Henderson said.

"My file says she is," Carver said.

I walked up to the judge's bench and motioned for Anna Beth to come stand beside me. Henderson opened his mouth to start in again, that is until the judge cut him off.

"Deputy, what appears to be the problem? We've been waiting for you for more than an hour and now we should keep waiting?"

"Judge, I need to pull everything together. I..."

"Deputy, I have a warrant with an affidavit in my file that you signed. I take it you are prepared to tell me about this charge. Now, what else is it we seem to need?"

Henderson started to speak, but Carver cut him off again.

"Let me help, deputy. Looks like you've charged this young woman with murder. Got any evidence?"

"Judge, we really need to hear this after lunch. You see..." Henderson said, but Judge Carver put his hand up.

"Evidence, deputy?"

Henderson told the Judge about the cell phone and then painted a gruesome picture of the murder scene.

"So, you have a cell phone in this young ladies' room? Her prints on it?"

Henderson started to speak and I cut him off. "No, your honor. Only those of the deceased and a Charleston police officer. If I may?"

"One moment, Mr. Parks. Deputy, request for bail?"

"Judge, no bail."

"She have any record?" Carver said.

"Judge, she's from out of state, and we can't be sure..."

"Good heaven's deputy, do you just go out and arrest people?

Didn't you run a records check?"

"I did, Judge."

"Well then, deputy, any record?"

I spoke up again. "Your honor, she owns property in the city and just signed a six-month lease on a local residence. I will be representing her as well. She has no criminal record, and in the last several months both her father and brother died. And now she has been charged with the murder of a lifelong family friend, despite a solid alibi. I understand that you must set bail with the seriousness of this charge, but please consider that all the state has is a cell phone found in her hotel room."

"Judge, she's charged with..." Henderson had a terrible habit of whining in bond hearings.

"Deputy, please. Bail is set at $250,000.00, cash or bond." He looked at Henderson when he said this, giving him a stern look.

"I'll get that posted with the Clerk of Court within the hour, Your Honor," I said.

The Judge gave me all of Anna Beth's documentation and had her sign her bail form.

A jailer led her out for processing. I headed out of the courtroom, Henderson on my tail.

"Think you're real slick don't you, Parks?"

I ignored him, but he continued.

"She'll go down, I promise," he said over my shoulder as I walked away. He followed me out into the parking lot.

"Better watch your ass, too. Might get sucked in."

I turned to face him. "What's that supposed to mean?" I said.

"You'll just have to find out, but I don't think Ms. Cross there planned this all on her own."

"Tell you what, I'll be back in an hour to get her. I'll say hi then."

THE TRUST

I left him standing in the parking lot as I went to get a cashier's check for a quarter of a million dollars.

CHAPTER 12

I gave Gabriel a call as I left the jail. He didn't answer and I left him a message. I drove on to my bank and walked up to one of the tellers. Charleston's not a huge town, but it is not a little village either, so I wasn't surprised when the teller became a bit flustered when she looked at the withdrawal slip for $250,000.00.

"If I could have a cashier's check, please."

She excused herself, saying that she would have to get a manager's authorization for the transaction. She appeared with a manager a few moments later who greeted me and provided the required authorization after verifying the balance in my account. I waited a few minutes longer and my cashier's check was ready. With the check for Anna Beth's bond, I was off to the Courthouse.

The Charleston County Courthouse is a newer building that opened less than ten years ago. However, given near constant major renovations, it was almost like getting a new courthouse every year. For decades the county's courthouse had been located in the heart of Charleston's downtown. However, in the closing months of the 1980's a huge hurricane, Hurricane Hugo, slammed the South Carolina coast and, while the building was not actually destroyed, it was damaged to the point where it was unusable. After that the courts were scattered all over the county, with the bulk of the operations ending up out of the downtown area in an old warehouse. A massive renovation was undertaken and a new courthouse facility was built. I parked at my office a few blocks down from the new facility and headed to the clerk's office.

I walked up to clerk's window with the check and paperwork in hand. One of the clerks that I knew was just finishing a phone call.

"Hey there Noah."

"And hey to you, Casie. I need to post a bond."

"Just posting it, no bail bondsman?"

"Nope, just got a check for you."

I gave her information on Anna Beth. Casie busied herself with her computer terminal. She glanced at me as she was working through the required paperwork to process the bail.

"You have a check, huh?"

I guessed she'd seen the amount of the bail.

"I do."

She smiled at me. "Got one for me too?"

I returned the smile to her.

It took her less than five minutes to finish everything. She gave me the required forms and told me, as I already knew, that she would also transmit the information to the jail electronically so Anna Beth's processing could get started. On the drive back out to the jail, I got a call from Gabriel.

"Seems you made quite the impression on Henderson."

"Meaning?"

"Meaning you're the talk of the town."

"Good, I hope?"

"Since most everyone feels the same way about Henderson, the talk is mostly good. But I can guarantee that you've got his attention."

"I figured as much, but he's an ass and deserves it," I said.

"You know he did, but he's going to be all over getting this murder pinned on your new friend. He'll probably try to pull you in, too. So watch out."

"You find out anything else on Thomason or Heather?"

"Don't worry about that, you just watch your ass."

"I have to run, I'm at the jail. I'll call you," I said.

"Just watch your ass," Gabriel said as he ended the call.

I pulled my car into a space close to the front of the jail. I sat for a moment and thought about what Gabriel had just told me. I didn't need Henderson digging around in my life, but I also didn't think Anna Beth deserved the attention she was getting from him. I went inside to get Anna Beth.

It took them about thirty minutes to process her out once I got everything squared away. I waited in the sparse waiting room, sitting on a metal bench with little to do aside from watching the jail's other visitors. The Charleston County Detention Center wasn't really that concerned with entertaining people who were waiting to see their guests. When Anna Beth finally appeared at the door she didn't really look all that different from when I had driven her to the jail a few hours earlier, though I had expected differently.

"Enjoy spending my money?" she asked with a smile.

"You're generally in a better mood than most people when I show up to give them a ride."

"I was petrified when they led me out of the courtroom, but I've really just been sitting in an office. They told me the bail was posted, so I just waited."

176

"Well, let's get you home."

We walked out of the jail to my car. I opened the door for her. She smiled as she got in. As I walked around the car I saw Henderson staring at us from the front of the jail. He glared as we drove off. Anna Beth didn't see him, and I didn't point him out to her.

It took about forty-five minutes for us to get to her house. We rode mostly in silence. We walked up the steps and saw that there was something on the door. I recognized it as a search warrant. I pulled it down and glanced at it. Her house had been searched while we had been busy through the day.

"The place is probably going to be a mess since the deputies aren't really subtle when they search a place."

She opened the door and stood for a moment before she went in.

They didn't appear to have done much more than dig through everything. It looked like they had touched everything in the house at least once, perhaps twice. While nothing was completely out of place, nothing was exactly where it should have been. She walked into the living room, I to the kitchen. I examined the warrant as I walked through the house. It appeared that they had gotten to the house probably not long after Anna Beth had left.

"Noah, would you put on a pot of coffee?"

I heard her going upstairs as I started the coffee. She came into the kitchen just after the coffee finished and I'd poured us each a cup. She had taken a shower and washed her hair - it was pulled up in a towel, and she was wearing a terry cloth robe. Interesting attire for the middle of the afternoon. She took a long drink of coffee.

"So what's next for me?" she said.

"First thing we need to do is get in that safe deposit box. All you have to do is see if you can relax a bit after being arrested for murder. Of course, I know that's a lot easier said than done."

She had walked over to the kitchen table where we had sat for dinner the last time I had visited. It was a beautifully clear day on Sullivan's Island. A mother and her children were playing on the beach. A shrimp boat paralleled the island, its nets in tow. A lone bicycle appeared in the distance.

"Noah, tell me this will all be okay."

I walked to her and sat across the table from her.

"I can't tell you that. I'd like to, but I don't want to lie to you. But we also won't make it easy for him, and innocent people don't go to jail. We'll get it worked out, but I can't promise you'll enjoy the ride."

There was silence.

"I want to help. I'll go crazy just sitting here."

"Well, I have an idea," I said.

"What?"

"I seem to be short a paralegal. I was thinking that since you spent some time in law school, maybe you'd like to spend some time at the office. I guess what I'm saying is that I could use some help. It's not exactly exciting, and the pay sucks. And you have to put up with me, and I can't believe I'm saying this, but at least you won't have to stay at the beach all day."

"Hum, sounds like a job interview. I haven't had one of those in, well, forever. Benefits?"

"I usually am good for a lunch or two a week."

"Sold. When do I start?"

"How about tomorrow?"

~~~~~~~~~~~~~~~~~~

I was at the office before 7:00 the next morning and Anna Beth was waiting for me. We went in and I showed her around as much as I could in my office. I'd stopped and picked up coffees on the way, so we drank them as we got started on her appointment as the Personal Representative of her father's estate. Only a few forms, which seemed to surprise Anna Beth, but we got them done and off to the court.

Anna Beth seemed to enjoy having something to do, and I enjoyed having someone in the office again. She was bright, and having spent a year in law school, she caught on quick. I couldn't help wondering about Heather, but Gabriel still seemed to think that she'd just picked up and moved along again like she did from Savannah on the way to Charleston. At the end of the day, with Anna Beth's help, I'd made a lot of headway in getting caught up on some of the work that had been piling up. When I decided to call it a day Anna Beth was still busying herself catching up on going through my mail, sorting it out in several different stacks for priority purposes.

"I'm heading out. You can go too, you know," I said.

"Is it time to go already? I didn't realize. Sorta snuck up on me. Give me a minute and I'll walk out with you."

She got up from the desk where she had been working, turned off the computer and walked to where I was standing.

"Okay, boss, do I get to come back tomorrow?"

"If you like. I'd love to see you."

"Then see you tomorrow morning."

We walked out the door together, and I watched her walk to her car and drive off.

The next few days passed much the same for us. I was working hard to catch up on the backlog of work, and with Anna Beth's help in sorting out and organizing things I was making great progress. She said she'd never worked in a law office before but she was a natural for the work. It wasn't that she was better than Heather, but just that she had an approach that was more comprehensive.

On her third day she walked into my office holding a fax.

"Noah, this just came for you."

I looked up from my desk. "Thanks, but you don't need to bring me everything right when it comes in," I paused. "That came out wrong."

"It's okay. But you may want to look at it."

I took the fax from her. It was from Low Country Legal Temp Services, the agency that had sent me Heather months back. Heather worked for me, but she was still paid through the agency that sent me a bill each month. I'd been meaning to switch her over to a full time employee of mine, but I hadn't gotten around to it. Generally after six months if a person is still employed as a result of a temp placement they like them changed over. Of course, they also get a fee for the placement of an employee. As I started to read the fax, I thought that was what it was about.

"Dear Mr. Parks:

Our records indicate that Heather Davis, earlier placed with your firm, remains in your employ. As you know, all paychecks sent to staff placed by our agency are sent Certified Mail; Return Receipt Requested. Recent paychecks sent to Ms. Davis have not been claimed and have been returned to our office. In an effort to maintain consistency in our placing and to ensure that the integrity of our agency is maintained, please give us a call to verify that Ms. Davis remains in your employ."

"Interesting," I said.

"Is that the woman that used to work here?"

"To be honest, I guess she still does. I didn't fire her and she didn't quit. She just sorta disappeared."

"Disappeared?"

"She went to visit family, called a couple of times and, well, I haven't heard from her in more than a month."

"That sounds like more than disappearing. You don't know where she is?"

"No. I talked to Gabriel about it and he thinks that she just moved on. She told me one time that that's how she ended up here - just walked out of her job and came here."

"She sounds kinda flighty if you ask me."

"She's a very smart girl, but it's strange, and her disappearing is even stranger. I remember reading about Agatha Christie disappearing for a couple of weeks one time. There was a huge search for her, then she just reappeared like it was nothing. I'm basically thinking that is what's going on here, only without the mystery novels."

"I guess that could be it, but have you tried looking around for her here? Like maybe going to her apartment or anything?" she said.

"As a matter of fact, I have. She wasn't home, but I think I may go talk to her landlord and see what he has to say."

"So you're an attorney and a detective?"

"You sound like Gabriel. Back to work, or the beatings shall resume," I said as she walked back to her desk.

I jumped on the computer and pulled up the tax records for the building where Heather lived. It took me a few minutes but I found the owner, and was able to run down the management easily after that. I looked up the phone number and a receptionist answered the phone. I told her the property I was interested in and got through to the management agent in charge.

I explained who I was and my concern about Heather.

"Parks was it? Well, sir, I really can't just go off and start giving out information about our tenants now can I?"

"I appreciate your position, but Heather works for me and has just sorta dropped off the face of the earth. All I'm really looking for is anything you can give me that would help me."

There was silence, then he spoke. "Let me look up something real quick."

I could hear him pecking away at a keyboard.

"Yes, here, Heather Davis, on King Street. Interesting, now what did you say your name was?"

"Parks, Noah Parks. Why?"

"You're listed here as her emergency contact, so looks like I can talk to you about whatever you need."

That was interesting. Me as her emergency contact?

"Like I said, anything really. I'm not really sure about anything specific to ask, but anything you have at all would help."

"Overall she appears to be a model tenant. Nothing here says otherwise."

"Nothing?"

"Really, nothing at all. Wait a sec, I remember this now."

"Remember what?" I said.

"Someone else called on her a while back, like maybe two, three months ago. I just realized it looking at her file. She paid a year's rent in advance, not too many people do that, so it kinda jogged my memory."

"Wait, wait, you said someone else was calling about her? And she paid a year in advance?" This was odd as Heather certainly didn't seem like the kind to have a year's rent sitting around, and it really didn't fit with her lifestyle and her story about how she ended up here from Savannah after leaving a job at a bar. I looked over to Anna Beth, who was still sitting across from my desk, intently listening to my side of the phone conversation.

"Yeah," he said.

"You remember who called?"

"I don't remember a name, but he was very matter of fact. And I didn't tell him anything, either."

"No, I would expect you wouldn't. What about her rent? Paid a year in advance?"

"I know, doesn't happen too often, but a whole year. Could've put a down payment on a house," he said.

"Yes, she could've. Listen, if you think of anything else would you give me a call? And thanks for your help."

I hung up the phone after giving him my contact information. I wasn't really sure if I was any closer to figuring out what was going on with all of this.

"So your Savannah waitress paid a year's advance on her apartment?" Anna Beth said.

"It would seem that is the case."

"How much were you paying her?"

"Not that much. You pick up on the part about someone else calling about her?"

"I did," she said. "Did he say who it was?"

"No. He didn't remember a name, but he described him as being very 'matter of fact.'"

"You look like your thinking something, Noah."

"I am. Tell me this, would you describe Thomason as matter of fact?"

"Noah, anyone would."

Things continued to work out well with Anna Beth at the office. Nothing new had come up with the murder charges and we were still waiting for her appointment as Personal Representative to come back from the Probate Courts. I was actually settling back into my routine. I looked forward to the start of the fall's college football season. I found myself thinking it might be a fun idea to have a party at the house on the first weekend of the season to get things going. About a week after Anna Beth had started working for me she was officially appointed as the Personal Representative for the estate. She brought the envelope into my office with a big grin on her face.

"I know you said I shouldn't bring in everything right when it comes in, but I thought that you'd want to see this."

"Let's have a look."

She handed me an envelope and inside was her appointment, though I suspected that she already knew.

"I say we go to the bank tomorrow and see what surprises are waiting," I said.

"I'm actually nervous."

"There's no need to be. We'll just go down and get it and at least take care of that question that's been bothering us."

I called the bank and spoke to Anderson King. I gave him an update and explained what had happened since we last spoke. I also told him that I'd like to come by and see him first thing in the morning. He most graciously agreed.

I looked to see Anna Beth standing in the door as I finished my phone call. For a brief moment she reminded me of Heather. For a brief moment.

"So everything's set?" she said.

"All set. Tomorrow morning at 9:00."

"You going to let me off work to go?" she smiled as she asked.

"So I have something serious to talk about." I pointed to a chair. "Sit."

"You do sound serious. What is it?"

"I don't think you need to stay alone tonight. Call me paranoid, but too much weird stuff has been happening lately to make me comfortable with you out at the beach alone after just getting appointed."

She sat, smiled and stared at me in silence. She crossed her legs and leaned back in her chair.

Usually I'm not one to break the silence, but she got the best of me.

"And?" I said.

"I'm just thinking. I'm wondering if you're really serious or if my boss is flirting with me."

I felt a bit of a flush come over me as my heart rate increased a bit. I wasn't flirting, but I was beginning to think I certainly could.

"What are you talking about?"

"Well, it's sweet of you to worry about me and even sweeter that you want to…"

"Hang on a second, I'm not suggesting that I stay with you. Well, I sorta am, but I want us to stay with Gabriel. If something does happen, I'd feel better if it wasn't just us."

"Oh. Now I'm just a little embarrassed."

I wanted to tell her not to be. I also wanted to tell her that she was thinking the same things I was, but I resisted the urge.

"Don't be. Not at all. How about this - I'll call Gabriel, then we can go pick up some things at your place. How's that?"

"I think I need to get my foot out of my mouth."

"No worries." I smiled.

I called Gabriel and he said he would love to have company.

We closed up the office and left for Sullivan's Island. I realized

I was probably being paranoid, but I wanted to make sure that Anna Beth didn't end up like everyone else who started getting close to that damn safe deposit box. We arrived at her house and she went upstairs to pack a bag while I waited downstairs. We left and drove back across town to my house. I left Anna Beth in the car and went inside to get some clothes. I called a neighborhood teen that watched Austin when I had to be away to let him know I wouldn't be home that night. Austin would have loved to visit Rudy, but I decided that springing Anna Beth on Gabriel was enough. Austin disappeared to the front of the house, then came back and offered an inquisitive look.

"Yes, company, and if you behave yourself maybe next time I'll bring them in and you can meet them," I said to him as I finished with my bag.

With a pat on the head I left to join Anna Beth in the Jeep. We headed over to Gabriel's house.

Gabriel was waiting for us on the porch.

"Hi, folks. Ms. Cross, nice to see you again."

"And nice to see you too. May I call you Gabriel?"

"Of course you may. Now see, Noah, manners. That's what I keep telling you - manners. Please, come on in."

We walked into Gabriel's house, immaculate as always.

"Ms. Cross, you get the guest room there," Gabriel pointed to a large room off of the living room. "Parks, you get the couch, but you do get the big screen."

I watched Anna Beth walk into the bedroom. Gabriel looked at me.

"You know I don't mind you staying, but what's up?"

I looked to make sure Anna Beth was out of earshot. "I'm probably being paranoid, but she was just appointed the PR for her Father's estate, and with all that's happened in this mess I didn't want her alone tonight. But I didn't feel right staying alone with her, either. If that makes any sense?"

Gabriel held up his hand to stop me then looked toward the bedroom. "You're probably overreacting, but I'm happy to have you, and I never miss a chance to have a woman stay at the house."

"Even if she is charged with murder?" I said.

"Not by me."

Anna Beth came out of the bedroom. "Show me to the kitchen - I'm cooking."

"I won't argue with that. All your clients like this?" Gabriel said.

"Let's just say there is a first for everything."

Gabriel and I went outside with Rudy after Anna Beth made herself at home in the kitchen - rather, after she kicked us out of the kitchen. She appeared a little while later and announced that things were well underway. Not wanting to miss an opportunity to show off, Gabriel ushered her over to the bonsai garden. I stayed with Rudy and his ball.

After dinner we sat up for a while until Anna Beth announced that she was going to bed. She thanked Gabriel again for having us and then walked into the bedroom, closing the door behind her.

"I know I keep warning you, partner, but be careful with that."

"Careful? What are you talking about?"

"She has that look."

"And what look would that be?"

"Oh, don't feed me that crap," he rose as he spoke. "You know what I am talking about - that look that's the reason attorneys can't sleep with their clients."

"You think?"

"Positive. Just keep that in mind. She needs all of your attention with Henderson crawling up her ass."

"You have a way with words, my friend. A way with words."

"See you in the a.m."

I stretched out on the couch after he walked into his bedroom.

The night passed without incident, and Gabriel was already up when I awoke the next morning. He already had the coffee going, too. Sounds from behind the closed guest room door told me Anna Beth was up as well.

Gabriel made us a great southern breakfast: scrambled eggs, bacon, grits, toast, coffee, orange juice - all served up piping hot. Anna Beth said Gabriel's was the best B&B she had ever stayed in, even better than the Planter's Inn.

~~~~~~~~~~~~~~~~~~~

We left about an hour later and headed to my office. I knew there was a problem as soon as I saw the broken window of the back door. Anna Beth didn't notice it until we got to the door.

"What happened?" she said.

"Look's like it's a good thing we didn't stay at the office last night."

I opened the door to broken glass all over the floor. I pulled out my cell phone and called the police. We waited outside the office for them. I also called the bank and left a message for Anderson King that we'd be a little late.

The police took about an hour and a half in the office before they had me come in to see if there was anything missing. As I walked through the office I saw nothing obvious missing. Nothing jumped out at me - there was just a lot of clutter. Then it occurred to me to check the Cross file. I walked into my office and took a crime scene tech with me. I had him pull out the file cabinet where the file was stored. It wasn't there. I told him a file was missing and he called in another tech. They had me look through the rest of the office, but everything else seemed to be there. They soon departed, leaving me with a trashed office, a business card with a case number, and no Cross file.

Anna Beth came in as I was dialing the Probate Court.

"Your father's file's been stolen," I told her as she walked in.

"You're not being serious are you?"

"Unfortunately yes."

I held up a finger as a clerk came on the line at the Court. I explained that I needed to get a certified copy of Cross' will and a Certificate of Appointment for Anna Beth. She told me she would get it together and give me a call when it was ready.

"Sorry, but it appears that someone just doesn't want us to get to that safe deposit box. Let's have a look around to see if anything else is missing."

While we looked around I asked Anna Beth if she had any idea who would want to keep us from getting to the bank, but she couldn't come up with anyone. Neither could I. However, I was starting to think she may actually be onto something about her father and brother - I was having a hard time explaining how things kept happening every time we were about to get into the safe deposit box. It didn't make any sense that someone would want to keep us out of it when no one knew what was actually inside. I was even more puzzled as to why someone would take the file as there was nothing in it that couldn't be replaced by obtaining a certified copy of whatever was needed from the Probate Court.

Our conversation was interrupted by the phone. I answered it. Anna Beth knew that it was the Court, and I could tell she was trying to pick up on what was going on. I finished the conversation and hung up the phone.

"This just keeps getting better. It appears that the Probate Court has misfiled your father's will."

"You're kidding, right?"

"Once again, unfortunately not."

"Well what do we do? We need a will to get in the bank?"

"Oh, ye of little faith. Follow me."

I walked into the library and over to one of the shelves.

"And this helps us how?" She had a puzzled look on her face.

"We need a copy of the will, right?"

She nodded her head as she watched me reach for a book. I pulled down a rather large volume and put it on the table. She studied it for a moment and looked up at me.

"So what's this, Black's Legal Dictionary?" she said.

I stepped beside her and started to flip through the pages. About a third of the way in I started pulling out pages that had been stuck in the book. She smiled as she watched.

"You have another copy."

"For some reason I do. I made it the first day I met Thomason."

"So why did you put it in this book?" she asked as she thumbed through a few pages. "There's all kinds of stuff in here."

"Long story, but I do that from time to time."

"So now we can go to the bank."

"I'll go call Mr. King and tell him we're on the way."

CHAPTER 13

After a stop at the Probate Court to pick up a copy of the Certificate of Appointment and to drop off a certified copy of the Cross' will, we drove to the bank, parked, and headed to the front door. As we walked in, my heart raced with anticipation. I told the receptionist we were there to see Anderson King and we took a seat in the lobby. Anna Beth sat on the couch, looking quite comfortable and relaxed. I, on the other hand, fidgeted and organized the magazines on the table in front of me. I was anticipating the answers that would come with the safe deposit box, but I was also wondering who the hell would have broken into my office.

"Not nervous are you?" she said.

"What?"

"That's the third time you have arranged those magazines."

"Hum."

"Noah, take a deep breath. In a few minutes we'll be in the safe deposit box."

"I know, I know. I just want to see the darn thing and get it opened. That, and I'm just wondering what could possibly happen next."

"So tell me, what happens after we open it?" She slid closer to me on the couch. "What's the first thing we do?"

"I honestly don't know. I guess it all depends on what's inside." I looked up to see Anderson King approaching. "Mr. Parks?"

"Mr. King, good morning."

"Please, call me Anderson. And let me see, Ms. Cross if I remember correctly?"

"Yes, it's a pleasure to see you again," Anna Beth said as she slid away from me slightly, adjusting her skirt as she did so.

He stepped aside and motioned to his office. "Please, let's sit in my office."

As he led us across the interior of the bank I realized I was looking around at the other people there and taking them in suspiciously, trying to determine if any of them were paying too much attention to Anna Beth or me as we followed Anderson. I caught myself, took a deep breath, and suppressed my paranoia as we entered Anderson's office. He closed the door behind us. If he knew anything about Anna Beth being charged with Thomason's murder, he let on nothing.

"Please, sit," he said, motioning to two familiar business chairs across from his desk. He walked around his desk, sat, adjusted a stack of papers, then looked at me. "Leonardo Cross, I believe?" he said.

"Yes. He has, or should I say had, a safe deposit box here. I have the appropriate authority allowing me entry and, in a nutshell, that's why we're here."

He looked toward Anna Beth then back to me. "I believe that last time you were here, there was some confusion with the

Personal Representative?"

"Was being the operative word. As dramatic as it may sound, the prior Personal Representative was murdered and..."

"Really? Murdered?" he said.

"Unfortunately, yes."

"I do apologize, please continue."

"Certainly. As I was saying, he was murdered, so we had to get another Personal Representative." I motioned toward Anna Beth. "Ms. Cross here took the job. I think you'll find that all the documentation is in order."

I slid an envelope across the desk to him, which he took from me and opened. He removed the contents and scanned each of them. He flipped through the will to the page that I had marked, looked at the death certificate, and spent enough time on the Certificate of Appointment that I was sure he had read every word twice.

"It does appear that everything is in order. So, how can I help you?"

"Well, there is a safe deposit box here in Mr. Cross' name, is there not?" I said.

"Yes. After you first came by I reviewed our records, and yes, there is in fact a safe deposit box here in that name. In fact, it is most unusual."

"How so?" Anna Beth said.

"It appears that the box was rented just over five years ago. It was paid in advance for ten years, with future payments assigned to automatic drafts from a trust in the state of Ohio..."

Anna Beth and I glanced at each other as he said this. Apparently he missed our reaction to the mention of the trust as he didn't miss a beat in his explanation.

"… Also, as I am sure both of you are aware, traditionally, to get into a safe deposit box we here at the bank have a master key for access. The master key is used together with the box holder's key at such time as they require access."

I had a sinking feeling in my chest when he mentioned this. We didn't have a key. I'd been wondering what the next obstacle would be - it seemed I had my answer.

Apparently the frustration was showing on my face, and Anderson picked up on it.

"And you don't have a key?" Anderson said.

"No, no key."

"When the box was first rented, part of the instructions at the time were that the customer key was to be held by the bank and used only upon the presentation to the current manager of proper documentation."

"And what, may I ask, is proper documentation?" Anna Beth inquired.

Anderson smiled. "This," he said, motioning toward the documentation I'd provided him. "You'd like to see the box, I take?"

We followed him from his office into a vault area that was illuminated by a single row of fluorescent bulbs that did a slightly less than adequate job of lighting the room. The dim light and the lack of any real distinguishing features made the inside of the vault more a place of questions rather than answers. It was about twenty by twenty feet and the walls, from floor to ceiling, were covered with numbered boxes of different sizes. Some were small, only a few inches high and wide, while others were quite large, measuring at least two feet square, and all sizes in between. At the rear of the vault was another barred door, and while the lights were out beyond it, by the shadows of the vault's light I could see that there were more boxes, only they appeared to be of a uniformed medium size.

Anderson approached the barred door, opened it, and flipped a switch that washed the room in fluorescent light. One of these boxes held our answer - the others all held questions and answers all their own.

Anderson approached a random box on the left. We followed him through the door.

"Pardon me a moment."

He opened the box, and inside it I could see there were many small numbered compartments. He ran his fingers down the far right-hand row, stopping on one from which he removed a small envelope.

"Your key, Mr. Parks," he said as he handed me the small envelope, which I passed to Anna Beth.

"Which one?" I said, looking at the wall of boxes.

"This way."

He turned to his left, stepped up to the wall and followed the numbers with a finger. About midway up he stopped at box number 387.

"Your key, please."

I looked to Anna Beth, who smiled and gave him the key. He inserted his, then mine, and turned each of them. The door on box number 387 swung open. Inside was a gray box that Anderson pulled out. The long box slid easily from within the safe deposit box. I couldn't tell from how he held it if it was heavy or not. He turned to me and held out the box. It was about eighteen inches long with a hinged top that allowed the contents to be accessed.

"Here you are. If you would like some privacy, there is a partitioned table just outside of the vault."

I took the box from him – light, very light. I followed him from the vault and walked to a table behind the partition. Anna Beth was right by my side. We stared at the small box on the table.

"It's not very heavy," I said as I pushed at the box.

"Open it," she said.

I took a deep breath and opened the top without lifting it from the table and peered inside. Empty. It was empty. I looked to Anna Beth and she back to me.

"Noah, what's going on here?"

I tilted the box and peered further inside, past the rear where the top was hinged. There I saw it, a single, small envelope. I looked at Anna Beth and then back to the box. I picked it up and tilted it, giving it a shake. The envelope slid to the front of the box. I turned the box over and it fell out.

"That's it, just an envelope?" she said.

It was a small manila envelope like you might buy at any office supply store. It measured no more than four by six inches. There was nothing written on it - nothing unique about it at all. The flap was tucked inside, but not actually sealed. I pulled it open and peered inside. There was a single sheet of paper inside, folded into thirds. I removed it and looked in the envelope. There was a thin metallic rod at the bottom. I turned the envelope upside-down and emptied the rod into my hand.

The rod was no more than five inches long. Half of it was decorated with a repetitive raised design that appeared to be Celtic, or at least Celtic inspired. The design was made up of a raised band of crosses with a flowing chain of diamonds against a background of runic-styled lettering. The raised design tapered toward the middle until the design faded completely, leaving only indentions and raised symmetrical lines that wound their way around the rod to the other end. I held the rod in one hand as I opened the paper with the other to see what it had to say about the rod. In the middle of the paper was a handwritten series of numbers.

340 3000 7853 400

Nothing else.

I turned the paper over and looked at the back, then turned it over and looked at the numbers again. A quick check of the envelope confirmed that it was still empty.

"You have got to be kidding me."

"What?" she said.

I gave her the paper and she did just as I did - looked at the number, then turned it over and looked at the back only to turn it back over to look at the number again.

"And this," I said as I held up the rod.

She peered at it and nudged it with her finger. "What is it?"

"Please tell me this means something to you."

I could tell from the look on her face that it didn't mean a thing. I turned the box over several times in my hand and looked inside again. I gave it another shake just to be sure that it was empty.

"Hang on a sec." I walked from behind the table toward Anderson, who turned as he heard me approaching.

"Yes, Mr. Parks?"

"I don't suppose there was another key, or perhaps we got the wrong box? Or perhaps any other instructions?"

"No. That was the only key, and box 387 is the only one here at the bank in Mr. Cross' name. Is there a problem?"

"No, just wanted to check."

I walked back to the table.

"That's it, the only box here in your father's name."

"What does this mean? It's just some numbers."

"I know."

I studied the numbers for a minute, then counted them. Fourteen digits, too many for a phone number. Too many for a credit card account, too. Then another thought occurred to me.

"Mr. King?" He looked at me as I called his name. "Would

there be any other accounts or anything else in Mr. Cross' name here at the bank?"

"I don't think so, but I can check."

He walked to the other side of the vault's ante-room and began pecking at a computer keyboard. He turned back to me rather too quick for my liking.

"No, sir, nothing else in Mr. Cross' name."

I looked to Anna Beth. "I was hoping it was an account number here at the bank. In fact, I bet that's what it is, but without having the name of the bank it's like the proverbial needle in the old haystack."

"So what do we do now?" she asked.

"I really have no idea, but we can certainly discuss it somewhere other than in here."

We walked out of the bank and went to my car, the proud new owners of a fourteen-digit number and a ubiquitous metal rod.

~~~~~~~~~~~~~~~~~~~~~~~~

We arrived back at my office. Anna Beth busied herself with cleaning up behind the crime scene techs who apparently aren't as tidy when examining a law office as they are at the Planter's Inn. I looked around several times just to make sure there was nothing else missing. It appeared the only thing that was gone was the Cross file. While I was quite upset over that, it really didn't matter. I had a copy of the will, a copy of the Certificate of Appointment, and really didn't need anything else since the estate was closed.

I made a copy of the will and Certificate of Appointment and put them back in my Black's. I wrote the mystery number on a sheet of paper and put that in there as well. I also wrote the number on a post-it sheet and put it in my wallet. I also saved it in my cell phone. Sure it was overkill, but given all that had happened, I wanted to be sure. Several hours passed in silence as each of us went about different things in the office.

"So, any more ideas on the number?" Anna Beth said as she walked into the room and sat down at the conference table.

"I've been thinking about that and all I can come up with is a bank account number, but that doesn't really mean a thing if we don't know which bank. Tell me, was your father one to play games?"

"Not really. I mean, I'm a bit surprised this is what we found. I don't have any idea what it may mean, and I've really been thinking about it," she said.

"I guess the good thing is that since everything is done it really isn't that important. And who knows, it might be fun trying to figure it out."

"If you say so, but it's sorta anticlimactic, wouldn't you say?"

"Actually yes. I was hoping for, well… I don't know what I was hoping for, but something more than this. At least an explanation as to why my name was in your father's will."

"Me too, to tell you the truth."

My cell phone rang.

I glanced at the number. It was Gabriel. He said he'd heard the office had been broken into and I told him the only thing that was missing was the Cross file. He agreed with me that it was odd that, given everything else that had been going on that would be the one thing that was taken.

"Something's come up."

I didn't like the change in his tone. "What?" I said.

"Seems Henderson received an anonymous package today - a shirt with some of your buddy Thomason's blood on it."

"Really? And how did you find out about this?"

"Son of a bitch called me. Called me to gloat. Says I needed to know what kind of company I keep, which means that he's been following you. At least the night you stayed here he did."

"So what does his getting something in the mail have to do with me?"

"You, nothing. Anna Beth, everything."

"Dammit, Gabriel, what the hell are you getting at?"

"Someone sent him one of Anna Beth's shirts. It has specks of blood, Thomason's blood, on it."

I said goodbye and hung up the phone.

"What was that all about?"

"Ever have one of those days when it... Well, let's just say that I have had better phone calls."

"Noah, who was it?"

"Gabriel."

"And?" she said.

"He got a call from Henderson. The long and short of it is that someone sent Henderson a blood-stained shirt. Thomason's blood, your shirt."

She sat in silence as I waited for her to speak, but words didn't come. Tears, on the other hand, didn't seem to be lacking. I walked around the table and put my hand on her shoulder. She raised her head and looked up at me.

"Who's doing this to me?"

"I wish I could tell you."

She cried as I brushed my hand down her soft hair. I sat beside her and held her hand. I wanted to talk to her and tell her it would be okay, that everything was going to work out and that she could soon go back to her life in Chicago with only an insane ex-husband to worry about. I wanted to tell her that I could make everything better, but I knew that I'd be lying to her. So I let her cry and kept my mouth shut.

After about half an hour she got up and walked out of the room in silence. I heard the door to the bathroom open, then shut. I sat alone in silence in the dark of my conference room. After a few minutes I stood and walked to the window. As I stared down Broad Street, I put my hands in my pockets. I felt the rod that had been in the safe deposit box. I took it out and examined it. While I wasn't an expert on symbols or designs, the engravings appeared to be of Celtic tradition and looked somewhat familiar. The other half of the rod had a series of indentions of random depths circling the rod all the way to the other end. I turned it over in my hand and rolled it between my fingers. I thought it might be a pendant for a necklace or some other sort of jewelry, but I couldn't figure out how it would have been worn or displayed. I was looking at it when I heard a noise behind me. I looked over my shoulder and saw Anna Beth standing in the doorway. She had a nervous smile and red eyes.

"I'm sorry for that," she said as she walked over to the window and stood beside me.

"Sorry for what?"

She reached down and took my hand in hers. "Sorry for that little breakdown."

"Listen," I began, but she put her other hand to my lips, then brushed it across my cheek. As she looked into my eyes I started to speak, but once again she pressed her finger to my lips. She pulled closer to me and whispered into my ear.

"Thank you for everything."

She kissed my cheek and hugged me tightly to her. I could feel her heart beating in my chest. I pulled away and reached for one of her hands.

"You're welcome."

She reached up to my face, but I probably ruined whatever

moment there was when I dropped the rod I had been holding in my other hand. We both looked and bent for it at the same time, bumping our heads in the process. We backed away from each other laughing.

"What is that?" she said.

"It's the other thing that was in the safe deposit box, and I have absolutely no idea what it is."

She bent over and retrieved it from the floor. She examined it and rolled it in her fingers just as I had been doing when she walked into the room.

"I've never seen anything like it before. It's actually very pretty, like a necklace or something."

"I had the same thought, but I can't figure out how you would wear it. I was really hoping that something about it would seem familiar to you, but no such luck, huh?"

"Unfortunately not."

"Well then I guess we have two mysteries. This," I said, holding the rod. "And the numbers."

"Actually, three."

"The other being?" I asked.

"Who sent Henderson my shirt."

"Then three it is. I guess we better get started on them." I looked outside, then checked my watch again. It was almost 5:00. "How about we go get something to eat and we can talk about this stuff, see if we can make any sense of it."

"Are you asking me out to dinner, Noah?"

"I guess so. Where do you want to go? That is, if you don't mind the company."

"Actually, I would love the company. Do you cook?"

"I do."

"Then, if you won't think I am being too forward, how about

your place?"

"If you don't mind being attacked by another guy, I'd love to have you."

"What are you talking about?" she said.

"Come on, I'll show you."

~~~~~~~~~~~~~~~~~~~~

I started to lock up the office when I heard Anna Beth call to me that she would be out in the parking lot waiting for me. From my office window I watched as she walked over to my Jeep. She glanced around, and I smiled to myself when she started adjusting her hair using the rear window of the Jeep as a mirror. It also looked like she put on some lipstick. Maybe there was something there. I certainly found her attractive, and the attention seemed to be reciprocated. I watched as she started on her hair again and realized that I was smiling. I had to decide on the next move. After the way things had gone in the conference room after she had started crying, I either needed to pursue things or just back off. Then I realized I was thinking too much. I took one more long look, then grabbed my keys from my desk and headed out the back door.

"Hey," I called as I approached the car. "Sorry I took so long."

"No, that's okay, vanity got the better of me. I was using you Jeep as a dressing room, so to speak."

For some reason knowing that was one hundred percent the truth was perhaps the most attractive thing I had seen about her so far. My mind was made up.

I headed out of the lot down Broad Street to a local gourmet grocery store. We went in and I bought fresh salmon, asparagus, risotto, sweet onions, peppers, some cheese and a couple bottles of wine.

"You're not planning on getting me drunk, are you?"

I couldn't tell if that was a warning or an invitation.

After a few moments of silence she said, "Okay, you've got to tell me, what do you mean when you talk about me getting attacked by another guy?"

"I guess you'll have to wait and see."

"That's hardly fair, but kinda interesting." She paused a moment. "Noah, you don't think I'm too forward by asking to come to your house for dinner, do you?"

"It was either that or back to Gabriel's, and I'd hate to impose on him again."

"Oh, planning on having me stay over are you?"

I stammered for an answer, then looked toward her.

"Well…"

"You're cute when you get caught off guard. That's not often, but… That came out wrong."

"What do you mean?"

"How about we forget about that and you tell me what you're making for dinner."

I wanted to tell her that she had to tell me, but I resisted.

I described the menu. I was going to fix cedar plank salmon with asparagus risotto. I cook the salmon filets on an oiled plank of cedar board that imparted a mildly smoky sweet flavor to the salmon. It was a minimalist approach, but the flavors, while subtle, were amazing. Then I told her about the asparagus risotto with smoked gruyere cheese and caramelized onions. I had once thought about being a chef before law school since I loved to cook. I had a few friends that were chefs, so I copied them whenever I had the chance.

"That sounds wonderful. If I'd known you could do all of that I'd have invited myself over sooner."

"You haven't tasted any of it yet. You may want to wait before you start with the praise - it might suck."

"Somehow I doubt that."

We arrived at the house and I collected the groceries. She waited for me to go up the stairs to the door.

"Okay, just remember, he really likes you and he's completely harmless," I said as I reached toward the door with my key. I was putting it in the lock as she spoke.

"Who's what?"

"Meet Austin," I said as I opened the door to a furry blur that shot out to greet us. "You do like dogs, don't you?"

Austin circled her, sniffing everywhere, his tail wagging so fast you couldn't tell if he was actually wagging the tail or if it was the other way around.

She let him sniff her, then when he stopped and crouched in front of her she knelt down beside him and let him sniff her hand. Softly and slowly she rubbed his head and scratched under his chin. He put one paw on her shoulder and nuzzled her hand with his head, then rolled over on his back so she could scratch his stomach.

"Seems you have a way with men," I said.

"I hope so."

CHAPTER 14

With Austin leading the way, we walked into the house. As I was heading to the kitchen with the supplies for the evening she asked if she could take Austin out back to play. Austin certainly seemed to have no objection, though I did warn her that she had to be careful or I might get mad after he decided to go live with her instead of staying with me. He led her to the back door, the deck, then the yard beyond.

They eagerly went out into the backyard and I wandered over to the window to watch. It was as if my thoughts from an hour ago had picked up where they'd left off. I decided I'd better stop watching lest my imagination get the best of me. I moved away from the window and went back into the kitchen. I put one of the bottles of wine in the freezer to chill and opened the other. I might have been a little presumptuous getting two bottles of wine for the evening, but I decided better safe than sorry. I started on dinner after I cut up some cheese and put it out with some grapes and crackers. After all, what was dinner without a little appetizer for snacking and conversation while you waited? After about half an hour of play Austin and Anna Beth came wandering back in, both looking as if the other had gotten the best of them.

"You guys have fun?" I asked.

I knelt down to pet Austin, who was clearly having a great time. He licked my face then pranced over to Anna Beth and pawed at her until she bent over and scratched his ears.

"I hate to be cliché, but I think he likes you."

"I love dogs. I had a friend when I was younger that had an Australian Shepherd that was the best dog ever, present company excluded," she said to Austin. "We never had a dog. My ex-husband was afraid of them. I'd forgotten how much I missed them."

She bent over again and gave Austin a healthy ear scratching.

"He's useless, but I love him to death. He was a rescue dog. I'll never understand how someone could have not wanted him, but I am glad they didn't."

Anna Beth had risen and Austin had gone to empty his water dish.

"He has the right idea, I'm kinda thirsty myself."

"What would you like?" I said.

"Unless you're saving that wine for a special occasion, I thought I might have some of that. And maybe a glass of water."

"I have white in the freezer and red on the counter," I said as I pointed back and forth between the freezer and the red.

"Let's start with white and see where that leads us."

I took the bottle from the freezer, opened it and poured each of us a glass.

We chatted about nothing in general while I cooked. She watched and commented on my almost every move, asking what I was doing, what a specific ingredient was supposed to do, how I was going to time everything to come together to be served. I have a way of getting consumed with the process when I am cooking, and several times while I was working on the risotto or while I was prepping the salmon I noticed the silence and looked at her to catch her watching me. The first few times she quickly broke my stare and shifted her attention to Austin or to something on the counter in front of her. Finally, I decided to get bold.

"So, you keep staring," I said without looking at her.

"Yes."

"I've been told it's not polite."

"If you want, I can always stop."

"But that would be rude of me to ask something like that of my guest."

"It probably would be. Do we have more wine?"

We'd finished the bottle of white and I reached to the bottle of red. I got a fresh glass from the cabinet. She watched as I poured.

"Thank you."

"For?"

"Just thank you. You've made me feel quite at home and relaxed when I didn't think I could, given all that's going on. This is nice."

"Well, it's my pleasure."

"Do you mind if I look around the house?"

I was a little bit surprised at this request. "No, just take Austin. He'll show you all the high points."

I watched her walk out of the room with Austin in tow. I busied myself with the dinner. I checked on the salmon and dusted it with a hint of cayenne pepper. I stirred the risotto, adding a touch of heavy cream to finish it. I decided to make a quick chutney to top the salmon and dug through the fridge until I found some mango, cucumber and, fortunately, some fresh cilantro. I was about to pull it all together when I looked up to see her walking back in the kitchen. She was wearing a pair of my boxers and a button down oxford dress shirt. She had pulled her hair up and was carrying several books.

"Don't be mad. Austin showed me your bedroom and I couldn't resist."

I had to look away to keep from staring, but I could tell she was thinking that I had something else on my mind.

"Oh, shit, I just made an ass of myself, didn't I?'

"God no, not at all."

"I'm sorry." She set the books she was carrying on the table in the kitchen and turned to walk out of the room.

"Anna Beth, stop."

She stopped with her back to me but didn't turn. I walked up behind her, stopping just short of touching her. I put my hand on her shoulder and moved my head until it was even with hers. Like she did earlier in the afternoon, I whispered in her ear.

"I really like that you decided to do that. I just don't want to make a fool of myself, that's all. Come back and let's eat."

"You're sure you don't mind?" she said without turning to look at me.

"Quite sure."

"Then, let's have dinner."

She turned and walked back into the kitchen, pulling me behind her. I told her where things were and she laid out the table. We had the red wine with dinner, but it was a Pinot and it was in my house, so I didn't mind if someone may have thought that I was committing a wine faux pas by having it with salmon. She talked through dinner about her life since her divorce and I listened, asking a few questions here and there. Mostly I found myself wondering about what would happen after dinner. That and, well, I watched her.

We finished and I cleared the plates and poured the last of the wine. I was in the kitchen cleaning things up when she called to me from my dining room.

"Wow, this is a neat dining room table. Where did you get it?"

"My great-grandfather made it."

"Really? Was he a Charleston furniture maker?"

"No, actually he just sorta fooled around with it. He made a lot for his friends and family, but he never sold any for some reason. I have a cousin in Columbia that has the most beautiful hutch-type thing. He tried stained glass for that and it's amazing. But I do love my table."

I realized I'd been talking mostly to myself and I looked into the dining room. She had spread out tablemats and had opened a couple of books on the table. I finished up in the kitchen and went to join her. "Wha'cha got there?"

"I found your library."

"Library? I don't think I've ever heard it called that before."

"You have a lot of neat stuff in there."

"Not everyone gets into history like I do." I looked over her shoulder and saw that she was looking at a book on the architectural history of Charleston. She had several other local historical books waiting in the wings, handy but not opened.

"What are you thinking?" I said.

"I was looking at that rod. The design on it is too repetitive, too symmetrical. Maybe it means something, but what is the question. Of course, I'm at a loss on the dots. I figured that I'd look through this and see if I could see anything similar."

"I don't think I'd have thought about that. Good idea."

"Father never just stumbled onto something, so those designs have to mean something. Since he spent so long in Charleston, I thought that building design wouldn't be a bad place to start. Problem is, he loved Chicago too, and there are a few more buildings there. There are even libraries completely devoted to the architecture of the city. So, I may be chasing a rabbit."

"No, that's a great idea. Gives me one myself. How does this sound - you take the rod and see what you can get, and I'll start on the numbers."

"Good idea, divide and conquer. Plus, I have no idea about the numbers."

"Neither do I, but that's what makes it fun. More wine?" I said.

"If you'll help me with it, sure."

I'll admit that this wasn't exactly how I'd seen the evening going. I had been hoping for something a bit more personal, but this made sense, and it couldn't hurt finding out what the rod was and what the numbers meant. Besides, I was beginning to think slow was a good approach with Ms. Cross.

She buried herself in the books and I logged onto the internet and started researching number sequences. I wished I'd paid more attention in my calculus and statistic classes. Mostly I felt like I was spinning my wheels, but she was engrossed in the books she'd found and I didn't want to interrupt her. For the next several hours we worked. Several times I thought I was onto something with the numbers, but each time I found a dead end. When I realized I was on eBay looking at guitars, I decided it was time to call it a day. I turned the computer off and walked into the dining room. She had four books open and had filled several sheets of a yellow legal pad with notes. I watched her for several minutes as she scribbled notes and flipped through the books.

"Find anything?"

"Sort of, but not really. Nothing close to our designs on this thing, but I found references to several other books that may help. Want to go to the library tomorrow?"

"Why not? But I think I need to call it a day. Tell you what, I'll cut through everything. You and Austin can have my bedroom and I'll take the guest room. Non-negotiable."

She looked at me for a moment and yawned. She stretched her arms and looked at her watch. "It is late. You won't get jealous if I take Austin from you?"

"I couldn't make him sleep anywhere else other than my bed even if I wanted to."

"Thanks for letting me stay," she said.

"Anytime you want."

"Don't tempt me."

"I mean it. Anytime you want."

"Really?"

"Yes, Anna Beth, really. Anytime you want."

"Okay, this is probably the wine talking, but would you mind if I stayed for a couple of days? I just think I would feel better if I had someone to stay with."

"Austin'll love the company."

She smiled. I showed her upstairs. After I got her situated I came back downstairs. I looked at the work she had been doing - it was quite comprehensive. She had been through a lot of information and had made about four pages of notes. It looked like she wanted to get another dozen books or so. We could go get them at the library tomorrow. I picked up her empty wine glass and walked into the kitchen. The empty bottles of wine sat on the counter. No wonder my thoughts were all over the place - I had a beautiful woman upstairs in my bed and I was downstairs cleaning up. My dog was going to sleep with her and I was going to end up in the guest room. I entertained the thought of her wandering into the bedroom in the wee hours of the night but dismissed it. After all, despite the fact that I was quite attracted to her, I did represent her, and it rarely turned out well when an attorney got involved with a client. I thought about watching some television but changed my mind.

I checked the back door and walked to the front of the house. I looked out into the cul-de-sac and saw a dark sedan parked in front of the neighbor's house. Henderson. Now I'd be sleeping with her. I thought about calling him and giving him a piece of my mind, but I was just too tired. I looked at my watch. No wonder, it was after 2:00 a.m. That made me chuckle thinking about him sitting there in his car watching me. I was a little surprised to see another car slowly driving down the street. I turned and went to the guest room, my thoughts still racing. I think I was asleep within ninety seconds of my head hitting the pillow.

~~~~~~~~~~~~~~~~~~~~~~~~

I woke up early the next morning and went downstairs. I was surprised by Anna Beth in the kitchen.

"Dammit, I was going to surprise you," she said.

"Don't worry, you did."

She'd made breakfast for us, us including Austin. She even cleaned up. While we had breakfast we talked about our trip to the library that morning. She suggested we do a few hours there then come back to the house and continue to work on the numbers and the design on the road. Apparently she'd also decided to close the office. I didn't protest. Austin was quite disappointed when we left without him. As we rode past the sedan that was still there I waved.

"By the way, just wanted to let you know that we're sleeping together."

"I'm sorry, we're what?"

"That car back there, Henderson. He's been there all night, and he'll tell everyone we're sleeping together."

"Seriously? Doesn't he have anything else to do?"

"Actually, no. He's pretty much all cop, just not very good."

"Oh God, Noah, will you get in trouble?"

"It'll be all right. If he starts the story most people will ignore him."

"Most people?"

"Yes, most."

"Great, just great. You're going to run me off before this is over," she said.

We pulled up to the library and went inside. I watched her disappear into the stacks with focused determination. I stood for a moment, decided to head up to the science section, then thought better and went to chase down my theory on a bank account for the numbers. I was thinking that I should go the route of numbered accounts and see if that got me anywhere. I found several reference books on international banking and numbered accounts, but nothing that put me any closer to understanding what the numbers meant. From there it only went downhill. After a couple of hours I decided that I'd go back downstairs and check on Anna Beth.

I put the books I'd pulled from the shelf back and turned to go downstairs. As I walked between the stacks I glanced toward the tables in an open area of the stacks. I did a double take. There was Heather, sitting with several books open in front of her. I started to call to her, but decided to go over to her instead.

I was a few tables away when she looked up. I had expected her to show some amount of surprise, but there was nothing. "Noah, what are you doing here?"

"Me? You? Where have you been? Are you okay? What are

you doing?"

"Noah, I, well… It's good to see you."

"Heather, is everything okay?"

She hesitated a moment, then got up. "I have to go."

"Heather, wait, I want to…"

But she walked past me, headed to the stairs and down toward the front door. I watched for a moment, wondering what had just happened, then moved to follow her. I made it to the stairs just in time to see her going out the door of the library to the main entrance. I raced down the stairs after her, almost falling as I reached the bottom, earning a sharp stare from one of the librarians in the process. I burst through the inner doors, down another set of stairs and out the front door. I was on Calhoun Street, but there was no sign of Heather. I looked up one way then down the other. Nothing, no sign of her at all. I stood for a moment then went back inside. I walked through the first floor stacks and found Anna Beth looking over her collection of books.

"I want to get all of these but it'll overwhelm me, and… Good heavens Noah, what's wrong?"

"I just ran into Heather upstairs."

"Heather? As in office Heather? What was she doing? Is she okay?"

"Well, yes, no… Well, yes, Heather from the office, but that's about all I'm sure of. I'd decided to come back downstairs to check on you and there she was. I tried to talk to her, but she ran off and literally disappeared."

"Where was she?"

"Upstairs in the stacks, why?"

"Did you get a look at what she was reading?"

We walked upstairs and I led her to where Heather had been sitting. There were two tour books on Costa Rica, a book on digital photography and a copy of Gray's Anatomy.

"This make any sense to you?"

"Not a bit. Maybe she's going to go study medical photography in Costa Rica?"

We looked around for a moment and riffled through the pages of the books she had been studying but found nothing.

"Let's go," I said. "We can pick up your books downstairs. I want to go home and work on this stuff."

We went back downstairs and checked out five books that Anna Beth had selected. As we walked out of the library I found myself looking for Heather. When we got to the car I dialed her apartment and her cell.

"I have to tell you something," I said.

"What?"

"I think I know part of what's up with Heather."

"You mean why she disappeared?"

"Yes. I think I did it to myself. Remember the night you called me to meet you downtown? I'd been with her before. I mean, we'd had some drinks and were back at her place. You called and I left. I think she's disappeared because she's mad at me for acting like I did, leaving, going home and all."

"Did you sleep with her?"

"No, but I think that she may have wanted that. Anyway, I think it was easier to leave and not have to see me every day. I feel bad for her."

"Noah, she's gone, don't worry about her. Let's focus on figuring this stuff out. She'll probably come around. What do you say? After all, she's what? Twenty-five?"

~~~~~~~~~~~~~~~~~~~~~~~~~~~~~

And from there that's what we did. The focus was on figuring out the numbers and the rod. I stopped going to the office. I called Gabriel and told him I'd run into Heather. He said he'd look into it. I also called a friend of mine and had him agree to take on most of my files so my clients wouldn't be neglected. Anna Beth began spending a lot of time at my house. Really, we pretty much stayed at my house and worked on figuring out the symbols on the rod and the numbers. Worked being the operative word. I'd been needing some time away from the office, but while I was enjoying this, it wasn't exactly what I'd had in mind.

It was slow going, terribly slow. Actually there was really no progress at all. If we could have found anything it would've been a major victory for us, but nothing on the rod seemed to bear any resemblance to anything we were finding in the books we'd checked out of the library. After a week we were exhausted and frustrated. I hadn't set foot in my office in four days, nor slept in my bed in a week. Austin, however, was quite pleased with our houseguest as he had a new friend and didn't seem to mind his new bedmate. The dining room table was buried under books, charts, maps and diagrams. And through it all we still had no idea what we had found in the safe deposit box.

We had been at it for over a week and we weren't any closer than we were the day we started. I chuckled to myself.

"What's so funny?" I heard a voice ask. Anna Beth had risen and was standing in the door to the dining room. She wore a pair of my boxers and one of my tee shirts, which was beginning to be a habit with her and was just fine with me.

I let out a deep breath. "This whole thing is just frustrating me. I'm starting to think we're missing something on these symbols. I wish I knew someone we could ask."

"Normally I'd take that as an insult, but I am starting to see what you mean. I just feel like we are overlooking something," she said.

I walked across the dining room to the far edge of the window. I leaned tight against the wall and slightly parted the blinds to peek out. There was the sedan again, and while I wasn't sure, the car I saw driving away looked like the one I had seen earlier.

"Looks like we have an audience again. He hasn't moved since last night."

"What's he looking for?"

"No telling. Maybe he expects you to hurt me."

"You've been funny lately. I laughed 'til I hurt when you sent him the pizza last night. Think he ate it?" she said.

"Positive he did, but I'm still amazed at how hard it is to order a pizza with anchovies." I turned back from the window and looked at her. I was beginning to think it wasn't possible for her to look anything other than stunning.

"What?" she asked, looking at me as if she had been caught doing something.

"I'm just overwhelmed by all of this. I don't know where to go or what to do. I'm supposed to be helping you end this thing and here we are holed up in my house trying to find out what some design on a piece of metal means. That and we're being watched 24/7 by an obsessive cop."

"Noah, let me say that this is the best week I have had in a long time, even with Henderson watching us."

I heard a big yawn behind Anna Beth and looked to see Austin coming down the stairs.

"What did you do to the dog?"

"Nothing. I was really surprised he didn't wake me up."

I bent over to Austin and called to him. "What's a matter boy? You okay?"

I ran my hands over him and he leaned against me. I decided he was just being lazy and turned my attention back to Anna Beth.

"You look great today."

"Really now, I just got up," she said. "So what are we doing today?"

"I think we should work on the symbols, but I don't feel like doing it. I don't want to go to work either, so how about we go to your beach house, take Austin and go for a walk on the beach? At least we can give Henderson a break or a change of scenery."

"That sounds wonderful. Let me get my shoes."

She was back in less than ninety seconds. She hadn't changed, but had retrieved a pair of sandals and had gotten a baseball cap (one of mine) and her sunglasses. We walked down into the garage and Austin beat us to the car. I opened the garage door and drove past Henderson. Both of us waved at him. I pointed the car toward Sullivan's Island and drove through town, basically ignoring Henderson in the car behind us as he followed.

We arrived at her house on Sullivan's without incident with our entourage in tow.

"Why don't you take Austin and get him a drink?" Austin was on a rampage to get out of the car. I got his leash on and gave it to Anna Beth, who took him and headed off toward the beach. I circled the Jeep, raised the back hatch and sat on the bumper. Henderson drove up to within about twenty feet of me. He sat in the car, and I stayed on the Jeep.

After about five minutes he pulled up beside me and rolled down his window.

"Cabin fever there, Parks?"

"No, just thought we'd give you a break. Figured you could use a change of scenery."

"Break, huh? Kinda like I broke this case open."

"Opening your mail the way I hear it."

"And what the hell is that supposed to mean?" he said.

"Great piece of detective work. What is it? Mail order evidence?"

"You're a funny guy, you know that?"

"Listen Henderson, we're going to head out on the beach for a while. Mind watching my car?"

"I got her, you know that. Better not get too close. You know a sinking ship's liable to pull you down with it."

"So you keep saying. By the way, you like the pizza last night? Maybe next time you'll want some warm milk with your anchovies?"

I looked up toward the house when I heard a bark. Austin was on the porch, impatiently prancing about. He loved the beach. "Sorry Henderson, my dog's calling me. Fun talking to you."

I jumped off the bumper, closed the hatch and headed to the house. Anna Beth was standing behind Austin. She looked great in the sun. Of course she looked great anywhere, I'd decided. She walked down the steps to meet me under the house with Austin on her heels. She waited on the steps as I walked around to them. Austin had wandered onto the beach. "Austin," I said. He looked, turned and trotted back to us.

"I think I like him," Anna Beth said.

"Who, Henderson?"

"No silly, Austin."

Austin had sat down beside her and she rubbed his head.

"I think you're bribing him, but it's pretty easy to see the feeling's mutual."

She peered past me to look to the front of the house.

"Was that him? Henderson?"

"It was. I bet you're sorry you missed him."

"What did he want?"

"More of the same, mostly just to harass us. Either that or he's really watching out for me, you being the dangerous killer you are."

"Do you need protecting?"

I was taken off guard by her question, surprised even. It may have been the fact that we were standing in front of an incredible beach house. It could have been that it was just a question. It could have been that I was ready to admit that I was attracted to her. Or, it could have been that I had no idea what she was thinking.

"I'm pretty sure I can take care of myself," I said.

"That sounds like a challenge."

I stepped over to her. She was standing on the second step, I on the landing, facing each other. I wanted to say something clever as a comeback, something to keep the moment going, something to... I leaned in and kissed her as she petted Austin. Part of me was concerned that I may have just pushed the envelope a bit too far, but I stopped worrying when she kissed me back. I started enjoying it when she put her hand behind my head. I forgot about the police officer in front of the house after a minute passed with our lips together. Slowly she pulled back, barely allowing our lips to part. She looked up into my eyes.

"You sure take your time, Noah Parks."

"Sorry?"

"I've been wandering around your house half clothed, sleeping in your bed and flirting with you for a week. What took you so long?"

"Let's say I move slow."

"Well come on, let's take a nice slow walk on the beach - we know the house and car will be safe," she said as she glanced toward Henderson.

She took my hand and led me through the dunes to the beach. The only thing that was missing was a sunset, but all things considered, I was pretty sure I'd be okay.

CHAPTER 15

Funny thing how a walk on the beach can make you forget about almost everything. Being beside the water gives you an interesting perspective on things. If you looked out to the ocean and the endless horizon beyond, anything that was on your mind or bothering you simply melted away. In front of you lay a blank slate with nothing to convolute or get in the way. I was thinking about this as we walked along.

The woman beside me had walked into my life with more than a few problems, more than a few issues, and more than enough to scare most men off. But there was something that made me want to find out more, even with a murder charge pending against her. I think I noticed it the first day we had met. I'd been thinking about Anna Beth and getting closer to her since the day I'd watched her from my office window. I'd been looking for a way to test the water with her and see if she was thinking the same as me. As much as I'd been anticipating this, it looked like it may actually be happening right before my eyes, and that was perhaps the thing that excited me the most. While whatever this was happened, I wasn't sure exactly what was going on. The only thing I was sure of was that I wanted to find out more. I thought back to Heather. With her it had always been more about the physical attraction. Even the night we almost ended up in bed we'd gone from zero to heat in the span of an afternoon. This thing with Anna Beth was different - very different. I didn't know what she was thinking, what she wanted, where this was going – and that didn't matter to me at all.

As we walked on the beach it was mostly silent as we watched Austin. He roamed around the beach as we walked, playing in the surf, running through the dunes, sniffing at things in the sand, following along with us as we walked. For the first time in more than a week we didn't talk about her father, the will, Thomason, Henderson, or any of the troubles that we were dealing with. For the first time in more than a week I didn't worry about the fact that my fragile law practice was slipping toward the brink of extinction. The beach was pretty much empty, as was generally the case this time of year. A few people were out walking their dogs, some late season surfers, the occasional jogger. Mostly we had the beach to ourselves, though. There was a cool breeze blowing in from the ocean, just enough to ruffle our hair and keep the temperature down. The gulls glided by, looking for food in the surf. It was low tide, and the scent of the sea spray carried in the air. During the summer there may be thousands of people on this beach every day, but it was times like this that I most enjoyed being at the beach. It was almost as if it belonged only to us. Austin was up ahead, barking at some ducks floating in a tidal pool. Anna Beth pulled close to me and put her head on my shoulder. We turned around when we ran out of beach and headed back to her house, where she went upstairs and made us coffee. We sat on the porch, side by side in rocking chairs, and watched the beach. Every so often I walked to the back of the house and looked out the window. Henderson was still there. If we had to actually go anywhere without anyone knowing about it, he was going to make it tough. But all things considered, I was more than content to stay put.

We stayed at her house all day, alternating between the rocking chairs and a hammock on the side of the deck. Anna Beth asked if she could stay a bit longer at my house and I said she could. In the early afternoon she excused herself for a shower. I thought about wandering into the bathroom but thought better of it, so I sat by the window, listening to the sound of the shower from the bedroom, and thought about my present situation.

I was falling for a client that was charged with the murder of another client. She had practically moved into my house, and since I'd met her my practice had essentially ceased to exist. That and I had a police officer watching my every move and threatening to arrest me. However, I don't think I could have been any happier. I knew I wasn't thinking like a lawyer, but I didn't care. I heard the water stop in the bathroom followed by the sound of her moving about in the bedroom, then footsteps heading to the kitchen. I thought it funny that after she had showered she put on my clothes again, even though she had packed a suitcase.

As sunset approached we decided to go back to my place to at least go through the motions of working on the problem of the designs on the rod. Who knew, maybe we'd actually make some progress. We stopped to get sushi on the way, Henderson in tow. Everything was just as we'd left it, as if we had never left our work at all. The research on the rod's designs took up the bulk of the table. As we walked in the house, I stopped and stared at the table.

"What?" she asked. "You not ready to get back to work?"

"I guess so, but the question is where do we start?"

She stood in front of me, raised herself up on her toes and kissed me.

"We'll start at the beginning, and I'm sure we can knock it out in no time."

I stayed in the door after she kissed me. I guess I had a surprised look on my face because after she turned and walked around the table to sit she looked up at me.

"What? I can't kiss you?"

"Oh, no, you most certainly can."

"Good, but now get to work. Maybe there'll be more of that later."

Austin looked up at me then walked over to Anna Beth, where he lay down at her feet with a sigh.

I picked up a book and headed into the living room.

"Where you going?"

"What?"

"What are you doing in there?"

"Working, why?" I said.

"Why in there?"

"You sound surprised. Why not in here?"

"Because we have sushi to eat."

She was sitting at the table with a book opened to Celtic symbolism. She had one leg underneath her and her hair fell down around her face.

I made a space on the table and opened up the sushi. As I was doing this she pushed back from the table and walked out of the room toward the kitchen. She appeared with a bottle of wine.

We ate the sushi and started anew on our problems, but soon found our familiar dead ends. Occasionally one of us would find a design that was similar or find mention of similar rods or staffs, but nothing that led further. We dug through book after book. Pictures started to look the same and sentences ran on, but still nothing. We'd made no progress on the numbers, either. All the while we were working the rod rested in the middle of the table. Occasionally one of us would reach for it and turn it over and over in our hand, as if perhaps some indication of its purpose would flow through to us.

We still felt the design was Celtic inspired, though we could find nothing similar to it. The runic lettering was unlike any actual runic symbols we had been able to find. Everything else about the rod was just as much a mystery as it had been the day we found it.

We looked at local architectural designs of various buildings; we studied Chicago architecture and even the history of Celtic design. All our efforts were met with the same result – frustration at best. Several days had passed since our walk on the beach, and while my architectural knowledge was growing by leaps and bounds, we still had a mystery rod and a series of numbers that made no sense and less than any idea how they fit together.

The one high point was that I was spending every moment with Anna Beth, who seemed to be thriving with our work and under the watch of Henderson, who was spending his time in his car parked in my cul-de-sac. Watching. Well, I say every moment - we weren't sleeping together, but we were staying up late, working on the designs, watching television and talking 'til the early morning hours when she would finally head upstairs to go to bed. She said she felt guilty for leaving Austin in bed alone. He'd generally go to bed about 8:00 o'clock each night. Although I told her I was sure he wouldn't mind, she didn't appear in a rush to move anything along between the two of us, and while I was really anxious to see where things were going, I was trying my best to be patient with her.

When we had first holed up in the house I received a few calls every day from my answering service about cases, which meant I had to call the attorney handling them for me. I had to make sure that my clients weren't neglected. As the days passed the calls became fewer and further in between. Soon it seemed the only things that were occupying my attention were Anna Beth, the rod and Henderson.

About a week after our beach trip the phone rang. I was on the back deck watching Austin in the yard.

"You want me to get that?"

I walked back inside and picked up the phone. "No, I got it. Hello?"

"Noah, got a minute?"

It was Gabriel. "Sure, what's up?"

"I haven't heard from you. Thought I'd check up on you. You okay?"

"Yes, why?"

"It's not like you to just drop out of touch. How's Anna Beth?"

"I think she's doing great. She's been staying here in case you're wondering."

"Thought so. Henderson called and let me know."

"Doesn't surprise me. He's been camping out in front of my house for the last week or so. Doesn't he have anything better to do?" I said.

"Word on the street is that he thinks you're sleeping with her and that she's pulled you in. With her money and your know how, you're going to get her out of town."

"Gabriel, we're not going anywhere. If I was, I'd let you know."

"You do that. Something else though. Heather."

"What about her?" I said.

"You absolutely sure you saw her?"

"Saw her and talked to her."

"Noah, she's a ghost. Not a trace of her anywhere. I mean, she's really vanished. If you hadn't seen her I'd be telling you forget about it, but that puts a little twist on things. You seeing her gives me some concern, 'cause I can't find her anywhere."

"Meaning?

"Meaning if you saw her then she's gotta be all right, but I'd feel a lot better if I knew where she was. Course, if it was someone that you just thought looked like Heather, that would explain it. I still think that she just split again and will pop up somewhere out of the blue."

"What do you mean, someone that looked like her?" I said.

"Just a thought, man. Don't take this the wrong way, but you know your stressing about stuff can make you see weird things."

"I know I saw her. I'm positive I did."

"Don't get touchy on me, I believe you. It just has me frustrated."

"Well, me too. Will you let me know what you find out?"

"Partner, keep me posted. Let me know what's going on. Tell Ms. Cross I said hello," he said.

"Thanks for calling, my friend."

I went back in. She was sitting at the table in thought. She looked at me and smiled.

"Who was that?" she said.

"Gabriel. He said to say hi."

~~~~~~~~~~~~~~~~~~~~~~~~

We were both becoming increasingly frustrated at the lack of progress and we were running out of leads. There were only so many times we could go back over the same things. We'd moved from the dining room table several hours ago and were sitting on

THE TRUST

the floor of the living room with Austin laying on the couch across the room. Suddenly she got up from the floor where we had been sitting, surprising both Austin and I.

"I'm going to bed."

Upon hearing this Austin jumped off the couch and headed to the bedroom.

"Okay," I said as I looked up at her and slowly rose from the floor. I shut the book I had been studying.

"So, goodnight."

"Goodnight," I said.

She walked out of the living room and headed toward the stairs. I looked at the door. She stopped at the base of the stairs, then turned to the door of the living room. She looked at me for a moment, started to speak, then turned and headed back toward the stairs. I followed behind her. She took two steps up the stairs and turned to me, looking me in the eye. She leaned forward and kissed me.

"Thank you."

"For?"

"Well, for helping, for letting me stay here and for not rushing things."

"Things?"

"You know what I mean."

I brushed a lock of hair from her face. "I do."

"Come upstairs with me."

I started to speak, but she put her finger to my lips.

"Sssssh. Just come with me."

I followed her upstairs and watched her get into my bed without taking her clothes off. I walked over and crawled in beside her. She rolled over and put her head on my chest. We fell asleep in each other's arms without saying a word.

~~~~~~~~~~~~~~~~~~~~~~~~~~~~~~~~~

There was silence when I awoke the next morning. It was as if we had closed our eyes and fast forwarded to morning in an instant. We were lying exactly where we'd been the night before. I slipped out of bed, leaving her to sleep. I stared at her for a moment before I turned to go. I walked downstairs and turned on the satellite radio. Miles Davis. We had slept with most of the windows in the house open, allowing us to enjoy the early fall weather. The scent of a crisp cool fall morning floated through on the breeze. Saturday morning. It was a perfect day for college football. I thought momentarily about the scores of South Carolina fans that would be traveling to Columbia to watch the Gamecocks. I stood for a moment in the doorway of the dining room, staring at the work that had taken up residence on my dining room table. I halfway wished that someone had come in during the night and taken it, but there was to be no such luck to be had, particularly with Henderson watching. I was surprised that the familiar sight of his cruiser was missing today. Austin nudged me as I stood in the doorway, and I walked him to the back door and let him out. I watched him for a moment from my deck as he patrolled the back yard. I went back inside and prepared his food and let him back when he announced his presence at the door. I looked back into the dining room at the work that waited on the table and thought of Thomason, my first meeting with him, and how this had all started. I was just beginning to smile with thoughts of Anna Beth when I heard her on the stairs.

"Hey," she said.

She was standing at the far door of the dining room. Her hair was a bit askew as she had just woken up. She was rubbing her eyes and she yawned. She had on one of my button downs and boxers, not the ones from the night before that she had worn to bed.

"Well good morning sleepy head, hope I didn't wake you," I said.

She walked over to the table and flipped through one of the books that lay open.

"Do you think we're just missing it or looking in the wrong place?

"I wish I knew. So what do you want?"

She looked at me and grinned.

"To eat," I said.

"Surprise me. I'm going to go catch up on what's going on in the world. Let's eat and then decide what we should do today.

"By the way, looks like our shadow has taken the day off," she called from the front room.

"Sorry, what was that?"

"Henderson, he's not out there. Looks like we wore him out."

"I'd imagine we haven't heard the last of him, but at least it seems that we'll have a little bit of privacy."

"And what is that supposed to mean?"

"We'll have to wait and..."

"Noah, come here quick," she said.

I walked into the living room. "What?"

"What do you know about hurricanes?"

"Sorry, hurricanes? Enough to know that you get out of the way of the big ones and that even a small one can be a pain in the ass. Why?"

"Look at this. There's one out in the Atlantic, see?" she said.

"Yeah, it happens all the time in hurricane season. They kick up and the entire east coast spends September glued to their computers and televisions hoping they don't get hit."

The local weatherman was talking about a hurricane kit that

you could pick up at a number of local businesses that would let the viewers follow the storm.

"What's the hurricane kit for?" she said.

"Not a lot of hurricanes in Chicago, huh?"

"No, not really."

"A hurricane kit lets you follow the storm. The news will tell you where the hurricane is, you plot it on the chart and follow its course. It's laid out on a grid and you just plot it."

"So you track them?"

"Yeah, not too exciting. Sort of a high tech connect the dots, but it lets you see where it's been and gives you an idea of where it's going."

"Hum?"

"What the hell are you getting at here?" I said.

"I have an idea, a thought at least. Say that the design on the rod is nothing of importance, maybe it's just a design."

"Okay, so? What's this got to do with hurricanes?"

"What if it's the numbers that are really important?"

"I think they almost have to be, but if they're an account number we need to know where to look, and…"

"But what if they're not a bank number?" she said.

"What else would they be?"

"How do you know where to put the dots on the hurricane chart?"

"You get longitude and latitude coordinates from the… Hey, wait a minute… It couldn't be that easy, could it?"

"Let's find out."

I followed her to the computer and watched as she did a Google search on longitude and latitude. She pulled up a site on plotting via GPS coordinates and followed the links to a screen that asked for a seven digit longitude and seven digit latitude. Interesting, given that we had fourteen numbers. She plugged in the numbers. Instantly it popped up showing mileage and time distance from our present location. It was a location less than two hours away from us. We stared at the screen in silence.

"Damn that's just up the road. What do you think?" I said.

"It's the first bit of progress we've had since we opened the safe deposit box."

"So what are you thinking?"

"Road trip?" she said.

"Let's go."

CHAPTER 16

Adrenaline's a funny thing. When it kicks in it's like a drug - better than a drug, even. You get focused, things just start to happen, clarity sets in and it all makes sense. But as quickly as it arrives, it leaves, and when it stops, the crash is like running into a brick wall. Sixty to zero in a split second. As soon as we decided to go there was a flurry of activity in the house. I turned off the stove and hastily cleaned up the kitchen. I put Austin in the backyard for a pre-trip potty break. Anna Beth disappeared upstairs, and from the sounds in the direction of the bedroom, she was packing a bag. I printed out the directions to where the coordinates said we were headed. I looked at the directions and a chill ran down my spine. This was when the adrenaline flow cut off. Then I saw the brick wall just before it hit. Anna Beth came downstairs just as the chill was setting in at the base of my spine.

"Noah, what's the matter? You look like you've seen a ghost."

"I... I mean... This place, where the, where we're going. I

know it."

"Know it, what do you mean?" she said.

"I grew up there. It looks like it's less than a mile from where I went to high school."

"What's going on, Noah?"

I could only shrug my shoulders and raise my eyebrows while I looked at the directions. She walked to me and took the map I'd been holding. She stared at it just as I had, pulled out a chair and sat down in the kitchen. She looked at it as though she expected the answer would jump out at her. She sat the map down on the table and turned her eyes to me.

"So what's there, where the coordinates are?"

"I don't know. It's funny, from looking at this map I know exactly where that is, but for the life of me I don't know what's actually there."

She looked back to the map then to me again. "We still going?"

"Like that?" I said as I pointed toward her, moving my finger up and down.

She looked down and blushed. She was still wearing my underwear and a button down.

"Give me a minute, I'll change."

I let Austin back in. He could tell we were getting ready for a trip. He loved to ride in the Jeep, so I decided to take him with us. Anna Beth came back down dressed a bit more travel worthy. She'd put on a pair of jeans, but still had on the button down.

"Mind if Austin joins us?" I said.

"A road trip with two guys? How could a girl say no?"

I got in the Jeep and picked up my cell phone. Gabriel answered on the first ring.

"Gabriel."

"What's going on with you today, my friend?"

"Listen, you know how you told me to let you know if we were leaving town?"

"Noah? What are you up to?" he said.

"Anna Beth and I are going to take a ride up the coast, hit Myrtle Beach for a bit. Just a day trip, no more than overnight."

"So what am I supposed to say?"

"Honestly? I don't know if there is anything for you to say, but since Henderson's been watching me, I wanted to let you know we were going to take a little trip in case he asked. And by the way, he's not out here. I think he gave up on us."

"Noah, everything okay?"

"Actually, everything's great. I'll give you a call when we get back."

I heard Gabriel take a deep breath. I could picture him walking out on his front porch and standing at the top of his stairs preparing to lecture me. "Remember a few months back when I told you I was the one that put them in jail and that you were the one that got them out?"

"Sure, why?"

"Just wanted to make sure you were listening. Just remember that we've both got our jobs and they're both different. Just drive safe and be careful. Call as soon as you get back."

I pressed the end button on the phone and looked at Anna Beth.

"What did he say?"

"He said have fun."

"You want me to believe that or just let it slide?"

"It's a long story, so how about letting it slide for now?"

"Fair enough. Hey, pull over there," she said, pointing toward the entrance to the Towne Center in Mount Pleasant, a huge upscale shopping area on the way out of town.

I put on the turn signal and pulled in. She directed me toward one of the large electronics stores.

"Wait here a minute. I'll be right back," she said.

I watched her hurry inside as I held Austin, who desperately wanted to follow.

"Loyal friend you are."

He looked toward her and whimpered, giving a single bark out the window. I worked to avoid his tail that was nearly creating a windstorm in the Jeep.

"Austin."

He lay down in the back seat and looked up at me, which was what he generally did when he'd been scolded. I scanned through streams on the satellite radio while I waited for Anna Beth. After about twenty minutes I looked up and saw her approaching the car with a large bag.

"Let's go. You do know the way don't you?"

"I do."

"Then off we go."

I pulled out of the parking space and headed onto Highway 17, which would lead us out of town and north to Myrtle Beach. Anna Beth sorted through the contents of the large bag, but I couldn't see what was in it. Austin had his head between the seats, studying the bag, easily as curious as me.

"What you got there?" I said.

"A surprise. So why's Gabriel worried about you? He concerned about me?"

"Like I said, it's a long story."

"You said we had a long trip, go ahead."

I looked over at her and saw that she was staring back at me, waiting for my response. "Any chance I get out of telling you about this?"

"Well, I don't want to pry, at least not too much, but I'd like to know. Besides, I'd be lying if I told you different."

She had her legs crossed in her seat with the bag in her lap. She was petting Austin gingerly behind his ear while I drove.

"You know he's going to end up spoiled and I'll have a mess on my hands if you're not careful."

"Don't change the subject." She kept on petting and scratching the eager canine.

"How about this? He's worried about both of us. He likes you, certainly doesn't believe you killed Thomason, but I've known Gabriel a long time. He knows how things get to me. He knows that I like you, probably more than I should, and let's just say that my past relationships haven't been without complications."

"And?"

"And that's it. He's doesn't want to see anything happen that causes problems with what is going on with you and he doesn't want anything to happen to me, either."

"That really doesn't tell me too much, you know?" She paused. "Other than what I was already pretty sure about."

"What's that?"

"That you like me, although the 'probably more than I should' has me a little intrigued."

"Well, after all, I'm representing you and the powers that be tend to frown on attorneys getting involved with their clients."

"Noah, I'm a big girl. I can make my own decisions." She turned to completely face me. "I've done a crappy job of hiding that I'm attracted to you. I mean I've practically moved into your house – thank you, by the way. I was sort of starting to think you were just being polite." She paused. "Or gay."

"I can assure you that I'm not gay. Not that there's anything wrong with that," I added as she smiled. "And I do try to always be polite, but why do you say that?"

"Noah, really." She adjusted again in the seat. "I've been wearing your clothes and sleeping in your bed for the better part of a month. You're starting to give me a complex. You're making me feel like I'm embarrassing myself. That you're not interested."

I looked at her and smiled. "Don't be embarrassed and don't worry, I'm interested." Austin gave a 'woof' as I spoke. "Course, probably not quite as interested as he is. He seems to have adopted you."

She smiled. "Good, I like having two new guys in my life. Now tell me why Gabriel is worried."

"Will you be too upset if I ask if I can tell you later?"

"It'll take a lot more than that to get me upset."

"So what's in the box?"

"I guess I can show you," she said.

She pulled out a large box that I thought was a portable DVD player.

"GPS. I thought it would be helpful. You know how to use it?" she said.

"I'm sure we can figure it out, but I actually have one in the console my dear."

"Okay, but this one is probably a bit more sensitive. It is supposed to get within a few feet of the specific coordinates. Something about tracking more satellites or some other type thing."

"Okay then Miss Nerd Herd, hook it up."

She shot me a playful look then opened the box, pulled out the pieces and began to plug parts together. She put in rechargeable batteries, plugged in wires and flipped through pages of directions. She plugged in the cigarette adaptor and then plugged it into the GPS unit. There was a window mount included and she attached it to the windshield above the dash. She turned the unit on to a series of beeps and flashes.

"There," she said when she was finished.

"You're pretty handy with that."

"My ex-husband used to have one of these things in all our cars. I always thought they were just expensive toys for big little boys, but I'm willing to admit that I may have been a little hasty in my judgment."

"So what does it say?" I said.

"It says you're speeding."

We drove on through the early afternoon, winding our way up the South Carolina coast, through the long expanses of marsh, through sleepy towns such as Georgetown, then Conway, bypassing the ever present traffic of Myrtle Beach as we headed into the rural parts of Horry County. Myrtle Beach is a vast, sprawling mecca devoted to golf, tourists and lots of neon. If you had to get from one end of the county to the next, Myrtle Beach was best avoided.

Anna Beth had programmed in the specific coordinates that we'd gotten from the safe deposit box. The GPS had determined a route and a chime sounded at each turn we were to make. The thing was actually quite amazing. With the number of satellites it was tracking it could lead us to within fifteen feet of the exact coordinates we had. But depending on what we were looking for, a search area of fifteen feet could be a lot of ground to cover, especially when we didn't know what it was we were after.

The marsh of the coast turned to woodlands, forest, country roads and open fields as we turned inland. As I approached my hometown of Loris, the sights became more familiar. We were on a two-lane country blacktop road.

After about forty-five more minutes I asked, "We getting close?"

"It's not far," she said. "Somewhere off over to the left, but there aren't any roads on the GPS, at least none showing."

"Sometimes the topographical maps that those things read don't have all the roads in them and..."

"You missed it."

"What?" I said.

"It says the coordinates are behind us, but I didn't see a road," she said.

"I don't think there was one."

Austin looked out of one side of the Jeep, Anna Beth and I the other. I did a three-point turn and slowly headed in the other direction. I looked back down the road where we'd just been. There was an opening in the brush that looked like it might be a dirt road, but nothing more than that.

"There's something back there a bit. I think we should've turned there."

Though we were stopped in the middle of the road, she had taken the GPS out of the car with her, looked at it, then looked back down the road. "I think that might be it. It looks like if we turn there it should be a straight shot. Do you know where we are?"

"Yes and no. Like I said, I grew up just a few miles from here and I've been down this road hundreds of times, but never in these woods. And I've got no idea what we'll find."

"There's a first time for everything. Let's go."

I watched her as she got back in the car. She met my gaze and the expression on her face said, "Come on, let's go!!" I got back in and headed toward the dirt road. As we got closer we saw that what we thought was a dirt road was more like a wide path with two worn tire-size ruts. I turned off the road and paused as I contemplated the path.

"So, what are you waiting for?"

"Just looking. What does the GPS say?"

"Says head on that way," she said, pointing off down the path.

I looked at her then to Austin, who seemed to be indifferent as to what I did. The pathway was really like a tunnel through the woods. The trees on each side joined their branches to create a canopy that covered the ground and shaded the way. It reminded me of the road leading to the boat landing where Thomason's body had been found. I decided to keep this to myself. There was no movement and generally off to each side, while there was not a lot of undergrowth, there was just enough to convince anyone heading our direction to stay close to the path. I slowly headed on but stopped after about fifteen feet, something having caught my eye.

"What is it?" she said.

"Hang on a sec."

I got out of the Jeep and walked around in front of the car, leaving Anna Beth and Austin inside. As I approached the brush I saw something protruding from behind the weeds. I bent over and brushed a fern and a rather large patch of high grass aside. There was a small sign, no more than eight inches square. It read "Patterson Cemetery." Anna Beth opened the door and walked up behind me. Austin was still in the Jeep, but I could tell he wanted to get out.

"Stay there boy."

"What is it?" she said.

"Looks like we're going to a cemetery." I pointed to the sign.

"Cemetery? Who's buried here?"

"No idea, but I've never heard of it. Shall we take a look?"

I walked around the Jeep and got back inside. I looked and Anna Beth was still standing by the sign.

"What's wrong?"

"Patterson Cemetery. You've never heard of it?" she said.

"No, should I have?

"Well, you did grow up here," she paused. "But I guess there's a lot of cemeteries in Chicago that I've never heard of. But then again, Chicago covers a little more real estate. Just interesting, the name and all."

"It's probably named after someone first buried here or whoever owned the land before it was a cemetery. Patterson's a fairly common name. I even went to school with some Pattersons. It's not that surprising."

She got in, shut the door and I slowly drove forward. As we moved on the woods opened, and we passed a couple of old fallow tobacco fields complete with old-fashioned flue-cured tobacco barns in various states of disrepair. There were no homes or other structures of any type. We pulled in the angle of view on the GPS and kept going down the path. About a mile from the main road the path opened further into a cemetery that was roughly half the size of a football field. I stopped the Jeep and looked around. There was no sign of a caretaker, but that wasn't surprising for an old country cemetery. While it wasn't what I would call well manicured, it wasn't overgrown with weeds or brush, and while it was quite old looking, it didn't look full.

"How far away from the coordinates are we?" I said.

She looked at the GPS and then stared out the window.

"Looks like about a hundred and twenty feet. That direction," she said as she pointed off away from where we were standing.

"Let's go."

She jumped out of the Jeep and followed me. Austin followed, sniffing the air as he walked away from the Jeep.

"Stay with us," I said to him.

I looked at Anna Beth and saw that she was staring at something she carried.

"What's that?" I said.

"Portable GPS. Package deal. Seventy five feet this way," she said as she walked past me, Austin in tow.

I followed and watched her walk, stopping every few feet to consult the handheld GPS. Finally she stopped.

"We're here," she said.

I looked around where she was standing. "Hang on a sec."

I jogged back to the Jeep and opened the back hatch and dug around in my tool kit. I found what I was looking for and shut the hatch. I ran back to where she was waiting.

"Here, hold this," I said.

I gave her one end of a long tape measure.

"So what does it say about accuracy?"

She looked at it again. "Eighteen feet."

I measured out twenty-five feet on the tape measure just to be sure.

"Hold tight and let's see what our circle looks like."

She held her end of the tape measure tight as I did the same. By pulling the tape tight on each end and walking the perimeter of the tape's length, I was able to walk a rough circle. I found a can of white spray paint in my Jeep, so every few feet I sprayed the ground. In less than five minutes, I had a search area marked out for us.

Anna Beth walked the perimeter and looked over my work. "It actually almost looks like a circle."

"Easy there. Let's get to looking and see what we can find."

"What are we looking for?"

"Haven't the foggiest idea," I said. "Hopefully we'll know it when we find it. You start over there and I'll look here."

I walked to the far side of the circle as Anna Beth headed the other direction. I was studying the headstones since they seemed the logical place to start. Patterson Cemetery appeared to be an old country cemetery that was quite common for this part of South

Carolina. There were easily a couple of hundred graves spread throughout the open field. In the search area I had marked, there were easily thirty graves. I wandered about, looking generally at most of them, looking for anything that might jump out at me. Austin had watched us for about the first hour as we walked about staring at headstones and memorial markers, but he lost interest and went off in search of something more entertaining. Part of the trouble was, we didn't know if we were looking for some clue, something tangible, or exactly what. So after my hour long overview, I decided to study the individual graves.

Some of the family names were familiar to me. I'd known people with the same names from when I lived in the area, but I didn't know any of the individuals whose names I was now reading. The dates of death seemed to go back no further than the early 1930's, with the most recent being more than a decade old. They all seemed like perfectly average graves. There was nothing unique about any of the headstones in the search area. In fact, there was nothing unique or that stood out the least little bit on any of the headstones anywhere in the entire cemetery as I could see. I stopped and looked around. It was quiet, peaceful actually. Anna Beth was wandering around on the other side of the circle behind me. I kneeled over and looked at the tombstone I was standing in front of.

"RANDOLPH ALLEN HARDEE – Born November 6, 1935 – Died March 12, 1979. Beloved Husband and Father. Rest Eternally in your Heavenly Father's Arms."

I didn't know him even though he had lived in my hometown for more than a decade after my birth. I thought about him as I looked at his grave. There were no flowers or anything around it. I pulled at some of the weeds from the ground and brushed the leaves from the headstone. I found myself wondering when it was that someone had last visited his grave. I wondered if I had ever seen this man before he died, perhaps passing him at the post office when I was younger or maybe at the local grocery store, or perhaps he had been to one of my little league baseball game. There was no way of knowing, but what I did know was that it had been a while since anyone had been to visit him. I stood up and looked around again. From the looks of Patterson Cemetery, it appeared that the rest of the residents shared an eternal plight similar to that of Mr. Hardee. It didn't look like too many people came here. At least not with any plans to leave.

"Noah, come here."

I turned and saw her standing over a grave. She had her hands by her sides with her eyes locked on the headstone.

I walked over to her. "What is it?"

"Look at this. I think this may be what we are looking for."

I walked up behind her and looked down at a non-descript headstone.

"RACHEL ELIZABETH PATTERSON – Born September 5, 1891 – Died September 1, 1971. Beloved for Eternity."

"It looks like one of the older ones, probably answers the name question," I said.

"No, that's not it."

"What then?" I said.

"That's my mother. Well, my mother's maiden name, anyway. Rachel Elizabeth Patterson."

"I see. So that's what got you about the cemetery sign?"

"Yes."

"You've never been here before?" I said.

"Never, why would I have been?"

"Point taken."

I looked beyond the grave and saw the spray paint on the grass.

It was definitely in the circle we'd plotted. I walked around the grave, looking closely at it as I did. It was a typical granite headstone. The condition of it was similar to that of Mr. Hardee's. Leaves and weeds cluttered about the stone. Other than the lettering, there was an inlaid seal on each edge of the headstone. But they contained no lettering, only a design that appeared to be a diamond. Nothing about the headstone stood out. Anna Beth watched me in silence.

"So, what do you think?" she said.

"I agree with you, this is too much of a coincidence for it not to be the place, but I can't see anything on here that looks familiar. Let's do this. We can look around a bit longer while we have light. I have a camera in the car, let's take some pictures of this grave, and by my count there're 15 or so others around this point. We can take shots of them, too. That'll give us work for tonight."

"I'll get the camera," she said.

I stood over the grave then looked around. I agreed with Anna Beth, this was where we were supposed to be. But the question was what were we looking for and what was I missing, and I was sure I was missing something. Part of me felt like I was looking right at our answer.

She came back with the camera and I took at least twenty shots of the Patterson grave. I gave Anna Beth the camera and told her to go take pictures of the other graves in the circle. I looked at my watch - we'd been at the cemetery for several hours staring at graves. The light wasn't going to hold out much longer as the shadows were already starting to creep toward us from the woods. This particular effect in a cemetery was a little unnerving.

"What do you say we get out of here?" I said.

"Sounds good to me. I've never really liked cemeteries after dark," she said as she slung the camera over her shoulder.

We got back in the car after we found Austin asleep under a tree. Anna Beth poured him some water in his car bowl and he laid back down again in the wayback of the Jeep. I slowly headed out of the cemetery and back up the path. I pulled almost up to the road and stopped just short.

"Hang on a minute," I said.

I got out and stepped into the bushes. I broke off a small branch from a bush and placed it in one of the tire ruts about twenty feet in from the turn in. I got back in the car.

"What were you doing?"

"Call me paranoid, but I want to know if anyone's snooping around behind us. I looked around the place while we were there and it doesn't look like a high traffic spot. But this cemetery is where we are supposed to be - question is, why?"

"Maybe the pictures will help?"

She was scrolling through them, looking at them on the camera's screen.

"Okay, here's the question. Where do you want to stay tonight? We can head back to Charleston, or we can stay up here. There are great places down the road in Myrtle Beach, more rustic places up here," I said.

"Do you have any family here anymore?"

"No, no one, but there's a motel on the other side of town. How does that sound? Not exactly the Planter's Inn, but we should have some privacy."

"Sounds rustic, I like that."

We headed into town and stopped to order a pizza. There was a grocery store in the same complex along with a pharmacy. We went in the pizza place and ordered. While we were waiting for the pizza, we walked over to the pharmacy and used their self-serve photo kiosk to print the photos from the cemetery. I felt sort of odd having a stack of thirty photos of graves, but no one else seemed to notice or care. We paid and then went to the grocery store, bought a couple of bottles of wine and some dog food for Austin. The clerk looked at us rather quizzically as we paid. We went back to the pizza place and picked up dinner, then headed out of town the few miles to the hotel.

We pulled up and I parked under the sign that read "Loris Motel."

"Hang on a sec, right back," I said.

I walked in the office and came back a few minutes later with the key.

"Tell me where else you can get a room with air conditioning, clean sheets and T.V. for thirty-nine dollars? Maybe it will qualify as the Planter's Inn North."

"Sounds like a bargain to me. How did you get Austin in?"

"It's generally easier to ask forgiveness than permission."

We parked the car and the three of us went into the room. We were greeted by two twin beds, a dresser, a small table and a television. There was a picture of a ship above each of the beds, faded green drapes and generic bed spreads. While the room was larger than most, the dim lights and the dark paneling made it appear small and somewhat cramped. Standing in the door, I wondered what it would have felt like to be a trucker stopping for the night after a long haul, a husband moving in after having been kicked out of his house or cheating spouses meeting for an hour of guilty pleasure. I studied the room for a moment, then went inside.

"Hardly what I had in mind for our first out of town trip."

"It's sort of romantic. Mind if I take a quick shower?"

"Don't expect monogrammed bath robes," I said.

"Don't worry, I came prepared."

She disappeared into the bathroom with a bag over her shoulder and I heard the shower start. I walked out of the room after putting out some food for Austin and looked around. The motel, a long ranch style house with a small office in the center where the owners lived, had four rooms off each side of the office. All looked identical. Outside of each room were two plastic chairs and a plastic table. The hotel offered a commanding view of a small pond and a tobacco field. I went back in the room and turned on the T.V. in case Austin decided to announce his presence. It looked like we were the only people in the hotel. I wandered down toward the office and got a bucket full of ice and an extra grocery bag full just to be on the safe side. After all, we did have two bottles of wine. When I got back to the room, Anna Beth was sitting on one of the beds in a white Oxford and a pair of boxers. Mine, of course.

"Nice outfit."

"Well, thank you."

Austin jumped up beside her. I walked into the bathroom and dumped the ice in the sink over a bottle of wine. I put some ice in two glasses and filled them with water.

We sat down at the table and ate the pizza under Austin's watchful eye. When we were done I got the last two glasses and opened the wine. I had to go out to the car to get a corkscrew.

"Nothing but the finest for you."

She laughed as I gave her the wine in the hotel glass.

"So what do you make of the pictures?" she said.

"I've looked through them and I'm getting nothing. Nothing at all. But you do take good pictures."

She smiled. "Thanks, but lots of good that does us."

She got up from the table and walked over to the bed, taking the photos with her. Austin was already asleep on the other bed. It was amazing how the dog could take up so much of a bed. She spread the photos out on the canine-free bed, sat and began to study them again. She brushed her hair back from her eyes and put her chin in her hands.

"All of these tombstones look alike. Except for the names, they're almost identical."

I'd taken the Patterson grave photos out and was flipping through them for what seemed like the hundredth time. I tossed them on the bed and got up to get some more wine. After filling my glass I emptied the bottle into her glass. I sat down at the table, put my feet on the other chair and sighed.

"What?" she said.

"Up then down, up then down. I was so sure that we'd show up and find what we were after."

"If it were easy, it wouldn't be fun."

She got up and opened the door.

"What are you doing?" I said.

She stuck her head out and looked one way, then the other. She stepped back in the room and grabbed my keys, walked out to the Jeep without saying a word, then came back with a black case. She stood over the table and stared at my feet. I moved them and she opened the case and removed a laptop - a nice laptop. She booted it up and inserted a wireless card.

"I don't think that there's a wireless setup here. I mean it's nice, but not quite there yet."

"Oh, don't worry, broadband will do the trick."

"What are we looking for?" I said.

"I thought I'd see if I could learn anything about this person who shares my mother's name. And you get to rub my neck while we look."

She kissed me on the cheek and sat down. I walked around behind her, brushed her hair aside and began rubbing her shoulders.

She spent about half an hour looking for anything on this

woman who shared her mother's name, but we came up empty. There were a few references to Anna Beth's mother, which I thought would upset her, but she moved on past them with no sign of emotion. After we had run into an all too familiar dead end, she asked if there was anything else that I wanted to look at on the computer. I said no and she turned it off.

We'd opened the second bottle of wine and were about half a glass away from finishing it. She turned off one of the two lights in the room and went in the bathroom, pulling the door shut. I watched the slow rhythmic rise and fall of Austin's chest as he slept. There was a show on the Discovery Channel about hurricanes. Fitting, I thought. I checked the weather channel and saw that the big storm out in the Atlantic had gotten bigger through the day and was now a tropical storm with the coast of South Carolina as one of several possibilities for landfall. I heard the water start and stop in the bathroom. She came out and left the door open. She walked by me without saying a word and sat on the bed. I looked at her a moment then walked in the bathroom. I brushed my teeth using a tooth brush from my kit.

Funny thing was it was already wet.

CHAPTER 17

I finished in the bathroom and turned off the light. I opened the door. The room was dark, the television off. I turned on the light in the bathroom again.

"Would you turn that off, please?" she said.

I turned it off and walked out of the bathroom, pausing to allow my eyes to adjust to the dark. I stood in silence at the foot of the bed where Austin was sleeping. Shapes slowly started to form in the room. I could see her on the other bed lying under the sheet with her back to me. I was about to wake Austin when she spoke to me.

"Coming to bed?"

I sat down on the bed beside Austin, who didn't move.

"Careful, you'll wake him. Come over here."

I stepped over to the bed and pulled the sheet back. I paused, then got in the bed. She rolled over, raised up on her side and kissed me, pulling me closer to her. I kissed her back and ran my hand through her hair. We stayed like this for at least half an hour, kissing, touching, holding each other without saying a word. She rolled on top of me, rising to her knees, straddling me. She was still wearing my Oxford, but had taken my underwear off. I put one hand on her hip and reached the other to brush the hair out of her face.

"So, now what, Mr. Parks?"

"I don't want you to think I'm easy."

"I don't think that - you've actually been pretty hard," she paused. "Okay, that came out wrong. You just haven't made it easy."

"I guess we just let what happens happen."

In the darkness, with the little light the moon provided, I could just make out a smile.

I pulled her close to me again and kissed her, long and hard, running my hands through her hair and down her back. We rolled onto our sides, facing each other, caressing each other as we kissed. I felt myself becoming quite aroused, and as much as I wanted to tear her clothes off, I shifted and I rolled onto my side behind her and kissed her neck. She edged closer to me as I put my arms around her. There was no sound in the room except for the breathing of Austin on the other bed.

We fell asleep side by side.

I awoke to the sun coming in through the window. I opened my eyes and looked around, first realizing that I was only wearing my boxers. She sat at the table looking at the photos, drinking a cup of coffee, her knees pulled close to her chest.

"Morning. How long you been up?" I said as I raised up on an elbow and rubbed my eyes.

"About an hour. Did you know you look peaceful when you're asleep?"

"Apparently you haven't seen my hair. You've been staring at me?"

"I have."

I glanced over at Austin, who was still asleep on the other bed.

"You're going to give me a complex if you're not careful."

"You're going to drive me crazy if you keep teasing me. Are all men down here such gentlemen?"

Not waiting for an answer, she leaned over and kissed me.

"I've been looking through the pictures, but I just don't see anything that helps us, nothing at all. So... I'm going to take a shower and we can decide what to do after that."

She stood from the table and walked to the shower. She took off her shirt, dropping it on the floor at the bathroom door - which she didn't bother to close.

I sat up in the bed and looked over at Austin. He was just starting to stir. He raised his head, yawned and stretched. There was coffee in the small pot on the dresser and I got up to grab a cup. I didn't have a headache, but I also didn't remember taking off my tee shirt or khakis during the night. I looked over to the open bathroom door and saw her shirt and her underwear just beyond it. I poured a cup and sat it on the table. My shirt was on the floor beside the bed, so I bent to pick it up. As I rose, my gaze fell on one of the pictures of the Patterson grave. It was upside-down the way I was looking at it as it lay on the bed. Maybe that was it, or maybe the shadows were different from this angle. I picked it up and looked at it more closely. At the base of the headstone there was what looked like a blade of grass or part of a weed, but from my new angle, I could tell it was actually a mark on the headstone. When I turned it right side up, it blended in with the grass surrounding the headstone. I quickly sorted through the other pictures of the Patterson grave and pulled them aside. In three of them the mark was visible if I looked at it from a different angle. On each one, as I rotated the photo, the mark became visible when the photo was upside-down. The arrow appeared to be pointing down on the headstone. How had I missed that before? I grabbed the first picture and walked into the bathroom. Since the door was open I didn't knock.

"Anna Beth. Look at this. Anna Beth."

"Noah, what is it?" she said.

"Look at…"

I looked up and saw her in the shower, naked of course, and quickly turned away, likely blushing at the same time. "I'm sorry, I'm so sorry. I just found something I wanted you to see."

She turned off the shower and pulled back the curtain. "Hand me that towel if you would."

I tried not to look at her, but when I turned to the sink her reflection in the mirror was all I saw. She was standing in the shower, naked, smiling at me. I felt around for the towel and realized I was still staring as I dropped the first towel and handed her the second one when I finally diverted my eyes.

"Why are you blushing? After all, you did sleep with me last night and the night before."

She wrapped the towel around her and stepped out of the shower.

"So what do you have to show me? Or was that just a silly way to see me naked?"

"No, it wasn't. I…"

"I know, I know it wasn't. What did you find?"

I showed her the picture, pointing out the mark I'd found. She studied it closely, her eyes lighting up as I showed her what happened when I rotated the photo.

"How did we miss that?"

"I have no idea, but guess we need to head back out there again and take a closer look."

"I'll get dressed."

I went into the bathroom and took a quick shower with a smile on my face. After I dressed I left Anna Beth to pack and take Austin for a quick walk while I went back to the office to check out. I paid and was surprised that the manager didn't mention anything about Austin. He smiled and said, "Come back to see us soon."

I walked back to the car and I saw that Anna Beth was kneeling over beside Austin, petting his head as he licked her face. Her hair fell down in her face, reflecting the sunlight. I stopped short of the Jeep and watched her with Austin. I found myself thinking that I should have perhaps taken advantage of the opportunities that had presented themselves the night before. That and wishing that I had my camera.

As I walked up Austin turned to me with what I was sure was a smile on his face. Anna Beth rose, reaching out toward me. I took her hand and she pulled me close. I kissed her as she scratched Austin's head with one hand and held mine with the other.

"You better be careful Mr. Parks, we've already checked out of the room and have to get to the cemetery. Where was this last night?"

"Well, I'm not sure."

"We can talk about that later," she said as she kissed me again, lingering for a moment longer than I would have expected.

I felt a slight flutter in my chest as our lips parted. I was even a little lightheaded.

"Okay, then," I said as I took a deep breath.

I reached behind her and opened the door. She got in with Austin leaping over her into the back. As I walked in front of the

Jeep to my side our eyes stayed locked. I smiled as I opened my door and got in.

"Are you okay?" she questioned.

"Very ok, actually."

I was still smiling as I pulled the Jeep out of the hotel's parking lot and headed back toward the cemetery.

~~~~~~~~~~~~~~~~~~~~

There was little traffic as we drove through town, not that there were all that many people in the little town to make a lot of traffic. The ride didn't take that long, and it was understandably much easier to find as we had been there just yesterday. Even still, we missed the road our first time by. I backed up and slowly turned into the pathway, stopping just as the car cleared the road.

"Hang on a sec."

I got out and walked up the path, stopping where I'd dropped the branch the day before. It was right where I'd left it. Exactly how I left it. I stood and looked around. It was as quiet as it had been the day before, with only the sounds of nature being carried by on a cool fall breeze. I turned back and walked past the car as Anna Beth and Austin followed me with their eyes. I looked up and down the road. Not another car in sight, so I turned back to the Jeep. I got back in and put it in gear.

"Everything okay?" she said.

"Actually yes. Doesn't seem that anyone else has been here, and I don't think anyone followed us."

We drove past the tobacco fields and back to the cemetery. We parked and walked over to the headstone. I knelt and brushed the grass aside, and there was the mark.

"Well, well, look here."

Austin walked over and sniffed at the headstone, and I had to brush him away before he decided to mark it. Anna Beth laughed at me as I ran him off. He looked a little bit dejected, but saw a squirrel across the cemetery and took off after it.

"Will he be okay?" she said.

"He'll be fine, but let's see what we have here."

I carefully cleared all of the grass and weeds from the mark and then did the same all around the gravestone. It was the only one on the grave. We both crawled on our hands and knees around the grave, but we ended up back in the front looking at the same mark. It was about two inches long, pointing straight down. We couldn't tell if it was new or if it had been made at the same time as the rest of the markings on the stone. I realized that we'd been on the ground for a while when my knees started to ache.

"Okay, now what?" she said.

"Hum. I haven't really got a clue."

I rose, offered her my hand and she stood beside me.

"Let's expand out just a little bit and see if we see anything else. And we probably should see if we can't clean up those white marks."

"I'll see what I can do," she said.

She headed toward the markings setting out our circle and started pulling the grass from the ground. In a few minutes there was no sign of the circle. I spent this time examining the other graves surrounding ours to no avail.

"There, good as new. Where's Austin?"

I looked around and agreed with her that there wasn't any real sign we had been there. I didn't see Austin anywhere, so I called for him. Nothing at first, but after a few minutes I heard a rustling in the woods, and then one excited canine came running out. He dashed over to me, stopped and sat at my feet. His nose was covered with dirt, as were his feet. I brushed him off, scratched his head and went to the car to get him some water. I returned to the grave carrying a putty knife and screwdriver from my toolbox.

"What's that?" she said.

"I think we may have been outsmarted, or at least out sleuthed, by your new best friend."

"What?" she said.

I knelt back down at the base of the grave and began to probe the ground with the screwdriver. I started in front of the arrow and worked my way around the grave. When I was back at the mark, I came out several inches and began to fan out my probes on the front of the grave. Nothing for several feet on either side. I went to the back of the grave and repeated the process. About six inches out the screwdriver hit something solid. I worked my way around what I had found and located the edges. Whatever it was, it was buried several inches below the surface. I went to work with the putty knife, pulling off the top layer of soil and grass in one piece so when we were done we could leave things as we found them. After about ten minutes I uncovered the top of what appeared to be a metal box. It took another thirty minutes to get it out with my rudimentary excuse for a shovel.

It was about a foot square and had some sort of a wax-like coating on it, similar to the coating over a block of cheese. It looked as if it would weigh a substantial amount, but looks were deceiving. We filled the hole with the grass Anna Beth had pulled from the ground that I had painted. This did a pretty good job of making it look like no one had been digging around the grave. I realized that Austin and Anna Beth were following my every move.

"It looks like we may have something here," I said.

We went back to the Jeep with the box. I opened the rear door and had Austin get out after he had jumped in once. I had him lie down under a tree with a bowl of water and a couple of dog treats. I took out a knife from my toolbox and contemplated the wax coating.

"What is it?" she said.

"I have no idea, but it looks like its been in the ground for a while. Any ideas?"

"Can you take that coating off?" she said as she reached out and touched it. "It feels like it probably isn't too thick."

I ran my fingers around it looking for a seam, but found none.

"I can't even tell how long this thing's been in the ground. I'm betting that the coating is some sort of protection or waterproofing for whatever's inside."

I ran the knife across it and cut into the coating about a quarter of an inch. I ran it over the cut again and felt it hit metal. It appeared that the coating was at least half an inch thick. I cut several more times and was finally able to work my hands under it, then I started to tear it off. It was mildly adhered to the box, but with a little effort it pulled free.

"Whoever packed this sure wasn't excited about having someone stumble into whatever this is."

"Don't stop."

I looked at her, smiling and giving a little laugh at the same time.

"What?" she said.

It took me several more minutes to get the rest of the coating off, and when I did, we found that we had a slightly dingy metal box. No apparent seams, no hinges, just a metal box. From its weight, or lack thereof, it had to be hollow. We rotated it and saw that all the sides were the same. Then Anna Beth reached past me and picked up the box. She turned it completely over, and we stared at what would have been the bottom of the box from the way it had been buried. It was identical to the other five sides - that is, except for the design in the middle. Etched into the metal was the symbol for infinity over a diamond. Inside the diamond were what appeared to be Celtic designs that were suspiciously similar to those on the mysterious rod which we had, of course, left in Charleston.

"I think the word you are looking for is 'Bingo,'" she said.

"My dear, I think you are right." I looked around and saw Austin sleeping again. "Let's get packed up and on the road back to Charleston. We can look at that on the way, but I don't want to hang around here."

"Sounds like a plan to me," she said as she headed toward Austin to get his things.

He awoke, shook off and bounded over to the Jeep, hopping in the back as I packed up my tools. He sniffed at the box, then at me, then laid down in the back watching Anna Beth and me. It only took us a few minutes to get packed up and to head back down the path to the road. I looked both ways and didn't see any other cars, so I pulled onto the road and headed back toward Charleston.

~~~~~~~~~~~~~~~~~~~

On the way home we rode mostly in silence, from time to time glancing back at the box in the back seat. I wasn't sure if it was because we were uncomfortable, tired, or each just excited we had found the box. As we drove into town, Anna Beth unhooked her seatbelt and took the box from the back seat, placing it on her lap.

"It looks like it should weigh more than it does. I can't even tell if there's anything in it," she said as she picked it up and hefted it to her ear.

I got the feeling she was going to shake it.

"Better be careful there, don't know what's in it."

"Good point. What do you make of these markings?" she said.

"Well, I'm willing to bet those designs match the ones on the rod, but the diamond and infinity are new. Was your father into riddles? You know, puzzles and things like that?"

"Not that I knew of," she said.

"We can see what else we can pick up when we get home."

I reached for my phone and dialed Gabriel. He answered on the first ring.

"I'm back. Anything exciting happen?"

"Welcome back. Did we have a nice trip?"

"Generally pretty ordinary."

"Henderson's barking up a storm. He's called five times wanting to know where you are. He thinks you and Anna Beth have jumped bail and put it in the wind. He's even watching the airport. Where the hell are you?"

"About five minutes from home. Where's he?"

"He's either at your place, the airport or in between. Say, Parks, still curious about your paralegal?"

"Yes," I said.

"Noah, you sure it was her you saw in the library a few weeks back?

"Positive, why?"

"I dug around a bit. You probably know a lot of this, but she hasn't been going to school, and I'm pretty sure she hasn't been to her apartment in weeks, but there's something else."

"So, do I have to guess?" I said as I pulled into my drive and opened the garage door. Anna Beth was looking at me as I talked to Gabriel with a 'What is going on?' look on her face.

Gabriel continued. "I got her contact information from the law school. No surprise, but she listed you as an emergency contact. No parent or next of kin information. I also got a number from the temp agency, a Savannah number, but it's disconnected. I dug around on the computer and got her back as far as Savannah. Last address matches the one she gave at the temp agency, but the apartment building there burned and it's a parking lot now. Long and short of it, she's gone."

"Gone, meaning?"

"Meaning that I wouldn't worry about it. I'm sure she's hit the road. Might never hear from her again, might turn up next week."

"Thanks, I think. It's just been bothering me."

"I'll keep you posted if I pick up anything else."

"Thanks, Gabriel. I hope that's all there is to it. I'll call you later," I said.

"What was that about?" she said.

"Seems our little trip got to Henderson, but no big problem. That, and Gabriel can't find anything on Heather. It's like she disappeared."

"She's probably heartbroken that she can't have you. But of course, I'm starting to wonder if anyone can."

"And what is that supposed to mean?"

"Mind if I don't answer that now?" she said.

I smiled at her and got the same back.

We went upstairs and everything was exactly as we left it. We cleared off a space on the dining room table and set the box down. I got the metal rod and compared the symbols. They were identical. I turned the rod end over end, then stared at it a moment. I put it down and went to the closet and returned with a wide angle lens from my old Nikon F3.

"What's that?"

"It's a lens from one of my old cameras. If I look through it in reverse it acts as a pretty good magnifying glass," I said as I put the lens to my eye. "I'll be damned."

"What is it?"

I handed her the lens and she looked where I pointed. On each end of the rod there was a light etching that we had both overlooked. One was an infinity symbol, the other a diamond.

"Well, I'll be damned too."

"Guess that means that we're on the right trail. But we still have the 'what next' question. Which seems to be a common for us."

"I guess this means these two things are related. So we figure out how."

"And we would do that by?" I said.

"No clue at all."

For the next hour we sat and stared at the box as Austin slept on the floor beneath the table. We'd examined the etchings and the box in as great as detail as we could. There were no hinges, no openings, nothing otherwise distinguishing about the box except the symbols on the one side.

"So I have a question," Anna Beth said, breaking the silence.

"Please, go ahead."

She was turning the rod over and over in one hand and twirling a lock of hair with the other.

"Why is it you don't have a girlfriend? I mean, you don't have one, do you?"

Taken a bit by surprise, as I was expecting a question about the box, I answered with a question. "And what makes you think I would?"

"Like I said, either you're the most polite man I have ever met, you're gay, or you have a wife or girlfriend. I guess there's another option - you might just not be interested in me."

"I already told you I was."

"Sure you're not gay?"

"Like I said, trust me, far from it."

"Wife? Girlfriend? Both? Neither?"

"No, no wife or girlfriend."

"Then, are you just that polite?"

"I like to think I'm pretty polite. Not that much, though."

"Playing hard to get then?" she said.

"No." I rose and turned to stand in the doorway. "You always so, well, aggressive?"

"Aggressive? Now that's a bit much. I don't think I'm being aggressive at all." She smiled at me. "Not that I can't be if the situation calls for it."

"And when would the situation call for it?" I said.

"I'm not going to tell you that. Not yet, anyway."

"I guess aggressive was a little strong, huh?"

"I like to think I'm persistent. Though the circumstances are a little different than what you would normally imagine, I guess."

"Persistent. I like that."

"Good. Hopefully I'll be able to find out what else you like."

"I guess it's like this - I'm attracted to you. No secret about that. Like Gabriel said, more than I should be. But I've got a little baggage that keeps me confused. But I, maybe even we, can deal with that."

"I don't have a problem with that. Not at all."

"But there is something I should tell you. About what Gabriel said to me the other day, telling me to be careful," I said.

"Go on, I want to hear it," she said, shifting her attention away from the box to me. I pulled a chair out from the table and sat down across from her.

"I got involved with a client once before. Actually another estate I probated. We spent a lot of time together. She was going through a divorce and no, I wasn't handling it. We started seeing each other, and though we didn't even meet until after she separated, her husband didn't see it that way."

"Did he do something?"

"Yes. A lot, actually. We decided to move in together; I mean, it was more than just a casual relationship for both of us. We felt we were supposed to be together. She had been away from him for almost a year. We'd been seeing each other for about eight months," I paused. "Then he found out about it. I mean, he'd known she was seeing someone, he just didn't know who it was. He had even come to my office once demanding I tell him who her boyfriend was. I told him I had no idea. When he found out it was me, I'm sure that since I'd lied to him he believed I was the reason they broke up."

I stood in silence for a moment.

"And what happened? Did he cause problems for you? Tell someone about you seeing his wife?" she said.

"If it had only been that," I said as I shifted in my chair, moving my gaze away from her. "I'd helped her pack up her apartment, and we'd been making trips over to my house through the day. We had one more load of things to get from her place. I told her to drive to my house and I'd stop and get dinner. She loved sushi, so I stopped for takeout. When I got back to my car there was a message from Gabriel on the phone. I called him as I headed home."

"What happened, Noah?"

"You know the sushi place is just around the corner. I got him just as I was about to turn on to our, I mean my, street. He was standing at the end of my driveway on his phone. There were at least half a dozen patrol cars, several detectives' vehicles and two ambulances. Seems her husband had been waiting at my house. He'd parked his car in the cul-de-sac and waited for us to arrive, only she showed up by herself. No one's sure if anything was even said, but he shot her twice then turned the gun on himself. He even called the police about the time she was pulling into my drive."

"Oh my god, Noah, that's terrible."

"In a word, yes. They found a note at his house, and it was clear that he'd come to kill us both. Me going for sushi saved my life, but cost hers."

We sat in silence for a long few minutes.

"How long ago did it happen?" she said.

"Almost five years."

"Then I understand why Gabriel is worried about you. And I feel absolutely terrible for acting like I have."

"There's no need to feel bad. And really, I want you to stay. Having you here's been the best thing in a long time. And I *am* interested in you, very much so. It actually makes me feel better telling you about her. I've wanted to for a while, but didn't know how."

She stood up and walked around the table to me. "Come here."

I rose and walked to her. She put her arms around me and hugged me tight. She gave me a light kiss on the lips.

"Slow, we'll go slow. How's that?" she said.

"It's been perfect so far."

"Let's go to bed. We can deal with that," she motioned to the box with her head, "tomorrow."

I followed her upstairs and we went to bed with Austin at our feet. Once again, we fell asleep in each other's arms.

CHAPTER 18

I dreamed about sailing. I dreamed of being on the open water. I was on the bow of a sloop leaning over the railing, stretching out, trying to reach something in the water. Something just out of my grasp. I couldn't tell what it was. I could hear a voice shouting to me from behind. I looked over my shoulder toward the wheel of the boat and could see a figure standing, pointing at me, shouting louder. I could see the figure's lips forming the words, almost in slow motion, forming words I couldn't hear. I knew they were meant for me, but what they were, I didn't know. As I strained to hear them I felt my grip slipping. I looked to my hand and could see my fingers coming loose, but I was powerless to do anything other than watch. I was still reaching toward the water with my other hand, but I couldn't make it move to catch my fall or do anything to keep myself from the water. I tried to scream, but no words came out. The figure was still shouting at me as I fell from the boat. The waves reached up to welcome me. It was cool as I slipped beneath the surface, still unable to make my limbs work. The light from the surface faded. The voice became clear.

"Noah? Noah, what's wrong? Are you okay?"

I awoke and looked around.

Austin was crouched at the foot of the bed, tense as he studied me.

"Noah?" Anna Beth said again.

I tried to speak, but no words came. I took a deep breath, rubbed my face and rose, propping myself on my arm. Anna Beth sat up beside me and rubbed my back. I reached out and took her hand, squeezing it slightly. Struggling, I managed a smile and drew in a deep breath. After a few moments I was able to talk.

"Bad dream. Boat, water, falling. Drowning, I think."

"Noah, the woman who was killed at your house, was her name Claire?"

The memory of the dream fled from my mind. I turned to face her.

"How do you know that?" I said. She drew her hand back.

"Noah, you were yelling it over and over in your sleep."

"I was?"

"Yes, almost screaming it."

"Sorry about that. I thought those dreams had stopped. It's been almost a year since I had one."

"You let me inside last night, it's not surprising. Are you sure you're okay?

"Yes, and thanks."

I leaned over and kissed her gently on the lips.

"I'm going to go make us some breakfast," she said as she got out of bed and headed downstairs, Austin in tow.

I put my head back on my pillow and rubbed my eyes to clear the last of the sleep from my head. It was nice waking up with a beautiful woman again after so long. Gabriel was right, though, I needed to be careful. The dream was proof of that. The few times since Claire's death that I'd been involved with any woman, the dreams had come. The longer I stayed with anyone, the more frequent the dream became. Now that Anna Beth was here, so were the dreams. But I decided that I had lived long enough in the shadow of a long lost love. Dream or not, I knew I wanted Anna Beth. Besides, there was breakfast cooking, and a strange metal box to deal with.

I pulled on some clothes and went downstairs to find Anna Beth working in the kitchen, the weather channel on. It seemed the hurricane that had stirred Anna Beth to think about the GPS coordinates was gaining strength and might just have plans to stop by for a visit.

"You ever been through a hurricane?" I said.

"No, can't say that I have."

"From the looks of things, that'll probably change in the next few days."

"Lucky me."

We ate under the watchful eye of Austin, and I stared at the box on the table in the other room.

"Any new revelations about what we do with that thing on the table in there?" I asked, motioning toward the other room.

"I don't suppose by chance your dream gave you any ideas?"

"Actually, no, but I guess we could always go back to bed and see if anything…"

"Noah, you're finally flirting with me! I like that. But let's see what we can do with our latest puzzle first."

"I wasn't being serious, just, like you said… flirting."

I filled up my coffee cup. We went into the dining room and looked at the box yet again. I ran my fingers around its edges and over the sides and the bottom. I turned my attention to the one design on the box - a diamond with facets and edges etched into the metal with Celtic designs etched into the face of the diamond. On the face above the diamond was the symbol for infinity. I reached for the metal rod on the table beside the box and picked it up. I shifted my attention to the rod. The symbols were definitely the same. I picked up the lens again and looked at the ends of the rod and compared the diamond and the infinity symbols etched on the ends of the rod. Anna Beth walked in and sat beside me.

"Finding anything?"

"Not really, just looking over everything again."

She took the rod and the lens out of my hand and studied the rod herself. I watched her as she looked through the lens, shifting to allow the light from the window to fall on the rod. I looked back to the metal box and then back to her.

"Be right back," I said as I got up from the table.

I headed into the garage and plundered through some boxes until I found what I was looking for. I took a slender box back upstairs, grabbed a flash light and went back into the dining room. She was still holding the lens and the rod, but was studying the box.

"Okay, I'm baffled," she said.

"Give me a sec here, I have an idea."

I moved a chair beside her and gave her the flashlight and had her point it on the top of the box. I opened the box I had grabbed from the garage and pulled out a magnifying glass similar to one a jeweler might use. Anna Beth looked at me rather quizzically.

"My grandfather, the furniture builder, he was a machinist, and he used this to work with the small parts and components. His work fascinated me when I was a kid and, well, I ended up with his stuff. This thing, like the lens there, does the same thing, just with more magnification."

She nodded as if what I had said meant nothing to her. I held the glass over the surface of the metal and studied it. The lens had been a help, but this glass was amazing with the detail it showed. Moving it slowly I examined the surface of the box, and realized I was scrutinizing a piece of metal that was absolutely unremarkable. Under the magnification it looked just the same, only larger.

"So?" she said.

"Nothing so far. Patience, my dear."

I moved the glass over the design yet again. Nothing, absolutely nothing. I shifted back to the box and the area around the symbols. Anna Beth shifted the light.

"Hold it. Do that again," I said as my heart jumped in my chest.

She moved the light again and I studied the surface. Something looked slightly out of place, a bit different. There was a slight variation in the surface at the middle of the symbol. I rubbed at it with my finger, and I could feel a slight difference between the symbol and the surface. If I hadn't seen it, though, I may have thought the variance was from the etchings in the metal. I peered closer at the imperfection, through the magnifying lens and without it. It was invisible to the naked eye and only slightly so with the glass. Suddenly, a thought came to mind. I reached around on the table and my hand touched the metal rod. I picked it up and pushed at the imperfection with the rod. The imperfection disappeared, revealing a hole in the surface of the box.

"Did you see that?" I said.

"What did you do?"

"I was just pushing against the surface with the rod. I thought that the rod would give me a little leverage. I saw a little dent that looked about the same diameter as the rod, and well, now we have a hole."

"You thinking what I'm thinking?"

"I think I am," I said as I put the rod in the hole, the end with the indentions first.

It easily slid in, but not straight down; rather, going in at an angle. It stopped flush with the Celtic designs that started halfway up the rod. The way the rod went in, the designs on the rod blended perfectly with the design on the box. I pushed against the rod, but nothing happened. I tried turning it, but was met with the same result. Anna Beth reached over and placed her finger on the rod and rotated it around the box. Part of the face of the box rotated and rose from the box.

"Seems our mystery rod was a key," she said.

The part of the box with the design etched into it had risen out in the shape of a circle no more than three inches across. I pulled and it easily slid out from the box. A cylinder came with it that was about eight inches long. On the side near the bottom there was another hole. I slid the rod out and into the second hole. It went in and easily turned in the hole. The bottom came off. I shook the tube, and a velvet bag fell out.

"What are you waiting for, open it," she said.

The bag was soft and delicate to the touch. It had a silk drawstring that was pulled tight, but with a little tug, opened easily. I turned the bag over in my hand and then upside down. A large gold coin fell into my palm. On one side was the symbol for infinity and on the other, not surprisingly, was the symbol of a diamond. Then there was the note.

Anna Beth picked it up, unfolded it and stared at it. A tear was running down her cheek, her hand slowly rising to her face. She sat down, dropping the note to the table.

I reached for the note, and my eyes fell upon an elegant script.

"Dear Chase and Anna Beth,

THE TRUST

Not to sound cliché, but if you're reading this, something has happened to me and I am no longer with you. All I can say is that I am sorry for all that has happened, or should I say, hasn't happened between us. I could go on about the mistakes that were made and the missed opportunities, but will sum everything up by simply saying that my love for each of you knows no bounds.

Now, as you probably know, there is a trust that I established a number of years ago. Up until now this trust has served its purpose well, and may continue to do so for some time. However, for one of you, one day this trust will be all yours to do with as you see fit.

But... the one thing that I cannot do is choose between the two of you, and for my own reasons I do not feel it appropriate to divide the funds between you. I have realized during the last months the one thing a father cannot do is pick a favorite child, and the thing a father should never do is provide an influence that could affect how his children perceive him.

Regardless of what our parting words may have been or how we may have left things between us, please know that I died fulfilled in every way except for the longing that filled my heart for every moment I was unable to enjoy with each of you.

As for the coin that is with this note, when you are asked, it will be all the authority you shall ever need.

Your Father."

I stared at the note for a moment and then looked to Anna Beth. "So much for thinking Dad wasn't one for riddles and games," she said with a smile and laugh.

I looked at her to see what she did next. She sat with her knees pulled to her chest, her chin resting on them as she stared at the note on the table, just as I was coming to expect her to do when she was in deep thought. I spoke.

"So you're telling me this all means something to you, right?"

"No actually, only that Father knew something was going on. I mean, the letter was written after Daniel died. It's only addressed to Chase and me."

"I noticed that."

"But other than that, nothing jumps out at me. Am I missing something?"

"The coin has me intrigued. Obviously it's our next step, but that last sentence about authority is the only obvious clue he left us. And the coin isn't a whole lot of help. I mean it's a diamond and infinity, the same things we've been frustrated with for weeks. What do you figure it means, 'Diamonds are forever?' Was he a James Bond fan?"

She chuckled. "Actually yes, but he's not that transparent. I would imagine that at some point that will be clear, but who knows."

I studied the coin again, turning it over in my hand. The infinity symbol was engraved into the coin, but the diamond was raised. It appeared to be a hardened substance, not soft enough to be gold. But other than that, there was nothing remarkable about the coin.

"It seems that the trust is the focus now," I said.

"Meaning?"

"It's the logical place to go from here. Want to go to Ohio?"

"It does seem we're being pointed there. When do we leave?"

I was watching The Weather Channel, and it seemed the new forecast on the hurricane was the eastern seaboard of the U.S., with

Charleston being the leading candidate for landfall.

"Why don't I jump online and get a couple of tickets for us. We can leave in the morning, take a few days and see what we can find up there."

"Another trip with you, how could I say no? While you get the tickets, I'll run back to the beach house and get some fresh clothes. I've been wearing yours long enough," she said.

"I'll throw some stuff together here and then run Austin over to Gabriel's so he can watch him. That and it'll give me a chance to let him know what we're doing."

She stood and, after wiping her eyes, walked over to me and gave me kiss. She pulled me tight and ran her fingers through my hair.

"I'll be back before you know it."

I walked her to the door and almost stopped her. After all, she had been wearing my clothes for the past few weeks, what would a few more days hurt? Besides that, the oxford really looked good on her. I smiled to myself with that thought as I watched her smile and wave as she backed out of the drive. Austin stood beside me, barking as she drove down the street.

"Some friend you are. Don't worry, she'll be back."

He barked a few more times before he returned to his nap on the couch. I followed him into the den and made reservations for two for the next morning to Cincinnati, where we would rent a car for the short drive to Oxford, Ohio, the home of Cross' trust.

I packed a bag for Austin and called him down to the garage where he jumped in the Jeep. We headed to Gabriel's. When I arrived, his cruiser was in the drive and he was standing in his front yard, his hands on his hips, gazing at his front porch. I stopped and opened the door for Austin, who rushed over to Gabriel and rolled over for a belly rub.

"Hey there buddy," Gabriel said as he bent to scratch the eager canine's belly.

"Morning," I said.

"Where's your lady friend?"

"Out at Sullivan's getting some clothes."

"You guys moving in together now?"

I could tell he was halfway being serious in his question.

"She's been staying at my place lately, but no, I'm not sure what's going on with that. Heard anything from Henderson lately?"

"Word on the street is he's hit a dead end with the shirt. He's tried to get a hearing to revoke Anna Beth's bond, but the solicitor shot that idea down. I think he's just waiting, hoping she slips up."

"You know that won't happen, but I do need a favor."

"Why doesn't that surprise me?" he said. Austin jumped up and ran to his front door.

"I need you to watch him for a couple of days."

"I take it you're going somewhere?"

"In fact I am. Anna Beth and I. We're heading up to Ohio to see the trustee of her father's trust. It seems that he left it all to her."

"Really? I imagine that's a pretty hefty sum for her there?"

"It is, but I don't think it is as easy as just showing up and asking for the funds. I've tried calling in the past and they wouldn't even talk to me. So we're going up there to check things out in person."

"Now wait a minute. If they won't talk to you now, what's going to be different if you show up?"

"We've got some new info about what her father was thinking that might help, and I want to confront the trustee in person so it will take a little more to get rid of us than hanging up the phone."

"Noah, sometimes you just amaze me. The lady's out on bond and you're leaving with her? What makes you think that is okay?"

"Hey, I sent the solicitor's office notice and provided them documentation on the travel arrangements. As far as they know, it's part of her defense."

"Slick, nice and slick. You do know Henderson will go through the roof? With that money up there, he'll be convinced your headed to Canada."

"Of course."

"Now that doesn't surprise me at all. Listen, you know I'll watch Austin, but you just watch yourself."

"You know I'll be careful, but there is something going on here, and I have to find out what it is. I'm pretty sure that Anna Beth's father's death is related to Thomason's, and if I can answer that, she'll be off the hook."

"I sorta figured that was what it was all about. That, and I think someone may have a little crush on one of their clients."

"Is it that obvious?"

"Just a bit. I know I'm preaching, but watch your ass," he said.

I smiled as I said goodbye to Austin, who was obsessed with Gabriel's door. I got back in my Jeep and headed back to my place. I expected Anna Beth to be waiting for me, but she wasn't there.

I went inside and started packing. I also did a quick letter to the solicitor's office saying that Anna Beth and I were going out of town to Ohio on matters related to her case. Since they were prosecuting the case, I could give them notice and bypass Henderson. I gave them our flight information and the location of the hotel where we would be staying. I called the hotel to make the reservations and got two rooms so the solicitor wouldn't get the wrong idea. Then I called my courier to take the message over to them. I can't say that the trip would excite them, but since we would be back before they got around to it, nothing would likely be said. This took about half an hour, but still no Anna Beth. I went to the window and looked out towards the street. Nothing. I went back to the den and checked The Weather Channel again. The new updates on the hurricane were in, and it was starting to look like I may want to extend the trip to Ohio to avoid the storm.

After an hour there was still no sign of Anna Beth, and I was starting to worry.

I walked to the phone and called her cell. I heard it ring upstairs. I raced up the stairs into my bedroom where I saw her phone ringing on the dresser. I called out to her, but there was no answer. I dialed her beach house, but got the answering machine. I picked up her cell phone and went downstairs. I left a note and her cell phone for her on the counter. I got in my Jeep and headed toward Sullivan's Island.

CHAPTER 19

I raced to her beach house and realized that the Ohio trip was going to have to wait - Anna Beth's car was parked in the drive with the driver's door opened. I walked up to the front door of the house and realized that no one had been inside in a while - at least two weeks of newspapers were stacked up on the porch, some propped against the door. I called out for her and walked around and looked under the house. I even looked out on the beach, but there was no sign of her anywhere. I pulled out my cell to make a call that I wasn't looking forward to.

Gabriel answered on the first ring.

"What's going on? Been a while. Austin says 'Hi.'"

"Listen, Gabriel, I have a problem."

"Why doesn't that surprise me, Noah?"

"No, really, it's Anna Beth."

"What's wrong?" he said.

"She was supposed to meet me back at my house after I got

back from your place, but she didn't show. I waited a bit then called her cell, but she'd left it at my house. I called her beach house and got the voice mail, so I'm over here. Her car's here but there's no sign of her, and it doesn't look like anyone's been here for a while."

"Damn. Listen, call Henderson right now. He'll be pissed, but I want him to hear it from you. I'll be there quick as I can and we'll see what we can find."

"Hurry."

I ended the call, took a deep breath and called Henderson. I got him at his desk. He didn't seem surprised that she was gone, but I think he was a little disappointed that I hadn't disappeared with her. After a few choice comments directed at me, he said he was on his way. Gabriel was right, he wasn't happy. There were going to be a lot of "I told you so's."

I looked around her place again, being careful not to touch or move anything in case Henderson wanted to process the area as a crime scene. However, he was likely to just say that she'd fled the jurisdiction and try to seize the place for the department. At least it was a rental. I decided to keep the news about the coin to myself and to be a bit vague on our trip to Ohio so I didn't accidentally fuel his suspicions. I went back to my Jeep and waited, frustrated that there was nothing more I could do.

Thirty long minutes later, Gabriel arrived.

"You touch anything?" he said.

"I knocked on the door and walked around the car once."

"Good, at least you won't be giving Henderson any ammunition to help him accuse you. I mean he'll do it anyway, but you don't want to help him now, do you?"

"Tell me about it."

Henderson drove up in the yard as my words hung in the air.

"Well, well, well, why am I not surprised to see you here

Gabriel? You've been sticking your nose in this from the start. Don't suppose you know where she is do you?"

"Now Deputy, I've been in on the Thomason case since day one, and since your suspect in this murder has disappeared, I thought I better be here in case your investigation goes deeper into the crapper."

"That's Detective Henderson."

"Tell you what Deputy, I'll wait back here with Mr. Parks while you look around and find our missing girl. A top notch deputy like yourself should have her found inside of, what Noah, thirty minutes? And that's with a coffee break or two."

"Guys, how about we just try to find her," I said.

"Find her?" Henderson said. "You probably got her out of here."

"Screw you, Henderson," I said, and took a step toward him.

Henderson took off his sunglasses. "You're pretty charged up there, Parks. Maybe your girlfriend did run off on you."

"Back off," Gabriel said as he stepped between us.

Henderson glared at him, then turned and walked toward Anna Beth's car. Then he went into the beach house after getting the key and permission to enter from me. I started to follow until he ordered me back to the car and told Gabriel to keep me there.

Gabriel tried to make small talk while I paced. We watched Henderson come in and out of the beach house time and again. He was joined over the next couple of hours by several more plainclothes deputies and a number of uniformed officers. About halfway into our wait, Henderson seemed to lose control of the officers on the scene. An unmarked cruiser arrived and a uniformed officer got out with captain's bars on his collar. Henderson's boss.

I had paced a path around his car when Gabriel stopped me and made me sit in the passenger seat, threatening to cuff me if I didn't stay put. About an hour after this, the media showed up and questions started getting thrown our way. The captain sent several deputies out to put up crime scene tape to keep them back on the street.

Henderson and the detectives all came out for what must have been the twelfth time and Gabriel told me to stay put while he walked over to them. While he was gone, I began running through everything that had been going on during the past few days. I knew the answer to Anna Beth's whereabouts had to be here somewhere. We had the coin, knew about the trust, but there was something besides Anna Beth I was missing. The feelings of frustration and anger that had been building in the hours since she had left my house were getting harder and harder to keep in check. I realized I was starting to lose my temper and control over this matter when I pulled Gabriel's rearview mirror completely off the windshield as I was tugging at it to look at the reporters on the street. When I turned my gaze back to the front of the car, I locked my stare with Gabriel's. He was standing at the front of the car, arms crossed, staring at me. The sun was starting to fall in the evening sky; there was no sign of Anna Beth, and I had no idea what my next step would be or even should be. He ignored the rearview mirror I was holding in my hand as he walked around to the passenger window and leaned down to me.

"You're not gonna believe this - course then again, maybe you will. Bad news is, Henderson is convinced you had something to do with her going missing. Good news is he's the only one that thinks it. They want you to come and walk through the house, see if anything strikes you as being out of place or missing. You up to it?"

"Sure, it'll make me feel like I'm doing something besides sitting."

We walked up to the house past her car, and as I glanced in it a scrap of paper caught my eye. I paused for a moment, looking at it. Something about it was familiar.

"Dammit it, Parks, get your ass in here," Henderson yelled, which prompted a barrage of questions from the media on the street. I lingered a moment longer at the car then headed to the house.

Henderson scowled at me as I climbed the steps to join the other officers, Gabriel in tow. I smiled at him as I walked by. Within five minutes of being inside, I knew she hadn't been in the house that day. Not that I had been there enough to be able to notice if any small items had been removed, but she hadn't spent any significant amount of time at the house in a few weeks and the house had the look of neglect. She'd been coming to get some clothes and there was nothing in her bedroom that looked at all like she'd been packing or had even been there. I joined the detectives in the living room.

"I don't see anything missing, and I don't think she was inside here today."

"Whatever, Parks," Henderson said.

I took a step toward him, but a deputy stepped between us.

"Henderson, shut the hell up," his captain said. Looking back to me the same time, the detective said, "What makes you say that?"

I looked at Henderson. "Everything looks pretty much exactly the same as it did the last time I was here. That and when I got here there weren't any footprints from her car to the door."

"What, you a detective now, Parks? God dammit, why don't you just tell us where she is. You get her hooked up and out of the country?"

"Henderson, for the last time, shut the hell up. What he's saying makes sense. It doesn't look like anything's been moved or taken, and you said there were papers propped against the door when you got here. Since she's out on bail we're going to get on looking for her as her going missing does make for a bit of a problem. Now, Mr. Parks, you have any plans for any travel anytime soon?" the captain said.

Someone had actually checked travel plans. That told me that Henderson wasn't heading this investigation up, which actually gave me a little comfort that Anna Beth may actually get some attention.

"I'd planned to go to Ohio with Ms. Cross tomorrow to follow up on a lead in her case, but I think I'll be staying here until I find out where she is."

I could tell the captain liked my answer. He was about to speak when Henderson started up one more time.

"I say we take him to the station 'til he tells us where she is."

"Excuse me a moment, Mr. Parks," the captain said as he walked toward Henderson. He walked him out of the living room and out of the house. I heard raised voices from the porch, but couldn't tell what was being said. A few minutes later the captain came back in the house. Without Henderson.

"Ok, Mr. Parks, I'm Captain Collins. Don't think we've met before, but I know you have a solid reputation." I shook his hand and nodded my thanks to him.

"Henderson's been handling this case and makes his feelings toward you pretty obvious. He'll be keeping the case, but I'm going to be handling Ms. Cross' disappearance. Now, I'm of the same opinion as you that Ms. Cross didn't come in the house, but that doesn't mean that she hasn't skipped bail. There's not a lot here to go on, and her car left like it was could mean she wants to make it look like something happened, or it could mean something did happen. I'm inclined to believe that you didn't have anything to do with it, but I'm also going to ask you to stay in town for a bit while we look into this. I'll probably have some more questions, but for now, why don't you go on home."

"Well, actually, if…" I started, but Gabriel, who had been standing off to the side of the room, spoke up.

"I'll make sure Noah gets home. Listen, Collins, if you would, could you keep me in the loop on this? You know, with the tie in to Thomason and all?"

"Sure Gabriel. I was going to offer Mr. Parks a ride if he wanted, but if you can get him home, I'd appreciate it. And I'll be sure to keep you up to speed."

"Come on, Noah," Gabriel said.

I started to protest, but he walked me toward the door. It was a moonless night, clear with a sky full of stars. With the hurricane coming, this would probably be the last we saw of the night sky for a few days. I looked up at them as I walked toward my car.

"I know you want to find her but Collins has it. Be glad someone other than Henderson's heading it up. Hell, if it was him, he'd probably have arrested you. Now, follow me home, stay at my place tonight. They'll be looking for her, don't worry. And before you say anything, there's not a thing you can do except stay out of the way."

I nodded as I got in the Jeep and followed him to his place. At least Austin was excited to see me as I walked inside. Gabriel asked if I wanted to talk about Anna Beth. I thanked him and told him that I'd rather just get some sleep. I was worried, frustrated, and was completely without options as to what I could do. I went to the guest bedroom, laid down, stared at the ceiling and wondered what the hell was going on.

I kept playing through the letter from her father, Anna Beth's reaction, everything over and over in my head. It was a lot of information and I knew that the answer had to be there, but I just couldn't put my finger on it. I didn't believe that Anna Beth had gone on the lam, it served no purpose. I knew someone had to have taken her. I glanced over to the nightstand where the coin rested upon the letter that had been in the velvet pouch. I'd picked both of them up when I left my place earlier in the evening to go to her beach house. It was going to be challenging enough to figure out what the coin meant, but now I had to figure out where Anna Beth was. The thoughts of all this danced in my head. I decided on a course of action that required me to be somewhere other than Gabriel's house. Looking at the clock, I saw that I had been there for almost three hours. I got up, slipped on my shoes and carefully opened the bedroom door. I peered out and started to walk slowly and quietly to the front door.

"Sleepwalking?" Gabriel said.

"Dammit, you're supposed to be in bed."

"Actually, I think it is the other way around."

I turned around and headed back to the bedroom and back to bed. At some point I drifted off to sleep. I knew that because the next thing I knew, I was sitting bolt upright. The bedside clock told me it was just after six in the morning. I got up and after a quick shower got dressed and went out to the kitchen, where Gabriel was making breakfast.

"I think I may have an idea about what's going on. I don't know where Anna Beth is, but I think I may have a good idea how to find her."

"Noah, what the hell are you... Wait, you're not going out looking for her."

"Just listen, I sorta need your help again," I said.

He rolled his eyes as I spoke.

"I'm going to head back over to my house, which, if I am right, will have been broken into and trashed, just like my office was.

From there I am going to go down to my office, and I need you to meet me there. I'll know more next time we talk, but I need to go now."

"Damn you're acting strange. And who trashed your house? I mean, how do you know that?"

"I don't know who, just trust me for a bit. As soon as I'm sure, I'll fill you in. I mean I'll have to because I'll need you to help me. Right now I need to find Anna Beth, and I don't think there's that much time."

"It's a good thing I've known you as long as I have, cause you're talking crazy right about now."

"I'll talk to you in about an hour," I said.

"No, you won't."

"What do mean?" I said.

He turned off the stove, walked over to his dining room table and picked up his keys. "If you think you're onto something, good, but, I'm coming with you."

~~~~~~~~~~~~~~~~~~~~~~~

We left and headed to my house. As soon as we drove up and saw the front door ajar, I knew I was onto something. I ran in and looked around. Just as I'd suspected, my place had been trashed. Surprisingly, though, the box was still there under the table where we'd left it, but the rod that had been my obsession for the last few weeks was gone. I smiled to myself and sat down at my computer while Gabriel looked through the rest of the house. It only took me a few minutes to type what I needed. Gabriel didn't find anything in the rest of the house, so we headed to my office. Before we left, I folded what I had typed and put it in an envelope.

We arrived at my office, went inside and retrieved a key from my desk. Then I went into my conference room and took my Black's off of the shelf. I opened it and pulled out several photographs. I laid them out in front of me and examined them. In each photograph, there it was - the infinity symbol or a diamond, just like on the rod and the coin. Gabriel looked confused, and a bit surprised.

"Let's go," I said. "Take me to Cross' house."

"You're serious?"

"Yep. Take me there then go back to my house. Not to sound too bossy, but the place is trashed and a few things are missing. See what else you can find. Hold by your cell and I'll give you a call as soon as I find what I need."

"Dammit it, Noah, what the hell are you getting at here? Letters, photographs, Cross's house... We're not going another inch until you tell me."

"You serious?" I said.

He turned the car off and pulled the keys from the ignition, dangling them in front of my face.

"Okay. I guess you are."

I took a breath and laid it out for him. Fortunately I'd been thinking about it enough to the point that it was fairly simple to explain. I was actually happy he had pressed me on it, because as I told him I realized that one thing I had been missing was a second opinion on my theory. I looked at him when I finished.

"Damn Parks, that just might make sense. But what the hell do I need to be back at your house for? If what you're thinking is really happening, I need to be trying to find out where Anna Beth is or watching your ass." He started the car and headed to Cross' house. "You find what you need at Cross's and I'll see if I can't figure anything out on where Anna Beth might be. I'll pull around the corner and keep an eye on the place while you're inside."

I had to admit, his plan made sense. There was no need to split up, and it made the most sense for me to go inside and look since I had the best knowledge of what I was after, leaving him free to watch my back.

"Okay, sounds like a plan," I said.

I got out of his car and watched him drive around the corner. I walked up to the door, pulled the key from my pocket and opened it.

~~~~~~~~~~~~~~~~~~~~~~~~~~~~~

I entered and looked around. It looked exactly the same as it did every time I had been in the house, but given my new theory, there were a number of differences that jumped out at me. Actually, there were lots of differences – mostly diamonds and infinity symbols. I started examining them one by one. They had been here all along, but I hadn't known what I was supposed to look for. It took me less than an hour to find what I had suspected was hidden in the house - a single page letter. It only took me a few minutes longer to read it and to confirm my suspicion. The answer I found was quite interesting.

I realized that most of my questions had been answered, and suddenly everything made sense. I was more than a little upset with myself for missing something that was now so obvious, but the one question that remained unanswered was where the hell was Anna Beth. I knew who had taken her, and this was all the more reason that Gabriel and I had to find her fast, but I still had no idea where she was.

Then it hit me.

I headed toward the front door, locking it as I left. Gabriel was waiting for me around the corner.

"Find what you were looking for?"

"I did," I said with a smile on my face.

"What's so funny?"

"I'm convinced that I'm right, and I think I know where Anna Beth is. Did you have any luck running anything down?"

"Unfortunately not, but what are you thinking?"

I told him my theory and was glad that I hadn't had him go back to my house. If I was going to avoid breaking any laws, I was going to need a cop with me. Surprisingly, he was driving before I was done. He said that from what I had come up with he had an idea that might just tell us exactly where to look for Anna Beth, but we needed to go back to his house to be sure.

He drove to his house and I waited in the car while he went inside. I pulled the letter I had done on my computer at home out of my pocket and read it again. After what I had found at Cross' house, I was confident that what I had just planned could work. I put the letter back in my pocket and pulled out the letter I had found at Cross'.

Mr. Parks:

I would imagine that by the time you read this you have become somewhat acquainted with me. If not through my friend Steven, perhaps through either my daughter or my son, or perhaps both. However, regardless of this, I do owe you an explanation as to why you are involved and are now reading this letter. I will start with Steven. I've known Steven for many years and always find it amusing whenever he first meets someone on either a professional or personal basis. He can be a bit standoffish and overwhelming. Thank you for what I am certain has been a great deal of patience on your part. I also want to thank you for your assistance as I would imagine, if you are reading this, you have completed, if are not nearly through with your work on my behalf.

I also apologize for the game of cat and mouse, but for reasons that you have likely come to understand, it had to be done. I love my children dearly and want to make sure that no outside influences, no matter how entitled they may think they are, interfere.

However, you are likely asking the question, "Why me?" Given the circumstances, that would be quite the reasonable question to ask, and one to which I believe you deserve an answer.

As you are no doubt aware, my life has been one of professional triumph but at the expense of personal reward in regard to my children. I have lived a life of reluctant distance and separation from my children, and that has been my one regret. When it came time to finalize my affairs, I realized I needed someone who was truly removed and had no personal stake in my estate to coordinate the legal aspects of my estate. This is where you came in. I lived in your fair city for some years and every attorney I met, not to demean your profession, only convinced me that I really didn't like attorneys. At the time I revised my Last Will and Testament, using the fine work Steven had done as a guide, I began a search for an attorney who could aptly serve as counsel to my Personal Representative. If you are reading this, then you are likely aware that I secreted certain items some miles from Charleston in a small town. Your small town. After I found the grave of a woman who shared my deceased wife's name, I needed an attorney who knew the area where I had located this grave and who was also from Charleston.

It seems you are the only Charleston attorney that meets these qualifications. I guess you could say you were chosen by the trust I have in the understanding of strangers.

As is many times the case, I wish we could have met under different circumstances, but after I learned of you and watched you for sometime, I was struck by your sense of dedication to your profession and the likelihood of your diligence in my service. I knew then that I had made the correct decision in you. Fate, it seems, was kind to us. I want to thank you for your assistance, and will end by asking only that you do what you feel is best in regards to my children.

Leo Cross."

I'd expected another message from Cross when I went to his house, but I really thought I would find something explaining the coin. I'd been a little bit surprised to find this letter, but it made sense that he'd have left it for me. However, knowing what I did now, it also made perfect sense that he'd want someone coordinating things that had no attachments and had no chance to form any opinions prior to undertaking the work Cross wanted done. I also knew it would be no problem at all to look after his daughter. I put the letter in the glove box of Gabriel's car.

The door to the car opened and a smiling Gabriel got in.

"Parks, I take it back."

"What?" I asked.

"Remember how I said you were the one that got them off and I was the one that put them in jail?"

"Yeah, why?"

"You hit the nail on the head. Seems we have a suspect in the disappearance of Ms. Anna Beth Cross," he said as he started the car and turned quickly into traffic. He handed me a piece of paper with an address written on it. I smiled in anticipation as we drove out of town.

CHAPTER 20

We headed out of town, away from the peninsula, past the business district on toward the outskirts of town into the industrial area that was dotted with shipping container depots, factories and strip clubs. We turned off the Meeting Street extension, past a row of abandoned houses and empty lots and into the parking lot of an old warehouse that had been divided into three separate businesses. The businesses were all closed and in varying states of disrepair. We stopped below a faded sign that read, "Newell's Drafting," "Allied Contracting, Inc.," and "The Velvet Cougar." Two blue collar establishments and a strip club, how appropriate for the area.

It had taken us less than fifteen minutes to drive to the address that Gabriel had dug up. On the way, I found myself wondering just how we were going to approach this once we arrived. I truly believed that Gabriel was behind me in my theory, but it was just a theory at this point. I was wondering if he was going to call in backup as soon as we got there or if he would wait to make sure I wasn't about to smear egg all over his face.

"I take it we're not in need of a builder or a draftsman," I said, looking at the sign.

"Well, like I've always said, you're a quick study. From what you've been telling me, this is probably where things got going, but it doesn't look like anyone's here. Tell you what," he said as he opened the glove box and pulled out a nine millimeter Glock that he put in his ankle holster. "Hang back here and let me take a look around. We can decide what's next after that. And Parks, that first part, I'm serious - keep your ass in the car."

"Dammit, Gabriel. Anna Beth might be in there and if…"

"Yes, she might be, and if she is, I damn well guarantee that she isn't alone, and I don't need to be watching your ass too. Let me do what I do. You got us here, now let me see what's up. If I see anything, I'll get backup and we can go from there."

"Okay, okay, just hurry, dammit," I said.

He got out of the car and walked past the door to the drafting business. He peered in through a tear in the newspaper-covered door. I watched as he tried the door, but it appeared locked. He removed the Glock from his holster and walked toward the side of the building, where an arrow under a neon cougar pointed toward the rear of the building. He turned, pointed at me and motioned for me to stay put. We locked eyes for a moment before he disappeared around the side of the building. I shifted in the seat and looked around the parking lot. Not another car in the lot. Not another car in sight, or another person for that matter. The sky that had been clear the night before was starting to cloud with feeder bands from the approaching hurricane. The wind had picked up to a brisk breeze, hinting at stronger winds soon to come.

I checked my watch every minute for the next ten minutes. My clock watching was punctuated with a rather unfruitful search of the car. The sole fruit of my search was a flashlight from the back seat. I checked my watch again – twenty minutes had passed, but still no sign of Gabriel.

I was starting to get anxious. Anxious and worried. Anxious, worried, and most importantly, impatient. I opened the car door and got out. I studied the building. Never having needed a contractor or any drafting, and not having been a patron of the local exotic dance halls, this was my first time visiting this building. I walked around the car once and put my hands on my hips. He'd been gone too long. I popped the trunk, hoping for a weapon of some type, but he didn't even have a tire iron in there. How does a cop not have anything other than a flashlight in his car? I shut the trunk lid, grabbed the flashlight from the back seat and carefully shut the door.

I walked around the building, halfway expecting, halfway hoping to see Gabriel walking back toward me, but there was no sign of him. I circled the building once, walking past a back door, hoping he'd be back at the car when I got back to the front of the building. Nothing. I looked around, hoping to see something that would give me a little insight as to what was going on inside, but nothing. And still no Gabriel. It was getting progressively darker from the clouds, even though it was only early afternoon. As I scanned the parking lot it struck me that, despite my careful efforts and my hope that something else was there, it really was just a garden variety parking lot. One you would expect to find at any abandoned building. I took a few steps back and looked at the surrounding buildings, but they looked as vague and abandoned as the one I was standing before.

I walked the building's perimeter from the front again. The strip bar had three doors; a main entrance on the side, a back door, and another set of doors in the front. As I approached the corner of the building on the end with the strip bar, I looked down and saw something in the parking lot that looked slightly out of place. I walked over to it and bent to examine it - it was small square of white fabric. I poked at it with my right index finger then picked it up. The edges were freshly torn, and it showed no sign of extra dirt or grime. It looked to me like it was a recent addition to the parking lot. I turned it over and saw it was a tag from a dress shirt, a dress shirt made from Egyptian cotton. A dress shirt made in a downtown men's store that I just happened to frequent. It also just happened to be from the same kind of shirt that Anna Beth had favored whenever she raided my closet.

She was here.

She had to be inside. I stood and walked back to toward the strip bar. Neither the front or side door were unlocked. However, when I made my way to the back, I found the rear door unlocked. I looked around again - still no sign of Gabriel. I took a deep breath, gripped the flashlight and slowly pushed the rear door open. With no sound it swung inward. The interior was pitch black save for a small sliver of light down the hall, and the few feet inside a door was illuminated by the waning light from outside. In between the door and the faint light down the hall seemed an eternity of blackness. I felt a trickle of sweat run down my neck.

Maybe Gabriel was right, I should be waiting in the car. What the hell was I thinking? He was clearly inside the building, so what choice did I have?

I looked around the rear of the building for something to prop open the door, but came up empty. I crossed the threshold and stepped inside, easing the door shut behind me. It wasn't until then that I realized how dark it actually was. As I started to click on the flashlight I took a step down the hall, but I tripped and landed on my face. The flashlight slid away from me down the dark hall, not having come on. Slowly it came to me that I must have hit my head in the process as it was beginning to throb. I also realized that I must have been out for a minute or two as I was lying completely still. I felt around on the floor for the flashlight, and after a few moments found it further down the hall. Grasping it, I struggled to my knees. As I did, I heard a faint whimper behind me. A check of my scalp came away with my fingers damp and sticky, warm, copper tasting. Great, I was bleeding. Fortunately, it didn't seem too bad. I turned my attention to the whimper behind me and remembered the flashlight. In the soft glow of the light, Gabriel was sprawled out just inside the door. I hadn't seen him there when I first opened the door.

There was a gash on the back of his head and a good bit of blood, but fortunately it didn't seem to be bleeding at the moment. I rolled him over. He seemed to be fading in and out of consciousness.

"Gabriel. Gabriel," I said, careful to keep my voice low.

He opened his eyes and tried to speak, but no words came out.

"Easy, buddy, I'll go call for an ambulance."

"Anna Beth," he said.

"What?"

He tried to speak, but it was too much for him and I couldn't make out the words he was trying to say. He raised his arm slightly, pointing toward the door at the end of the hall before he collapsed in my arms as he lost consciousness. I thought he was dead until he started to take shallow breaths that, after a few more, became regular. His pulse was strong, but he was out cold. Looking him over I couldn't find any more wounds or other signs of trauma, not that the head wound wasn't bad enough.

Music was coming from down the hall behind the door Gabriel had just pointed to. A guitar – "Sleepwalking" by Johnny and

Santo, which was rather spooky given the present circumstances. I'm pretty sure it was probably fairly loud, but the sound of my heart pounding in my head was overpowering. I started to rise when I remembered Gabriel's gun - it wasn't in his holster. Looking around, I didn't see it on the floor either.

Great, I thought to myself. This was going to have to be on charm alone. It reminded me of bringing a knife to a gunfight, or in my case, a flashlight to a gunfight. I knew that I should go call for help, but I was sure Anna Beth was down there, and I wasn't going to let her wait.

I stood up and felt my head again - the bleeding seemed to have stopped. I checked the walls for a light switch and found nothing. I held the flashlight out to the side and walked slowly down the hall. There were no other doors between the entrance and the door with the faint light at the end of the hall. As I approached it, I realized that the light I had been seeing was actually a light from a taped-up sign over the door shining from where the tape had peeled back over time. In reality the hallway leading from the entryway to the second door wasn't even ten feet, but from the first door, the darkness had made it seem further, and the light from the sign had created an odd perspective for me. I felt the door first, then put my ear to it and listened. The music was louder, actually winning out over the pounding in my head, but the pounding was still a close second. I tried the doorknob - it was unlocked. I slowly opened it, crouched to the side, looked through the opening and pushed it open.

Another hallway. At least this one was lit, well relative to the first. I glanced back down the hallway from where I had just come. I checked each side beyond the doorway and didn't see anything. It was dark, lit by another "Exit" sign at the far end of the hall. There were several doors along the hallway on each side, none of them open. Over each there was a single number, and over the "Exit" sign was another reading "Stage."

My heart pounded in my chest to complement my head. With my back to the wall I worked my way slowly down the hall, resisting the urge to yell Anna Beth's name.

Door number one.

No light behind the door. The doorknob turned - it was unlocked. Being careful to stay to the side of the door, I opened it slowly, crouched again and looked inside. More darkness. Inside the door I found the light switch.

Click.

The room was instantly bathed in a lavender hue. It was a dressing room for the dancers. Looking to the ceiling, I saw that the lavender hue came from the filtered fluorescent bulbs. I stuck my head inside, checking behind the door. Nothing. The room was empty, with no sign of anyone even having been in the room for some time. I stopped and looked at a mirrored wall lined with bulbs. The mirror was covered with scrawled symbols. Almost immediately diamonds and infinity symbols jumped out at me. I backed out into the hallway.

One door down, three to go. I worked my way down the hall with my back to the wall. I stopped just across from the next door and quickly stepped across the hall. I stood beside it and placed my ear against it. No sound, nor did I see a light from under the door. I tried the knob - unlocked. I crouched, reached up slowly and pushed. It opened. There appeared to be nothing inside. I reached inside with my hand.

Click.

Light filled the room. This appeared to be a storeroom, an empty storeroom. Nothing behind the door. I stepped inside. The walls were lined with empty shelves. I backed up to the door, glancing over my shoulder as I did so.

I slid into the hall with my back to the wall as before. Johnny and Santo were starting over for the third time as I looked to the next door. There was no sound other than the music from the far door. This door was locked. I placed my shoulder against it and pushed. It gave a slight bit then suddenly exploded inward. I crashed through, falling to the floor for the second time in the last half hour. Somehow I managed to keep a grip on the flashlight as I landed, though I hit my head again. I paused and looked at the door, thinking that with all the noise I was about to have a visitor, but no one came. If anyone was there maybe they hadn't heard me over the music. I rose to my feet and looked back to the wall where the light switch should be.

Click.

Nothing. On came the flashlight. Another dressing room, but this one was a little different. Someone had been in here. Recently. There was a mess at one of the makeup stations, lots of torn scrap bits of paper that appeared to be labels torn from the jars and bottles on the counter. A cot sat against the far wall. More scrawling on the mirror. But there was no Anna Beth. Three doors down, one to go. I felt my head again. At least the fall hadn't caused me to start bleeding again. I walked back to the door and glanced into the hallway. Clicking off the flashlight, I stepped into the hall. I didn't bother with putting my back to the wall. I was certain that whatever I was here for was behind the last door. I walked to the end of the hall and stopped under the sign that read "Stage."

"Okay, and behind door number four," I said as I took a deep breath.

I reached to the knob – unlocked. I wanted to think I'd snuck up on whoever was behind the door, but I was smart enough to know that I was headed right to where I was wanted. I tried to think up a plan, but I came up blank. All I could think about was Anna Beth and getting to her. I turned the knob and pushed the door open. The music got louder as it opened. I stepped through the door into complete blackness. I backed through the open door and slid down the wall inside, closing the door as I did so, being careful that it didn't latch since I didn't want to cut off my one sure path of escape. I stood for several long moments letting my eyes adjust to the darkness that slowly morphed to a rather nondescript and featureless gray. I was in the backstage area of the club where the entertainers waited before going into the spotlight.

From a narrow, faint sliver of light in front of me I gathered that the stage was that direction, through the curtain that was before me just out of arms reach. I looked around, but could make little out in the way of details. I walked to the curtain before me, adrenaline surging. Parting it slightly, I looked through it to the stage. A spotlight shone onto an empty stage that made it impossible for me to see into the bar beyond. With few other options, I stepped out onto the stage, holding the flashlight in my right hand and squinting my eyes. I was quite astonished that this was the best plan I had been able to come up with. Hopefully it was foolish enough that it would confuse whoever waited beyond the stage. I walked to the edge of the stage, shielded my eyes from the spotlights and looked out to the floor. Nothing. That couldn't be, I thought. I jumped down from the stage and my eyes adjusted to the dim light.

The club could have held about three hundred people between maybe twenty-five or thirty tables, barstools and general standing room. Except for a few of the tables in the shadows, I could see almost everywhere in the place. I walked over to the bar, set down the flashlight, leaned over and looked behind. Nothing. This was all starting to become quite confusing. No one in the bar, but Gabriel was out cold at the back door. The stage was awash in the light from the spot above. I crossed my arms in thought as Johnny and Santo started over yet again. Damn song was starting to grate on my nerves. I turned to go investigate the front entrance of the bar, then it hit me – the DJ booth. I looked around and saw it on the far side of the bar. There was no way to get to it other than walking straight across the room.

The booth was raised and, in total, about nine feet high. It was solid from the floor up to about the height of six feet, then enclosed by plexi-glass on all sides. Keeping far enough back so I could see if there was anyone standing in the booth, I walked to it. On the far side of the booth, away from the bar, there were three steps leading up to a door. Everything about this place was another closed door. It was unlocked -the DJ booth was empty.

"Dammit," I thought.

I stepped in and looked around. There was a control panel with a mixer. I quickly located the master volume and ended Johnny and Santo's run. Silence filled the bar. I also found the controller for the stage spotlight, but didn't turn it off as this was the only light illuminating the room. I looked over the controls two more times, but there were no switches or controls for the house lights. I gazed back toward the bar. The house lights had to be there. Awash in silence, the bar took on an eerie quality. Whoever was in here had to be about to burst from holding back their laughter watching me bumble around.

Looking around once more, I decided that the best move was to head to the front door and get to Gabriel's car. This was looking more and more like a trap when suddenly I saw a shape in the shadows on the wall opposite the DJ booth. A figure sat at one of the tables. I couldn't make out a face, or even if it was a man, woman, or maybe even a cardboard cutout. My heart went into overdrive and the adrenaline that had subsided surged once more. I ruled out the cardboard cutout as the shadow turned slightly. Even though I couldn't see a face, I could feel the figure's gaze burning into my stare. A chill ran down my back. I realized that the flashlight, my one excuse for a weapon, was on the bar across the room.

"So, you know why I'm here. Care to fill me in?" I said.

Nothing. I waited for several long seconds, my heart pounding even harder. The chill kicked back in.

"Going to make me guess? Tell you what, we'll sit down and talk it over."

I opened the booth's door and walked down the three steps, stopping at the bottom to face the figure. I waited for some response that didn't come.

"If you're not going to invite me over, I'll just do it myself."

Taking a deep breath, I walked over to the table, my heart rate increasing with each step, the pounding in my head returning. The figure's features slowly started to come into focus with each passing step. I was about three feet away when I realized it was Anna Beth.

"Good god, are you okay?" I said as I rushed to her. When I got to her, I realized her mouth was taped and her arms were tied behind her. She had a terrified look on her face, and her eyes looked past me to the DJ booth.

Anna Beth's eyes grew wider.

"Hold on, I'll get you loose."

I smiled at her, hoping to calm her, but from the look on her face I realized I had failed. Miserably. She started to shake her head as I knelt beside her. I placed my hand on the side of her face, but that didn't help either. I reached up to her mouth and grabbed the edge of the tape.

"Take a deep breath, this'll hurt a good bit."

I pulled the tape hard and fast. Anna Beth gasped as I did. As the tape came off, she took a deep breath. I threw the tape aside and reached behind her to take the tape off of her arms. As I did, she bent her head to my ear and whispered a single word. It was soft and faint, but clear as a bell. It was also the last thing I heard before everything went black.

"Heather," she said.

CHAPTER 21

"*I'm not nearly over you. I'm not nearly over you. Don't know what to do now, because I'm not nearly over you.*"

A song, I knew this song. God did my head hurt. I didn't remember going out drinking last night. Wait, Anna Beth. Gabriel. Something was wrong with them. Where the hell was I? I couldn't clear my head. I needed to concentrate and get my thoughts under control.

I opened my eyes, but nothing was in focus - everything was a dark, gray blur. My head was heavy. I tried to raise it and pain exploded behind my eyes. My arms flew to my head, or should I say my arms wanted to fly to my head, but for some reason my arms weren't working. I realized that the reason they weren't working was that they were tied behind me. I shook my head and discovered that was entirely the wrong thing to do. This effort was greeted by yet another explosion of pain behind my eyes. When I opened them again, the CD was several more songs along, so it was apparent that I had once again passed out. I took a deep breath, moved my eyes from left to right and slowly began to raise my head to look around, being careful to keep one step ahead of the pain that was lurking in the reaches of my mind.

I remembered finding Anna Beth.

I was able to keep my head up. I was still in the strip club, tied to a chair in the middle of the stage. The spotlight was on, with me as the main attraction. I tried to look over my right shoulder, stopping just as the pain started to rush back. I shook my head once more and saw Anna Beth tied to a chair a few feet beyond me, just out of the spotlight. Her head was slumped to her chest, her hair falling haphazardly around her face. I glanced around the club but couldn't see a thing. I squinted my eyes against the spotlight and looked to the front door. I couldn't be sure, but the faint light I'd seen when I'd been standing at the bar earlier seemed to be gone. I guessed it was after nightfall - that or the storm had darkened things up. I had no idea how long I had been out, what time it was or even what day it was.

I needed to do something, but I'd come across few options since I had started to come to my senses.

I called to Anna Beth, but there was no response. I pulled against what I guessed was duct tape on my arms. Nothing but a dull ache. I called to Anna Beth again. Nothing. I turned my head toward her, waiting for the all too familiar explosion of pain that thankfully never came. I didn't see any obvious signs of injury on her, though with her out I couldn't be sure. I heard a slight groan escape her lips. I hoped that meant she was coming to.

"Anna Beth. Anna Beth," I said.

"Poor Noah," a voice said. "All alone in the spotlight and no one to share it with. Story of your life, isn't it?"

I remembered. I remembered the last word I had heard Anna Beth say before I had fallen into the darkness.

"Heather. I've been worried about you."

I looked to where I thought the voice had come from, but the glare of the light was all I could see.

"And I've been worried about you too, Noah."

The voice was coming from everywhere. The PA - she was on the PA. I looked toward the DJ booth.

"So how have you been?" I said.

I squinted my eyes again and thought that I could just make out her figure behind the booth. An uncomfortable silence set in as I waited for her response.

"How's your head?" she said.

I started to answer as a chill ran down my spine. Fingers running through one's hair have a way of doing that.

"Noah, it's so good to see you," she whispered in my ear.

"Nice place you have here, Heather. Never figured you for a patron of the arts."

I turned my head to her voice as I saw her appear from the shadows. As I watched her I found Gabriel's gun - it was in Heather's hand.

"What have you been up to Heather?"

"Oh, Noah, I think you know."

"I have an idea, but why don't you tell me."

"Noah, this isn't easy. You know I really like you, but you certainly know I have to kill you if I'm going to pull this off. What's actually going to happen, at least as far as everyone else is concerned, is that Anna Beth is going to kill you just before I escape trying to save you," she said. "Only you won't quite make it."

"I sorta thought it would have to work out like that. I mean, how else can you explain everything and tie it all together?"

"Now Noah, I know you love the movies where the villain explains everything just before his downfall, but that's just not going to happen here. I needed you and Anna Beth here, and now I can wrap everything up. There's no need to draw things out, I just hate too much drama."

"I guess I played that right to you, huh? Well, if you're not going to tell me, how about letting me tell you?"

"Interesting. If I hadn't stopped your friend out there I'd think you were stalling for some time, but no one's coming. Unfortunately, we're on a tight schedule. Tell you what, I have to move things around in here. If you want, go ahead and tell me what you think while I work. For old time's sake?" she said.

"I've been wondering how much of it I got right. Let's see, I take it you have the medallion. You probably took it out of my pocket just now since it wasn't at my place last night."

"Good for a start," she said as she sat down several tables over from Anna Beth. She reached into her jeans pocket and held it up in the spotlight, the gold reflecting as she studied it. She was facing the stage but also looking at the door to the club. I was trying to buy some time, but I was running out of options.

"It is a neat looking thing isn't it?" she asked as she sat the medallion down on a table.

"I thought it was," I said.

She moved tables around and knocked chairs on the floor, making it look like a struggle. My questioning didn't seem to be working.

"I'd been wondering about that actually, you finding it and all. Mostly about how you did it without anything to help. That was good, impressive even," she said.

312

"Wondering about what? You mean who broke into my office? I mean, I know you weren't wondering who did it."

"Now Noah, it pretty obvious that I was the one in your office. I mean, there's nothing in there that anyone would ever want. I'm a little surprised that you didn't pick up on the fact it was me before today."

"Nothing in there that anyone would want unless you count the Cross file."

"Right, except the Cross file. That's what I was wondering about. See, about that time I knew you were onto something, so yes, I took the file. I needed to slow you down until I could figure out how to get into the safe deposit box, but somehow you still managed to get in. That was good, I must say," she said.

"Yea, it was wasn't it?"

"I thought about it a while and all I can figure is that you had another copy of the will at the office."

"Bingo," I said. "Though your getting the probate file from the Court, that was impressive."

"That was pretty good, wasn't it? It was really pretty easy - came on to a clerk and asked for a late night visit to play in the Courtroom. Though I wouldn't have had to do that if you had been a little more cooperative yourself. I threw myself at you which would have taken care of all of this, might have even made you and me partners, but, good god, Noah, you started screwing this..." she pointed at Anna Beth. "I was actually convinced you were gay. It was easier with my clerk at the probate court. One time in the sack and his keys were mine."

"Which really didn't help you any," I said.

She stopped her work and turned back to me.

"No, and it didn't even slow you down. I was astounded when you found the medallion. Thanks, by the way. You did all the work for me and I didn't even have to follow you on your little trip. I hope the two of you had fun."

She slid a chair over from the side of the stage, the back of it facing me. She sat down and rested her arms on the back, still holding the gun.

"Noah, what am I going to do with you?"

"I'll admit, I am stalling for time, but why I'm not sure. Although, I do have one more piece of the puzzle that you will need, and I can promise that I won't be helping you with it."

"That's the best you can do? I'd hoped for at least a little more. That, or maybe a little begging." She ran her fingers through my hair, lingering a bit longer than I was comfortable with.

"Tell you what, want me to shoot you first, or do you want to watch me shoot your girlfriend here?

A chill ran through my body, and I decided that it was now or never.

"I'm not going to beg or plead, but look in my back pocket. There's a letter there. Read it, and if you don't believe me, have at it."

"Weak, Noah. Weak."

She stood and put her hands on her hips, circled the chair and stood behind me. My head exploded in pain as I fell to the floor, still in the chair. I came to a few moments later and, as my vision cleared, I saw her standing with the letter in her hand. She sat in the chair and leaned over toward me. She was turning out to be a bit more violent than I had expected.

"Ok, you got my attention. What the fuck is he talking about here?"

I fought the urge to smile.

"It's taken a while for me to put this all together, but that medallion you have is only half the equation. The medallion gets you in, but you need the key to get what you'll want to leave with."

"That's bullshit. I've spent years working through this and never found anything about a key. You're fucking with me and it's pissing me off."

She walked over and kicked me in the stomach. For a small woman, she had a one hefty delivery.

"I was just as surprised as you when I read the letter. But, I know what he's talking about, and I am guessing you don't. And you're damn right that I am going to use it to get us out of here."

"Fuck you."

"Whatever it takes to get me out of here," I said.

"Noah, you may have a letter, but I'm betting that you don't have anything else. I'd have found it in the office or your house, but there's nothing there. Nothing else at all."

"You're forgetting about two things. Cross's house and a certain safe deposit box."

"What?"

"You should've ransacked Cross's house like my place and my office. Seems the old cuss liked to hide things all over the place. And remember the safe deposit box? Just because I visited it once doesn't mean that it just went away. I figured as hard as it was for me to get into it would be pretty safe, pardon the pun. Especially after the recent rash of break-ins I've had to endure."

I realized as she kicked me again that I may be making some progress.

"Heather, I want out of this, but I think we can make a lot more progress if you just stop kicking me every time you realize that you're not as smart as you think you are."

"You've got no room to push me, Noah," she said as she paced the stage. I glanced toward Anna Beth who was still out, tied up in her chair a few feet away.

"It's simple. You get Anna Beth and me out of here, let her go and I'll get you what you need. Keep me with you and that way you can get the money. I'm pretty sure you'll still kill me, but at least I'll have a few days to try to get away. Or to try to convince you not to."

"Noah, ever the saint - save her and throw yourself in the fire. Still feeling guilty about the last one that didn't quite work out?"

I'd never told her about Claire. She'd done her homework, I thought to myself.

"Hit a nerve there, did I? You didn't think it was just a coincidence that I ended up working with you, did you?" she asked as she sat down in the chair again. "It took me three different times going into Cross' house to find his will, which does make me a bit skeptical about your finding something there. When I did, I knew the answer was in the safe deposit box and all roads led to you. Sorry to disappoint you though, I have no idea why Cross chose you."

"That's really not important is it? But if you want to finish what you've started, you need to let her go so we can get going. See, you should have looked around more in Cross's place when you had the chance."

"Noah, Noah, that just isn't going to happen. I know you think you know everything, but you don't. If you did, you'd realize how foolish you were being, and I'm still not convinced you're doing anything other than screwing with me."

She was right. I was flying blind, but I had to keep pushing.

"Think what you want, but you've read the letter and…"

"Yes, yes, maybe it's a problem, maybe it isn't, but you're not leaving here, Noah. I can go back to his house tonight."

"Then we have a problem, because the only way you're getting anything out of me is if Anna Beth leaves."

"See, you don't get it, do you? That's the key to everything - she can't leave."

"If you want anything from me, she will."

"Poor Noah. You just don't understand. You're all caught up in this, but even as one of the most important players and you don't have the slightest idea of what's happening. I'll give you this, you're going to get me to do something that I hadn't planned on, just so you can see how far in over your head you are. That, and so you can realize why neither one of you is going to be leaving."

"Tell me what you want, but you're not getting a thing from me," I said.

She laughed.

"Okay, I'll tell you a little story. You know about the trust and that Cross in all his cat and mouse crap set it up so it takes a fucking medallion to get to. I mean, a medallion, whoever heard of that?" She looked at the letter. "It wasn't a problem getting a job with you, and I didn't have to wait all that long for Thomason to show up since Cross's will led him to your doorstep. I had to wait on you to find the medallion after you got into the safe deposit box. After I stole the files, I went round and round on how to get in that box, but I finally realized that you're the only one that could do it. And Noah, let me say, it fucking took you long enough."

Anna Beth groaned from her chair. Heather walked over and raised her head. I turned and saw that her eyes were still closed. Heather dropped her head, where it bounced on her chest.

"Sorry to disappoint you. Listen, not to appear bored or flip, but I really don't see where you're going here. You certainly haven't convinced me to tell you anything else."

"Let me see if I can make it really simple for you. You know it's about the trust?" she said.

I nodded my head.

"You're missing the main point. The main reason your friend Ms. Cross, and well, you, can't leave here alive."

I had to admit, she had me there. "Now you sound like the one that's pulling at straws," I said.

"Noah, didn't you learn anything about Cross in the last year? He hated to pick favorites. He'd never choose. I mean, in the whole process you were the only one he actually picked. He was never going to split the trust up between his children."

I remembered the letter that had been with the medallion.

'However, for one of you, one day this trust will be all yours to do with as you see fit.'

She must have seen the light come on in my head.

"That's right," she said. "You know Daniel was murdered. I mean, all he'd have had to do was trust me, but he felt so guilty about his father. He felt like he'd abandoned him. So he had to die. Chase was a fool, and Thomason was the most loyal of them all. I was wondering about how I was going to take care of you and Anna Beth, but you took care of that for me."

"So you killed them all? Even Cross?"

"No, actually, he died all by himself, but if he hadn't I was ready to help him along."

"But why? How did their deaths benefit you? How would you ever get the money from the trust? The medallion was left to Anna Beth and Chase, and..." Then it came to me. I remembered Cross' letter. He had said that he wasn't going to pick between them. That meant that if he wasn't going to pick either they would or...

"I see you've realized what this all hinges on," she said.

"The trust was sort of a 'last man standing.' The last child gets it all."

"Very good, Noah, very good. You're probably wondering how I found that out."

"Actually, given your methods, I'd gather you made some young Ohio boy happy for a few days."

"Young Ohio woman, actually. And it was only for a night."

"So kill me, kill Anna Beth, pose as her and the money is yours before they find our bodies. Okay, not bad, but it still doesn't explain why I couldn't come with you." I was pulling at straws now.

"Mostly right. Kill you. Kill Anna Beth. I don't really care if they find your bodies…"

"But if they find the body the trust could find out. I mean, even with the proper documentation and items, I don't think that the trust is just going to hand over millions and millions of dollars. Unless…" I paused.

"Exactly. Unless Cross had another heir," she said.

"But you can't be his daughter, you're younger than Anna Beth – even younger than Daniel."

"Yes, I am. And I never said I was his daughter."

"But what then?"

"I lived my childhood in the shadow of Leo Cross and his three spoiled, arrogant, stuck up children. You know, I don't even believe Cross ever knew he had a granddaughter."

"Granddaughter?"

"Cross was quite the playboy when he was younger. I can only imagine how many abortions he paid for before he got married. I wouldn't be surprised if that was why he never remarried and why he tried so hard with his children. He gave my grandmother money for an abortion, but as you can see, it didn't take. My father was born and, sadly, my grandmother died in a car accident shortly after. He was raised as a bitter young man in an orphanage just a few miles from where Cross lived with his family in Chicago."

"So your father was a pissed off man," I said. "And you a bitter, bitter woman."

"Maybe, maybe not. But I decided after I learned about the trust and after father died that if anyone was going to have that money it might as well be me. I've got everything I need to, shall we say, prove my pedigree and get my money. My father killed himself, and he earned that trust. He should have had it, but never even tried. Now, I'll have it."

"Damn," I said.

"Yes, damn. Tell you what, tell me what else I need and I won't make you watch me make your girlfriend there really, really suffer. So what's it going to be?"

She was right, I had only part of the equation. She also knew that she had me. My bluff, while convincing, had shown that I didn't have all the pieces of the puzzle. Maybe it was time to start begging.

We stared at each other for several long minutes. She finally stood.

"Okay. I'll take that as your answer."

She walked over to Anna Beth, who was just starting to open her eyes. Her chair was only a few feet away from me, near the edge of the stage, but with my hands taped together behind me there was no way I could make it to her. Heather walked over and stood in front of her, her footsteps hardly making a sound on the stage as she moved. I could just see her as she ran the gun around Anna Beth's face, under her chin and down her torso. She used the barrel to spread her legs apart just enough to put the pistol between them against her body. Anna Beth groaned. Heather looked at me and smiled. Actually it was more of what I would have called a sick and twisted grin.

"That's where I'll finish, Noah, but that will be a while. Tell me or I start."

I stared at her. Time, I needed time.

She raised the gun to Anna Beth's head and placed the end of the barrel against her right shoulder. I could just imagine a nine millimeter police issue, full metal jacket slug slamming into her collar bone at point blank range. She was going to torture Anna Beth until I told her, and as soon as I told her she was going to kill both of us. She looked back to me. I turned my head.

I closed my eyes just before a shot rang out.

CHAPTER 22

I had always been told that the span of a few moments, in times of stress, can sometimes seem an eternity. If the moments following the shot had only seemed an eternity, I'd have felt a bit better. I fought to keep from opening my eyes, not wanting to see Anna Beth covered in blood, but I couldn't keep them closed any longer. I looked over to her. Her head slowly shook. She was still not completely awake, but I didn't see any blood. I also didn't see Heather. I heard the sound of heavy footsteps falling on the stage behind me. I pulled against my bonds in an attempt to turn to see who was there. Then it hit me - Gabriel. I'd forgotten him. Once again, he had come through. I felt his hands pulling against the tape that was binding my hands.

"Forget me, help Anna Beth," I said.

"She's fine," a voice said. A voice that didn't belong to Gabriel.

I twisted to look back and was dumbfounded to see Henderson.

"What the hell?"

"Goddammit, Parks, hold still so I can get these off."

"What the hell are you doing here?"

"Someone's got to look after your ass," he said as he got the last of the tape off my hands. "You okay?"

"A little shook up, but yeah, I'm fine."

Henderson reached into his pocket and pulled out a telescopic baton called an Asp. It was no more than six inches long and hardly looked dangerous; however, by holding it in your hand and flicking your wrist, it would snap open to a steel rod about two and a half feet in length. It was most excellent for knocking the crap out of someone.

"Go take care of her," he said, motioning toward Anna Beth. "And if anyone you don't know comes by," he handed me the Asp, "knock the shit out of them. I'll be right back."

He disappeared off the front of the stage.

I stood, surprised that I wasn't dizzy, and walked to Anna Beth. She was still tied and not yet conscious, but there wasn't a mark on her. It took me a couple of minutes, but I got the tape off of her hands and feet. I paused, wondering how I could wake her, shrugged and ripped the tape off of her mouth. That did the trick.

"Ouch. Noah? What... Where is she?"

"Hang on, I don't know."

I was just about to call for Henderson when he appeared back on the stage.

"She's gone," he said. "I know I hit her, but she's not out there. The front door's open. It was locked a few minutes ago, so I am guessing that's where she got out. No blood, though." He shone the flashlight around the perimeter of the stage, his gun, unholstered, in his other hand.

I pushed Anna Beth behind me and flicked my wrist to open the

323

Asp. I started to back up toward the rear of the stage. I didn't have to say a word to Anna Beth, who followed my lead and guided me backwards.

"Parks, what the hell are you doing?" Henderson said.

"Leaving, if you don't mind."

"Hold on a minute. We need to talk about a few thing, but first…"

"But first my ass. Where the hell did you come from?" I said.

"God dammit, Parks, don't be indignant. You ought to be thanking me for saving your ass and your girlfriend's, too."

"I ought to be wondering what the hell you're doing here, and surprisingly enough, I am."

I broke his stare and looked to the Glock in his hand. He looked down at it, back to me and put it in his shoulder holster.

"Sorry about that." He took a step toward me. I raised the Asp.

"Parks, listen to me a minute. I know you're pissed at me, but remember your buddy, Gabriel? He's back there bleeding. Think maybe we better get him some help?"

I paused for a moment.

"Yeah, good idea," I said.

"Then come on." He pushed past me, ducking his head under my raised arm, not even glancing at the Asp as I held it above the stage. As he did, he pulled a walkie-talkie and started speaking into it.

Within five minutes there were three ambulances and a dozen county and city police officers at the scene. They'd done it all without the media showing up. The police worked quickly when one of their own was involved.

The EMT's took care of Gabriel, who had a nasty head wound and a concussion but was stable. Anna Beth and I sat on the back of an ambulance sipping coffee while two more EMT's looked us over and patched my head. I was surprised - the coffee was actually pretty good, though I found myself wondering why first responders always had fresh coffee. Despite Heather playing soccer on my ribs, none of them were broken, but they were going to hurt like hell for a few days. Collins came over and talked to Anna Beth and me for few minutes. Henderson surprised me and stayed out of the mix and actually coordinated getting Gabriel into an ambulance. We watched as the deputies and officers came in and out of the bar. After several hours of this, Collins came back over to us.

"No doubt the two of you've had quite a day. Ms. Cross, you've had a couple of them. We've been pretty lucky so far, keeping the media in the dark on this, but that won't last," he said. "Mr. Parks, we've had a few officers over processing your house, and if you don't mind I'd like to have the two of you go back there and, if you're up to it, debrief all of this."

I looked over at Anna Beth who, despite the events of the last several days, was looking quite energized.

"You up to it?" I said.

"Why not? It's the first time in weeks that the police want to talk to me and don't want to arrest me. Let's go." She paused. "But only if it's okay with my attorney."

"First, how's Gabriel?"

"He's doing fine. Might be in the hospital a day or two, but looks like he'll be fine," Collins said.

"Let's go then. But we need a ride, and I need to go by Gabriel's house and pick up my dog."

Collins smiled, turned and called to Henderson. Seems we had a reluctant chauffeur in the deputy. To my surprise, he briskly walked over to us and helped Anna Beth to his car. He didn't even complain when Collins told him to take me by Gabriel's to pick up Austin.

~~~~~~~~~~~~~~~~~~~~~~~~~~~~~

After the detour to Gabriel's, we arrived at my house. I'd expected to find a convention, but to my surprise the house was dark. Henderson reached in his pocket and took out a remote control and opened one of my garage doors. I started to say something, but he cut me off.

"The detectives who were here earlier brought it to me." He turned and handed it to me as we went in the garage. I shut the door as he got out and opened the door for Anna Beth. I studied him for a minute, then headed up into the house. As I was going inside, with Austin, Rudy, Anna Beth and Henderson in tow, I saw another set of lights drive up outside. Collins and another deputy got out and walked up the steps where they were greeted by two curious canines who led them into the living room. The place was a mess, but I couldn't tell if it was from Heather or from the deputies.

"Sorry for the mess, Mr. Parks, but seems that Ms. Davis was intent on finding something here."

"She was and she did," I said.

I motioned to the couch for everyone to sit. Henderson was still making me uncomfortable.

"Okay, Mr. Parks, best way to go about this is to tell us what happened," Collins said.

"No problem, but if you don't mind, I'd like Anna Beth to start. I think Deputy Henderson might find that interesting."

Henderson stared at me. I waited for it to turn to a scowl, but he just smiled.

"I'd love to hear it, but only if Ms. Cross is up to it," Henderson said.

I was pleasantly surprised at this from him.

326

"It's pretty straight forward. Day before yesterday Noah and I decided to go to Ohio to find out more about my father's trust. He was going to make reservations while I went to my beach house to get clothes. When I got there, Heather was sitting on my front steps," she paused as Austin walked over and jumped on the couch beside her. "I got out of my car and was walking toward her to find out what she was doing at my house when she pulled out a black box and touched it to my chest. Next thing I knew, I couldn't move. She tied my hands and pulled me across the yard and put me in a car. She didn't blindfold me, but I was lying down in the back seat of the car and I really couldn't tell where we were going."

I reached over and put my hand on her knee. She smiled and kept going.

"We stopped, and by this time I was able to stand. We walked into that bar and she locked me in a dressing room. I stayed there until earlier today when she took me out and taped my hands and mouth. I saw Noah come on the stage and watched him wander around before he ran over to me. I tried to warn him, but she hit him on the back of the head then put us both on the stage. She put that black box on my chest again and I don't remember anything other than that until Noah pulled the tape off of my mouth."

Collins cleared his throat and pulled an evidence bag out of his jacket pocket.

"That black box look like this?" he said.

"Yes."

"It's a Streetwise stun gun, similar to a Taser. Shocks the hell out of you and incapacitates you. You remember anything else?"

"I heard her moving stuff around and wandering around the bar, but other than that, no."

"Hum," I said.

"Yes?" Collins said.

"She was using Anna Beth as bait."

"It looks that way," Henderson said.

I looked over to him then back to Collins. I decided to tell them everything since what they did know really didn't make any sense with Anna Beth and the trust.

"I agree with you, actually. Gabriel and I showed up out there. I'm still not really sure how he found the place. He made me stay in his car and went inside. I should've called for another officer, but I think Heather was counting on me not to do that. I waited until I couldn't wait any longer and went looking for him. He was on the floor when I went through the back door. I tripped over him, made my way to the stage and found Anna Beth, then Heather found me."

"Not the brightest of moves on your part, Mr. Parks," Collins said. "You're lucky."

"Tell me about it. She made it really clear that she planned to kill us. She admitted to killing Thomason and pretty much admitted to killing Anna Beth's brother, Daniel. I found some things that make me believe she killed Chase and his attorney, too."

"Found what?" Henderson said.

"That's actually how I decided that Heather was the one that was behind all of this. Anna Beth and I had been working on a puzzle, a riddle of sorts that her father left, and we kept running across the symbol for infinity and a diamond. We were on the trail of a trust established by Anna Beth's father in Ohio. After Anna Beth disappeared, I went to my office and pulled out a bunch of pictures I had – some related to this case, some of Heather. There were diamonds and infinity symbols all over them. I think what Heather had been doing was leaving a calling card of sorts with all the things she did. There was one in the car Chase died in. Thomason was holding a scrap of paper with a diamond on it. The kicker was when I noticed a picture of Heather she'd left at the office. She had on earrings – one infinity, one diamond. So I was pretty sure it was her that was behind all of this. I'm betting that if you look back to Daniel's murder, there will be an infinity or a diamond symbol involved somewhere. Then, Gabriel somehow found out where she was."

"Property records," Henderson said.

"What?" Collins and Anna Beth said at the same time.

"When Parks here and Gabriel disappeared, I have to admit I figured they were both in on it with Ms. Cross. I called city dispatch and asked if Gabriel had called in. They said he had, but was off radio. They told me he'd called on a property check in the name of Heather Davis. Apparently Ms. Davis owns that building out there."

"I'll be damned," I said. "That makes sense, too. Heather seemed to be surprised it took me so long to find her. I never thought to see if she owned any property."

"So?" Collins said. "What happened?"

"She knocked the shit out of me," I said. "Then she told me she was going to kill Anna Beth and me and make it look like Anna Beth had kidnapped her and killed me when I came to rescue her. That would have left Heather the only one alive. She was going to make it look like she saved the day from the crazy woman from Chicago that came down here with dollar signs in her eyes. I bet she had a plan to pin all of the deaths on Anna Beth."

"Thing is, I think we'd have believed that. With you reporting to Gabriel that Heather was missing and Anna Beth here charged with Thomason's murder, we'd have believed her. The question is why'd she go to all that trouble?" Collins said.

"It goes back to the trust." I looked to Anna Beth. "This won't be easy, Anna Beth."

"What are you talking about?" she said.

"Your father."

"What about him?"

I looked around the room at the deputies, coming to rest my eyes on Henderson. He stared back at me.

"Don't worry, I heard enough from the good Ms. Davis at the Cougar to know that Ms. Cross here didn't kill anyone, if that's what you are worried about," he said.

"Actually, no, but that's nice to hear. The charges will be dropped I take?"

"I'll see to it myself," he said.

"Good. But this is rather private and personal about Anna Beth's father, and…"

"Noah. Go on, tell us about what happened," Anna Beth said.

I looked around again. "It all goes back to the trust. Seems it had some unique provisions. If you're documented appropriately, then the trust ends and goes in its entirety, its rather large entirety, to the last of Mr. Cross' heirs. I was trying to stall Heather for time when I learned this," I said. "Before Gabriel and I went out there, I had a suspicion it was Heather behind everything, but I didn't understand how it all fit together to benefit her. Basically I figured she was going to pose as you. For insurance, I typed a letter that was supposedly from Cross to the trust in Ohio. I wrote it to explain that in addition to the letter, the bearer also needed another item we had found. To my surprise, Heather bought it, but unfortunately I didn't know all of the facts, and it almost backfired on me. I missed the most important part. I was banking on this letter keeping me alive, but it seems the way the trust is set up, the letter wouldn't have made any difference. The only way anyone can get the money from the trust is if they are the last living relative of Leo Cross."

"So she was going to kill us both and pose as me?" Anna Beth said.

"That's what I thought. It seemed the only possibility."

Anna Beth looked at me, confused.

"Leo Cross had another child?" Henderson said.

"Seems so. Before he met Anna Beth's mother, he was involved with a woman who told him she had taken care of things. She hadn't. She gave birth but died soon after, and Cross apparently never knew he had another child. This woman gave birth to a boy who knew Cross was his father. He spent his whole life growing bitter about all that Cross had and all that he didn't have. Then he learned of the trust. And all of this rubbed off on his only child, a daughter... Heather." I looked around the room as everyone gazed at me in silence. "She actually went so far as to break into Cross' house before he died. She saw the will and that lead her to me. After she started working for me all she had to do was wait, though I think she would have sped up your father's demise if it hadn't happened naturally. So, even after I tried to trick her, she was prepared to kill us because she needed you dead to get the money from the trust. She was about to start torturing you when Henderson walked in. When he shot her, I thought she'd shot you."

Anna Beth was silent for a moment.

"So this woman is my niece?"

"Seems to be the case," I said.

"Where is she?" Anna Beth said.

Henderson stood and scratched his head.

"First, Ms. Cross, I want to apologize. Seems that this woman did a pretty good job pointing the finger at you. Mr. Parks, same to you."

I nodded. He continued.

"To answer your question, we don't know where she is. But I promise you, I hit her."

"So she's gone?" Anna Beth said.

"Hardly," I said. "There's a lot of money sitting in Ohio that she wants. She still has the medallion - oh, you need that to access the trust as well, so I can promise you she'll be looking for you because she can't get the money until you're out of the picture."

"You mean this?" Collins said.

I looked at him and saw that he was holding an evidence bag with a gold coin in it. I smiled.

"Looks like we need a plan," I said as I looked at Henderson. He smiled.

Collins stood and handed the coin to me. "What about a little bait and switch?"

"Depends on who the bait is, I guess," I said.

"Well," Collins glanced at Anna Beth. "Hardly a job for a lady, so I guess it would be you."

"I sorta figured you'd say that. We'll give her a dose of her own medicine."

"How ya feel about a news conference?" Collins said.

"Let's work out the details," I said.

~~~~~~~~~~~~~~~~~~~~~~

We worked through the night planning our approach. Anna Beth took Austin and Rudy upstairs and left the deputies, Collins, Henderson and me working until the wee hours of the morning. We finished our plan just before dawn and the deputies drove off, leaving one officer to watch the house. I went upstairs and found Anna Beth asleep on my bed with a canine on either side. She rolled over and stretched as she opened her eyes.

"How you doing?" I said.

"Actually pretty good. It's nice to sleep in a bed that I'm used to."

"Did she hurt you?"

"She didn't do anything to me."

"Good. You hungry?" I said.

"A little, yes. You?"

"A bit. I mostly feel like I've been hit by a bus." My head was throbbing and my ribs ached. I'd been downing ibuprofen all night, but I still felt like crap.

"So what's the plan?" she said.

"I'm going on the news in a few hours and we're going to break the story. Henderson is going to announce that the charges against you have been dropped and that this was all related to the trust. We're going to have Collins pose as the trustee and have him make a statement that he's met with the police and has been briefed on everything. Based on this information he's prepared to release the entirety of the trust to you. We'll say there's a suspect who was attempting to pose as an heir, but some quick research has proven that she's an insane woman who had family that once worked for your father. I'll be waiting for her with the PD at the Planter's Inn, and I'm pretty sure she'll get right over there."

"Sounds like a pretty good plan."

"From my discussion with Heather, it should piss her off beyond words."

"So what do I do during all of this?" she asked.

"You're not staying here. I'll feel better if you come with us. There'll be enough protection in case anything does happen."

She got out of the bed, walked over to me and kissed me.

"When do we have to leave?"

"Not for a few hours," I said.

She took my hand and led me to the bathroom. She turned on the shower. I looked over my shoulder and saw there were two dogs watching our every move. In unison, their eyes moved to the floor of the bathroom. I looked back and saw a pair of jeans on the floor as the shower door opened. I smiled and walked across the room toward her. I may have felt like I had been hit by a bus, but I was pretty sure that this was going to be just what the doctor ordered.

Things had gone slow for long enough. I undressed and joined her in the shower. After we ran out of hot water, we moved to the bed. Her touch, her kiss, her body made me feel human again. Later, as I lay on my back in the bed with Anna Beth's head on my chest, one of her legs draped over my body, I realized we were breathing in unison. She rolled on top of me, her hair falling to my face as she kissed me. The second time was better than the first.

We got dressed, taking our time, and then went downstairs to get in the car. Anna Beth got in and I realized that I had forgotten my keys. I ran upstairs and chuckled as the dogs watched me. I went back down and got in the Jeep. I looked over at Anna Beth and saw that she was crying.

"What's wrong?" I said.

"No, No, Noah, even with all that's happened with that woman, being with you makes me smile," she half cried and half smiled.

"What?"

"That woman. I mean, I met her at your office, I talked to her, I even laughed at her jokes. She wants to kill me. And she's related to me. I mean, how do you hate someone that much? How can you just act like that and then have no regard for them, be prepared to kill them, torture them? And you, you only helped her! You were even interested in her and she was going to kill you."

"Anna Beth, don't try to understand her. You can't and you won't. You didn't hear her, hear the contempt in her voice. I'm pretty sure that while she was growing up, not a day went by where she didn't hear from her father about how he'd been cheated. About how you and your family had everything and how they had nothing.

Then he died, and I can imagine that only fueled a fire that had been burning for years. She only sees you as an obstacle in the way of what she thinks is her money. This may sound a little lofty, but you personify everything she hated about your father, her grandfather. All she knew was the suffering of her father, and his anger has apparently been multiplied in the mind of a mad woman."

"I know, but I just don't understand."

"And you won't."

I reached over, brushed her hair from her face and kissed her. She laughed and fanned her face.

"I'm sorry, Noah. I guess I'm just overwhelmed by this."

"You seemed to be taking it a little better than expected."

"Thanks, but I guess that it all really hasn't set in yet..."

CHAPTER 23

The press conference took longer than we anticipated. It seemed that one of the local news stations picked up a leak from the port police about the response to the strip bar. No one was talking, so they did some research and came up with Heather's name on the deed to the strip bar. They found out that she'd been in law school and that she had been working with me. From me they traced things back to the Cross estate and came prepared with question after question. I was impressed with Collins, who kept the press conference on point. He did a great job, with Henderson's help, of painting Heather as a psychopath who'd been obsessed with Anna Beth her whole life. Henderson even mentioned that she'd probably even been abused and molested by her father. Collins had been in touch with the trust in Ohio, and while they wouldn't acknowledge anything about the trust with Collins and me on a conference call, they agreed not to interfere as we laid the trap. What we had hoped would be a fifteen minute exercise turned out to be a two hour question and answer session.

We finally made our escape. Anna Beth, Collins and I headed to the Planter's Inn, where it had been leaked that Collins was staying while he was down from Ohio. Henderson was going to check the strip bar again and the airports in case it turned out that Heather tried to leave town. Our trip to the Planter's Inn was slow going as the weather worsened as the hurricane made its way to what was shaping up to be a hit on the South Carolina coast. The wind and rain were picking up, and by nightfall we'd start to feel the worst of the winds and rains, if not a full hurricane.

We'd made arrangements to stay in the same room Anna Beth had been in when she was last there. We had lunch sent up and made ourselves comfortable in the suite. We watched The Weather Channel as the conditions outside worsened. Other than that, about all we did was wait.

And wait.

And wait.

I'd never met Collins before the day at the beach house, but knew him by reputation. We talked about Henderson for a while and had a good laugh over him. I even spent about an hour telling him all that had happened while I had been working on the estate. After another hour the conversation turned to more small talk about the hurricane. Anna Beth was becoming obsessed with following the storm. I expected her to ask for a tracking chart.

At 6:30, after a full day of waiting, I decided the plan wasn't working quite how we thought.

"So, Collins, what do you think?" I said.

"I think she isn't coming, at least not here. About the only thing I'm expecting now is this storm."

The winds outside were at least tropical storm strength, and the rain was starting to get heavy.

"Maybe she was expecting us to do this," Anna Beth said.

"I think you might be right. She'll turn up, but it doesn't look like it will be here. She also might be watching, and we've stayed here about as long as we can to make it look like the real thing. Maybe too long," I said.

"If my opinion counts at all," Anna Beth started, "I think you need to walk us out to Noah's car, say good bye and have a deputy meet us back at Noah's house in case she shows up."

"Okay," he said. "As much as it pains me to say so, I think you're probably right. Let's do this, head back to your place. From the looks of it, you'd better make it quick - looks like this storm might just get pretty nasty in the next little bit. Call if anything out of the ordinary happens. I'll have a deputy waiting. Stay inside and we'll touch base tomorrow. That'll give me time to get out the appropriate APB and maybe that'll get things moving," he said.

I looked at Collins then back to Anna Beth. I really didn't like the plan, but couldn't think of anything else.

"Let's go," I said.

We headed down to the lobby. Collins spoke to the two plain clothes deputies that had been waiting there and they left. Collins accompanied us to my car, parked on a side street down from the inn. He gave Anna Beth a hug, turned, shook my hand and said he'd see me in the morning. We waved as he walked back to the inn. The rain had let up, but the wind was gusting.

"This storm's probably going to get a bit worse. We need to hurry, but how about we pick something up on the way home? If you feel like eating?"

"God, I'm glad you asked, I'm starving. How about sushi in bed?" she said.

"I'm up for that. Could you drive?" I said. "My head's killing me."

"Sure."

I tossed her the keys and she unlocked the doors. She started the engine and pulled out of the parking space onto the street. We were the only car that I saw on the street. Hurricane's had a way of thinning traffic.

"Sushi in bed? Sounds romantic."

A chill ran down my spine. Heather's voice had that effect lately. Another chill followed when I felt the cold steel of what I presumed was Gabriel's Glock on the back of my neck.

"Just drive, Anna Beth," I said.

"Listen to your boyfriend, dear. Drive."

I glanced over at Anna Beth, but she looked pissed when I expected her to look anything but that.

"Dear god, Noah, how long were you planning on staying up there with that deputy? Do you realize how cramped it is in the back of this Jeep? My neck's killing me. And Noah, I must say, you really disappointed me, letting them tell all of those lies about my father."

"Were they lies?" Anna Beth said.

"Anna Beth," I said, hoping she would catch the caution in my voice.

"Noah's right. Be quiet while I talk to your boyfriend."

"Oh, you be quiet! I'm getting fed up with you! Just because your bastard father was pissed and had some sort of entitlement attitude doesn't mean a thing to me. Besides, you'll never see a dime of my father's money."

"My, my, you've gotten bold since the other day. And I'll see oh so much more than a dime."

"Screw you."

"Anna Beth," I said.

"Dammit it, Noah, I've had enough of this woman. She's used

and abused you, killed my family and friends, and she wants to kill us."

"That last part is most definitely right," I said.

"She's pretty good isn't she, Noah?" Heather said.

"Noah, she won't be killing us today. She doesn't have Father's coin and we don't have it to give. She doesn't have the key, either."

"Very good, my dear, and that's why you're still alive. For now, anyway. If you don't piss me off," Heather said.

"Heather, we don't have anything to give, the police took it."

"I know that, but don't you worry about that. I'll be going to see Deputy Collins in a few minutes to get that taken care of. For now, why don't we just head to your office. There's going to be a tragic accident – a lover's quarrel. And Noah, just keep quiet, don't try to talk yourself out of this. I believe you know the way to his office, don't you, Anna Beth?"

Anna Beth headed down Meeting toward Broad and cut through the alley on the side of my office. She parked the car in the empty lot.

"Anna Beth, be a dear and hand me the keys," Heather said.

Anna Beth looked at me as she turned off the car and tossed the keys over the seat to Heather.

Heather got out, keeping the Glock pointed at me. She threw my keys over the fence into the next parking lot. The wind was starting to whip things around. Heather stepped back from the car, the gun still pointed at me.

"Out, and keep your hands where I can see them," she said to me.

I glanced at Anna Beth who was still sitting, staring straight ahead.

"Just do what she says. I have a plan," I said.

She didn't say anything as I got out of the car. I'd actually lied to Anna Beth about having a plan - I had no idea what I was going to do. I got out and turned to look at Heather.

"Don't suppose that I can talk you out of this?"

"Noah, shut up. We're going in the office. I'll shoot both of you and then I'm going to go get my medallion from the good deputy. Then I'll go get my money. See, it doesn't matter how Anna Beth dies, I get it. It'll all be mine. Mine and father's."

She was delusional. She'd lost it. She was as wrong as wrong could be on this. She had to know we had been in touch with the trust.

"Heather, I…"

"Noah, be quiet. You won't confuse me again. I have to kill you and that's that. If you just hadn't gotten involved with that woman I could have brought you with me, but now that you've betrayed me, I have to kill both of you. Let's go."

I stepped toward her. The rain had started as we'd been standing in the parking lot. It stung as it was blown against my face. As I stepped toward her, the street lights illuminating the parking lot went out with a bright flash. Apparently the storm had blown out the electricity. I started to run.

"Don't you dare move," she said as a flashlight came on. It was Gabriel's from the strip bar.

I raised my hands in defeat and walked past her, turned (putting my back to her), and walked behind my Jeep. I stopped as I turned the rear corner to the driver's side.

"Keep moving," Heather said.

"Shit," I said.

"What's the problem?"

She walked around the side of the Jeep, swinging wide behind me. She trained the flashlight on the open driver's side door - and the empty driver's seat.

"God dammit! Where is she?"

I kept my mouth shut.

"Noah, where the fuck is she?" Heather said. "Look at me, God dammit!"

I turned to face her just as the two by four crashed down on the back of her head. She fell to the ground.

"Hi," Anna Beth said.

"Where the hell did you go?" I said as I stepped by Heather's crumpled body toward Anna Beth.

"I figured you were trying to stall, so when the rain started and the lights went out, I slipped out. When we pulled up I saw some boards by the door, so I grabbed one."

"Good girl. Let's find something to tie her up with, then call Collins," I said.

I bent to examine her - she was out cold. "I think she'll be out for a while."

We headed down the alley toward Broad Street.

As we stepped onto the sidewalk, a car pulled up in front of us and slid to a stop.

It was Henderson.

"Ya'll are out a little late in some nasty weather tonight, aren't you?"

"Heather. She's back there, behind my office. She was in my car and Anna Beth knocked her out," I said.

"Show me," he said.

We headed back down the alley and he followed behind us in his cruiser. She was still on the ground beside my Jeep as he pulled to a stop. Henderson pulled out his light and walked over to her. He bent and felt her pulse.

"She's okay, just out." He pulled out a pair of handcuffs and locked them on her wrists.

The wind and rain were picking up.

"You got any lanterns or battery lights in your office, Parks?"

"Yeah."

"Give me a hand dragging her in there so we can get out of the weather. I'll radio for back up."

We half carried, half drug her to the back door of my office. I unlocked the door, Anna Beth having retrieved my keys from where Heather had thrown them, and we laid her on the floor in the reception area. I then went to the storage room and rummaged around in the dark until I found a battery operated lantern, which I then set in the window between Heather's old desk and the reception area. Turning, I saw Heather standing beside Henderson, rubbing her wrists.

"Nothing like another twist, huh, Parks?" Henderson said.

Anna Beth was sitting down in the reception area, rubbing her head.

"Why don't you have a seat beside her there," Henderson said as he pointed to the open chair beside Anna Beth.

I shook my head as I walked over to the chair and sat down.

"Okay, how much? How much did she agree to pay you?"

"Now that's not any of your business, but let's just say that I'll be doing pretty good. No more police work in my future."

"And let me guess, you already got the coin?"

"Yep, that and Ms. Davis' Taser. Seems she's attached to it."

"What? Did you kill Collins?" I said.

"Good god no. I may be greedy, but if I kill a cop they'd hunt me down so I couldn't get about at all. This way, I just have to be able to get out of the country. And believe me, with this hurricane, I'll be in the Caribbean tomorrow morning."

"Why doesn't this surprise me? When'd she get to you?" I said.

"Not that it's any of your business, but about the time

Thomason was murdered. She made me the same deal she tried to make him, and I guess I was just a little smarter. All I had to do was arrest Ms. Cross and then make an appearance at the strip club. Worked out pretty well, huh?"

"Henderson, you know she'll never let you out of here, don't you?"

"Parks, save it," Henderson said. "Me and Ms. Davis have a deal here, don't we?"

"That we do, Detective. And now, if you'd just take care of these two, we can get on with things."

He turned to smile at Heather. I felt Anna Beth press something against my leg. It was a gun, a pistol - Gabriel's Glock. I took it and slid it under my shirt, hoping neither Henderson nor Heather had seen it in the dim light. I also hoped it had a shell in the chamber.

"Can't do your own dirty work, Heather?" I said.

"Oh, no, I'm perfectly capable of handling all the details," she said, taking a step toward Henderson and sticking the Taser to his neck. With a surprised look on his face he tensed and crumpled to the floor.

"Told you she wouldn't let you out of here," I said.

She stood over him, staring down, several feet from Anna Beth and me.

"Follow my lead," Anna Beth whispered.

She stood and walked toward the front door, moving away from Heather, who was still standing over Henderson.

"I think I'll be leaving now," she said.

"Hold it, bitch, you're not going anywhere!" Heather stepped over Henderson and moved toward Anna Beth with the Taser outstretched. As she did, I stood and raised the Glock to her.

"Hold it Heather, it's over," I said, being careful to keep enough distance between us to keep her from using the Taser gun.

"Noah, sit down and…" she said as she turned to face me, then her eyes fell on the gun. "Where did you get…" her voice trailed.

"Anna Beth, get Henderson's gun and his cell. Heather, drop the stun gun."

It was no surprise to me that she didn't. I kept the gun pointed at her, but she didn't move. Anna Beth slid behind her, out of reach of the stun gun, and over to Henderson.

"Got'em," she said.

"Call 911," I said.

"Noah, we can both have the money, you and I. We can pick up where we left off that night - we can be together. Finally. Just like you've always wanted."

"Heather, drop it."

"Noah, don't you want to run away with me?" Heather said.

She took a step toward me as she was speaking. I backed up, keeping the gun on her.

"Drop it Heather."

"Noah, you know you want to be with me. We can have everything you and she could have had. That and more. You'll never be happy with her, she's evil, pure evil. Her and her whole family. Everything about them. They killed my father."

Two shots rang out as Heather lunged at me. The shot from the Glock hit her in her shoulder, the shot from the gun Anna Beth had taken from Henderson hit the stun gun. It flew out of her hand, crashing to the floor. Heather slammed against the wall and slumped to the floor. She was bleeding, but she was still alive. I looked back at Anna Beth, who kept the pistol pointed at Heather.

"Damn," I said.

"Noah, get the cuffs and cuff her to Henderson. She already got away once."

Without asking a question I did as I was told.

As soon as they were cuffed together, Anna Beth called 911 on Henderson's phone and was patched through to Collins. She spared the details and told him to get to my office as soon as possible. He was there in less than three minutes, during which we didn't take the guns off either of them.

"What the hell happened here?" Collins said as he came in.

We explained how Heather had been in my Jeep and had had us drive here, how Anna Beth had slipped away and hit Heather on the head with the two by four, how Henderson had mysteriously appeared and brought Heather inside and how he had been her inside man for some time. Anna Beth had stumbled across the gun in the parking lot and, thinking it a little odd that Henderson had just appeared, had kept it quiet.

"Good thing you did, seems that made all the difference. But I'm one of the good guys, so how about you let me have those guns," Collins said as he took a pistol from each of us.

More police arrived, followed by EMT's. The EMT's got Heather off to the hospital, and after Henderson came to (with a different attitude, I might add), the officers cuffed him properly and took him off to the jail. At least he knew what to expect.

Anna Beth and I waited out by my Jeep as the police and EMT's went about their business. We laughed as we sipped coffee while watching the same thing again for the second time in as many days. Collins came over after they put Henderson in a car.

"Henderson had us on that, had everyone fooled. We knew that he had it in for you, but how he ever got hooked up with her, I just don't know."

"Well, he always struck me as a bastard," I said.

"A greedy bastard," Anna Beth added.

The wind and rain were starting to fade. "Looks like the worst of it passed us by. It's headed to North Carolina," Collins said.

I looked about and rubbed my head.

"You sure about that?"

"Touché," he said. "You folks okay getting home?" he said.

"Unless you're going to be coming after us."

"You're pretty safe there. Figure there'll be some news folks that want to talk to you, but after tonight, I think you can take care of yourself. I'll call you tomorrow," he said as he turned back toward my office and the officers waiting there for him. As he did, the power in the downtown came on.

"So, my dear, where to?" I said.

"Hang on a sec," she said, and ran toward Collins. She spoke to him for a moment, kissed his cheek and came back to the car.

"Let's go. I'll drive," she said.

We got in the Jeep and headed down Broad and cut over to Calhoun. I was a little surprised when we parked outside of the Medical University Hospital.

"Collins tells me that Gabriel's up. Thought we might stop and say hi. I bet he has a few questions."

We went inside and asked for his room. Even though it was late, we found out that Collins had called and spoken to a doctor friend of his. We were in his room in less than five minutes.

Gabriel was propped up in his bed watching TV. A bandage covered most of his head.

"Damn, Parks, you look like you been through the ringer."

"Strong words coming from someone with a hat like that."

"Hi, Gabriel," Anna Beth said as she leaned over to kiss his cheek.

"And hi to you. So, anything interesting going on?"

We both laughed.

"What? Don't screw around with a black man with a head injury, no telling what I might do. What's going on?"

I pulled up a chair.

"This will take a few minutes, but I promise you'll like the way it turns out."

Anna Beth laughed as we began to tell him about what had just happened.

We told the story twice for Gabriel, not because he didn't believe it, but because he just wanted to hear about Henderson going down hard. As much as cops didn't like hearing about other cops getting hurt on the job, they loved it when a bad cop got caught. We'd been there about two hours when the night nurse came in and ran us off. We promised to come visit again the next day. I also promised to take care of Rudy until he got out of the hospital.

We made our way back to the car and I walked to the driver's door and started feeling my pockets for the keys.

"Looking for these?"

I looked at her and saw her dangling the keys. I reached out for them and she put them behind her back. I stepped toward her.

"Yes, I'm looking for those."

"Tell me why I should give them to you?" she said.

I pulled her close to me and kissed her - then kissed her again.

"Because if you don't, it'll look pretty odd when I start to take your clothes off right here in front of the hospital."

"Ok, I guess that's a good reason," she said as she slid the keys into my hand. "So, I take it you want me to stay at your place tonight?"

"If you're free?"

"Absolutely."

"I'm pretty wide awake right now, and have a lot of energy to burn off if you're up to it."

"Really now?" she said.

"Is that okay?"

"Let's just say that you better have a lot of energy," she said as she smiled. "Then what?"

"Well," I reached in my pocket and pulled out a coin, turning it over between my fingers. "I thought we might take a little trip to Ohio."

THE TRUST